Between the Devil and the Sea

Chani Lynn Feener

ALSO BY CHANI LYNN FEENER

*For a list of YA books by this author, please check her website. All of the books listed below are Adult.

Bad Things Play Here

Gods of Mist and Mayhem

A Bright Celestial Sea

A Sea of Endless Light

A Whisper in the Dark Trilogy
You Will Never Know
Don't Breathe a Word

Abandoned Things

Between the Devil and the Sea

Chani Lynn Feener

This is a work of fiction. Names, characters, places, and incidents are the product of the author's imagination, and any resemblance to actual events or persons, living or dead, is entirely coincidental.

Between the Devil and the Sea

Copyright @ 2023 by Chani Lynn Feener.

All rights reserved. No part of this book may be reproduced, distributed, or transmitted in any form without written permission from the author.

Front Cover design by @the.ravens.touch .

Printed in the United States of America.

First edition — 2023

Author's Note

Dear Reader,

Even if you've read one of my books before please do not skip this note. As some of the triggers couldn't be included on the book's main listing, I wanted to take the time to include them here.

This book is a lot darker than any of my other books. Neither of the characters are what can be considered great people, Shade has seriously bad mental health which he hides from the world, and Apollo is...well. If you're looking for a hero, a knight in shining armor, or an ending where the villain becomes the superhero, this isn't the book for you. That being said, it does have a HEA.

Apollo is not morally gray, he's black all the way. He's willing to do whatever he wants to get what he wants. He's possessive and manipulative and if you've read the blurb you already know, a serial killer.

I want to just get out of the way that I do not condone anything that takes place in this book in real life. This book is purely fiction. These characters aren't real and this takes place on a made up planet in a made up galaxy. If you or anyone you know is ever in a toxic relationship, please seek help. You deserve better. And if you ever meet an Apollo, run.

Now onto the triggers. **If you aren't easily triggered or you want to avoid any spoilers, feel free to skip the rest of this note.**

If tried to note down all of the ones I can think of, but please keep in mind that I may have missed one or two. Your mental health is important, if any of these don't sound appealing or may put you at risk, please skip this book. I have other MM books that don't fall under the dark category that may be better suitable for you.

Most, but possibly not all, notable triggers include: Non con, dub con, knife play, choking, rejection from family, serious self-loathing and low self-esteem from one of the main characters, murder, torture (not shown on page), mention of child abuse (both sexually and otherwise, never shown on page and only briefly mentioned), mention of child death (never shown on page), kidnapping, stalking, conditioning of the main character, Stockholm syndrome, sadism, masochism (pain, not humiliation), and very graphic sex scenes. Seriously. There are more sex scenes in this book than any of my others. Physical intimacy plays a big role in binding the two main characters together. While it's not just about sex for them in the end, sex is used as a tool by Apollo. Finally, lube is only sometimes used. I understand that's a big one for some people. Please keep in mind, while they look basically the same as humans, these are aliens, and while I don't go into great detail about anatomy in this one, I like to think they aren't exactly built the same as humans. In my contemporary works lube always plays a very big role, but this isn't contemporary, and also…one of the main characters has an attraction to pain anyway.

Again, **this book does have a HEA**. It features two people who, by the end, decide to put their relationship above everything else, including the bad things that may or may not have transpired between them. This relationship is messy, twisted, and in many ways, wrong. To reiterate, I in no way, shape, or form condone anything mentioned above in real life. This is purely fiction.

This book is intended for a mature adult audience only.

Remember, your mental health and well-being is more important than reading this book. Always put yourself first and be responsible for your own triggers. You're worth it and you matter.

Blurb

What happens when a devil claims a demon?

Detective Shadow Yor hates his life.
He spends all of his time, day after day, struggling against the demons in his head that tell him he's a worthless, unlovable person. This doesn't change when he's sent on a new assignment with his partner to solve a series of murders. He's good at his job and will find whoever did it, there's no doubt there. The only question is whether or not he'll be able to keep himself together during, or if his empathic abilities will finally be the death of him.

Apollo Orobas is bored.
He's bored of his secret nighttime proclivities and bored of playing the part of charming neighborhood do-gooder. Apollo isn't good, never has been, but just when he's starting to think life holds no interest, Shadow Yor stumbles into his sights. It doesn't take long for him to figure out the detective is also hiding his true self, and suddenly coaxing Shade's monster out into the light is all Apollo can think of. As obsession sinks its claws in, he decides it's time for a new game, one Shade is going to play with him. Whether he likes it or not.

Kidnapped and forced to endure whatever twisted plans Apollo has in store, Shade struggles to hold onto his idea of right and wrong, but the more he tries to resist, the more those lines start to blur. What chance does a mere demon have against an actual devil? Especially one who soothes those twisted voices in his head and makes him feel for the first time ever that maybe he isn't as unlovable as he's always believed.

Chapter 1:

"How long has the body been like that?" Gael asked, a thread of disgust in his tone. He kept his distance from the corpse, standing a good ten feet away from the crime scene as he grimaced.

Shade wasn't as squeamish and was already making his way slowly around the poor woman they'd been sent out here to investigate. Although, poor may be an over-exaggeration, considering the thick packet that had been left with the body—printed on paper, a novelty on this planet.

It wasn't his job to judge though; he was here to catch the killer and nothing else, which meant ignoring whatever shady morals he had and focusing on the cold facts.

A person had been murdered.

Her limbs were bent at odd angles and her killer had stripped her bare before dumping her at this construction site. Without clothes, it was easier to see all the injuries she'd sustained in life, like the burns up and down her arms and the deep gash in her side. Her legs were facing the wide entrance to the main level of the office building that had been in the process of being built, her head tipped and facing the opposite end where another opening large enough to fit the machinery needed for the job was located. Through it, a copse of dense trees could be seen.

A small glass orb circled the body at a faster pace than Shade, a beam of red light shooting from it to scan the body as it did. It made contact with the side of his boot once it was done, but he hardly noticed, too busy staring at the woman's face.

Her eyes were empty and glazed over, but wide as if she was locked in a perpetual scream. It was hard to tell though since the entire bottom half of her jaw was missing.

"Workers found her early this morning," Dario Braylon, the police officer from Ux station who'd been assigned this case before them, replied to Gael. "Whoever did it picked an operational worksite."

The killer had wanted her to be discovered, and sooner rather than later.

"Are they all this…gruesome?" Gael made a face as Shade snatched up the glass orb, a device known as N.I.M., and returned over to them. "You didn't mention this was a psycho we were after."

The first comment had been made to Dario, the second to Shade, but Shade answered.

"I wasn't aware," he said. "You know I just go where they tell me to."

Which usually meant they did the work no one else was willing to do. This case was no exception. A string of murderers had taken place on the planet Pollux, usually a dream job since solving something like this meant possible promotion, but it was trickier than that.

The murderer only killed other bad guys, and not just, the worst of the worst.

Shade hadn't gotten the chance to look over much of the information sent to them, but he'd scanned the brief. This killer caught people who hid amongst society, who blended so well, even the people around them had no clue of their deviance.

With each body, a packet of evidence was left behind, more often than not, revealing the horrible things that they'd done. Some were perps for open cases who'd covered their tracks too well to even be considered suspects. Others had committed crimes no one was even aware of. It was the last part that interested Shade the most.

Whoever they were after, this person was somehow in the know, more so even than the actual police. He would have taken on the case anyway because he never turned down a job, but that tidbit had piqued his interest.

Everyone else had passed it over because a criminal taking out other criminals was sort of like "the trash cleaning up itself", or so their chief had explained when he'd called to ask Shade to handle it.

Gael made a sound of frustration. "We could be picking our own cases, we're high up enough."

"Sounds a little like you're in the wrong line of work, Inspector," Dario teased, patting the younger blond man roughly on the back once. "You guys just arrived on planet, didn't you?"

Shade nodded. "That's why we haven't yet had a chance to go over the case files."

"We were on our way back to Percy when we got the new assignment," Gael explained.

Percy was a manmade planet where many of the Intergalactic Police Force, or the I.P.F, in the Dual galaxy lived. When a person signed up for this job, they agreed to cut all ties to their home world, and relocating was deemed the easiest way to successfully do that.

Truthfully, Shade wasn't any happier about this than his partner was. He'd only gotten a few days on blockers, and they'd been spent on their ship heading back to base. Even though he'd been trying his damndest to avoid looking over at the gathering crowd outside in the parking lot, the migraine was already starting to prick behind his temples.

The forensics team moved in, and Shade quickly glanced away, but not before making eye contact with one of them.

Outwardly, his expression was blank, like this was just another Tuesday, but inwardly…

Shade could see and feel people's true emotions, whether they—or he—wanted to or not. Direct eye contact was needed for most of his kind, but it was a lot harder to avoid meeting someone's gaze than it seemed.

It was hard to describe what he saw when he read a person, but he'd been asked enough times he'd mostly come up with a decent description. There was the outward expression as he liked to call it, the expression a person wore on the outside to conceal his true feelings from those around him. And then there was the inward one, the one that couldn't be hidden and showed what the person was truly feeling. Like everyone else, initially when he looked at someone he saw their outward face, but if the emotion didn't line up with what they felt inside, the image would alter. It was almost like seeing the screen of a computer glitch, pixels and lines flickering over their features a split second before a new image took the place of the old.

The man on the forensics team was gagging on the inside, no doubt trying to hide that he was every bit as squeamish by the sight as Gael.

There were a few different empathic species in the universe, but Shade was known as a Chitta. They were the only ones who experienced the glitch. They also had the same regular abilities as other empaths, however. For most, in order to lock on and reads another person's emotions, eye contact was still necessary, but not for Shade.

Trauma-induced PTSD had left him a bit…unstable, as his doctors liked to put it. The end result was a constant influx of other people's feelings that left him discombobulated at the best of times, and barely functioning at the worst. Hence, the blockers.

Too bad it was illegal for him to be on them during working.

"Everything all right, Detective?" Dario asked when Shade turned away from the team.

He'd already read the other man to get it over with and had been pleasantly surprised to find that the officer's outer and inner emotions matched up. At least for now, he wasn't hiding anything. Probably used to things like this and being transparent enough on the job with his co-workers, which was what Shade and Gael currently were.

The I.P.F had been called in to take over this case after a slew of terrible murders had terrorized the streets of Ux. The police had done their best but had hit dead end after dead end and had eventually asked for help.

Shade had never been to the planet Pollux before, but since it was within his galaxy and he was technically still on the clock despite having completed another assignment only four days ago, he'd been asked to take on the case. He used the term ask lightly.

"Just give him a minute," Gael said, sending Shade an apologetic look. The two of them had been partners for going on five years now, friends for twice that, and he was used to the physical toll Shade's empathic abilities took on him.

Another man approached then, stride determined as he came directly over to them. He called out, getting all of their attention at once.

Inadvertently, that had Shade lifting his head, catching sight of several people in the crowd over the man's shoulder. He sucked in a sharp breath and pressed a palm to his left eye where the stinging sensation had increased.

The new arrival faltered for a second before recognition dawned on him. "Oh, that's right. You must be Intergalactic Detective #167. Shadow Yor, yeah?" He held out his hand to him. "I just read your file. You're a Chitta."

"I'm Draxen," Shade corrected automatically. Technically, all that did was tell the other guy that he was a Chitta from the planet Drax, but he hoped it made his point.

He hated being reduced to that one thing. Chitta. In school, kids had whispered it when he'd passed in the halls, gossiping about him, teasing him. Some had even been afraid, knowing that he could see their deepest, darkest emotions with a mere glance. Things hadn't gotten much better when he'd joined the Academy.

Children, young adults, adults…age range didn't matter. No one liked the idea of another person getting in their head. Period.

"You are?" Dario blinked at him, momentarily caught off guard.

In return, Shade stared him down, almost daring him to have a bad reaction to that information. He was pleasantly surprised, however, when his ability didn't pick up on any change in the man. The news was a shock, but that was all.

Chitta were an empathic species that cropped up randomly within most of the known galaxies. There was no way of ever telling why, how, or when one would be born. It didn't matter if one or more of the parents were Chitta or not, it didn't mean anything when it came to whether a child born of them would be.

Shade's parents had been as normal as they came.

Which was why they'd only lasted a handful of years with their freak son before abandoning him to the system.

Swallowing down the bitterness he still felt about that, Shade cleared his throat and turned back to the new arrival. "And you are?"

"This is Axel," Dario answered for him, "my partner."

Dario was probably in his mid-forties, his hair already starting to pepper. He was a good foot shorter than Shade, with wide shoulders and a muscular body.

His partner was on the slimmer side, younger too by at least ten years, still a bit older than Shade and Gael. He seemed apologetic for bringing up the Chitta thing now and shifted awkwardly in his gray suede shoes.

"I go by Shade," he held out his hand to the other guy, hoping to move past the weirdness. It bothered him when what he was got called out so blatantly, but it wasn't something worth holding a grudge over, especially not when it was clear Axel hadn't been looking down at him or afraid of him for it.

There were stranger things out there than Chitta. Maybe he'd seen a few of them.

"It's nice to meet you," Axel motioned with his chin toward the body, "well, except for the circumstances, of course."

"Of course."

"I was just about to tell them about the others," Dario said. "She's the eleventh, as far as we know."

"Murdered the same way?" Shade asked.

"That's the frustrating part," he shook his head, "it's always different."

"Why do you think it's the same perp then?" Gael frowned. "Just because of the information packets? Could be a group effort."

"They're all tortured before they're killed," Axel answered. "The methods of torture vary as well, but there's always one physical similarity."

"What's that?"

Axel moved closer to the body which was being swabbed and photographed by the forensics team, pointing to a spot just above the back of her right hip bone. "That."

Gael kept his distance. "What?"

With a click of his tongue, Shade lifted his multi-slate, the body-borne communications and computer device most people wore strapped to their wrists, and clicked to access the specs he'd just had N.I.M. create when it'd circled the body.

An image of it projected a few inches above the long rectangular screen of the multi-slate and he held his arm between them so they could all see as he rotated the image and then zoomed in to the spot on her body Axel was talking about.

"What the Light is that?" Gael wrapped an arm around Shade's shoulders so he could lean in and squint at the projection. "An hourglass? Bowtie?"

Something had been carved into the woman's skin. Because of the position of it, it did look a lot like a bowtie, only the top parts of the triangles at either side were larger than the ones at the bottom.

"No idea," Dario confessed. "We've been trying to figure it out but so far it's just all guesses."

"And it's been on every single victim?" Shade asked.

"Yeah, same place and everything."

"So it's his signature." That was gross, but not entirely unheard of. Serial killers tended to leave something of themselves behind to help claim their kills. He'd worked a case once where the nail of the left big toe was always removed. When he'd finally found the culprit, the guy had strung them up around his apartment like they were fairy lights.

"Anything else?" Gael dropped his arm and stepped away. Though he'd been his partner when they'd worked the toe-nail case, he'd never adjusted to blood and gore. More often than not, he joked about retiring early and finding a water planet to spend the rest of his days fishing and purging his mind of all the shit he'd seen.

They both knew that was never going to happen though. Gael liked helping people too much. Plus, he came from a long line of I.P.F agents, all the way back to his great-great-grandmother. This was sort of the family business, and he'd grown up dreaming of following in their footsteps.

A commotion over by the crowd had them all looking a second time, Shade wincing all over again when his gaze connected with a few of the onlookers and the reporters being held back by a line of officers.

Their emotions were already weighing on him, heavy, like a wet blanket tossed over his shoulders, but the glitches made it ten times worse.

Word of the murder had gotten out and many held up their multi-slates or their professional cameras, snapping photos of anything and everything they could, even though the body was too far away for any of them to get any real good shots.

"Vultures," Dario hissed, glaring at the mass of reporters, many of whom were clearly trying to negotiate with the officers keeping them at bay to allow them to get closer. "I swear it's like they have a nose for blood or something. Every time."

People, no matter what planet they were from, had a sense of morbid curiosity ingrained in their DNA, it seemed.

"Is it always that bad?" Axel risked asking Shade, keeping his voice down as if that would somehow help to not offend him.

"It's because I'm recently off blockers," he explained, knowing exactly why that officer was referring to. He'd noticed Shade was in pain every time he looked at someone. It still hurt but had finally settled into a dull ache, allowing him to scan the crowd with only minor discomfort. It sucked sorting through the mess of expressions, not to mention having to deal with actually experiencing the zips of those emotions himself whenever he did make a connection, but this was also part of his job, and he wasn't about to shirk his duties.

Chitta and other empathic beings were hired for this job specifically because their abilities came them an edge in the field.

Just like leaving a signature or taking a trophy, killers also tended to revisit their crimes.

The crowd seemed chaotic however, some of the reporters overly eager for a scoop. No one was feeling any weird twists of guilt or dark glee. Nothing to cause Shade to suspect them.

"Blockers make it worse?" Axel frowned. "Why take them then?"

"They make it better for a while too," he stated absently, not wanting to get into it when they were meant to be here working.

He was about to give up on the crowd when his gaze passed over a tall man standing toward the end. There was a large camera hanging over his neck as well as a badge that showed he was a reporter, but his hands were tucked into his pockets and unlike the rest in his profession, he didn't seem all that interested in snapping photos of the crime scene.

There was too much distance between them for Shade to get a good look at his features, but the man tipped his head slightly in his direction, clearly catching notice that he was being watched. Their eyes met and Shade braced himself…

Only, nothing happened. No rush of emotion, no glitch over the man's face. There was just…nothing.

His brow furrowed.

There were two separate layers to his ability. The first was the glitch, where he could visually see a person's true emotions. The second was actually being able to feel them himself. Most Chitta were able to turn their abilities off at will, at least for a little while. Unfortunately, Shade was an exception. Without the blockers, the most he could do was focus all of his attention on a single person to narrow the swell of feelings bombarding him at any given moment.

When he'd first met Dario, there'd been no glitch, so he'd tuned into him just to be certain and had felt the swell of nerves and pity and anger the officer had been feeling. The exact emotions written all over his face.

Shade tuned into the guy with the camera now, sending out his mental feelers, thinking there had to be something wrong.

But he still felt nothing.

"All good, S?" Gael squeezed his shoulder, jolting him.

Shade gave a silent nod then quickly glanced back over to the crowd, only to find the man with the camera had vanished.

"What?" Gael stepped closer. "Someone seem suspicious?"

He considered trying to explain what had just happened, but even he thought it sounded crazy. Must just be the lingered effects of the blockers he'd been popping like candy up until six am this morning. People weren't immune to Chittas. That wasn't a thing.

"No." He sighed.

"Let's let them finish up here and meet at the station," Dario suggested. "We can go over the case files and answer any other questions you may come up with there."

They'd taken a taxi directly from the shuttle port but were now led over to one of the police cruisers. The station was supposedly on the opposite side of the city, a good twenty-minute drive, which meant they had some time to go over the information packet they'd retrieved from the I.P.F upon their arrival on planet.

Just as he was about to climb into the vehicle, a shiver raced down his spine and he turned back, scanning the crowd one last time.

No one was paying him any mind now that he'd moved away from the crime scene.

"Coming, Detective?" Axel leaned out of the passenger's side and asked.

"Yeah." With no other reason to keep him there, Shade slid into the back seat and left.

Chapter 2:

They held a press conference the next day at the city hall. Up until this point, the police had refused to make any public announcements of that grandeur, other than to request citizens to be vigilant and keep safe. Since there was no obvious pattern in how victims were chosen, Dario had smartly refused to hold a conference before, not wanting to needlessly cause panic in the streets.

But that was before Shade's arrival.

There was a reason being a Chitta almost guaranteed a position in the I.P.F. Transparency. If a detective could see through a person's lies, their job was a lot easier to complete. And faster as well.

The Ux police had been working this case for six months already with no solid leads. In the beginning, it was Shade's understanding that the cops hadn't taken the killings all too seriously. As soon as they'd confirmed the information in the packs left with the bodies had been true, they'd been disgusted with the victims'. Some had even quit the case altogether, refusing to help solve the murder of a murderer. Though, they weren't all murderers. Some of them had done worse things than that, at least, in Shade's mind.

But the killings hadn't stopped, and with each new body, it had become harder and harder to keep news out of the media. The head of the Ux police was starting to get pressure from those above him who wanted this solved before it blew out of proportion. Dario had taken over and had been the first one working on it who'd taken it seriously. Still, after months of dodgy police work, they were past the point of desperation and open to suggestions.

Since they knew the person they were after had a thing for marking up his kills, it was safe to assume he'd show an interest in a press conference. At least, that's what Shade had figured. It was worth a shot, if nothing else, and if they happened to get lucky? Great.

Even though it was well known that the I.P.F had taken over, Dario led the conference, standing at the front of the room, center stage, leaning over a podium with a microphone on it. He explained to a room packed full of reporters as well as members of the public who'd been allowed in under the guise of—ironically—transparency. Really, they'd just hoped the culprit would be amongst them and they'd get a hit.

Which was where Shade came in. He stood off to the side, blending in with a group of other officers who'd been working the case already. He kept as far from the crowd's notice on purpose, scanning through the faces as their attention was glued to the front, on Dario.

Any lingering effects of the blockers had worn off completely and he was able to use his ability with a clear mind. He'd only have an hour or so before the headache crept in anyway, but they were estimating the conference would be winding down to a close by then.

He and Gael had spent the better part of yesterday combing over all of the information on the past murders that Dario's team had collected. There was a lot, and yet nothing that pointed to anyone definitive as a possible culprit. No DNA samples had been left at the scenes, and they were pretty sure that every body discovered had been left there to be found.

They were all killed somewhere else and then moved after the fact. No clues on where the kill site could be located either. Just a whole lot of blanks. Whoever they were dealing with, they were good.

Meaning they were very, very bad. Even Shade, who could typically stomach anything, had choked up flipping through some of the pictures of the other murders. Gael had excused himself to vomit in the tiny bathroom attached to the suit they'd been given in a hotel nearby the station.

But it wasn't just the crime scenes of the victims that'd been left that were hard to stomach.

Information on each of the victims' secret crimes had been carefully compiled and printed before being stuffed into a manila envelope and left atop each body. That info had been scanned and digitalized, making it easier for Shade and Gael to work their way through it and…it was every bit as gruesome as what their serial killer was capable of.

Out of the eleven known murders, not a single one had been a decent person during life. They'd faked it, fooling those around them, but somehow the killer had seen their true selves and reveled it to the world.

They'd opted to refrain from disclosing that bit to the public, worried that if they did, people who hadn't committed any crimes would assume they were safe. While it was true only horrible criminals had been targeted so far, there was no telling when or if that would change. Even if highly unlikely—serial killers very rarely altered their M.O.—it wasn't worth the risk.

"Can't you tell us anything else about this possible murderer?" one of the reporters asked Dario, Shade only partially listening as he continued to search the room. "How worried should we be?"

"Unfortunately there isn't much I can say with any real certainty," Dario replied, "other than people should avoid going out alone at night. Travel in pairs or groups."

"Any particular areas that are a bigger threat?" another reporter stood up and questioned.

The bodies had all popped up in different places all around the city, so there was no way of narrowing down any particular hunting ground. They were prepared to get a lot of shit for this conference and the lack of crucial information they could provide, however, they'd decided to word it as a public announcement in order to alert them to the possible danger. Hopefully, that would be enough to slacken the blow.

Shade sifted through various faces, some of them bored and dragged here by their friends or family members, others alert like the reporters on a mission. Some were scared, as they should be, and—

There. Shade homed in on a man in the back. The guy was wearing a black baseball cap pulled low over his face and while his mouth was set in a firm line, the Glitch showed differently.

He was laughing. Not a casual chuckle or a boisterous kind of laugh either. In the man's mind, his hand was covering his mouth as he laughed and laughed as if he knew something no one else did.

Shade shifted along the wall, traveling around the edge of the crowd, eyes locked on the man.

He was hardly the only civilian in here with a hat on, so it hadn't drawn suspicion from anyone else. His clothing wasn't anything particularly noteworthy either, dark blue jeans tucked into work boots and a plain black t-shirt.

He'd almost made it to the very back when the man took notice of Shade and stiffened. When he turned and marched out the wide double doors, Shade was already in motion.

Shade rushed after him, catching sight as he took a right down the branching hall. The man was running now, glancing over his shoulder once back at Shade to see if he was being chased or not.

There weren't many people out in the hallways, but there were a few, and Shade breezed past them, desperately trying to keep the suspect in sight as they raced down hallway after hallway. The city hall building was used for many different events and had more twists and turns than he'd anticipated. They'd already taken several turns and the man in the cap didn't appear to be losing speed in the least.

He disappeared around a sharp corner and Shade cursed, ignoring the slight burning sensation in his thighs as he tore after him.

And slammed into what felt like a solid wall.

The force of the impact sent both him and the man he'd just crashed into falling to the ground. He landed on his ass and scrambled to right himself, glancing around the body he'd just smashed into to catch sight of the man in the hat.

The guy was gone.

Shade debated taking his chances and giving chase again, but then a smooth voice like warmed honey spoke, catching his attention.

"Sorry about that, Detective." The man he'd run into stood and dusted off the thighs of his black jeans, holding up the camera hanging around his neck once he saw that Shade was looking at him. "I wasn't paying attention. Bad habit."

Shade stilled. "I saw you," he found himself saying, "yesterday. At the crime scene."

"Did you?" The man gave a light chuckle, the sound reaching his dark blue eyes. "If you run into my boss next time, do me a favor and tell him as much. I didn't get a single shot and he keeps insisting it must be because I got cold feet and didn't show."

They two of them were roughly the same height, with the other guy maybe having an inch or two on him. His hair was an inky black and slightly curled at the ends, his brows thick, nose long and straight. He was wearing a violet dress shirt tucked into black jeans and dress shoes. An expensive multi-slate with a golden case sat on his right wrist, typically indicating that he was left handed, and the camera slung around his neck was top of the line. The man's lips were the shade of freshly ripe cherries, but on the thinner side, tipping up slightly at the side in an almost embarrassed way.

Shade realized with a start he'd been staring and cleared his throat, retreating a full step in the process. Even after all of that, his ability hadn't picked up on a single thing. The only emotions he felt were his own and those closest down the halls.

He tried to think of something, literally anything, he could say to cut through the awkwardness he'd just created purely on his own, but was struggling.

Fortunately, Axel chose that moment to dart around the corner, coming to a stop a bit out of breath. He rested his hands on his hips and glanced between the two of them, nodding familiarly at the man with the camera before turning to address Shade.

"There you are," he inhaled. "By the time I realized you were chasing someone you were already like ten miles away. How fast are you?"

"Cleary not fast enough," Shade drawled. "He got away."

"Do you run for fun, Detective?" the man with the camera asked, still with that same friendly, honey-dripped tone.

For reasons completely unknown to him, Shade found he liked it, the sound of his voice.

"Yeah," he replied. Running helped to keep his head straight when the influx of other people's emotions got to be too much for him to handle. Sometimes, like if he was ever in a crowded room, the sensations could become overwhelming. When he ran, he had an excuse to avoid the eyes of any passersby and could just focus on the way the air burned in his lungs and the wind whipped at his cheeks.

"Apollo is the BH1's track star," Axel said, referencing the number one news agency on all of Pollux. It was so large it was broken up into separate, smaller branches, many of whom had sent reporters currently packed in the conference room listening to Dario. "Last summer when we had a friendly competition between our station and there's, he wiped the floor with all of us."

"I got lucky that day," the man—Apollo—laughed.

"If you're looking for someone to run with on your off time you should ask him," Axel continued. "He knows all the best trails, including ones that will have less foot traffic."

"Are you not a fan of people, Detective?" Apollo kept that friendly smile on his face as he waited for an answer, the cheerful glimmer in his dark eyes never wavering.

"I'm not a fan of pretenders," he found himself saying, being a bit more honest than he'd meant to. For a split second, he thought he saw Apollo's smile widen, but when he blinked it was back to the easy, polite upward curve of his lips and nothing more.

"Who were you chasing?" Axel seemed to recall what they were doing there, standing in the middle of the empty hallway.

"That's my cue." Apollo bowed his head at them formally and moved around the officer. Just before he was about to leave, however, he turned back and caught Shade's eye. "Let me know if you ever want to go on that run, Detective."

"You should hurry," Axel warned, grinning, "the conference is almost over. Don't get chewed out by your boss again."

Apollo laughed and lifted a hand in a wave before disappearing out of sight.

For a moment, Shade stared after him. He'd never been unable to read a person before, but that wasn't reason enough to be suspicious. Still…

"How well do you know that guy?" he asked.

"Who, Apollo?" Axel shrugged. "A couple of years now probably."

"He was at the crime scene yesterday," Shade said, still clinging to how off-putting it was he couldn't read him. Killers tended to return… "Is he usually the first to arrive? Has he been at any of the other murders?"

Axel finally seemed to connect that Shade was apprehensive and frowned. "No way, man. This isn't even his area of expertise. Apollo is a beat reporter for the art scene, one of the best. Huge knowledge base. I heard one of his seniors got into an accident and was hospitalized making them short-staffed. He must have gotten the short end of the stick and was simply selected by his boss to take this story over in the meantime."

"An art reporter?" Shade couldn't hide his surprise. "Covering a murder case?"

Axel glanced up and down the hall even though they were alone. "You didn't hear this from me, but his boss is an ass. Used to be this really committed woman named Cin Brice, but she's out on maternity leave, and the guy they got to replace her…yikes. He's a Royal and does he act like it. Super underqualified for the job."

"Nepotism?" Shade asked, only somewhat interested.

"You got it."

Imperials and Royals tended to think they owned the world…mostly because they sort of did. Shade would usually have to have an official meeting with the Imperial Emperor of Pollux, but since he was located on the opposite side of the planet in the capital country Ot, he'd gotten out of that. It was always a mere formality and complete and total waste of time too, so he was glad for it.

"Who were you chasing?" Axel sighed disappointedly. "Our first lead and he got away."

"He might not be a lead," Shade reminded. Though, innocent people didn't tend to run, not like that anyway.

"What made you go after him?"

"He was laughing." He moved to head back toward the conference, going the same way that Apollo just had. "Where's the security room located?" The cameras had been filming in the conference and in the halls, so there was a good chance they'd caught the guy on them. "If we can get a facial ID we'll be able to check him off the list of suspects at the very least."

It was a long shot, going after a guy for laughing, and in his head for that matter, but as far as Shade was concerned, it had to take a certain kind of sicko to find anything about how that poor woman yesterday had been butchered funny. And to everyone listening in that room, that's all she'd be, a poor woman, since they were keeping the fact she was apparently also guilty of poisoning several people in her family a secret.

Axel lead him to the security room, which was mostly on the way back toward the conference, with a left turn thrown in just before they would have made it. More people were in the halls now, letting them know that Dario was most likely winding things down to an end. Since they doubted the man Shade had been chasing was still in the building anyway, they weren't really in any rush.

Shade took the opportunity to inspect everyone that he passed, using both the Glitch and opening himself up to their emotions as he walked by. When they finally made it to the room with the words "staff only" painted across he gave up.

That's where Gael and Dario found them twenty minutes later, hunched over the massive row of screens, each showing a different feed from the building.

They'd managed to sort through most of the footage and had only just found a useful image of the guy Shade had chased. He tapped on the image and ordered the security worker sitting in the chair who'd been helping to send it to him directly.

"I'll have N.I.M.. run it through facial recognition," Shade told the others after filling them in on what was going on.

"It's a good a bet as any," Dario said, running a hand through his graying hair. He heaved a sigh and motioned toward the door. "Let's get out of here before we're hounded by reporters and trapped for the rest of the day. I don't know about you three, but I could seriously use a drink."

Shade would much prefer to slink off to his hotel room where he could be alone and nurse the oncoming headache he felt, but since it was only the second day of working together, he knew keeping up appearances was more important.

Most I.P.F teams were made of three to four members, but Shade and Gael had operated on their own since the beginning and had refused any other teammates whenever the offer was made. They worked well together and they liked including local forces whenever they were on a job. More often than not, that was hardly the case and the I.P.F completely took over.

Dario and Axel knew more about what was going on here than Shade or Gael, so staying on their good sides was important.

Which meant going to what was no doubt about to be a crowded bar that would exasperate Shade's headache and have him wishing he were dead in under a half hour.
Fantastic.

Chapter 3:

N.I.M., which stood for Networking Intelligence Machine, was a top-of-the-line, somewhat new creation that only some teams of the I.P.F had received. As one of the first, Shade had gotten used to the device and how handy it could be. But N.I.M.. didn't work miracles and was still limited in certain areas.

Like time.

The bar Dario took them to was a brief walk down the street from city hall, but the whole way Shade kept hoping he'd get a notification saying that N.I.M.. had ID'd their suspect so he could get out of having to socialize. No such luck.

He'd programed the device to start by searching the databases on planet, and if it didn't get a hit, it would slowly work its way outwards, using Demeter Station, the information hub of the universe, as its source. An automatic report would be sent to his superiors as well as those working the station at the same time, which would allow him access in a timely fashion, should it come to that.

Demeter Station was located in another galaxy, but with technology as advanced as it was, he'd ideally get approval before nightfall.

Shade just hoped their guy was a citizen of Pollux. It would make things so much easier all around.

As he'd feared, the bar was packed when they arrived, the chatter loud enough to worsen his oncoming migraine within seconds of entering. It'd been decorated in old-timey fashion, mostly wood and metal, with projection screens hanging in intervals on the walls playing different kinds of sports games that must be popular with the Polluxians.

Aside from running and the occasional trip to the gym to ensure he stayed in shape, Shade wasn't interested in sports or anything else that involved strenuous physical activity. The upside, he was in the minority amongst this crowd, and most people kept their eyes on the screens even as he and his small group made their way through the main floor trying to find seats.

Even though it was only mid-afternoon the bar was almost at full capacity, the smell of beer and fried foods tickling Shade's nose. There was also the mixture of sweat and more cologne and perfume than he cared to mention, but to each their own. There was an equal amount of men and women as well.

A female screamed at one of the screens across the room then, as if reading his mind.

"Cloudball," Gael said, motioning with his chin toward the screen she was watching with his chin. "That's the sport. It's the most popular one on planet. Everyone has a team and the two playing are rivals. Explains why there are so many people here today, even though it's the middle of the week."

As the Inspector, it was Gael's job to research the culture, tradition, and laws of whichever planet they'd been assigned. He was meant to act as a buffer between Shade and the laws here, to ensure that no one up top was offended and things didn't go south and land them in an intergalactic jail cell. Since every planet was different, an Inspector was assigned to every Detective which was why the lowest number a team could be was two.

"Look who it is," Dario said boisterously as they approached one of the long bars on the far left side of the room. There were a few empty seats there and he stopped their group in front of them as the man he'd addressed turned his head their way.

It was Apollo. He held a half-empty glass aloft casually and gave a warm smile at the officer. "Great minds think alike it seems."

"Mind if we join you?"

"Not at all." He waved toward the empty stool chairs, gaze flicking over to Shade briefly before returning to Dario as he was asked another question.

"Drowning out your sorrows, kid?" Dario tapped the bar surface to get the man tending on the other side's attention. "I saw you come in toward the end of the conference. Bet your boss wasn't pleased."

"Celebrating, actually," he replied, pausing to nod in greeting at Shade when Axel all but shoved him onto the empty stool directly next to the guy. "Because of that, he finally realized I was a terrible fit for the job and he took me off it. I'm back on art, just in time too."

"Right," Axel sat on Shade's other side, leaving the only empty seat the one on the end by Dario, which Gael took, "Vice's showing. It's this weekend, isn't it?"

"It is." Apollo shifted a bit to better face them, his leg bumping up against Shade's momentarily before he pulled back a little. He didn't seem the least bit affected by the contact, if he even noticed, and ignored Shade's look as he continued to speak down the length of the bar with Axel. "Are you a fan? Not to brag, but I have an in with the artist. I could get you tickets if you'd like."

"Could you?" Axel laughed sheepishly. "My girlfriend would really appreciate it."

"I'll have them sent to your office."

"Suji likes art?" Dario asked, and the conversation shifted to the three of them at the end, leaving Shade sitting there feeling like an idiot.

He didn't even bother checking the menu, ordering the same thing that Axel did. When the dark blue glass bottle was set before him, he eyed in momentarily before figuring fuck it. With the way his head was currently feeling, he'd take what he could get. In one gulp he drained a third of the bottle, only aware of what he must look like when the man on his right let out a low chuckle.

"Thirsty, Detective?" Apollo held out his hand, ink from a wrist tattoo partially visible as his sleeve slipped up. "I didn't catch your name earlier."

"Shadow Yor," he accepted and shook, trying not to make it obvious he was curious about the design. It wasn't like him to be interested in people's personal business or their appearance if it didn't have something to do with a case, yet he found himself wanting to know. "But everyone calls me Shade."

"Apollo Orobas," he leaned in as if to divulge some great secret, "but my boss calls me Useless. It's nice to meet you, and it's a butterfly, by the way." He grinned when Shade didn't immediately reply. "The tattoo? Random decision made one night in college after too many. Do you have any?"

Shade hesitated, which was dumb, because there was no reason not to be honest. It wasn't like the other guy was a mind reader or anything and would instantly peg why Shade had tried it. "Yeah. One."

"Any great meaning?"

"What about yours?" he countered.

"Rebirth and resurrection," Apollo replied. "It was a dark period in my life. I needed something that would help me feel like I regained control of myself."

"Why not a phoenix?"

"Too on the nose."

He wasn't sure what that meant.

"Thought you said you were drunk?" Shade made sure to keep his tone light so he'd know he was only joking. "Sounds like you've been through some stuff."

"Haven't we all." Apollo didn't push Shade to tell him about his own ink. "First time on Pollux?"

"That obvious?" Shade took another drink. His tattoo had also been the result of a drunken night. Only, he'd been chasing after a feeling, not trying to escape one. He'd hoped the sting of the needle would help him find some peace.

All it'd done was hurt.

"You just seem a little skittish, that's all."

He snorted. "It's not the atmosphere."

"Isn't it?" Apollo hummed, not seemingly like he believed him, and sipped at his drink before adding, "And here I thought you were going through Repletion. My mistake."

Shade choked on the alcohol, feeling it burn down his throat as he swiveled to face him, wide-eyed.

"I'm sorry," Apollo said, "I assumed you'd realized. I'm also a Chitta."

"What?" That was… "Seriously?"

"Yeah." He grinned. "You're acting like you've never met another before."

"That's because I haven't." Shade swallowed the sudden lump in his throat. "Have you?"

"Once or twice. We're not as uncommon on this planet as some others. I'm surprised your Inspector didn't inform you of that fact."

It did seem a little odd that Gael would miss it, but since they'd had this case tossed at them last minute, he'd most likely been hyper-focused on the important details instead. It would have been nice to know, if only so Shade could have tried to meet one of his kind sooner.

"I've always been curious about meeting another in person," he admitted, eyes roaming up and down Apollo, taking in the way his shoulders stretched out the tight material of the shirt he was wearing.

He'd changed out of the outfit he'd been in for the press conference and instead was in a dark gray t-shirt, a maroon jacket, and black jeans. There was nothing flashy or unique about the clothing itself, and yet Apollo stood out like a lit beacon in the night.

And Shade wasn't the only one who noticed. A glance around the bar proved as much. There were eyes everywhere peering over at them, some with mild interest, others with obvious jealousy toward Shade for being seated next to the gorgeous reporter. For what it was worth, Shade wasn't an unattractive person. But people tended to shy away when someone dropped their gaze in their presence or went out of their way to outright ignore them the way Shade always did.

It was due to his fear of migraines and, ultimately, Repletion that caused him to do it, but he couldn't exactly go around saying "sorry, it's not you, it's me". Every now and again someone might take his mistaken aloofness as a challenge and approach him anyway, try to get under his shell, but that never worked in the long run either.

People always left the second they realized how unstable his abilities made him.

Shade wondered what it would be like to have the type of attention Apollo got. To walk into a room and have your pick of conversations without fear of what the consequences might be.

"Hey," Apollo tapped the side of his arm, watching him closely, "everything all right, Detective?"

"Yeah," he feigned a laugh. "Sorry about that. I'm just surprised to meet you, that's all."

"I've never met one of us who was in the I.P.F before."

Shade frowned. "Really? It's not that unheard of. It's one of the few jobs that'll take us just for being Chitta. Many others shun us."

Apollo frowned. "That hasn't been my experience. That's unfortunate that it's been yours."

"Do they," Shade indicated the officers sitting on his other side, "know?"

"About me being Chitta?" Apollo nodded. "Yeah. Most people in my life do. I don't keep it a secret."

"That sounds nice," he tried and failed to keep the edge of bitterness from leaking into his tone. Sighing afterward, he downed the rest of his drink in one go before tapping the bar to indicate he wanted another. "I apologize. That's not fair of me."

"Being fair is overrated." The corner of Apollo's mouth tipped up.

There was something intense about the look, something that had Shade almost squirming in his seat, so he cleared his throat and kept the conversation going. "Is that why I haven't been able to read you? We're both Chitta?"

While he'd never met another of his kind, he'd done plenty of research and was active in a few online forums. There'd never been any mention of Chittas being unable to sense the emotions in each other, but that would explain it. Considering how different every body in the universe was, it also wasn't like that situation couldn't occur.

"Most likely," Apollo confirmed. "Others had trouble reading me as well. I think I just have strong mental walls."

"Is that how you figured out what I was? Can you still read me?"

He tapped his temple. "It was the wincing, actually. Gave it away."

Shade searched his face, but the other man seemed calm as ever, relaxed even. "You don't seem to be experiencing the same problem."

"I rarely go into Repletion," he shared. "I'd like for it to be because of my mental walls, but honestly, I'm not the strongest Chitta. I can't get any kind of reading without making eye contact."

Repletion happened when a Chitta used their abilities in too crowded of a location, overstimulating them. Some suffered from it constantly while others only experienced it occasionally or not at all. It was one of those things that couldn't be predicted. Some brains handled the influx of outside emotions and the constant Glitches interfering with their vison more than others. If Apollo didn't feel anyone else unless he was looking at them, it was safe to assume he never dealt with overstimulation.

"Lucky." Shade sighed.

"You get them a lot then?"

"Only when I'm breathing." Shade repeated his earlier move and ordered a third drink.

"Can you handle your liquor, Detective?"

"Usually," he replied. "Though, every planet's alcohol is different."

"Guess we'll have to wait and see then." Apollo gave him that friendly smile again.

Axel laughed with the others next to Shade, reminding him they were there. For a moment, he'd forgotten that he and the reporter weren't alone, which was…Unheard of for him.

Shade was constantly being bombarded by the emotions of others, making it impossible for him to ever "forget" their presence. Was it because Apollo was also Chitta? Did that make a difference where their abilities were concerned somehow? Was it dimming it or something similar?

Or was he just entirely distracted for other reasons.

Like he had back in the hallway, Shade acknowledged that Apollo was a very attractive individual. Everything about him screamed appeal. He had the perfect proportions, was well dressed, friendly…

Nice. Safe.

Two things Shade could use more of, if only to help ground his inner demons, the ones he was always struggling against. But he wasn't here to meet someone and saddle them with his burden. Apollo came off as a well-rounded individual who had a lot going for him. The last thing he needed was for someone like Shade to throw a wrench into the mix.

Still…It wouldn't hurt to get to know him a little better, at least right now, purely because this was his first time coming face-to-face with another Chitta. He had to take advantage of the opportunity, right? It didn't have to mean anything more than that or go any further.

"Are you seeing someone?" The question left his mouth so quickly, it took him a second to process he'd been the one to ask it. How unprofessional.

"No," Apollo answered, and if he'd been offended he didn't show it, "believe it or not, I'm actually a pretty private person. I haven't found the right one yet."

"I don't," Shade said. "Believe it, that is. Axel seems to know you pretty well." He'd been able to tell Shade about the other guys running proclivities, and he seemed well-liked by the older officer too.

"He probably tried to set us up earlier because he knows we're both Chitta." Apollo propped his arms on the edge of the bar. "I tend to keep to myself on my off time, so I bet he's trying to look out for me too."

"That can't be true." Shade couldn't picture someone who drew this much attention from others sitting at home all weekend alone twiddling his thumbs. "What about your family? Friends?"

"I don't have the first, and as for the latter…" he shrugged. "I have them, sure. But I like my space more often than not. You understand. My abilities aren't nearly as intense as yours, but sometimes it's nice to just get away and enjoy the quiet, you know?"

He did know.

"Not a fan of being in the limelight?" Shade asked.

"I prefer to blend," Apollo replied. "What about you, Detective?"

"I'd prefer to live in a hole far from civilization," he joked. Mostly.

"Sounds like you're in the wrong line of work."

"It was one of the few careers that would have me," he admitted. "I was put in the system at a young age, so my status as a Chitta was pretty public knowledge at the orphanage. That made my options for advancement limited."

It'd also made adoption impossible. No one had wanted him and he'd been forced to watch time after time as he was passed over for one of the other normal kids. Even those who'd almost aged out of the system were chosen over him. There was still some lingering resentment when he allowed himself to think back on those times, so he tried not to. Unfortunately, the past was a lot easier to let go of in theory than in reality.

"When I figured out I'd be stuck there until eighteen, I did the only thing I could think of. Focused on my studies. I ended up graduating almost four years ahead of the rest of my class and was accepted into the Academy at sixteen, and—" he stopped himself, running his fingers through the short hairs at the base of his skull, "I have no idea why I'm telling you all of this. I'm sorry."

"It's fine," Apollo said. "I'm interested."

He shook his head. "What about you?"

"My family died," he divulged without skipping a beat.

"My condolences."

"It was a long time ago."

"What happened?"

"Fire. I was at the library at the time. My sister was supposed to come with me, but she decided not to at the last minute and stayed home. She and our parents died from smoke inhalation. Yours?" Some of the light had left Apollo's eyes, but that was the only indication that the subject was hard for him to talk about.

And he'd just asked him why he hadn't gotten a tattoo of a bird that rose from ashes. Suddenly Apollo's comment made sense and he felt awful for it.

For the first time in a while, Shade found himself wishing he were able to get inside someone's head. If he could read his emotions, he'd know how he was truly feeling and whether or not it was appropriate for him to comfort or change the subject. As it were, without that ability, he was forced to react the same way any regular person would.

Instinctually with hope for the best.

"I was abandoned," he admitted.

Apollo didn't apologize like most people would, or even give condolences like Shade had. He merely stared at him beneath hooded lashes for a stretch of silence before drawling in that honey-toned voice of his, "Aren't we the pair, Detective?"

Usually when that story was told, Shade received pity. Even Gael had been unable to hide that emotion from him when he'd first discovered it halfway through their first semester as roommates at the Academy. But

Apollo didn't look like he pitied him. He didn't ask if being Chitta was the reason his parents had dropped Shade off at that orphanage and never come back. Didn't pry for how that'd made Shade feel or call them names and give empty platitudes like how it was their loss, or look how well he'd turned out without them.

Though their circumstances were entirely different, Apollo appeared as though he…understood. Staring into his eyes, the boisterous noise in the bar seemed to fade into the distance, the cries and curses as some team on-screen scored sounding almost as if they were underwater.

Along with the quiet, a sense of calm settled over Shade, easing the tension in his shoulders. A sigh slipped past his lips, drawing Apollo's attention down to them and before Shade even knew what was happening, his chest was constricting and he felt a familiar pulsing heat in his groin.

What the actual hell was going on with him?

He was getting turned on by a man he'd only just met in a crowded room after talking about their *dead families*.

There was a reason he hadn't hooked up with anyone in years, other than the fact his being Chitta made it hard to connect with someone when he was constantly forced to feel whatever they were feeling. Maybe it was the fact he'd already taken a stroll down memory lane thanks to Apollo's line of questioning, but he thought back to his first time and how bad it'd been.

About how, because it'd been bad, parts of it had been good…

Which was why he'd played it safe and only participated in vanilla sex ever since, and always with carefully selected partners. If that meant he hadn't enjoyed sleeping with anyone as much as he had when he'd lost his virginity? So what. It was better than it getting out that the well-respected, quiet, and cold Detective #167 preferred it rough in the bedroom.

Shade would never kink shame anyone for their sexual proclivities, but he was a damn I.P.F agent for Light's sake, and he hadn't struggled to build his reputation, one that had finally helped him make Chitta a part of his identity instead of its defining feature, just to acquire whispers and odd looks because he liked a little pain and dominance in the bedroom.

It was okay for other people to be into that sort of thing, so long as it was consensual. But that was another part of the problem.

Getting out of his own head was so difficult for him, half the time the pain he sought out didn't help. The tattoo was a testament to that fact. Sometimes the sting from the needle helped him focus on his feelings and block out everyone else's. But mostly it did nothing. By the end of the two-hour session, he'd been pretty overwhelmed by the five other people in the building.

Pain was a trigger if his past was any indicator, but there was some secret formula to it that Shade had yet to figure out on his own. Not only because when was he supposed to find the time? But also, again, because his profession kept him from giving in to those types of temptations.

Sometimes, when he was at risk of Repletion and it was really bad, he'd swear to himself that he'd sign up at one of the sex clubs Gael frequently mentioned. As soon as he felt better, however, he'd chicken out. His reputation was the only thing he had going for him, and the mere thought of tarnishing and losing that left him terrified.

He wondered what a nice and friendly guy like Apollo would say if he heard any of this. Most likely he'd think there was something wrong with Shade.

Shade certainly believed there was something wrong with himself.

Before the disgust could truly sink in, his multi-slate went off, a harsh pattern of beeps and whizzing sounds that had him jolting in his seat. Thankful for the interruption, he quickly checked it, getting to his feet in a hurry when he saw what it was.

Shade bumped his shoulder against Axel's. "N.I.M.. got a hit. Hey, Gael. Let's go."

"Come to the Vice Gallery showing this Saturday," Apollo said, catching Shade's attention when he would have stepped away from the bar.

In his haste to get back to the case, he'd forgotten his manners. He was all over the place today. One second he's picturing jumping the guy and the next he forgets all about him and is going to leave without saying goodbye.

Sleep. Shade needed sleep.

"I'd love to," he said truthfully, "but I'll most likely be too busy working on the case."

"I'll have tickets dropped off," Apollo told him, shrugging casually. "If you can make it, great. If not, no hard feelings."

Events that included crowds, like gallery showings, fell into the category of things best avoided in Shade's mind. Yet, he found himself nodding, and as he followed the others back out onto the street, he realized with a bit of surprise that he was actually hopeful that he *would* find the time to attend.

If only so he could see the reporter again.

Chapter 4:

From the very moment their eyes had met he'd known there was something special about the detective. Shadow moved through the crowd like a predator, spine straight, mouth set in a firm line as he concentrated on his surroundings, looking for something.

Looking for *him*.

But he didn't want to be found just yet, so the detective was going to have to be patient.

It wasn't the confidence in the other man's strides that drew him though. It was the way he was barely holding himself together beneath that unapproachable demeanor. The strain in his muscles and the wincing whenever he thought no one was looking gave him away.

He'd come out to check on the progress of the case. Now that the I.P.F was involved keeping a closer eye on the investigation was the smart move. He was careful with his tracks, always had been, and was certain it wouldn't be easy for anyone to stumble upon his identity, but the I.P.F were going to look at this case a lot more closely than any of the Ux police had bothered, including Officer Dario Braylon.

The man had a noble heart that bled for the victims, even if they were all vile and rotten to the core. Dario had tried his best to catch him but that nobleness that spurred him on when most of the rest of his department would rather turn the other cheek was also what got in his way.

It was impossible to recognize a devil in the dark if you weren't willing to become a little monstrous yourself. Dario? He probably kept himself up at night thinking about that one time he J-walked as a preteen.

No, Dario didn't have hope or a prayer of ever catching him.

But Detective Shadow Yor...

There'd been a look in Shadow's eyes when their gazes had locked and a tremor had skittered down his spine, pleasurable and warm. For the first time in a long time, he'd felt well and truly seen.

He wanted more of that.

He'd glimpsed the monster lurking behind those eyes and he wanted to drag it out to play. Coax it into his hand and watch it dance as he set fire beneath the pads of its delicate feet. Everyone had a demon inside of them, but most people snuffed them into silence or caged them in a corner.

Shadow was trying to hide his, and while the rest of the world around them might not see, it was obvious that he was failing.

He didn't usually target people like Shadow Yor, people who clearly hadn't done any wrong. People who would bring down a world of attention if they suddenly went missing.

And yet...

He wanted to know what made the detective tick. Wanted to see inside that head of his and play around, find out just what had made him so closed off from the rest of the world. What an odd job to choose for someone who clearly hated being around other people.

He'd already chosen his next target and put that process into motion, but he could make this work.

He'd fit the detective into his schedule and satisfy this strange curiosity that had awakened within him. It wasn't like the one he usually felt when he discovered someone's dirty secret. That always left him with this elation, like a dark high, because he knew he'd be able to let his true self out from behind his carefully crafted boy-next-door-persona.

Many years had passed since he'd first concluded that he was different from the rest of society. In the beginning, he'd tried to pretend that it bothered him, but eventually the fake frowns and mock disappointment he showed his family got tedious and rather dull.

Why should he have to change for others anyway? There might be something wrong with him, something that made him different, but he was hardly the only one with skeletons, proverbial or otherwise, stuffed into his closet.

One of his favorite pastimes was riffling through someone else's junk and unearthing those skeletons for the whole world to see.

He was a devil in a universe filled with demons, and like hell would he ever allow any of them to forget it.

But he was strict with himself, disciplined, because that made all the difference between a devil and your run-of-the-mill everyday monstrosity. He kept himself in check, only went after those like him. Normal people were too boring to waste his time on anyway, good for both them and him. Normal people tended to be missed when they disappeared. That was one of the major reasons he made it a point to uncover as much dirt on his target before he actually made his move.

He'd gone to catch a glimpse of the I.P.F agents in charge so he'd know what he was dealing with and whether or not he should put his latest hunt on hold. Locking gazes with the detective hadn't been on the agenda.

Being unable to get the other man off his mind definitely hadn't been.

True, he wouldn't mind taking the detective apart, but it was more than that. There was something about those eyes, hazel and wide, so that they stood out on the detective's perfectly proportioned face. His hair was the shade of mahogany, shiny and soft in appearance. He wanted to run his fingers through it.

Wanted to wrap his hand around his neck and see how hard he could squeeze before those pretty hazel eyes bulged out of the detective's head.

Would they change color? Flicker between greener and browner?

He wanted to know.

He wanted to know everything.

It made sense, too. He'd been trying to figure out how to get close enough to the case to keep tabs on things without coming off suspicious. This was a good start.

Keeping an eye on the detective could be the ticket he'd been waiting for.

Opening a fresh page on his multi-slate, he typed out the detective's name, taking in the look of it in writing. Then he deleted it because only an idiot would keep physical evidence lying around. Even once he'd cleared it and there was nothing but a white screen staring back at him, he could still picture the letters clear as day.

Shadow Yor.

He was coming for him.

Let the games begin.

Chapter 5:

While they waited for a warrant to search the man's home, they reconvened at the station. Shade's team had been given a meeting room and were currently spread around the wide white table, the blinds all closed to block out the windowed walls that would allow onlookers walking throughout the rest of the station to see inside.

Dario and Axel had given their thanks again for allowing them to remain part of the case, but Shade had waved them off and gotten started on researching their one and only suspect.

"Maxen Schwan, age twenty-six, born in Gred, moved to Ux to attend college," Axel read the information off of the projection on the wall they were all staring at.

N.I.M. had provided the facial ID and Axel had gotten Maxen's file. A copy had been sent to all of their multi-slates, but the projector in the center of the table displayed it large for them all to go over together.

"Major?" Dario asked.

"Didn't choose one. He dropped out his second year."

"What's he been up to since?"

"Odd jobs here and there. Nothing set."

"Looks like the longest he's stayed in one place is a year," Gael read with a low whistle. "Either he's the restless sort who still hasn't figured out what he wants to do with his life—"

"Or he's a serial killer who stays on the move to avoid getting caught?" Axel suggested.

"Let's not jump to conclusions," Shade stated, scrolling through the information on his multi-slate. "He was laughing during the press conference, but there are a lot of weirdos out there who aren't murderers. We could be chasing another dead-end."

"Well," Dario sighed, "we won't know until we look into it further. And this is still more than we've gotten on our own in months. Whoever this bastard is, he's clever."

"And disgusting," Gael added, glancing at the screen that made up the surface of the table where photos of the crime scenes were displayed along with information text.

"Which is why we have to find him before he gets the chance to hurt anyone else."

"You sure we can get a warrant without providing a motive?" On most planets, Shade was allowed access to anything and everything he wanted simply by flashing his I.P.F badge, but Pollux took their citizens' rights seriously and required he still go through the proper channels before he was allowed to enter someone's private residence.

They were trying to hunt Maxen down so they could at least speak with him, but he was listed as currently unemployed, and since he'd run from Shade at the conference, there was a good chance he'd either gone straight home or was in hiding. They were hoping it was option A so they could get him and search the place all in one trip.

"For killings like these?" Dario motioned to the photos. "Hell yeah. Everyone wants this settled and over with."

That didn't mean Shade was willing to pin it on the wrong person. They didn't have anything tangible to go on and they all knew it. He glanced across the table at Axel. "Have you found any connections between him and the victims?"

"His house is located on one of the streets where public transit stops," he said. "I haven't checked all of the victims, but I remember that at least three of them, including Bee Wik, traveled on hoverbus to and from work."

Bee Wik was the name of the woman they'd found the other day. According to all of her friends and family, she didn't have any enemies. She'd recently gotten a promotion at the marketing firm she worked for, but the competition hadn't been steep and the guy she'd beat out for it had a solid alibi the entire week leading up to the discovery of her body.

She'd been reported missing by her sister the day before she'd been found, but they estimated she'd been taken sometime over the weekend when there was no fear of anyone at work calling in her absence. Since she'd lived alone, there was only worry once her sister had called a few times and hadn't gotten a call back.

Of course, as per usual with these victims, the people in her life had been shocked to learn about Bee Wik's secret pastime.

She was the onsite manager of a long-term care facility, dealing with residents who, for one reason or another, were unable to look after themselves. Bathing, feeding, and even turning bodies to help avoid bed sores were all part of her job description. From the outside, it appeared as though she loved her job and cared for her residents. But the killer they were after had uncovered the truth.

There was video footage of elderly people who couldn't walk on their own left in the bath tub for hours on end. Records of food denial and threats had also been submitted. She'd convinced the people she'd mistreated to keep quiet by warning them that they wouldn't be believed due to their old ages and circumstances.

As someone who understood the struggle and suffering not being able to trust yourself could cause, Shade was furious that she'd been able to get away with this for so long. Though the evidence only showed events of the past month, it was obvious by her cockiness that she'd been at it for a much longer time than that.

And the scariest part was that no one had known. No one had even suspected.

It was like that with every single victim. The information left behind with their bodies exposing their dirtiest, most horrifying true selves to the world. It had made it hard to feel bad for them, even when the photos of the crime scenes were right in front of Shade like they were now.

The coroner had been able to tell them some of the injuries Bee Wik had sustained were most likely from as early as Saturday. As far as the timeline went, that meant she was taken either late Friday night or Saturday morning, brought to an unknown location, tortured until Monday when she was eventually murdered, and then her body was left at the drop site, discovered Tuesday morning.

Shade had gone over the other cases, trying to check if the timeline was important, but it was like Dario had said. The only thing any of the victims had in common was the mark that was carved at the back of their hips.

"The three you're talking about," he pointed out, "didn't take the same bus."

"No," Axel confirmed. "But their buses did all pass that street. I'm not sure if it's a lead or not, but right now it's the only connection that I've found. I'll keep looking."

"They're all taken during a time it's least likely they'll be missed," Shade said, tapping on his notes to bring them up and send them over to the projector. Maxen's file minimized, his typed notes taking up the wall in its place. He scrolled through the list of names of the last several victims. "Er Welsh, missing at least two days before reported by his neighbor. Posie Nook, four days, reported by her girlfriend. Henry Ight, three days. His mother. They all lived alone."

"We know for a fact that the killer is stalking them beforehand," Dario pointed out. "Some of his evidence against his victims comes from their own homes even. The problem is we've never been able to catch anyone on security cameras. There's never anyone even remotely suspicious looking on the footage."

There were dash cams on hovercars and security cameras on pretty much all of the streets, both commercial and residential. Ux was a large city and security was important to the people who lived there. According to the reports, none of the cameras had been tampered with, meaning they'd filmed with no problems, and yet none of them had caught anyone appearing odd or strange.

"Do we have anyone double-checking and searching for signs of Maxen specifically?" Shade asked and Gael nodded.

"Put a team on that already. They'll let us know if they find anything, but it didn't seem all that promising when they checked in last."

"What about the places they'd visited leading up to their abductions?" Axel suggested. "If the killer didn't follow them home, he had to have gotten info on where they lived and whether or not they lived alone some other way."

"And the footage from inside their houses?" Dario said.

"Hacking." Shade had already been playing with that idea. It made the most sense since everyone used a multi-slate and had an at-home computer. "As for the rest, social media?" He brought up another page of his notes. "Every single one of them was fairly active on Imagine."

The social media app could be downloaded to a multi-slate and was one of the most popular on the planet and in the galaxy. It allowed people to post photos and comments, as well as tag other people and locations.

"Even I'm on Imagine," Dario told him.

"Sure," he pulled up images he'd saved and compiled, "but do you post photos of your house with the number and tag its exact location in maps?"

Some of the pictures had the victims in them, standing in front of an apartment door, the number clear as day, or at the end of their driveway with a great view of their house. Others were literally just of the home itself. One showed a man's hand holding up a set of keys—mostly for show since everything was electronic now, even house locks—in front of a red house with a white door.

"If you scroll through their feeds," Shade continued, "most of them mention at some point that they live alone."

He pulled those up too, screenshots of comments like *Another day going home alone. Anyone out there want to bring me pizza and cuddle?* Or *Can't wait to chill with just me and my cats.*

Dario straightened in his seat and frowned over at Axel. "I thought we had people comb through their social media?"

"We did," he said, turning to Shade, "how far down their feed did you have to go to find all of this?"

"Some of it was further back than others." He crossed his arms and leaned in his seat. "What matters here is that it would be pretty easy for someone to find out where they all lived without ever having to meet with them in person and have a real conversation."

"Could be why there's no security footage." Dario rubbed at his face, frustrated and clearly a little put out that his team hadn't made this discovery on their own.

"We went through all of their messages and comments," Axel said. "There weren't any strange ones, and they didn't share any of the same contacts."

"All of their multi-slates were found somewhere near their bodies," Shade mentioned. "The killer could have deleted any chat threads between them." He'd been smart enough not to leave any DNA behind or anything that could help them narrow down where the actual kill site was located. No loose leaves or bits of dirt. The only things not clean about the scenes of the crime were the dead and mutilated bodies.

"Maxen Shwan has an account." Axel sent the screen he was looking at to the table and his profile popped up.

"Doesn't look like he uses it much," Dario said. There were less than thirty posts, and when Axel clicked on the most recent, it showed the date as over a week ago. "What is that?"

The image was of the corner of something, shot in black and white which only made it harder to figure out.

It sort of looked like something hanging on a wall, but not enough of whatever it was had been captured in the picture for them to run it through a trace. He also hadn't set the location.

"He only has fourteen followers?" Gael clicked his tongue. "Poor guy."

Most accounts had over a hundred just because.

"Outcast maybe?" Axel shrugged. "Out for revenge because he couldn't connect with anyone?"

"What's his home life like?" Dario asked.

"Parents are dead," Gael answered. "He has a younger brother, but the two of them are estranged. Should I try and get a hold of him?"

"Not yet." Shade really didn't want to jump the gun here. As someone who understood the danger of having the public turn on them, he didn't want to risk giving Maxen's only family the wrong idea if this wasn't their guy. "Let's talk to Maxen first."

If only their warrant would hurry up and get approved.

Chapter 6:

Come the next morning, they still hadn't gotten approval and Shade found himself in his running clothes quietly exiting the hotel room he shared with Gael. The shower worked sometimes to drown out the outside feelings seeping through the hotel walls, but now and again he needed to run to get his mind to clear properly, and with any luck, later on today they'd finally get the go-ahead to search Maxen's house. He needed to be in top shape when that time came.

He'd asked Axel last night for a couple of good running spots, refusing to take him up on his offer to call Apollo, trying to convince himself that he didn't need to involve the reporter in his life. Besides, Shade would only be on planet for as long as the case lasted. There was no point in making friends.

The thought had him chuckling darkly to himself as he made his way to the path behind the hotel that Axel had told him about. Supposedly it led on for a few miles away from the city, perfect for people who wanted a little escape from the hustle and bustle. To better ensure he avoided a crowd, he'd gone just as the sun had breached the sky. There was just enough light for him to see and not fear running into something and that was about all.

Shade had been like this since his parent's abandonment, the type of person who would rather risk running in the near darkness than have to make eye contact with someone else. He wished he liked solitude more, but the truth was he didn't. He hated being alone, in fact. Hated being trapped with nothing but his thoughts and the tight cinching in his chest that seemed to always tell him what an epic loser he was.

At twenty-seven, most of the people he knew had close friend groups or were dating or settling down. Even his co-workers back on Percy got together and hung out whenever they weren't off-world working a case.

Shade had Gael, and he was grateful for even that, he was, but…That didn't stop the loneliness and the feelings of self-deprecation. Aside from being a Chitta who couldn't control his abilities, there was nothing overtly wrong with him, and yet he couldn't form attachments. Half of that was his own fault, he acknowledged, because he was stiff around others and pretended not to notice them to avoid making eye contact if he was already in the throes of a migraine—which was often.

But the other half…

People didn't like being around someone who could easily get into their heads by reading their emotions. Regular Chitta dealt with this as well, but since they could usually turn most of their ability off the avoidance wasn't as strong. Everyone he'd spoken to on the forums had dealt with bullying at one point or another in their lives, but were also all now living well and comfortably.

With family and friends.

Shade wanted someone. He just didn't know who he could trust. Didn't know who he could get close to enough without risking Repletion being in their company. Who wanted to be with someone constantly in pain? It killed the vibe.

That's all Shade ever did.

Drain the life of the party.

He'd been told as much by a couple of the upper classmen at the Academy and it'd always stuck with him because it was tru—

"Detective!"

Shade startled and came to a stop, realizing that at some point he'd gotten onto the trail and had begun his run without even noticing. He turned, eyes widening slightly when they landed on Apollo making his way toward him.

The reporter was coming from the same direction he'd been running and was dressed in black shorts and a violet tank top. His golden skin was covered in a thin sheen of sweat by the time he reached Shade, and he smiled at him brightly, coming to stop with his hands on his hips.

"Hey, fancy meeting you here." Apollo glanced over Shade's shoulder down the path. "Are you just getting started? Mind if I join you?"

"Did Avery tell you where I was?" All he could think about was how the officer had insisted he give Apollo a call last night.

Apollo frowned slightly though. "Nope. Why? Was he supposed to?"

"No," Shade shook his head, "no, just wondering that's all."

"I run this trail a lot," Apollo explained as if wanting to clear the air before Shade could get any ideas.

Which only made Shade feel like an asshole for insinuating that the guy had come here for him in the first place. Apollo didn't need to chase after someone like Shade. He had the entire city ready and willing to spend time with him.

"So?" Apollo cocked his head.

"So?" he parroted back. Like an idiot.

"Can I join you, or," Apollo held up his hands and took a single, deliberate step back, "did you want to be alone? I can go if—"

"You just said you run this trail all the time," Shade somehow managed to claw his way out of the hole of embarrassment he'd sunk into, pleased when his voice settled somewhere between friendly and indifferent. "If anything, I should be the one to go if *you* want alone time."

He smirked. "I think there's plenty of path for the both of us."

They started into a light jog, keeping stride side by side. No one else was out this early, and the sun had just raised high enough to cast its golden glow on the surrounding tree tops when Apollo finally broke the silence between them.

It'd been a comfortable one too, with Shade easily falling into step next to him, the tension easing from his shoulders, any earlier discomfort at seeing the perfect reporter gone. For the second time since meeting the other man, Shade wondered what it was about him that managed to do that. Even with Gael, it'd taken Shade months to warm up to him enough, and even then, his presence in their shared dorm room had always been there, scratching at Shade's consciousness as if afraid to be forgotten.

But with Apollo there was nothing. An absence of presence that allowed Shade to focus on maintaining his breathing and the burn in his thighs as they ran.

"I have a confession to make," Apollo said.

Shade glanced at him, silently telling him to go for it before returning his gaze to the path straight ahead. It was paved but there was always the chance of a fallen branch or something and he didn't want to trip in front of the other man.

"I asked Avery to give me your contact details," he told him, "but he refused to do it."

Despite his careful attention, Shade ended up tripping anyway, though only a little, and over his own feet. He stopped before he could really fall and turned to Apollo, who came to a halt with him. "You what?"

"Yeah." He ran a hand over the back of his head, clearly embarrassed. "I'm sorry, is that too much? Am I being creepy? I was sort of hoping you'd call me after yesterday but when you didn't I got a bit impatient. Then when I saw you here I thought maybe it was a sign to just gather my courage and outright ask you."

"Ask me for what?"

Something on the top of Shade's head caught Apollo's attention, and instead of answering, he ended up plucking whatever it was off. He held up a small leaf between them and with a smile, let it drift to the ground. It twirled, landing on the asphalt between their feet.

"You're flirting with me," Shade said.

"Picked up on that, did you?"

"You shouldn't." Even if he liked it.

Apollo tilted his head. "Why not?"

"You'll be wasting your time."

"What makes you say that? Is there someone else?" Apollo's eyes seemed to darken in the next instant, though the easy smile never left his lips. "That partner of yours?"

Had he mistaken the hint of jealousy just now? He must have, but that didn't stop Shade's heart from skipping in his chest. His skin felt too tight all of a sudden, and he became hyper-aware of the fact that it was just the two of them out here, with no one else for half a mile—he could still feel the lingering feelings of guests back at the hotel, but he tried not to focus on them. Everything was calm, with just a light breeze causing the trees to sway, and their leaves to chime.

Shade could count on one hand the number of times he'd felt at peace in his life. It was harder to find a two-mile radius devoid of others than it sounded, especially when his work required him to constantly be on the move, hopping from one planet to the next.

The Academy in this galaxy was based on a fully functioning planet all its own, unlike most other galaxies.

Because they were smaller, the Intergalactic Conference, those in charge of the I.P.F, had decided it didn't make sense to create a man-made planet solely for training purposes. So Shade had attended the Academy in the same city as an elite university, where there were people left and right. It'd been a struggle just to make it through, but somehow he had.

After graduation, they'd been able to select their own team since both he and Gael had perfect scores. Keeping it to just the two of them helped during the travel on the ship, but Gael was still constantly there, blurring the lines between what Shade felt and what he did.

Half the time, Shade couldn't tell what he was personally experiencing at all. More than half, if he were being honest.

But not right now. Right now the interest and the lighthearted feelings swirling through his chest were all his own. The fact of the matter was, he did want to flirt back with Apollo. Having the other man's attention was both flattering and managed to stroke against the secret part of himself he tried so desperately to keep hidden from the world—Gael included.

That didn't change things though.

"Gael and I are just friends," Shade said.

"Then I'm not seeing the problem." Apollo eased a step closer so that there were only a few inches separating them. "Unless I'm not your type?"

"I'm pretty sure you're everyone's type," he drawled but retreated anyway.

"I like you, you like me, what's the issue?"

"You're very forward, huh?" Shade wasn't used to it, and it was taking all of his energy just to keep himself responding in a normal tone.

"This is nothing," he told him. "I'm actually holding myself back at the moment."

"Why?"

"So I don't scare you away?" Apollo laughed, giving off the impression he'd been joking. "I don't believe in pretending. If I want something, I go after it. And if I'm interested in getting to know someone, I do. If you're hesitating because you're technically working, and you don't plan on sticking around once you're finished, don't worry about that. I know what I'm getting into. You're an I.P.F agent, after all. Staying in one place isn't in your guys' mission statement."

Should he be insulted that the reporter was basically admitting he was only interested in a fling? Shade wasn't sure, but he wasn't. They were two grown adults with lives of their own, and if someone like Apollo had been looking for something serious, no doubt he would have found it already.

"Can I try something, Detective?" Apollo asked, and without giving himself time to pause, Shade nodded.

In the next instant, Apollo's lips crashed against Shade's. Everything else vanished as he surrounded him, the smell of linseed oil and moss choking him the same way Apollo's tongue was.

He swirled it against the roof of Shade's mouth and stepped even closer, hands falling to his hips to pull him until their chests were flush against one another. The hard ridges of his body weren't lost on Shade and he was hit with the undeniable urge to rip Apollo's shirt off so he could get a look.

Apollo's teeth nipped at his lower lip, lightly at first, until Shade groaned. Then he bit down a little harder, enough to draw blood.

Shade yanked back, fingers going to his lip. They came back red, though it wasn't all that bad. The sting was already starting to fade.

"Sorry, Detective," Apollo's voice sounded far away even though the tips of their running shoes were touching, "did I hurt you?"

"No," he shook his head, and pressed to the wound again, applying a little more pressure to reignite that minor bit of pain, "it's fine." Realizing what he was doing, he dropped his arm back to his side, but when he glanced at Apollo, his breath hitched.

There was a raw intensity in the way the reporter was watching him, almost like he knew exactly what Shade had been after. There was no disgust on his face, however. He looked like he'd just made a fascinating discovery.

Just as Shade was beginning to fear he was imagining that, Apollo pounced.

He dragged Shade back again with a hand at his nape, clutching him close in a tight enough grip there was no chance Shade could escape even if he wanted to.

Not that he did. Especially not when his mouth was recaptured with more fervor than before. There was something possessive in the way Apollo consumed him, an urgency that hadn't been there the first time. He was rough about it, the hand at the back of Shade's neck squeezing when he didn't get the response he wanted.

Shade's eyes fluttered closed as Apollo tipped his chin up to change the angle, unable to sum up even a slight bit of embarrassment at having turned to putty in the other guy's arms.

He'd kissed people before, but it'd never been like this. No one had ever made him feel like his mouth was their favorite meal and they'd gone months starving in the desert. Kissing had always been a means to an end in the past, a precursor for the bland, boring sex he and whatever partner had chosen him would have.

Nothing had ever set fire to his blood, and when Apollo nipped at him a second time, easily cracking open the wound on his lip that had only just begun to seal, Shade let out a shameless moan he felt rocking all the way to his core.

The pain was...perfect, the reporter's mouth sinful, and if Shade had any say in things, the two of them would end up naked and entwined in the bushes over there before—

The chiming of his multi-slate ripped through his lust-filled haze as if dousing him with a bucket of ice-cold water. He stiffened against Apollo, eyes snapping open and widening as one of his palms lifted and pressed against his chest.

They were outside in public. Anyone could have stumbled upon them and then his reputation, literally the only thing he had going for him, would have been destroyed.

Apollo didn't look like he was going to let him go for a second, but then he sighed and dropped his arms, watching as Shade bolted to the side.

He needed to put distance between them, needed to get a hold of himself and remember what he was actually doing here. A little attention and he was completely losing his mind? Damn it.

Shade made a big show of checking his multi-slate, pretending that it required all of his focus and that's why he could no longer meet the reporter's gaze. In reality, he felt like he'd been caught up in a tsunami and couldn't regain his baring with Apollo's intense blue gaze so hyper-focused on him.

"I need to get back," he said, moving in the direction they'd just come.

"See me again later," Apollo stopped him, but when Shade finally forced himself to look at him, any hint of the possessiveness that he'd seen here before was gone. The charming, friendly guy from the bar had replaced him, his hands slipped casually into his short pockets as he smiled at Shade.

"I…" He cleared his throat. "I don't think that's a good idea."

"What are you so afraid of, Detective?" he asked it nicely enough, but it had Shade flinching anyway.

He *was* afraid. Afraid that Apollo would figure out how damaged he actually was and run, but not before twisting Shade's insides again, like he'd only just done a moment ago with his mouth and those damn fingers on his nape.

A little bit controlling, the stinging of teeth, and the softness of those lips…It was the perfect combination for Shade.

Gael was always telling him it was all right not to get turned on by vanilla sex, but Shade only partially believed him, because at the end of the day, it wasn't so much about what he liked in the bedroom as it was what he'd do if anyone else ever found out.

No one would trust an I.P.F agent if they heard he liked being hurt, even if it was only a little. No one would take him seriously.

Hell, Shade didn't take himself seriously.

His multi-slate dinged a second time with a message from Gael telling him to meet at the station.

"You should get going," Apollo said. "I'll see you later, Detective."

Shade hesitated but then spun on his heels and began running back the way they'd come. He tried not to think about how he felt the other man's gaze on him.

Or how a thrill shot through him at that fact.

Chapter 7:

"Twenty hours," Gael complained as they made their way up the stone steps leading to the small single-story home at the end of High Street. "Unbelievable."

Shade wasn't exactly pleased by the turnaround either. They'd spent most of the night going over the case details *again*. By midnight, they'd all given in to the fact they wouldn't hear about it and had gone off to sleep. He'd gotten a total of three hours in before he'd given up and gone out for a run where he'd met Apollo.

There was a lot to unpack there, and he didn't have the time to do it now so he tried to push it from his thoughts. After learning their warrant had been approved, he'd ordered the nearest patrol team to check out Maxen's home first, not wanting to waste any more time. The team was waiting for him when he and Gael finally arrived.

"No one's home, Detective," one of the officers said as soon as they made it to the top landing of the long set of stone steps that led from the street up to the front door. "We've knocked a few times. My partner is around the back double-checking and making sure no one tries to sneak past us."

"Hey," Axel called from the driveway where he and Dario had just parked their cruiser and were getting out. "Anything?"

"Not yet," Gael said while Shade motioned for the first officer to move out of the way of the door.

Shade pulled N.I.M. from his pocket and set the device at his feet. "Can you hack the system?" he asked it, listening to the positive beeping tone letting him know that the bot would try.

"What is that?" the officer asked, staring down at the glass orb.

"A.I.," he replied. "Rien Inc made it."

"And that thing can hack the door?"

"Maybe," he shrugged. "It's still fairly new. I haven't encountered any bugs yet, but still trying to figure out its limitations." There was a click and the light on the control panel next to the front door turned green. "Which apparently doesn't include something like this."

At his command, N.I.M. entered the home first, rolling silently across warped floorboards, sounding an all-clear that pinged on Shade's multi-slate. It continued to move down the hall, stopping to roll into any rooms that didn't have the door shut to them as Shade and the others entered.

They were allowed to search even without Maxen present and quickly got to work, careful in case the man was hiding somewhere inside. N.I.M. returned to Shade less than ten minutes later, however, and let him know that it hadn't found any other heat signatures, meaning wherever Maxen was, it wasn't here.

"This place is a mess," Axel noted, scrunching his nose at the cluttered kitchen table. Tupperware, some with old food still in them, littered the surface. The sink wasn't in much better shape. "Getting DNA from this place is going to be a nightmare."

They might not need to take things that far, but Shade didn't bother saying anything, moving from the kitchen further down the hall. He opened a closet on his way, but unlike the rest of the small home it was pretty empty, so he kept going. At the very end he found the bedroom, the sheets twisted over the mattress, a pile of dirty, crumpled clothing in the corner by a desk with a single computer on it.

He turned the device on and set N.I.M. between the keyboard and the mouse, letting him scan for anything that may be useful or related to the case.

"Anything?" Gael asked as he stepped in and glanced around at the posters of music bands they didn't recognize hanging on the beige walls.

Shade shook his head and picked N.I.M. back up. "Nothing on the computer that seems suspicious. No mention of any of the victims or even the usage of keywords in his search history."

"Well," he rested his hands on his hips, "it's not like we assumed we'd find a pool of blood or a signed confession stating he was the killer."

"Hey, Detective," the officer who'd already been there called from a room over, "you should probably see this." He was standing in front of an open door and motioned with his chin when they arrived.

Shade moved over and glanced in to find it was a walk-in closet. There wasn't anything particularly odd about it, aside from the fact it was empty save for a single thing hung on the wall. "Found what the photo on his feed is of."

The painting was roughly three by four feet, done in various shades of red. It was chaotic and messy, with no discernable pattern that Shade could see, but looking at it made him uncomfortable. Gave him a rush of anxiety. It reminded him a lot of how people looked when they Glitched and he saw their screaming faces superimposed over the fake smiling expressions they were making in public.

"That isn't..." Gael's voice trailed off and he made a gagging sound. "It's not right?"

In the bottom corner, a symbol had been carved through the layers of paint. Two connecting triangles with wider points on the top.

The murderer's signature.

Shade stepped back. "Have this tested for blood and see if any of it matches with the known victims."

"Good Light." Gael covered his mouth and turned an off shade of green.

"It could be paint," Shade tried to comfort him, though even he knew it was moot.

"It doesn't *smell* like paint," the officer with them said.

Even dried, there was a twinge of copper in the air. It must have accumulated within the tiny space of the closet since the door had been closed.

"Shade," Dario appeared in the door way and held up a postcard between two gloved fingers.

Most things were sent digitally now, but some fancy events still used paper and had them delivered by post. The card Dario was holding up didn't have an address or postage on it, but it was clearly an invitation.

"I hope you boys brought suits," he said, waving the card in the air.

It was an invite to a black tie event being held this Saturday.

The Vice Gallery Showing was written in swirly black lettering at the very center of the card.

Shade hated himself for it, but his first thought wasn't about getting the chance to catch Maxen.

It was about Apollo.

Chapter 8:

Shade didn't understand much about art. That mixed with the crowd of people dressed elegantly in shades of black, white, and gray, made him feel extremely out of place as he slowly made his way through the gallery.

He and the rest of the team had only arrived a while ago and had spread out, keeping their eyes peeled for any signs of Maxen. The invitation they'd discovered at his house was the only lead they had to go on, and after the painting from his closest had come back confirming that it was in fact done in blood, it seemed likely this was his type of scene.

There'd been no mention of him having an interest in art in his history, and aside from that one photo of the corner of the canvas that he'd posted to his social media, he didn't have an online art presence either.

"All exits have been secured," Axel's voice came through the clear earpiece at Shade's right ear. It connected to all of their multi-slates and could be activated by a simple touch at the wrist. "Anyone got eyes on the target yet?"

"Nothing so far," Gael replied.

"Same," Dario said.

Shade didn't bother answering, moving from the painting he'd been standing in front of, pretending to inspect. He stopped in front of the next one, scanning over the thick dabs of green paint that covered a swath of blue. Whenever someone drew near, he tipped his head in their direction and caught a glance at them. Since he'd been the one who'd given chase the other day, there was a chance that Maxen would recognize him, so his part in today's search was to be incognito.

"Are you interested in art, Detective?" Apollo stepped up to his side, drawing his attention off the large painting.

Like the rest of them, he was dressed in a suit, the three pieces a silky black that hugged him in all the right places. He'd styled his hair so it curled over his forehead, and when he smiled, the lights hanging over the painting they were standing in front of reflected brightly in his dark blue irises.

He looked good, really good. Certainly better than any of the expensive works pinned to the walls.

"I like it," Shade said, then cleared his throat and turned back to the painting, "but I don't really get it."

"What's to get?" Apollo shifted closer, slipping his left hand into the pocket of his dress pants as he stared at the swirls of blues and greens before them. He was holding a champagne flute, suddenly close enough to Shade that he could literally hear the bubbly golden liquid fizzing inside the glass. "Art's all about feeling."

Shade made a noncommittal sound in the back of his throat. "I have enough of that, thanks."

"Not other people's feelings," Apollo corrected. "Your own. Just yours."

"Well therein lays the issue then," he said. "I hardly ever know what *I'm* feeling."

"Have you tried using a grounder?"

A grounder was something a Chitta focused on when they started to feel overwhelmed—similar to a worry stone. Supposedly it helped to distract them so their brain could sort through the onslaught of emotions and stabilize.

"They don't work for me." Shade had tried many, but his problem was greater than a little overstimulation.

"What about a tether? Found one?"

"Have you?" There'd been a couple of people on online forums he'd spoken to over the years when the loneliness had gotten too much for him to deal with on his own, but there was a big difference between listening to the cadence of someone's voice and reading impersonal black and white letters off a backlit screen.

A grounder was an item, but a tether was usually a living being, either another person or even sometimes an animal. Unlike with grounding objects, there was no choice when it came to making a tether connection. It was rare, though possible, and Shade had spoken to a few supposedly in that type of relationship as well over the years.

Sometimes two people, or two creatures, just clicked. Tethering with someone was a lot like that apparently. It was always mutual, but typically there was a change in power dynamics, as in one person always had a stronger ability than the other. There was a huge scientific explanation behind it, but Shade hadn't really bothered with memorizing it. Something about brain waves syncing just right or whatever. It all came down to chemistry, always did.

It didn't mean tethers always ended up in romantic relationships, but it wasn't uncommon for that to be the result. Supposedly the connection was…intense. It helped to quiet the onslaught of foreign emotions in their bodies, providing relief from the empathic ability in a similar fashion that blockers did, only without dimming the person's own feelings.

For the average Chitta, this could be nice. Like coming home from a busy day at work and slipping into a bath in the peace and quiet kind of nice. Typically, they didn't hate what they were, because having empathic abilities for them was the same as being able to smell or see or hear for regular people. It was just an extra sense, a bonus.

But for Shade things were different. Since his brain couldn't sort through the emotions he felt or dim them properly like most others, he was in constant torture. Having something like a tether wouldn't just be nice for him. It'd be like a saving grace.

Too bad it wasn't something he could choose for himself.

"No, I haven't used a grounder and I've never met anyone or thing who I then became tethered to. But then, I've never needed one before," Apollo said.

"Right," Shade shook his head, "you don't experience Repletion." Research showed if a Chittas abilities were weak, there was even less of a chance of them making that random connection with another. The belief was that it was nature's way of creating balance for them, giving them a chance to recalibrate in a sense.

"There are other reasons to have a tether," Apollo shrugged but didn't say what any of those other reasons could be. Instead, he pointed to the painting. "What do you feel when you look at this?"

"You really just asked me that."

He chuckled. "I'm an art reporter, remember? Come on, help me out. Give me something to write so my boss doesn't decide I'm not good at this either and I find myself without a job."

"It makes me feel..." Shade considered it, "remorse."

Apollo made a face like that was the strangest answer he could have possibly given. "Why remorse?"

"Don't know." He smirked. "Maybe it's not even my feeling at all. Maybe I picked it up from someone else."

"The only person's eyes you've met in the past five minutes are mine," Apollo stated, "and I can assure you, I've never felt remorseful a day in my life."

"No, I don't suppose someone like you would."

"Someone like me?" Apollo quirked a brow.

"You know," he circled a finger in the air at him, "the friendly, overly likable type. Tell me the truth, you don't even kill bugs when you find them in your bed, do you?"

Apollo snorted. "What horrible people have you been ending up in bed with, Detective?"

"That's not—" He laughed. "I meant literal insects."

"I've made an impression, it seems." Apollo drained his glass and then reached back as a waiter passed with a tray. He deposited the empty and grabbed two full flutes, handing one over to Shade.

"Thanks, but I'm on the clock." He took it anyway, since it would help keep up appearances, but didn't sip. "Anyway, that's not how it works for me."

Apollo cocked his head, silently asking for him to elaborate.

"I can read anyone in this room," Shade motioned around them, "without moving from this spot. It's just the Glitch that only works through eye contact. The rest of it comes without prompting at all. I can dim it. Make sure I don't feel things as intensely, but it's always there, scratching at the surface of my mind."

His eyes darkening ever so slightly was the only change that came over the other man. "No wonder you go through Repletion so frequently. How do you even stay functioning?"

"Ask myself that same thing every day."

"And?"

"I guess there's just no other option?" He shrugged. "What else can I do? Give up and die? No thanks."

"So you're in constant physical and emotional pain," Apollo said, "but you don't want death to be the cure. Interesting. Many others would have succumbed by now and ended it all."

"Most of us are like you," Shade pointed out, trying to keep the conversation positive. "Able to block it or avoid overstimulation. There's just something wrong with me, that's all. I'm an extreme case."

"I'll tell you a secret, Detective," Apollo shifted closer, bringing his mouth close enough his lips almost touched the curve of his left ear. "No one is like me. I'm one of a kind."

Shade couldn't help it, he shivered, and to cover up the wave of embarrassment he felt at that reaction, he said, "But lacking in the modesty department."

"What's that?" he joked. "Can you eat it?"

"I've got eyes on him," Dario's voice crackled through Shade's earpiece, cutting their conversation short. "Who's in the far room on the left? He just walked in there."

"I am," Shade said, tapping his multi-slate to send the response and turning to check the entrance.

The gallery was split into multiple sections, each showcasing a different artist's work, and Shade had remained in the same spot. There were a lot of people, but the space was wide and everyone was busy facing the art hanging on the walls, so it was easy to avoid catching the eyes of too many others as he looked for Maxen.

"Sorry," he said to Apollo, still searching.

"Don't mind me, Detective. I'm fine standing by and watching."

He would have responded to that odd choice of words, but then he spotted the familiar dark mop of hair and moved to follow after the man as he made his way through the gallery.

Maxen was slim, tall, and dressed in a suit, though one not nearly as fancy as most others there. He obviously couldn't wear the baseball cap, so it was easy to catch sight of his face and ID him. He was ignoring the artwork but seemed to be looking for someone, his lips pursed, brow furrowed in a slight frown.

Shade was only a few feet away, planning on pulling the man off to the side to tell him he was wanted for questioning, when Maxen turned to look over his shoulder and saw him.

It only took a second for recognition to dawn on the other man, and then he took off, shoving a woman out of the way instead of going around her.

She hit the ground with a hard thud and people screamed in surprise.

Shade swore. "He's making a run for it!"

Ignoring all of the attention that was now on him, Shade raced after him, determined not to lose him this time like he had back at the city hall. The spaces were wider in this building at least, which benefited him, making it a lot easier to keep the other man in his sight even with people mingling here and there.

"Headed to the back," he told the team, in case one of them was there already so they could help cut Maxen off. He picked up the pace just in case, almost slipping in his dress shoes against the polished marble flooring more than once.

He almost crashed into a statue of an armless woman, twisting to avoid that disaster at the last second.

"Wait," Gael came through the comms then, "back to the left or the right?"

"Right. No," Shade watched as Maxen suddenly switched directions, "left!"

"Shit! Shade, don't—"

The warning came too late as he was already at the opening in the wall that led into the other room. He turned and ran in after Maxen, coming to a halt in the center of it.

It was a lot smaller than any of the other sections, and instead of facing the walls, every single person inside had their eyes trained on the doorway. They were packed in there like sardines, so that at least three dozen eyes suddenly landed on Shade all at once and before he could help it, he connected with them one after the other.

The Glitches came fast, like flashes that discombobulated him and had him stumbling backward a full step without meaning too. His breath quickened, a heavy and thick sensation of dread enveloping him like a warm blanket in the middle of a sweltering summer spent in the desert. There were bits of surprise thrown in there, and worry—for him, he realized—but discomfort was the over-encompassing emotion.

He slipped into the worst stage of it all rather quickly, his throat closing up as his brain struggled to make sense of what was happening to his body and sort through all the outside input. He gasped, trying to suck in oxygen only to flounder. His face was no doubt turning red and he clawed at his throat as if that somehow would help.

He was going to suffocate, in this room, surrounded by strangers.

In less than a minute he forgot all about Maxen or even what he was doing there, grabbing at his skull as a piercing pain shot through the spot between his eyes. It felt a lot like what he imagined getting struck by lightning would, and it actually brought him to his knees.

Just before he was about to hit the ground, however, strong arms banded around him, catching him and holding him tight.

He blinked, trying to see who it was but all that did was cause him to accidentally connect with another onlooker and he hissed and squeezed his eyes shut.

"Hold on, Detective," that voice, rich and honeyed, drifted over him like a balm as he was half carried have dragged from the room, "I've got you. Hold on."

Miraculously, he was able to gulp in a breath, then another as he clung to Apollo's arm, silently begging him to speak again. Something about his voice helped, and though he didn't understand it, Shade wasn't exactly in the position to act like it didn't.

"What the fuck?!" Axel exclaimed, somewhere off to the left. Shade wasn't going to look though.

"I tried to stop him." Gael.

"I'm taking him somewhere quiet," Apollo told them.

"Thanks, kid," Dario. "Shade, don't worry about this. We've got it."

He was clenching his jaw too tightly to even try giving a response, and in the next instant his arm was lifted and rested around Apollo's shoulder and he was being brought away from the chatter and the noise. He kept his eyes closed all the while, until he heard a ding and felt a slight pressure that indicated he was inside an elevator. He blinked, groaning against the pounding in his skull, but pleased at least to find that the two of them were alone.

The numbers were going up, and he frowned at them, trying to make sense of what was happening through the pain.

"Roof," Apollo said, as if he could read Shade's thoughts. "Almost there."

"Keep," he sucked in another breath, "talking."

Apollo cocked his head. "Does that help?" The elevator came to a stop and he pulled Shade toward it. "Come on. Outside."

It was pouring, rain splattering against the rooftop. Dark clouds filled the sky, blocking out most of the light so that only the ones set up on the side of the building were there to help them see.

A stone awning lined the enter wall of the building, and Apollo brought them at least ten feet away from the door and then rested Shade's back against the cool stone. The wind whipped around them and some of the rain was blown their way, but for the most part, they were able to avoid the downpour.

"Breathe." Apollo was close, the warmth from his body and the palm he kept on Shade's shoulder a solid presence amidst the chaos of the storm raging around them. "Let the rain clear your mind."

Shade had never done anything like this before, but he obeyed, closing his eyes again as he tried to even out his breathing. He listened to the torrent, the staccato rhythm somehow seeming to seep into his very being the longer he stood there and let it.

His raging mind started to sort through the noise he'd collected downstairs, the flashes of unease peeling away bit by bit so that it lessened and he grew lighter and lighter. That weight on his chest vanished and he sucked in a deep breath, slowly exhaling as his frazzled nerves righted themselves.

He had no clue how long it took, how long the two of them just stood there, getting lightly splattered by the rain, but eventually Shade's axis fully righted itself, and the sound that slipped past his lips was one of pure and total relief.

He'd never been able to rid himself of a Repletion like this before. Not ever. In the past, if it got this bad, it was usual for him to pass out even and wake hours later in the hospital with Gael by his side.

The drugs the doctors gave him to help stabilize him always left his throat feeling dry and his mind as if it'd been filled with cotton. That wasn't the case now. He felt more present than he had in weeks. His thoughts and emotions clear and tangible.

And *his*.

Just his.

"You looked like you were choking," Apollo said then, soft and intense, quiet enough that the words were almost drowned out by the storm.

"Yeah," Shade sounded like he'd swallowed sandpaper and then hacked it back up again, "that happens sometimes. It feels like someone's got their hands around my neck." He brought one of his up and rested it there to emphasize, laughing humorlessly.

The reporter was silent a moment and then asked, "Are you feeling better?"

"Understatement." He wished he could launch into a whole explanation about how he was almost certain he'd never felt this centered in his life, but his throat still hurt from all the gasping and he didn't want to push his luck for something that would no doubt embarrass him anyway.

His skin had cooled, the layer of sweet he'd broken out in now causing him to feel chilly but in a good way. It was weird, but it reminded him he was alive and himself and he couldn't get enough of that. Blindly, he extended an arm, smiling when he felt the pattering of water on the tips of his fingers.

"It's cold," he murmured, pleased. "I usually hate the cold."

When he got cold his mind tended to struggle to compute even simple things. Since he already gave up so much control of self when he experienced a Glitch or others' emotions, he tried to avoid things that took away his mental autonomy as well. Avoiding the cold was a lot easier than steering clear of any and all people.

"Can I kiss you?"

His eyes popped open and he went still, certain he'd misheard.

Apollo was less than a foot away, watching him closely, an enigmatic expression on his usually open and friendly face.

"What?" Shade asked when he didn't repeat the question on his own, but the reporter must have misunderstood it for rejection, because he took a pointed step backward, away from him. Without thinking, he grabbed onto his wrist and tugged him back in. "No, that's not what I meant." He laughed, a real one, not one spurred on by embarrassment or social awkwardness. Damn, he really must feel good. He couldn't even recall the last time he'd actually found something truly amusing. "It's just funny that you'd ask, is all."

"Why is that funny?" Apollo didn't mirror his mirth, face still set in that enigmatic expression. He did, however, move in closer, planting his palms against the wall at either side of Shade's head. "You're an enigma, Detective. Always surprising me. I admit I'm a little bit fascinated by you."

He grunted in disbelief. "You don't have to ply me with compliments just for a kiss."

Apollo tilted his head, seemingly finding something interesting about that as well. "Most prefer me when I'm sweet and amicable."

"I'd much rather accept people as they really are."

"That's how you end up surrounded by unmentionables."

"I said I'd accept them," Shade corrected. "I didn't say I'd stick around."

The corner of Apollo's mouth twitched up, but it was different from any of the other smiles he'd given before. Almost imperceptible, somehow coming off private. "See, that's the problem then. I want to keep you around."

Shade opened his mouth but Apollo didn't let him get a word out before he was sealing his lips over his and kissing him like the world was coming to an end.

Chapter 9:

When was the last time he made out with someone—aside from a couple of days ago when Apollo had kissed him that first time? Shade struggled to recall, but his mind, which had been so clear only a heartbeat ago, felt suddenly cloudy all over again, only this time in a good way.

The rough stroke of Apollo's tongue tangling with his and the hot breaths fanning across his cheeks were all-consuming sensations. The reporter trailed his hands up his sides, slipping beneath the suit jacket that was already slightly rumpled from being half dragged up here like a sack of potatoes.

Apollo tasted like champagne and something a little bitter, maybe a dark roast coffee blend, and Shade found himself chasing after the flavor. He smelled fantastic too, the brine of ocean spray and moss.

The kiss was a thousand times better than the ones he'd fantasized of since their run—which he wasn't ashamed to admit he had thought of a lot. Even though he'd tried to remain focused solely on the case, his thoughts had wandered, especially when he'd pictured getting to see Apollo at the event tonight.

This wasn't like him. None of it. Kissing strangers in the near dark while his team worked on their own a few floors below? Shade may not love his job, but he was good at it and he took it seriously.

Fingers slipped into the back of his waistband then and he pulled away, pressing a palm to the center of Apollo's chest.

"I'm working," he said, breathy and not all that convincing. His eyes scanned the top of the awning hanging over them.

"There aren't any cameras up here," Apollo reassured him, knowing exactly what he was doing. "Relax, Detective. Relax, and forget about right and wrong and all the things you're supposed to be doing. Just focus on feeling."

Shade hesitated. "I shouldn't be doing this. I've got—"

He kissed him again, this time biting on his lower lip, hard.

Shade flinched, taken aback by the sudden roughness but...His eyes fluttered shut and when Apollo's tongue teased over the sting, he parted his lips, welcoming it in deeper. Something in the center of his chest started to unfurl, and he shivered in anticipation, even knowing this wasn't right.

"Sorry," the reporter mumbled against his mouth.

"It's okay."

"So you're fine if I'm a little more unrestrained?" Apollo pulled back just enough to meet Shade's gaze, waiting for him to peel his eyes open again.

Shade should put a stop to this, but the stinging from his lip and the racing of his heart got the best of him and he found himself nodding his head.

Apollo flipped him around faster than he could protest, flattening him against the wall with his hand on his lower back. He slid his palm down until it was at the top of Shade's pants, then without waiting a beat he shoved inside, cupping him through the thin material of his boxers.

A moan slipped past Shade's lips at the roughness of it all, but he caught himself and tried to bank the sudden onslaught of arousal. When Apollo squeezed, Shade jumped and tried to push back, but the reporter was surprisingly strong, standing firm and keeping him from wiggling free from between him and the solid surface.

"Do you want me to stop?" Apollo leaned in and asked, nipping lightly at his earlobe. "Really? Think about it. What do you want, Detective? I'll let you tell me."

He wanted to point out that was a weird thing to say, but he felt Apollo brush up against the swell of his ass then, the full, hard length of him pressing between his cheeks even through the layers of clothing, and the only sound that managed to leave his mouth was a sharp gasp.

Shade's semi-hard cock lengthened in Apollo's hold and he sucked in another breath when he was squeezed a little harder.

"Have you ever slept with a man before?" Apollo asked, seemingly unbothered by the fact Shade never answered his other questions. "I'm pretty sure I didn't misread the signs and you're into me."

"I am," Shade said, resting his forehead to the wall when that hand slipped beneath his boxer briefs next and made skin-to-skin contact. Stars burst behind his eyelids.

"It won't change anything," Apollo said as he felt around, as if he was testing out the length and shape of Shade's cock since he couldn't see it from where he stood, "but I'd like an answer about the people you've potentially fucked in the past."

He cursed, and for the first time since they'd come up here, Apollo laughed.

"What's wrong? Too," he cupped his balls and rolled them in his palm, causing Shade to squirm, "dirty for you, Detective? Let me guess, the people you usually do it with say things like make love and sleep with."

Apollo flattened his other palm against the globe of Shade's ass and kept it there for a second, racking up the tension before suddenly the hand was gone, only to come back with a vengeance.

Shade gasped at the first slap of his ass, shock rolling through him. No one had ever spanked him before, and the spot was already starting to burn after only a single hit.

"Answer the question," Apollo ordered, smoothing those fingers over the sting, the silent warning there.

He shouldn't find this hot, should be shoving the other man away and pointing out that it was his job to deal with things like violence and abuse, but...This couldn't really be considered that if he was enjoying it, could it? Even if they hadn't discussed it prior and he was inexperienced in this department.

It was something he'd always been curious about, and this was his chance to experience it so...

"I—" Shade shook his head and tried to concentrate, but it was growing more and more difficult with Apollo still stroking him from tip to balls. The movements had grown lazy, like they had time to spare, and instead of cooling him down it was working Shade up. The crass way he spoke wasn't hurting either, pricking at something Shade had desperately tried to keep hidden. The sting from the spanking coupled with the pleasure in his dick created a fissure within him and now it felt impossible to seal it back up. "Once."

"What was that?" Apollo rested his chin on his right shoulder, the move causing his front to seal more firmly against Shade's back. Which also meant his cock also pushed his cheeks further apart, settling between them in a way that was impossible to ignore.

Shade could feel him back there and they were both still fully clothed. The guy felt huge, and a zip of reality sliced its way through the lust-induced haze. He blinked, focusing on the gray-painted siding of the building.

"I slept with a guy once," he found himself answering despite his sudden trepidation. "It wasn't..." He couldn't find the right words to describe the experience. It hadn't been awful, but he certainly hadn't felt the need to rush out and do it again. Or, at least, that's what he'd always told people if asked about it. Truthfully, there had been parts of that afternoon that had been amazing.

But they were the parts that would have been horrifying to regular people, and he'd always been smart enough to keep them to himself, especially after seeing the reaction he got from the boy he'd been experimenting with.

"You didn't enjoy it," Apollo surmised, humming.

Shade felt the vibrations from his throat rumble down his shoulder.

"What about women? Do you prefer them?" He rolled his thumb over the crown of Shade's dick as he spoke, the move somehow possessive, as if it didn't matter to him what Shade's response was and he wouldn't stop even if that was the case.

"I—" He gasped again when Apollo rotated his hips, humping against him. "I don't have a preference."

"No? Interesting." It didn't sound like he was all that interested, actually, at least not in his opinions about women.

Frowning, Shade put his hands flat on the wall and tried again to push away from it, turning his head to peer at the other man over his shoulder when he was forced back into positon. "Apollo? What are you doing?"

"Feeling," he said matter-of-factly.

"You're trying to distract me." Thunder ripped across the sky, followed by a bolt of lightning so bright it lit up the entire rooftop, momentarily blinding Shade.

When he got his baring back, he was shocked to find that in that short period of time, Apollo had undone his pants and pushed them to his knees. He glanced down at himself, staring at his swollen dick like the traitor it was.

"I'm on the clock," he repeated dumbly. But Apollo wasn't giving him a hand job anymore and he realized he wasn't happy about that.

"Should I stop?" Apollo asked, and without waiting for an answer, he pressed a finger against Shade's hole. His palm gripped his ass cheek, pulling it aside as his finger slid in, forcing its way past that tight ring of muscle.

Shade made a gurgling sound at the intrusion but didn't demand he pull out.

"Does it hurt?" His finger glided free slowly before stroking back in all the way to the knuckle. Back inside, he felt around, corkscrewing his digit to hit all of Shade's inner walls until he found that spot that had him writhing. "I used my precome as lube, hope you don't mind."

Holy hell, why was that so hot?

"It doesn't really sound like you'd care if I did," Shade theorized, only partially paying attention to the conversation, mostly just hyper-focused on the zings of pleasure zapping through his entire body. The stretch stung a bit, and it took everything in him not to beg for more. Beg to make it hurt a little more.

His first time he hadn't been able to control those urges, and when the guy he'd been sleeping with had forced his way inside without prepping him first, he'd panicked over Shade's obvious cries of pain.

He wasn't a masochist, he just liked a small burn to help him focus on himself and his own feelings, that was all—but the pain had faded as soon as the guy had settled his heavy form over top him, pinning him down to the desks they'd pulled together in the closed classroom, and the first thing Shade had said once that happened was *harder*.

Apollo chuckled behind him. "Picked up on that did you? Oops. What are the chances you're in the right state of mind right now to remember that when we're done?"

"Slim," he answered honestly. "What are we even talking about?"

"Wow, poor thing. You really haven't been touched in a while, huh?" He added a second finger, not pausing to allow him to adjust, stretching him and working him brutally through the pain until it started to shift into warm pleasure on its own.

For a split second, Shade actually feared he'd accidentally spoken out loud and voiced his proclivities after all, but then Apollo asked him another question, and it was clear that he hadn't.

"What was he like? The other guy that you fucked?"

"You are way too nice of a person to be saying things like that." Shade wished he could claim to be too nice of a person to get off on hearing them.

"You think so?" Apollo scissored his fingers, making Shade cry out. "Even with my fingers shoved up your ass like this?"

"He was boring," Shade replied, thinking back on his one and only male sexual partner. It'd been just before he'd left for the Academy, thankfully. "Wouldn't stop staring at me during class. Tried to hide it, but he'd Glitch and I'd see his face in the throes of passion, feel what he was imagining. Eventually I did it with him, mostly just to see what all the fuss was about."

"You were pressured into it," Apollo read between the lines. "You into that sort of thing?"

"What?" He shook his head even as his heart leaped at the suggestion, knowing denial was the appropriate response. "Of course not. The sex was awful." It wasn't a complete lie. Shade wasn't interested in being made to feel obligated to put out for anyone. But the concept that someone could be so interested in him they'd try…For a person who'd spent his entire life desperate for attention and acceptance? Yeah. That worked for him.

"Because you felt like you had to do it?" Apollo asked next.

"Because he had no clue what he was doing, lasted less than two minutes, and—"

"Hurt you?" he guessed.

"Well, sure, there was that." The guy had torn him a bit. Having to deal with the after-effect had sucked, but the initial pain...He stopped himself from saying that he'd liked it, not wanting to scare Apollo away when his hand felt so good stretching him. "But I was going to say he left without making sure I came too."

"So pain is all right," Apollo hummed, and there was no judgment in his tone, "but don't like to be left hanging, Detective? Noted."

Shade stiffened some, feeling exposed despite his efforts and swallowed the lump in his throat.

Apollo must have felt the change in him, because he settled in closer and nipped his earlobe. "There's no reason to be alarmed, at least not about my finding out something as minuscule as that."

"Miniscule?" he snorted. "I was practically laughed out of school because of that."

"Did that asshole tell people he hurt you?" Apollo's voice darkened slightly.

"And that I kind of started to like it?" Shade said before he could think better. "Yeah."

"Fucker."

"He wasn't exactly a prince charming, no."

"From the sounds of it, prince charming isn't your type anyway." He nipped at him again. "Too boring for you."

Shade frowned for what had to be the millionth time since the start of all this, opting to believe for now that he didn't think poorly of him. "I can't see your face because you're behind me, but why does it sound like you're enjoying learning that?"

"Must be the rain," Apollo told him. "It's distorting sounds, that's all."

It was still pretty loud. It was really a wonder, even with the two of them pressed this close, that they could hear each other at all, more so now that it'd started to thunder.

"Distraction time is over," he announced, pulling his fingers free and lining up the flushed head of his cock to Shade's hole before the sentence was even fully off his lips.

Shade realized with a start that he *had* been distracted, pushing back into those prying fingers, enjoying the warm, pleasant sensation of them, but more focused on the sound of Apollo's voice and the confession he'd put out there.

Sex had never been all that life-altering. His head was always spinning, sorting through the feelings of others, trying to locate the ones within himself that actually belonged to him. If he could tune it out for a few minutes and focus on sex with whatever partner he'd chosen for the night, it could be a pleasing experience that left him lighter at the end. But it'd never been anything awe-inspiring. Even losing his virginity hadn't been, and yet that was still the most excitement he'd ever felt in the bedroom.

Up until now, when Apollo pinned him more tightly against the rough wall and repositioned his hips almost roughly for a better angle.

His cock felt huge behind him, a lot bigger than two mere fingers, and now that pain had been brought up, Shade was reminded of how much it had hurt back then. After so much time avoiding situations like that, his hesitation was palpable.

He opened his mouth to tell him to wait, to give him a moment to brace himself, but Apollo didn't give him the chance.

With one sharp flick of his hips, his cock slammed straight through him, spearing him practically in half in one go.

Shade's breath caught in his throat and his face connected with the wall once more. His dick, now trapped between his stomach and the cold concrete pulsed and he couldn't tell if it felt good or not through the searing heat scorching through his lower region. He floundered, no doubt looking like a fish, as that too-big cock within him slid free all the way to the tip and then rammed back in.

Now he understood why Apollo had kept referring to it as fucking.

His thrusts were rough, deep and hard enough to have Shade's body quaking. With every stroke he was sure to hit his prostate, growling into his ear when that soon had Shade mewling like a kitten, unable to form full words or even moan properly by the intensity of it all.

He had no idea when it stopped hurting, but one second he was clenching his teeth against the pain and the next his hand had reached back to cover Apollo's ass and pull him in harder. Shade lifted his hips and pressed into every forward stroke, meeting him thrust for thrust.

"I'm trying not to be vocal so I don't scare you away," Apollo said, sucking on the side of Shade's neck before licking the mark he'd no doubt left behind. "But you feel amazing around me and you're so responsive, you're making it really hard to hold back."

This was holding back?

"You're literally taking me against a wall right now," Shade managed to say, a chuckle dying on his lips when Apollo plunged into him with even more force.

"There you go, purr for me. This is nothing. I can think of a few dozen things I'd like to do to you."

"So do them," Shade challenged.

"You wouldn't be saying that if you could read my mind."

"Can't," he shook his head as best he could with it pressed to the wall, "not your mind or your emotions."

"And that, Detective, is why we're playing it your way. For now." He reached around and found Shade once more, stroking him with the same harried pumps as his hips. His other hand dove into the hairs at the base of his skull, gripping tight enough to pull at the scalp. "Come, Shadow. Come for me."

As if obeying him, the orgasm hit, ripping a loud cry from his mouth as he came in Apollo's hand and against the wall. He clenched around the cock still burying deep inside of him, muscles squeezing, and then moaned when he felt Apollo hit his peak, warm jets painting his insides.

The guy he'd slept with in high school had pulled out, so this was an altogether new sensation for Shade and he groaned as he was filled, as the sparks of electricity raced through his entire body. He felt both light and heavy at the same time, even when he lost feeling in his legs and collapsed against the wall, only kept from falling to the wet ground by the hot body at his back.

Apollo's breathing was wild as well, sharp bursts of air puffed repeatedly against the curve of Shade's throat. He held them there for what felt like an eternity, still partially inside of him even though he'd shrunk in size.

When he did finally separate them, they both let out a low groan, and Apollo dropped his forehead between Shade's shoulder blades and waited for another beat as if recovering.

A part of Shade was turned on all over again by that concept. By the possibility that he wasn't alone in this, in these feelings, and that Apollo was every bit as gone to the world right now as he was.

That *he* could *make* another person that way.

All his life, Shade had been a prisoner to other people's emotions. A slave to their feelings. He'd never been on the other side of things. Had never been the one making someone else feel something, at least, not anything as vibrant and visceral as *this*.

And that slight sting from being opened too soon and too quickly? That burn between his legs only helped to anchor him more, to the moment and himself. He felt *real*. Not merely an amalgamation of other people's sums and parts, *their* emotions and *their* desires. But of his own.

He was still blissed out when Apollo eased him off the wall and turned him around, barely registering that he'd already tucked himself away and had sorted his clothes in place. He remained still as the reporter's hands danced over him, cleaning him up as well, making him presentable.

Shade snorted.

"Something amusing, Detective?" Apollo asked, hands tugging at his collar to straighten it. When he was satisfied, he lifted his gaze.

His eyes were so dark they were practically black. Like pools of ink that threatened to swallow Shade whole and never release him.

He snorted again, finding that idea just as hilarious as recalling where they were.

Since when was he so damn poetic?

"They're going to come—" The sound of the metal door bursting open cut him off, and he turned to face it as Apollo released him and took a deliberate step back.

Gael glanced between them and exhaled in relief. "Thank the Light. I was worried I was going to come up here and find you unconscious. You weren't responding."

Shade lifted a hand to his ear but the communications device was gone. He found it on the ground by his feet, crushed and in pieces. He hadn't felt it fall out.

"We chased him a couple of blocks," Gael continued, unable to contain his excitement now that he'd seen that Shade was okay. "Axel got him just before he was able to hop on a speed train."

"You got him?" Shade pulled away from the wall, heading over to him with determined steps. Or, at least, he meant to. He only made it about three before the pain in his rear had him stumbling.

Apollo was there in a flash, helping to steady him with one hand on his waist and the other on his arm.

"What happened?" Gael asked, making to move closer.

Shade was grateful for the dim lighting of the storm because he was certain he went beat red. He sure as hell wasn't about to tell his partner what had happened was he'd just taken a cock up the ass for only the second time in his entire life.

"He's still a bit disoriented from earlier," Apollo jumped to his rescue and said. "I've got him. He just needs help to the elevator and some rest and he'll be fine. He shouldn't be moving too much though."

"Okay, no problem," Gael nodded in understanding. "We're escorting Maxen back to the station already but they're planning on waiting for you to start the questioning since you're in charge of the case. Should I tell them to begin without us so you can—"

"No." Shade refused to allow a personal matter to interfere with his job. "No, it's fine. I can do it."

"Detective," Apollo leaned in and lowered his voice so the Inspector couldn't overhear, "you didn't get a chance to see it this time, but I'm not exactly of average size. You should really reconsider and get some rest or you're going to find it difficult to sit comfortably tomorrow."

Shade felt a twisted thrill snake its way through him at that and forced his expression to remain blank. "One," he somehow managed to keep his voice even despite the way his heart was now pounding in both anticipation and mortification, "didn't have to see it. I felt it. Two, remember that thing I mentioned earlier? About your lack of modesty? I'll be fine."

It was just sex. Tons of people had mindless, meaningless, spur-of-the-moment sex all the time and woke up the next day still fully functioning adults. He wouldn't be any different.

"I just fucked you on a roof, Detective," he stated bluntly, causing a shiver to race up Shade's spine. "And you loved every second of it. Clearly modesty is overrated."

Chapter 10:

The good news was the blood used to create the painting found in Maxen's house matched one of the victims, Posie Nook. So they had their killer.

Bad news, they didn't actually, physically have their killer.

The day of the Vice Gallery showing, by the time Shade had made it to the station Maxen had already gotten away. During the drive, he'd attacked Axel and the other officer that'd been escorting them and made the hovercar crash into oncoming traffic.

Axel was currently in the hospital in a coma, and the officer who'd been driving had been pronounced dead on the scene, so they had more bodies and more questions. CCTV footage on the roads hadn't been able to capture anything useful. All they knew was one second the car had been driving fine and the next it'd made a beeline for the next lane.

They'd been waiting the week since for Axel to wake and explain, but his condition, while stable, wasn't improving.

Everyone, including the public, was high-strung and rightly on guard. Maxen's face was plastered all over the city, reported on every news station, and they'd been getting calls in on the tip line for days, yet nothing. None of the leads ever panned out. It was almost as if they were looking for a ghost.

Shade leaned back in the leather chair in the living area of the hotel room he shared with Gael. The Inspector was out picking up food since they planned on having another long night in, just them and the copious amount of notes they'd collected since their arrival on planet.

There was something that they were missing, there had to be. He refused to believe that all leads had run dry and they were as screwed as it was starting to seem. Sure, the Ux police hadn't been able to solve it on their own, but that's why Shade had been brought it. He wouldn't fail. He never had before.

That was one of the major reasons his superiors overlooked how frequently he went into Repletion, how he could barely function off the clock unless he was drowning himself in blockers. When it was time to work, Shade showed up and gave it his all. He was consistently one of the top agents in their galaxy, also why he hadn't had to deal with a rookie being forced onto his team.

Unlike other agents of his rank, Shade wasn't picky. He'd take whatever assignment came his way without complaint. Robberies, murders, missing persons, didn't matter. If something needed to be solved, he'd solve it.

Working gave him something else to focus on other than the ragging emotions crushing him from all sides or the splitting headaches. The downside was, of course, those two things always increased in occurrence whenever he was on a job, since being a detective meant putting himself out there and often talking to as many people as possible.

Not for the first time, an image of the reporter flashed in his head and he groaned, clasping a hand over his eyes as the familiar embarrassment quickly followed.

Since the moment he and Apollo had gone their separate ways, him heading toward the station to interrogate Maxen, he'd felt shamed and humiliated. All that work to climb the ranks and what had he done the first time someone had shown interest?

Had sex on the roof of the building he was meant to be watching. During an arrest. And not even soft, romantic, or quick and passionate sex either. It'd been…probing. Almost as if Apollo had used it as a means to learn more about Shade while he'd been distracted by lust and near out of his mind, and it had worked. It'd worked so well, the other guy had even known to hurt him toward the end there.

Depraved didn't even begin to describe it. More than once he'd almost confessed to Gael, if only to get it off his chest and have someone to talk it over with, but even knowing it would probably help, he couldn't do it.

What would the Inspector say? Would he look at him differently? Clap him on the back and tell him good for him?

Gael was constantly on him about dating, wanting him to put himself out there, but Shade had always shaken the suggestions off and coldly reminded his friend that they were too busy for things like relationships.

Not that he for a second believed what had happened between him and Apollo meant they were in a relationship. Casual sex, that's all it'd been. A onetime thing done in the heat of the moment when he'd been loopy due to the Repletion and adrenaline rush of having just chased a suspect. That was all.

Apollo was gorgeous, sexy, fun and flirty and somehow managed to put Shade at ease, but that was also part of the problem. He was a good guy.

He didn't deserve to get saddled with someone like Shade, who couldn't stand being in a crowd for longer than a half hour without complaining about head pain. Who didn't even know the difference between his own anger and the person's twenty feet away half the time.

Sex on the rooftop had been the most exciting thing Shade had done in possibly his entire life, but he doubted Apollo would say the same.

Hell, with a face and body like his, one-night stands were most likely the norm for the reporter.

Though…

Shade's gaze wandered to his multi-slate, which he'd unstrapped from his wrist and set on the coffee table before him. Apollo had called twice and sent four text messages, all of which, accept the last, had been ignored. And when he had sent that last response, Shade had simply apologized and said he was busy at the moment working the case. That was all.

He was a child.

But this was for the best, and anyway, the last he'd heard from the other man had been two days ago. Perhaps Apollo had taken the hint and given up. If that made Shade feel a little disappointed? Well, it was his own damn fault, and, really, it was what he wanted, wasn't it?

Wasn't it?

With a low growl, he forced himself to his feet and headed for the bedroom he'd been occupying. The hotel suite was nice and spacious, with a living and dining area as well as a kitchen and two separate bedrooms. They had to share a bathroom, but that was neither here nor there, though Shade's toothbrush had gone missing the other day which annoyed him.

Since they were working on classified information cleaning services weren't allowed to enter, which meant either he or Gael had misplaced it. When he'd asked, his partner had claimed to know nothing, but it wouldn't be the first time Shade had caught him absently knocking something onto the bathroom floor and then tossing it for sanitary reasons.

When they'd been roommates back at the Academy, three hairbrushes and several flossing picks had been sent to an early grave due to Gael's clumsiness.

Shade entered the bathroom and stripped carelessly, wanting to get under the hot spray of the shower as fast as possible, hopefully to wash these unwanted thoughts away. Clearly, the Inspector wasn't the only clumsy one here. As far as he knew, Gael had never slept with someone while on the job.

Fucked, Apollo would correct.

He grunted and flicked the shower spray on, leaving his clothes in a heap on the ground by the closed door. While he could care less about the rest of their living arrangements, Shade was admittedly a big fan of the shower stall and often retreated here in an attempt to sort through his thoughts.

He was like that on most cases, but this time there was more for him to deal with. More for him to feel guilty for.

Usually, he'd wallow about how his ability got in the way of an investigation by limiting his time out in the field. Logically, he was aware that him being Chitta was his ace, not his shortcoming, but when he got like this, low and depressed and self-loathing, it was always a bit hard to drown out that voice in his head that said otherwise.

That told him he was useless and a freak.

That reminded him that not even his parents could love him.

Apollo had seemed like it didn't matter when Shade had implied he liked things a little rough, but that'd been then, when they'd both been in the throes of passion. Now that he wasn't thinking with his other head, Shade had to wonder…

Maybe the reporter had realized he was too big of a weirdo to match with him anyway. It was the same conclusion Shade had come to, so it shouldn't bother him.

It did though, and he hated that.

This was exactly why he'd stuck with boring, missionary sex. The farthest he'd gone since the first time had been letting a girl stick a finger in his ass while they'd been doing it. It'd been more fun than all the other times and he'd left more satisfied, but it'd still been nothing in comparison.

He wished he could account that to the fact Apollo was a man, wished he could snap his fingers and conclude, oh, it wasn't because he wanted to be dominated and owned and, yes, punished, it was because he was gay and just hadn't recognized that before.

Truthfully though? Shade wouldn't mind it if a woman held him down either.

So, no. It wasn't a gender thing, sadly.

It all stemmed from his abandonment issues. His need for love and affection. He was almost desperate for it, pathetically so, and he tried really hard to keep that fact locked down. When people knew they could manipulate you simply by pretending to care, it left you vulnerable, and Shade wouldn't allow himself to be taken advantage of like that.

But that'd never stopped him from fantasizing about being wanted so badly by someone that they'd do literally anything to him to have him. Tie him up, pin him down…His mind wandered to the slaps Apollo had given him and he bit his lip as his dick twitched at the memory.

Which was so fucked up.

Apollo was *nice*. He was a nice guy who would most likely be mortified if he knew Shade was imagining him roughing him up like that. He'd said it himself he'd never met another Chitta who was an I.P.F agent before. That must have been where the interest stemmed from. He'd hooked up with Shade to appease that curiosity, and was probably laughing about how the detective, the guy who was meant to catch criminals, was into being spanked.

The shower stall was large enough to fit three grown men with ease, giving Shade plenty of room to fill the space with his self-hatred, the one emotion of his he never seemed to have trouble identifying and picking out from the mess that belonged to others.

Shade Yor hated what he was, not the fact that he was a Chitta, the fact that he was a *broken* one. He hated the migraines and the constant fluctuating emotions that made it impossible for him to ever pinpoint how he was personally feeling. The one good thing about his job was that being a detective gave him something to focus on other than his inner turmoil. He didn't need personal emotion to solve crimes, he just needed to be attentive.

Some psychiatrists specialized in helping Chitta deal, but he'd seen a few already and no one had been able to get to the root of his issues, other than to discover that his heightened and over stimulated abilities were supposedly mental. Perhaps he'd been more normal before his parents had abandoned him, he couldn't really recall. He had memories of his mother and his father and their lives, remembered his favorite toy and Hy Lori, the girl who always picked on him for being an empath. But when it came to his abilities…it was blank. He'd been asked multiple times by doctors and psychiatrists alike but he could never give a straight answer.

Had his abilities always been this way, or was it a result of being abandoned on the side of the road like an unwanted pet?

After extensive tests, doctors had told him that his inability to sort through emotions like a normal Chitta was what caused him to enter Repletion so often. Typically, feelings were felt in layers, the lighter overlapping ones belonging to the people a Chitta was reading. This difference allowed them to always be in touch with the heavier layer beneath, which were their own emotions. Repletion only happened on the rare occasion when the body was flooded by too many outside emotions, and the layers piled up, confusing and stressing the brain's ability to sort through them all and locate the body's root emotion.

Shade didn't have this ability. There were no separate layers that felt like different weights for him. There were just droplets, all coming together to form an ocean in which he'd either drown or struggle to stay afloat in. Somewhere within that sea, his emotions mixed with the rest, so that it was only upon occasion that he could reach down and cup the correct droplets in his hand.

PTSD and trauma were words thrown around in regards to why this happened to him, linked to his abandonment issues and the fact he was love-starved—something he'd never been able to hide from a medical professional. They'd touched base on how part of the problem was how Shade never trusted anyone enough to get close, but the real kicker, the one that always had the doctor or the psychiatrist clearing their throat in social discomfort, was that very few people ever even bothered to try.

All of those women Shade slept with? Not a single one had asked for his contact info after the fact. They'd gotten off on the idea of sleeping with a high-ranking I.P.F agent, even told him as much, and the bragging rights that came with it, but they didn't want anything else to do with him once he'd made them come.

His coworkers who lived with him on Percy? Polite, friendly when the situation called for it, but no one ever went out of their way to invite him over to their place or out for drinks. When he was on base—which admittedly wasn't all that frequently since he kept busy with cases—he was either at home alone or hanging out with Gael.

Gael was the only person who'd ever stuck by Shade. The only person who enjoyed his company past a quick conversation or congratulations on a job well done. He said part of the problem was that Shade didn't put himself out there, but they both knew the truth.

It wasn't because Shade was rude or too closed off. He could be introverted, sure, never the first person to strike up a conversation in the middle of the grocery store with his neighbor. But when he was working a case, he took control and was a strong leader, a fact everyone on Percy knew. What it really came down to was the fact he was a Chitta who didn't know how to control his shit, and everybody knew that too.

No one was comfortable with the notion of being around someone who always knew what they were feeling. It was intrusive. Shade got that. It sucked that being alone only helped feed into his problems, but he did understand.

Ironically, he needed to figure out a way to let go of his desperate need for love and his self-deprecating nature in order to find the balance to restore his mind's mental shields—which is what the layering system was often referred to, the brain's natural way of compartmentalizing emotions to keep the body functioning. Supposedly, it shouldn't be all that difficult and yet, here he was, standing under a shower spray hot enough to have his skin turning a beat red, wishing the world outside the tiled walls would burn to the ground and cease to exist.

Honestly, with how big of a mess he was, it was a wonder he was allowed to work for the I.P.F. at all, even with his record. The Intergalactic Police Force dealt with cases throughout the universe, with branches set up in each of the known galaxies. It was tough work, but prestigious as well, and through it, Shade had managed to scrape together respect from the people around him.

There was still prejudice, of course, but he'd never even dreamed of fully escaping that. People were cruel and judgmental, holier than thou, he knew that better than anyone. But for the most part, his badge gave him the honor that nothing else in his life or about him could or had. Being a ranking detective meant people bowed their heads when he walked by and whispered less about him being a Chitta and more about all of the cases he'd solved.

He *should* feel good about that.

But mostly? He just felt crushed, like he was constantly on the defensive, needing to defend his skills and his title. Constantly proving his worth to the agency and his co-workers and the other officers he came into contact with on each new case.

Half the time, it felt like he was sunk at the bottom of that vast and dark ocean, water smothering him on all sides, lungs struggling to find air…

Shade gasped, realizing with a start that he'd had his head under the spray for too long and had indeed been holding his breath.

Idiot.

He was an idiot. The kind of idiot who fucked a man he'd only met three times in the middle of a job and then felt horrible for it for days afterward.

"I hate this," he said, slapping a palm against the tan tiles, wishing he could punch them instead and feel them shatter beneath his knuckles. Feeling anything, *literally anything*, else would be better than this never-ending self-abasement always there, on the outskirts of his mind, threatening to swallow him whole.

Gael was the only other person, aside from the psychiatrists he'd tried to get help from, who knew how he truly felt. Shade had confessed one night after they'd gotten wasted with some of the seniors from the

Academy and he'd completely lost control of his sense. He'd sobbed like a baby and had spewed a ton of the nonsense that was always filling his head, about how he was useless and unlovable and a freak.

His partner—roommate at the time—had wrapped his arms around him and held him close and let him cry on his shoulder. Like they were friends and not just two guys who'd been assigned to a room together at random.

Every now and again Gael would tactfully bring it up, just a brief check-in where he tried to make it sound like he wasn't concerned for him, but the worry would show through and Shade always ended up lying.

Gael was a good person. He didn't deserve to have a partner that needed coddling.

And neither did someone like Apollo, a man who was clearly liked by everyone he came into contact with. At least Gael got something out of it—advancement of his career—Shade had nothing he could offer the reporter.

Sighing in defeat, Shade reached to shut the shower spray off, a slight clicking sound causing him to freeze. Rubbing water off his face so he could see better, he turned, popping open the clear glass stall door to check outside. For a second, nothing seemed amiss, but then he noticed the door leading out of the bathroom wasn't fully closed.

He'd made sure to was when he'd walked in, just before removing his clothing, since he had no way of knowing when Gael would return.

Finishing up quickly, Shade wrapped one of the crimson terrycloth towels around his waist and stepped from the room, padding down the short hallway until he reached the main living area.

"Gael?" He'd expected to find him here, setting out the food, but the apartment was silent and still. Shade frowned and went to pick up his multi-slate, pulling out the earpiece attached to the side and shoving it in before calling his partner.

"Sorry, a bit behind," Gael's voice came through the line, slightly out of breath. "I chose the wrong restaurant, they were so backed up. Apparently some dude ordered enough food to feed the entire station."

"No problem," Shade glanced around, uncomfortable for some unknown reason. "Don't rush." He ended the call and slowly set his multi-slate back down on the end of the table. Was he just being paranoid?

The front door was locked when he checked, and both bedrooms were left undisturbed as well. By the time he'd returned to the living room, Shade was feeling a little crazy.

That was it. No matter how badly he needed to maintain his track record in the I.P.F. in order to stay positive about himself, he very obviously needed a break. As soon as they were done with this case he'd put in for a two-week vacation. Hopefully spending some time away from people—especially of the criminal variety—would be the reset he needed to get his shit together.

His nerves had settled by the time Gael finally arrived with the food, and he found Shade dressed and seated at the kitchen table, going over case notes.

"Find anything?" he asked as he plopped a plastic bag onto the corner of the glass surface, one of the few places where the built-in computer screen wasn't showing a piece of digital notepaper. He grimaced when he caught sight of some of the crime scene photos and held a hand up in front of his face. "Aw, come on, man, right before we're about to eat? Seriously?"

"It doesn't bother me," Shade said, but he closed most of those image files and then motioned to Gael it was safe. "And no, I haven't found anything. It's all just...pieces."

"No wonder they called us in." Gael slid a Styrofoam container over to him before taking the seat at the end.

"We've been so helpful."

"Uh, yeah," Gael stabbed a fork into what appeared to be a chunk of some kind of meat over a bed of leafy greens, "we have been. You caught the guy, remember? Or, well, you ID'd him, which is more than they can say."

"It was luck." The same odd square meat was in his container as well and he frowned at it. "What is this?"

"No clue," he admitted, taking another bite. "They called it kraken but it's obviously not the kind we know. It's their best seller and supposedly spicy as all hell so I just grabbed whatever by the time I made it up to the counter."

"Why didn't you just go somewhere else?"

"You know my motto."

"Right." Shade clucked his tongue. Gael always selected the most crowded restaurant he could find, citing that it meant the food had to be the best around. Typically, he wasn't wrong, and Shade had never minded having to wait a little extra for him to return with food.

This had been their setup since the Academy, with Gael understanding Shade's desperation to avoid crowded places—like restaurants or the school cafeteria—as often as possible. They'd settled into a routine where he'd go out and get the food, and Shade would eat whatever happened to be brought back with no complaints. It worked for them, and they'd weirdly gotten closer over the tradition.

It was the closest thing Shade had ever had to a family dinner routine his whole life. Sad, but true.

"Funny thing about that though," Gael snapped his fingers as if he'd just recalled he'd wanted to say this earlier. "The person who placed that huge order and made the rest of us have to wait? Guy never showed."

"Really?" He winced thinking about the cooks and how upsetting that must be for them.

"Asshole."

"Seriously." Shade was even gladder he'd stayed in and avoided having to feel the rush of anger that had no doubt flooded the restaurant. "Have you heard anything about Axel today?"

"Not yet," he sobered instantly. "You?"

Shade shook his head.

"We'll do better tomorrow," Gael assured him, and he sounded like he believed it.

Maxen was their killer, and they'd managed to tie him more closely with the bus routes that passed his house. They still hadn't found any links between his and any of the victims' social media accounts, but Shade's theory that he'd deleted all of those chats before dropping the bodies made sense. The company was refusing to check their backlogs and claiming they couldn't access any conversations that'd been deleted by their users, so...dead end there.

"We have to figure out how he's choosing his victims," Shade said. That was the most important thing, the biggest missing piece. The second they found that out, he was confident the rest would fall into place.

"Thank goodness you can look at this stuff," Gael made a face at the screen even though the photos had been set aside. "If I had to work this on my own, they'd be shit out of luck. How do you do that anyway?"

"You mean because us empaths are usually too emotionally connected to others to stomach seeing them in pain?" Shade snorted. "Doesn't work that way. But also," he tapped the table, "these are bodies now. No emotions."

"Please don't follow that up with something like 'just meat'," Gael joked, since that wasn't something Shade would ever actually voice and they both knew it. "I envy that. Being able to separate yourself from the work is what makes you so good at your job."

Shade narrowed his eyes. "Why the sudden praise?"

"What?" He shrugged innocently, but a wave of humor wafted off of him, mixing with the emotions of the people in the surrounding hotel rooms that Shade could all feel, giving him away.

"You know I hate this job," Shade said. "Telling me I'm good at it doesn't change that, which means you're trying to start up a different kind of conversation and buttering me up to do so. What is it?"

"Hate is such a strong word," Gael practically pouted, but it was merely another stall tactic. "Come on, we have fun together. We make a good team."

"You're the only good part about any of this," Shade agreed.

"Aw," he blew him a kiss which had Shade grimacing, "thanks, partner. I'm rather fond of you too. But," his tone deepened and a glint entered his eyes, "I can think of another good part you're pretending not to be considering right now."

"Which is?"

"Meeting sexy reporters with smooth voices and a sunshiny disposition," Gael stated, laughing when Shade stiffened. "You didn't think the chemistry between you guys went unnoticed, did you? Why are you making that face? This is exciting! The last time you showed an interest in something it was a new flavor of coffee. Five years ago."

That had to be an exaggeration…probably.

"Let me guess," he continued, not giving Shade the chance to speak, "it's that last part that has you hesitating, am I right?"

"He's too good for me," he muttered, dropping his gaze to his food, suddenly really invested in eating the mystery dish when he'd only been picking at it a second prior.

"Shade," Gael turned serious, "how many times do I have to tell you that there's nothing wrong with you?"

"A guy like that isn't interested in—"

"I like tying people up," he interrupted, and when Shade's eyes rounded he lifted a hand. "See?"

"Since when?" They'd spoken about Shade's first time before, and how icky it made him feel thinking back on how everyone had treated him after and Gael had never mentioned anything like that any of those times.

"It's a newly discovered proclivity," he shrugged. "My point is, I like tying people up during sex, and the people I've done it with like being tied up. There's nothing wrong with wanting a little spice in the bedroom."

"You didn't see the look on—"

"Fuck that guy who took your v-card," Gael told him, "and fuck everyone at your school who listened to him when he went around talking about it. The gross one in this story isn't you, my friend, it's him. Don't kiss and tell is a pretty universal understanding. He told them you liked it when he held you down and kept going even when you cried that it hurt? Sounds like he sexually assaulted you. Who sides with someone like that?"

"And if I said I didn't care if he had?" Shade forced the words past his lips. "That getting to feel like myself in that one, fleeting moment, was worth all the physical pain he caused? What would that make me?"

"You're not the only one in the entire universe who enjoys receiving pain during sex, Shade," he said, he was silent a moment, lost in thought before suggesting, "I know the people at the orphanage didn't mean to, but they really messed with your head by feeding you all that bullshit about needing to be perfect and normal to be adopted."

"Except, I wasn't either of those things and ended up not being adopted."

"Shade."

"Gael."

He blew out a breath and switched tactics. "After we wrap this case, why don't we take a vacation to Alter?"

Shade shook his head. "An entire planet of sexually charged feeling people? No thank you."

"They have these new buildings with dampeners built into the walls," Gael explained. "You select potential partners through a list of them, without having to meet anyone face to face, and if you match, you're directed to a room where you're left to…explore however you like."

Alter was a manmade planet, considered a World Ship, that acted as a safe space for people all over the universe to come and either find potential sexual partners, life matches, or even to vacation with their significant other.

"You know that BDSM is a thing, and you know that many people enjoy it. So why are you so hell-bent on torturing yourself like this when you could be letting someone else do the torturing for you and actually enjoying it?"

"Yes," he drawled, "I'll just explain to the captain that I'm putting in leave so I can take a trip to Alter to get my dick wet. That'll go over well."

Gael scowled. "And why shouldn't it? It's none of his damn business what his agents do off the clock, who they do, or even how they do them for that matter. If he judges you—"

"It'll get around the base and I'll be the talk of the town just like back then," Shade said. "Yes, BDSM is a thing and people are allowed to enjoy that. But not me. I can't afford to let myself go there."

"Because you're afraid about being brought back to that place you were forced into when you were a kid?" To his credit, since they were talking about Shade's trauma now, Gael sounded more like he understood.

As much as Shade wished that was all of it though, it wasn't, and he couldn't lie to his only friend. "You know you love spicy food?"

Gael frowned but nodded. "Helps me relieve stress."

"That's because it triggers your body into thinking it's in danger," Shade said, "so your brain releases endorphins to make you feel better. Whenever you're feeling a negative emotion—sadness, stress, anger, annoyance—"

"I get it," Gael stated.

"—You instinctually crave something spicy, and if you don't get it right away, you become a walking nightmare to be around."

"Thanks, friend, love you too."

"My point is, it makes you feel good and whenever you feel bad you need it. I can't be rushing off to Alter every other day because my ability has read the negative emotions of half the planet. I'd get too caught up in feeling grounded that I'd consider quitting the I.P.F and I can't do that."

"Don't take this the wrong way," Gael told him, "because I would hate having to find a new partner, would be pissed for a while, and would miss you like crazy, but…You don't care about this job. If quitting would make you happier, why not?"

"I'd have nowhere to go," Shade reminded him. "Our salaries aren't exactly enough to allow me to relocate and live without needing to get other work first. Then I'd be right back in the same situation, except with lower self-esteem because I don't have the fancy title I worked my ass off for anymore."

"I can't tell if you're very self-aware," he clucked his tongue, "or not self-aware enough. You said it yourself, it's not like you like intense pain, and you're not into humiliation at all. Just find yourself someone who's into tying you up in the bedroom and whipping you a couple of times and you'll be good to go."

Shade lifted a brow. "No thank you."

"I don't mean me," Gael laughed.

He'd known that, but trying to lighten the mood was just about the only thing he could do right now. "I just…I wish I didn't want to be wanted so badly."

"Everyone wants to be wanted, Shade."

"Can we stop talking about this?"

"Only if you promise you'll consider it," Gael insisted. "We can always lie and tell the captain we're heading somewhere else. They don't check the travel logs. That would be a breach of our privacy rights."

"If it means putting an end to this conversation, sure whatever."

"I'm serious."

"I am too." Shade blew out a breath. "I'll think about it."

He was tired of always feeling this way about himself. Maybe his friend was right about him having to risk putting himself out there more instead of always complaining and feeling lonely and unwanted on his own.

"Cool. Subject change coming in, three…two…one. Dario mentioned he's working a possible angle on the gallery, right?" They'd both received the message from the officer earlier that afternoon. "Did you request any other details?"

Thank the Light for Gael. If he didn't have him, Shade probably would have gone full-on insane by now. He made him face his demons, but never pushed him too hard to confront them, knowing he had that, that he had someone who legitimately cared about him made him momentarily feel warm, and he tried clinging to that feeling for as long as possible as they went back to talking about the case.

"No," Shade had been tempted but then he'd thought about how the older man might ask him to come back to the station and have it explained there and the idea of stepping back outside and dealing with people… "I told him to gather everything and present it to us tomorrow."

"Smart. See? Told you. We'll do better tomorrow."

Shade sure as hell hoped so.

Chapter 11:

"What've you got?" Gael slid into one of the rolling chairs set in front of the long conference room table and swiveled to face Dario, who was already seated at the far corner.

Shade was less enthusiastic as he sat with them, though he was curious as well.

"We're still combing through the tips," Dario said. He'd started every conversation off with this information so they'd know if there'd been a legitimate sighting, though they would have been notified immediately if there had. "He knows how to hide, have to give him that. Which got me thinking, what if he isn't working alone?"

"It's possible." Shade had considered that himself, but with no proof to help back the theory, there wasn't much they could do about it but sit here and make assumptions. "Someone to help move the bodies, maybe. The actual killings themselves…" He licked his lips and shook his head. "He'd want to handle those on his own."

"You think?"

"They're messy, but clinical if you look close enough." And he had. He'd stared at those images so many times and for so long that he could picture every minute detail vividly in his mind when he closed his eyes.

"He wasn't just torturing them for fun. He had a reason. A purpose."

"Don't they all." Gael let out a low whistle. "Maxen's unhinged. What possible reason could a person have to do something like that?" He motioned to one of the crime scene photos of a man whose face was set in a perpetual laugh. It'd obviously been manipulated and forced into that expression.

"That's Er Welsh," Shade said. "Have you forgotten what he did to his victims?"

The information packet exposing Welsh for his crimes was one of the thickest they'd received.

"Sounds like you think these guys deserved it, Detective," Dario drawled, and Shade shrugged his shoulder.

"Someone had to take down the monsters. If not for our serial killer, we wouldn't even know these people existed. They'd still be out there on the streets hurting others."

"That's why no one took this case seriously. You seem to be different though."

Shade wasn't, really. He just couldn't afford not to succeed. Couldn't stand even the thought of his chief back on Percy being disappointed in him. Since he couldn't be that honest, he ended up saying, "Just because I don't feel too badly for the people he's killing, doesn't mean I don't agree he needs to be stopped."

"We've been assigned this case," Gael cut in, holding Dario's gaze a bit more seriously, "and we'll see it through."

"Actually," Dario sighed and clicked his multi-slate, a file opening on the table, "since' you've brought it up, after some further investigation, someone's finally come forward with some less than stellar information about Mr. Henry Ight."

For the most part, the evidence left in the packets was irrefutable, but that didn't mean they weren't checking up on it. Apparently, they'd been able to confirm most of the crimes, but Henry Ight, the last victim before Bee Wick, had been tricky. There'd been no thumb drive containing footage and though the paperwork had been detailed, that hadn't been enough.

Either their serial killer had gotten lazy, or he'd run out of time and had to kill the man ahead of schedule for one reason or another. They'd most likely never know.

Shade's eyes scanned the new document, brows winging up and then furrowing in deep disgust. "Has any of this been verified?"

"We're running some more checks now, but the victim was able to show us their chats, and even had some footage captured by her car's dashcam in their office's parking lot."

A woman who worked with Henry Ight had made claims that he'd been sexually assaulting her for months leading up to his disappearance and murder. It'd started as unwanted touches on the shoulder or thigh during company outings, but had escalated during a business trip.

"Why'd she wait so long to come forward?" Gael asked.

"Didn't want to get blamed for it," Shade guessed, and Dario nodded.

"Yeah, that's what she's saying. At first, when he went missing she was scared that he was planning on sharing photos he'd supposedly taken of her. She says she tried contacting him over a dozen times but never heard back."

"No signs of that on his multi-slate either?"

"Nope. Helps solidify the theory that the killer was wiping info off of their devices before dumping the bodies."

"Unless he did it himself to avoid detection," Shade offered. "He might have destroyed the evidence before our killer could get to it, setting him up and causing him to move up his murder timetable. Would explain why we weren't given as much proof as with the other bodies."

"You think the killer was paying that close attention to them?" Dario nibbled on his lower lip in thought.

"Makes sense."

"Why'd she come forward now?" Gael pressed his fingers against an image of the woman taken from her resume and expanded it. She was smiling in the photo, pretty and roughly around their age. "Henry was discovered six weeks ago. That's a long time to wait. What changed her mind?"

"This is the interesting part," Dario told them, a gleam entering his indigo-colored eyes. "Miss. Sung claims that she's been talking to someone online from a support group. That person convinced her to come to us and confess. This person told her about the Rose Protection Act, which she hadn't previously been aware of."

"The what?" Shade hadn't heard of it before, meaning it must be a law specific to Pollux.

"The Rose Protection Act was established ninety years ago," Gael explained, proving once again why he was a great Inspector to have around, "set in place to protect victims of, well, other victims. So long as Miss. Sung can prove an alibi for those days Henry Ight was missing, she doesn't have to answer any of our questions specifically about the abuse she suffered under him, aside from telling us that abuse occurred."

"There was a really famous case," Dario said, "where a poor man was dragged through the media after a woman was found murdered. Turned out, the woman had been abusing him for most of their relationship, really bad stuff too, and blackmailing him with photographs she threatened to show his family. Of course, as soon as the press got word, they did everything they could to uncover those photos and plastered them all over the papers. Poor guy ended up jumping from a skyscraper shortly after. Hence, the law."

"And the murdered woman?" Shade asked.

"Guy had nothing to do with it. It turned out to be a robbery gone wrong. She was just in a bad part of the city at the wrong time of night and it cost her. They caught the killer and he admitted he was just after cash and panicked when she fought back. Damn case resulted in two deaths because people couldn't keep their thoughts to themselves."

"Basically," Gael folded his arms on the edge of the table, "Miss. Sung has a solid alibi so can't be the killer herself, but came to tell us that she was abused by Henry Ight so that we'd know he was a shit person?"

"There's a chance there are others he was abusing as well," Dario said. "She isn't sure, but wouldn't put it past him. She's not the person who killed him, but despite what everyone else at their office claims, she says he was a real piece of work when the lights went off. I've ordered another, more thorough, check through his home computer and his social media accounts. Maybe we'll get lucky and find something on the first that the killer wasn't able to get to."

"She could still be an accomplice," Shade mentioned, though he didn't really believe that. Still, best to put it all out there now so they could officially check it off the list of possibilities. "If he does have someone helping to move the bodies, she could have easily been that someone."

"Checked where she was that entire week," Dario reassured him. "She was never alone."

"Never?" Gael frowned then motioned between himself and Shade. "Even we find time to be alone." The door to the conference room clicked open behind him, but he was too distracted by the teasing lift of Dario's brow to notice, throwing up his hands and adding, "Alone from each other I meant, not *with* each other!"

"Am I interrupting?" Apollo asked from the doorway, drawing their attention.

Shade had already noticed him the second he'd walked in, his chest going tight and his shoulders stiffening. What was he doing here? Not only was this meant to be a locked investigation, but they were also in the middle of a police station.

"They told me you were waiting and said I could just head back here," Apollo continued a bit sheepishly, reaching back to run his fingers through the short hairs at the base of his skull. "But if this is a bad time—"

"No, of course not." Dario stood and motioned toward the chair at the opposite end of the table, which just so happened to be nearest Shade. Then he turned to Shade and replied to his questioning glare, "I forgot to mention that I asked him to come."

"Yeah," Shade drawled, "it must have slipped your mind."

Inwardly, he scolded himself. He'd already made the mistake of mixing business with pleasure. He couldn't allow himself to slipup like that again, which meant separating the part of him that was nervous and embarrassed around the reporter from the part of him that was here to do a damn job.

"Nice to see you again," Gael smiled at Apollo, who returned the gesture warmly as he took a chair.

He was carrying a camera bag with him, which he set on the table. "I brought what you asked for, though I can't guarantee it'll be any help. With everything going on, I haven't had the time to sort through them all myself."

"Did something happen?" Gael asked before Shade could.

Which was for the best. He shouldn't sound interested. It was a dick move, but drawing a line between himself and the reporter was the smartest thing do to. He'd already decided he wouldn't be seeing Apollo again, for multiple reasons, and after one glance, hearing the sound of his lulling voice, his conviction was already wavering.

Maybe he should have taken Gael's advice sooner and gotten laid before their last case. Was that what this was? This minor obsession he had with the other man? They have spur-of-the-moment, meaningless sex one time and suddenly he's all Shade can think about. That wasn't normal, right? Normal people were capable of having a one-night stand and moving on with their lives without hating themselves or second guessing every little detail of the act itself, wondering if they'd been bad and—

"Is everything all right, Detective?" Apollo's low tone sliced through Shade's spiraling thoughts like a machete.

He'd been staring.

Again.

Shit.

"Something happened?" Shade was pleased with himself when his voice came out steady and strong.

Apollo nodded. "The Vice Gallery was vandalized."

"What?" He hadn't bothered checking the news this past week, too busy working the case. Local news was hardly an interest of his anyway, since it always involved people and celebrities and companies he didn't know, not being a citizen of whatever planet he was currently working on. "When?"

"The night after the showing," Dario answered for him. "All the security cameras were busted and the place was destroyed. We're still trying to find out who did it, but it's not looking good. That's why I asked Apollo to come in and give us a hand."

Shade wasn't following. "Do you suspect Maxen had something to do with it?"

"No," he said, "but I suspect something else."

He silently waited for the older officer to elaborate.

"Don't you think it's strange how he knew to lead you to that room specifically?" Dario asked. "He bypassed several on his way to it, and the second you entered that particular exhibit, your abilities practically had you on your knees. Which gave him the perfect opportunity to slip away."

Shade hadn't really considered that before. "My file is sealed. Only members of the Uk police have access. How would he know?"

"No clue," he admitted, "but I'm pretty sure he did. The Room of Terror—that's what that exhibit was called—was meant to show people their biggest fear, and the space was made small on purpose so that everyone would have to pack themselves in together. There was even a suggestion written on the side of the entrance that it would be more affective if a group entered than if a single viewer did it alone. Depending on how long he'd already been at the showing before we spotted him, Maxen could have easily figured out that was the best place to lead you."

Sure, *if* he'd discovered that Shade was Chitta. But that brought up the question of how? How could he know? They weren't a common breed, so even witnessing what had happened when he'd entered that room, no one there would guess it was because he was an empath. Hell, most empaths didn't have the same problem he did.

The only people who were aware of what he was were sitting in this room or unconscious at the hospital so—

Shade turned and frowned at Apollo, unable to help it.

"Officer Dario asked me to come because I have pictures of the gallery before it was destroyed," Apollo told him, holding his gaze with a steady one of his own. It was obvious that he understood Shade's silent accusation, but if he was offended by it, it didn't show.

Dario most likely didn't realize that Shade had told Apollo about being Chitta, so of course he wouldn't have brought him here to accuse him of being a leak.

He'd jumped to conclusions, but he didn't get the chance to apologize.

"He also took tons of shots of the guests," Dario added. "We may get lucky and find a few pictures of Maxen. See if maybe he was speaking with someone while there."

They still didn't know why he'd gone to the showing. Had he been meeting an accomplice or stalking a new target? If they were able to figure out which of those it was, they'd get a leg up for sure.

Apollo pulled out his camera and opened the bottom base, where the scanner was, so that he could set it on the table and make a connection. After pressing a few buttons, his photos began to appear in a stream on the surface of the table, spread out at first before overlapping at the vast quantity.

Gael clicked his tongue. "Damn. You took a lot of photos."

"It's my job," Apollo said a bit apologetically. "But maybe that'll work in your favor and you'll be able to find something."

"Why didn't you just leave the camera at the front desk?" Shade asked, realizing too late how rude he sounded. Still, it was a valid question. He turned to Dario. "I requested this conference space to ensure details of the case remained confidential. We can't just have non-team members walking in and out."

"Ah," Gael began randomly sorting through the photos as he spoke, "looks like the real Shadow Yor has entered the planet's atmosphere."

Shade sent him a dark look.

"What's that mean?" Dario frowned between the two of them, clearly uncomfortable with having just been scolded by someone who was technically his superior.

Gael motioned to his head. "The blockers have completely worn off and he's recovered from that horrible Repletion he experienced the night of the showing. Meaning he's back to his typical sunshine self now that his focus isn't split between us and trying to hide the amount of pain he was in. That whole nice act he's been fooling you with all this time? Yeah, that's just what it was. An act."

"Shut up," Shade ordered.

Dario chuckled, realizing that he was only teasing his partner and then started sorting through the photos as well.

"You should have some coffee," Gael suggested, making to get to his feet, "I'll go—"

"I'll get it," Apollo cut him off, standing himself. "The Detective is right. I shouldn't be here. I'll go." He bowed at them and then left without so much as glancing in Shade's direction.

As soon as the door was sealed behind him, Gael motioned to it with his chin.

"I thought you liked him?" he said, and at Shade's look, rolled his eyes. "You're not good at hiding your emotions, just FYI, so it's not like I'm outing your crush to the officer here."

"Sorry." Dario didn't sound sorry.

"It's been obvious to everyone from the start," Gael continued. "Besides, we were there to see how Apollo rushed to your aid at the gallery."

He didn't want to, but his eyes trailed over to Dario.

The officer shrugged and nodded. "I apologize for asking him to come without running it by you first. I assumed because the two of you were getting along so well, it wouldn't be a problem. I won't make that assumption again."

"No," Shade rubbed at his temple, mostly out of habit since his head felt fine at the moment, "no, I overreacted. I mean, I was right and no one should be allowed to see any of this, but I didn't need to be an asshole about it."

"You should probably go after him then," Dario replied, grinning when Shade didn't immediately move. "Go on. You're no good here if all you can think about is how you may have hurt the kid's feelings."

Since he wasn't really needed there and he probably could do with walking it off, Shade took their advice. He found Apollo down the hall, waiting in front of one of the coffee dispensing machines.

"Hope this is all right," Apollo said as soon as Shade approached, reaching down to pick up the small paper cup filled with steaming liquid. "It was the closest I could find."

"Worlds that have coffee, in any capacity, are my favorite," Shade stated lightly, accepting the cup. He was quiet for a minute while the reporter punched in some buttons for another, and then cleared his throat. "I'm sorry."

"For?" Apollo didn't turn his way, busy with the machine. "Ghosting me? That I showed up when you were trying to avoid me? Or for being blunt back there?"

He blinked, unsure where to start or what was most important to address first. Eventually he just settled on going in order. "I wasn't ghosting you, I really have been busy."

"Overthinking about things," Apollo agreed, "sure."

"With the case," Shade corrected, but after a lingering look exhaled and admitted, "Okay, and overthinking. But you're wrong about my not wanting to see you. It's not like that. And the reason I was so blunt is because this has to do with my job, and counter to what happened on the roof that day makes it seem, I take work seriously. Too seriously, in fact."

"I wouldn't leak confidential information," Apollo told him, "even if I am a reporter. Though," he grunted, "I suppose considering my occupation your reaction does make sense."

"So we're good?"

Apollo snorted, and when Shade clearly didn't get the joke, he laughed outright. "Shadow, if you think making a slightly firm statement counts as being a bad guy, you've got a lot to learn. Plus, you were ignoring me all week. Why do you even care if you hurt my feelings with what you said back there? Weren't you trying to get rid of me anyway?"

"No, I—" He stopped himself, and collected his thoughts before he dug a bigger hole and went with, "You're great."

"Wow." Apollo grabbed his coffee and went to walk past, headed back toward the conference room, only stopping once Shade had his hand on his arm.

"Look, I'm really bad at this, okay?" Shade shifted on his feet. "It's been a while since I've ever flirted with someone, let alone," he waved in the air, "do what we did."

"We fucked," Apollo said, rather loudly.

Shade slapped a hand over his mouth before he knew what he was doing and glanced up and down the hall. They were still alone, but there was always the chance those words had echoed.

"Relax," Apollo pushed his hand away but held onto him by the wrist, "we're two grown adults. No one is going to care even if they do find out."

"I was on—"

"The clock," he nodded, "right. So?"

"So? What I did was super inappropriate. "

Apollo cocked his head. "I think I get it now," he murmured to himself, and Shade frowned.

"What?"

"Why your abilities are so twisted," he replied. "I've been trying to sort it out since we met, I've never heard of anyone having it as bad as you and was curious what the reasons could be."

"And you think you've suddenly had an epiphany?"

"What did Gael mean back there?" Apollo asked instead of answering. "When he said you were acting like the real you?"

This conversation had more jumps than a trih race, and he was finding it difficult to keep up. He tried his best though. Typically, people left right away when they found out Shade was Chitta. He'd assumed the reason Apollo had stuck around was because they were one and the same, and there was no fear of him being read since Shade didn't appear like he could read another of his kind.

Then he'd dodged his calls and messages after sleeping with him. If there was a better reason to call someone an asshole and leave, he couldn't think of one at the moment. Yet, Apollo didn't look like he was gearing up to tell Shade to go fuck himself. He didn't even appear to be even remotely upset, almost as if their whole conversation up to this point he'd been simply going through the motions and saying what he thought should be said instead of what he really wanted to.

Shade's brow furrowed deeper. What an odd thought to have…And he didn't have the time to pick it apart right now. The reporter was still waiting for an answer.

"He likes to say I'm not as nice as I pretend to be when I first meet people. Since I care too much about what others think of me. According to him, there's the version of me when I'm on blockers, the version of me just off blockers, and the *real* me." Why were they talking about this? "It's just a joke."

"What are you like when you're on blockers?"

"There's no pain since I don't have to worry about Glitches giving my ocular migraines or the empathic connection overstimulating my senses. But in order for them to work, I need to take the strongest dosage available, which has the nasty side effect of dimming my emotions as well."

"You can't feel when you're on them?" Apollo seemed to find that fascinating.

"Not really," he clarified. "It's sort of like I'm floating? It's not great but it's better than the alternative. Typically by the time we're gone with a case, I'm willing to do just about anything to stop the pain, even if it means cutting my feelings off in the process. The result of that is I tend to be more selfish and uncaring about the people around me."

"You don't drop your gaze or get that sky look about you, you mean," Apollo surmised.

"Pretty much. But I'm still not happy. When I'm on the blockers, I can't feel, and when I'm off them, it's hard to know what I feel when there are several dozen other people's emotions racing through me all at once. For a day or two when I come off the blockers, they make my ability worse until I can readjust to feeling. Anyway, this is an elaborate way of answering your question. Gael says the real me is the one who doesn't care about pleasing others and is less cautious about picking and choosing the right words. I don't know if that's true though."

"Why not?"

"I don't really know myself," Shade admitted. "I guess you don't have that problem."

"No," Apollo said, "I don't. I know who I am, and I like who I am."

"Everyone does." Shade sighed. "Everyone seems to like you."

"Jealous?" Apollo inspected him. "Of me or of them?"

"People don't like me," Shade gave as his response. "They tolerate me."

"Gael likes you."

He couldn't argue with him there. Gael did like him, but… "He's the only one."

"Dario seems to like you too," Apollo corrected. "And Axel spoke highly of you. It's not that people don't like you, Shade, it's that *you* don't like yourself. It's kind of hard to see the world with your head always tipped down."

For a split second he was offended, but that indignation fizzled out pretty quickly. "I thought you couldn't read me."

He'd been mostly joking, but Apollo's next words had him going still.

"I never said that. You can't read me, and I told you I'd noticed."

"Wait…" Shade's stomach clenched uncomfortably. "Can you read me?"

"Like an open book, baby. Why?" This time when he tilted his head, there was an edge to the movement. "Got something you want to hide from me?"

Was it just him, or had it suddenly gotten tense between them?

"It does seem like Gael has a point. You care too much about what others think of you. Why does it even matter?"

"Abandonment issues and PTSD from when I was left on the side of the road," Shade confided. It wasn't the first time they were speaking of it, so he didn't see a reason not to, especially since he was busy trying to ignore the strange feeling he'd just gotten, certain that he'd misread the room. Apollo was so friendly and upbeat, there was no way that darkness that formed in the air between them had come from him. It was all in Shade's head. "That's why it's so important to me to do things by the book. I don't want to get in trouble with my superiors because being a top agent means people smile when I walk into a room instead of trying to hide their gazes. It's why I'll push myself too far sometimes, like I did last week. I should have rested more between cases, but I didn't and the result was me causing a seen at the gallery."

"You mean when you fell apart in that room in front of all those people," Apollo shifted an inch closer, the move almost imperceptible, "or when you fell apart on the roof in front of me?"

He swallowed the lump that formed suddenly in his throat. "Both?"

"If I'm understanding correctly," another step, so that the tips of their shoes were now touching, "when you've recovered from the blockers your body adjusts more naturally, meaning you can go longer periods between overstimulation."

"Yeah." Shade nodded.

"Then why the blockers at all? Sounds like they're more than half the problem."

"Because I can't shut it off," he said. "Someone else is constantly there, scratching at my insides, filling me up with their feelings, and I hate it."

"I don't know," Apollo glanced at his mouth, "seemed like you rather enjoyed having someone filling you up."

"How do you do that?" Shade asked. "You're having two conversations at once."

"You're following along just fine."

"You're hitting on me."

"Yup."

"But also interrogating me."

"Correct again."

That caught his attention and Shade held his gaze. "Do you usually interrogate the people you hit on?"

"Truthfully? I've never treated anyone the way I've been treating you. I'm still trying to decide if I like it or not."

"What does that mean?"

"It means everything has been pretty tame," Apollo said. "I should have gotten bored a long time ago. Instead, I find myself thinking about you constantly. Wondering what you're doing, who you're with, if that panicked look in your eyes, the one you had when you ran into that crowded room, is back or not. Back to the blockers."

"What?" Was something wrong with Shade, or was something wrong with Apollo? Was this just how people hit on one another now? Messy and intense and all over the place?

"You take them to feel normal and aren't happy with yourself when you're off them. But you handle your abilities for longer stretches of time than I was led to believe initially because the aftereffects of said blockers. Correct so far?"

"Yeah. Wait." He held up a hand. "It's not like I lied to you."

"If I thought that you had, we wouldn't still be talking," he told him cryptically then moved on. "How long? If you run into that room right now for example, how long could you deal with all of that attention on you before you started to get overwhelmed?"

"Since I've only seen the few people here at the station all day, and only made eye contact with a handful of them," he thought it over, "probably an hour. I'd be able to meet with them individually and question them through the Glitch and whatever they were feeling. I'd use their feelings actually, try to get a rise out of them to see if someone might slip."

"Find out if they're nervous or working with Maxen?" Apollo hummed. "You think he has an accomplice."

"It would make sense if he did."

"Because?"

"Bodies are heavy?"

He chuckled. "Why does that sound like you're asking me, Detective?"

"Probably because you're starting to make me nervous."

"Good nervous," Apollo rested a hand against his hip, "or bad nervous?"

"This is really an interrogation, you know that, right? Like, you could switch jobs with me right now and anyone would believe you were the detective and I was your suspect."

"Person of interest," Apollo corrected, smirking. "You're my person of interest at the moment, Shadow Yor. How unlucky for you. But you're also making it pretty damn easy, which is earning you points for sure."

"Did you just call me easy?" Shade went to push him away, but Apollo moved to grab his hand to stop him.

"I'm pointing out you're inexperienced with relationships," he said. "Are you denying it?"

"I'm twenty-seven and have had one real friend my entire life," Shade drawled. "No, I'm not denying it." It was better that the reporter know in any case, because after this he was even more confused than he'd been initially. "There's a good chance I'll end up hurting you without meaning to."

He wasn't socially awkward in general, but when it came to personal matters and forming attachments that didn't have anything to do with work…Then things became difficult for him. That's what happened when you grew up the social pariah of each and every school you ever attended. He didn't know how to make friends because he'd never gotten the chance in the past. Gael had befriended him, and the rest of the people he was friendly with were really just co-workers he got along with.

They certainly weren't throwing-surprise-birthday-celebrations for one another kind of close.

"Don't worry about that," Apollo told him, voice dropping to a low whisper, "there's a great chance I'll end up hurting you on purpose."

Shade frowned all over again. "Do you mean because this is going to have to end? When the case is done and I leave—"

"That's your plan?" Apollo asked. "Get off planet as soon as the case is closed?"

"Well, yeah. That's how it works. I either go back to base for a bit or they send me off on another assignment. I was thinking about taking a vacation though. You saw how bad it was the other day. I clearly need it."

"If you stopped using blockers—"

"I said I could last an hour in that room as I am now," Shade reminded. "I could maybe stretch that to two, but I'd start feeling sick. My chest would feel tight, like something heavy was sitting on me, and my head would start to pound. I'd probably be short of breath by the time hour two was up. And lasting through a third? Not likely. Being off the blockers makes me more normal, more like other Chitta, but it doesn't make me *normal*."

"Normal is overrated."

"That's easy for you to say." Apollo was the most regular, normal guy Shade had ever met. Literally everything he'd ever dreamed of finding in a partner. Everything he'd ever wanted to be himself. "It's not jealousy," he said with little thought. "It's envy."

"How very honest of you." It didn't sound like an insult or like he was upset by Shade's comment. He sounded…pleased. "If only you could be so honest with yourself, I'd solve a lot of your problems."

Gael appeared at the end of the hall then, waving his arms to get their attention.

With a start, Shade realized how closely they were standing and put space between them, nodding over at his partner when that had Apollo's eyes narrowing. As soon as the reporter realized they were no longer alone, however, his expression softened back into the easy-going friendly one he so often wore.

"We need you back in the conference room," Gael said once he'd reached them.

"Then I'll—" Apollo went to step back but was stopped.

"No," Gael looked at them soberly, "you too. We found something. Something you both need to see."

Chapter 12:

Shade hadn't gotten the chance to look at the exhibit when he'd raced in after Maxen, but now, staring down at the dozens of photos he understood why everyone in that room had felt so uncomfortable.

The Room of Terror had been posed as an art piece that exposed everyone's greatest fear. Most of the space was empty, just four crimson walls and the black marble floor. But the wall where the door was located was different, and where the actual piece was displayed.

The whole wall had been redone in mirrors. Pieces and shards, all of varying sizes, with large cracks and small, jagged edges and smooth surfaces. There was no discernable pattern, but it was easy to see that was more than half the point.

Apollo had captured the true purpose of the exhibit splendidly, the photos showing the reflections of groups of people, all staring at their reflections. Some were frowning, others were wide-eyed. They, like the glass, came in all shapes and sizes, but crowded together the reflections mixed, all of them broken and shattered.

"Who was the artist who came up with that?" Gael asked.

"It was done by Anonymous," Apollo answered. Everyone else was staring down at the images, but he hadn't taken his gaze off of Shade since they'd walked in here. "He's a pretty famous artist who started out doing illegal street art. He collected a following on social media and was offered a few spots in gallery showings throughout the city. He's done a couple, but not all."

"No one knows what he looks like?" Dario rested his hands on his hips.

"Are you thinking he might be the accomplice?" Shade knew the officer didn't have enough to suspect Miss. Sung, especially since there was no connection between her and the other victims, but a street artist who didn't want to show his face?

It was a long shot, but hadn't everything in this case been so far?

Dario considered his words before speaking. "Honestly? No. That would be too easy, right?"

"Usually the most obvious answers are the right ones," Shade said, only to have Apollo snort at his side.

"Come on, Detective," he drawled, "you know better than that. As a Chitta you've seen how easy it is for people to cover up their truths. It's a simple matter to plant 'obvious answers' that are actually just pretty lies tied up nice with a bow."

"Don't think I've ever heard you say anything so jaded before, kid," Dario let out a low whistle, clearly just teasing him. "But seriously, you've never seen this Anonymous guy either? Know anything about him that may be able to help us out?"

Apollo thought it over. "There's a rumor going around that he's actually a high schooler and he's keeping his identity a secret for now to avoid angering his parents. I can't confirm that for you though. The gallery gets in touch with him through his Imagine account and any contact from there takes place on the app. He doesn't give out his private info or his number."

"Does he have a signature?" Shade asked. He'd been trying to find one in the photos, but it was difficult to do since they were mirrors.

"Yeah." Apollo stretched an arm around him instead of asking him to move, momentarily hugging his body close as he tapped on the screen.

Shade felt the tips of his ears heat but refused to look over at either Dario or Gael to see their reactions to the other man's proximity. It didn't last long, in any case, one second he was there, the brine and forest smell tickling at Shade's senses, and the next he'd moved away again as if the moment had never happened.

Apollo had selected a photo that was taken closer and had zoomed in to the corner of the piece. At the bottom, a capital A was scrawled in Sharpie. The lines were loose and flowy.

"It's nothing like the signature on the bodies," Gael was the first to point out, flinching when both Shade and Dario sent him withering glares.

"Promise I won't be reading anything about this in the papers tomorrow, kid," Dario warned Apollo.

"Not that kind of reporter," he assured them, "and I would never do anything to get in the way of your investigation."

"If he's really in high school it's highly unlikely he's the accomplice." Dario sighed. "And Gael's right. The style is completely different."

"It's also done in a pen and not a knife," Shade reminded. "Could be he just doesn't have as much control over a blade."

"You can't actually be suspecting a minor?"

"I'm suspecting someone I don't know the identity of," he corrected. "I don't like when people hide in the shadows. There's a reason, and it's almost always a bad one."

"Something you and Anonymous have in common," Apollo said, motioning to the photos with his chin when that had Shade frowning. "That's the point of the piece. The Room of Terror. They're all staring at themselves, in pieces. When they look around, they see everyone else is in the same state. What's scarier than that? People always try to hide their faults. This piece exposes them for being the broken creatures they are."

"Yet," Gael pointed out, "Anonymous is hiding."

"He's not perfect either." Apollo shrugged. "No one is. I'm sorry I couldn't be of more help, officers. There isn't much I know about this artist either."

Dario and Gael shared a weighted look then.

"Actually," Dario confessed, "that's not why we asked you in here."

"This is." Gael tapped the screen, sending the photos of the exhibit off to the side so another set could fill up the space. One by one, pictures appeared in a clean line, so that each was clearly visible with no overlap.

In every photo, Maxen could be seen somewhere in the distance or off on the sidelines.

And he was always looking directly at the camera.

At Apollo.

Shade sucked in a breath and dropped his palms to the table, leaning in closer to scan over the images rapidly. Every single shot was the same, Maxen unmistakably there watching. He'd done a somewhat decent job of staying out of Apollo's direct line of sight but was impossible to miss in the photographs.

"You didn't feel like you were being followed that night?" Dario asked.

Apollo appeared perplexed but didn't seem nearly as concerned about this turn of events as Shade was. "No, I didn't feel a thing. But then, that's pretty typical when I work. I tend to zone out and only focus on the world through the camera lens."

"There were hundreds of photos and he only appeared in thirty of them," Gael said. "It makes sense you didn't notice him in the shots either."

"We can't know for certain he was following you specifically based on that," Dario concluded. "But there's a good chance you've at least caught his notice. Especially after you rushed in and dragged Shade out of the Room of Terror. Honestly, it's fortunate you haven't already been attacked. Best guess is Maxen is laying low for the time being now that he knows we're after him."

Apollo pursed his lips but shifted a little closer to Shade. "I'm not sure why a serial killer would be after me. I'm sure it's mere coincidence that he got in so many of my shots."

"That's not a chance you should be willing to take," Shade chided.

The reporter gave him a soft, pleased, smile and lifted a hand to the back of Shade's hip, resting it there lightly.

With the way they were standing, the other two couldn't see it, but Shade still stiffened under the public touch.

If Apollo noticed his reaction, however, he didn't do anything about it, glancing back at the photo spread instead. "Better safe than sorry has never really been my motto."

"Well it is ours," Dario said firmly. "Besides, can you imagine what would happen to us if something did occur and word got out that we let Ux's favorite reporter walk out of here without any kind of protection? They'd tear this whole station to the ground is what, and with budget cuts already what they are…"

Apollo gave the appropriate laugh. "All right, officer. I understand. What would you like from me?"

"Cooperation," Dario stated, then he turned to Shade, "from the both of you."

"Excuse me?" Shade quirked a brow. Last he'd checked he was the one in charge here.

"Told you he wasn't going to like it if you posed it like that," Gael mock whispered to the older man.

"Problems with authority, Detective?" Apollo asked, grinning. "Not the type to take orders?"

"Just," Dario held up a hand before Shade could answer, "hear me out. It's our job to do the grunt work," he motioned between himself and Gael, who nodded emphatically, "and we've got a lot of it now thanks to the kid."

"I'm fairly certain he and I are the same age," Shade pointed out, only to have Dario clear his throat awkwardly and continue on as if he hadn't been interrupted.

"We'll be here for at least an entire day combing through the rest of these photos in case the computer missed something. I assume during that time, Apollo has better things to do than sit around in police custody."

"I do, actually," the reporter agreed.

"There's no way he's a target." Shade and the rest of them knew what Apollo didn't, and that was that the killer only murdered other monsters. Apollo? A monster? Come on. Even Dario had just pointed out how well-liked he was by the entire community.

"Still. He shouldn't be left alone," Gael took over solemnly. "It's too dangerous. You've seen what Maxen is capable of, and if Apollo is his target, we still have no clue what his motive typically is. For all we know, seeing him run to your rescue at the gallery pissed him off. Knowing we're after him might not be enough to keep him in hiding for long."

"You want me to work protective detail." Shade didn't do that. He ordered others to while he continued to investigate, which Gael was very aware of. He narrowed his eyes. "Out in the hall. Now."

Gael blew out a breath and clapped Dario on the shoulder before rounding the table.

"I'll be right back," Shade told Apollo, following after his partner. Once the two of them were far enough away from the door to the conference room that he felt confident they wouldn't be overheard, he turned on him. "What are you playing at?"

"Nothing," Gael blinked, but the innocent act was clearly faked. After a moment when it became obvious Shade wasn't buying it, he exhaled. "Dario isn't a bad guy, but he's worried about your condition. I told him that you've fully recovered, but he's still nervous that it might happen again. He's invested a lot into this case, half a year's worth of blood, sweat, and tears. You can't blame him, S."

"He's discriminating against me because of what I am," he stated. Things between him and the older officer had been going so well, he'd fooled himself into thinking it wouldn't be a problem this time. Swearing he turned and rubbed at his temple, tempted to kick at the wall for good measure.

"You could have him removed," Gael said calmly. "But I truly believe he's coming from a good place. He just knows that we're going to have to do a lot of interviews of people who are seen in these photographs, and that's not something that you need to bother with. This is why you and I have always involved local police, remember? So there are other people there to do the legwork we don't want to."

"Who says I don't want to?" Shade snapped. It bothered him that logically, his partner made sense. They were going to have to interview everyone in the pictures standing near Maxen, on the off chance that someone remembered him or anything that could be useful about him. "I'll be fine. You know I will be."

"For a couple of hours," Gael agreed, "sure. But this could go on for a couple of days and you know it. And it's the only thing we've got going for us. The only thing that is, aside from the reporter in there."

Shade paused, narrowing his eyes all over again as everything clicked into place. "You want to use him as bait."

"I mean," he shrugged, "if the shoe fits?"

"It doesn't."

"All of the other victims were good at hiding their true natures as well," Gael said quietly. "I haven't spent nearly as much time with him as you have. You sure he's not a target, or do you just hope he isn't?"

"Seriously?" Shade scowled at him. "Now you think Apollo is some secret criminal mastermind?"

"No," he exhaled, the first gleam of frustration showing, "of course not. I'm just saying we can't rule anything out. That's usually your stance on things, remember? I'm taking a page from your book here. And, if it turns out Maxen is targeting him, that doesn't necessarily prove it's because Apollo has done anything wrong. Murderers change their M.O. sometimes."

"Not without good reason."

"Maybe he has one." Gael lifted a shoulder. "We don't know. We still don't know why he's doing this at all. My point is, this could be a chance to catch him so we can get the answers we need."

He closed his eyes and prayed for patience. "So you sided with Dario to appease him *and* so someone could keep an eye on Apollo in the hopes that the killer after him will show up?"

"Not *someone*," he corrected, "you. This is our case. And he's—"

"What?" Shade said, almost daring him to continue.

Gael knew him well enough though to know his anger wasn't lasting. It never was. Like all other emotions, they filtered through Shade at a rapid pace, making it impossible for him to cling to anything for longer than a few moments at best.

"You like him." He placed a hand on Shade's shoulder and squeezed once. "When was the last time that happened? Huh? Was it Becca Hue, the second year of Academy?"

"Shut up." Shade swiped his arm off but couldn't help when the corner of his mouth tipped up slightly. "I thought her hair was super pretty."

"Wow," Gael laughed, "that's so sad, dude. Come on. Is that what it is this time? Do you think the reporter's hair is pretty?"

Yes. It was so black and shiny, like spilled ink.

Shade was smart enough to keep that thought to himself, however.

"Look, I'm sure you're right and Apollo hasn't don't anything to warrant Maxen's attention, but he may have it, and this could work in your favor either way. You may be able to catch our killer, and if he doesn't show and you can't, at least you have an excuse to spend more time with the reporter."

"Are you trying to get me to agree to play bodyguard as my Inspector," he drawled, "or as my friend?"

"Can't it be both?"

"That's not very professional."

"Says the guy who was caught making out on the roof."

Shade's eyes went wide and he stepped a little closer, slapping a palm over Gael's mouth. All that did was remind him of how he'd done that same thing to Apollo a half hour ago for the very same reason. He dropped his hand. "You—"

"You were flushed and had this dazed look in your eyes," Gael said. "I know that look. We've been friends for over ten years, remember?"

"So you guessed I was up there making out with someone on the job," Shade replied, partially fishing to be sure that kissing was all Gael suspected took place up there, "and you…don't see anything wrong with that?"

He looked at him bewildered. "Why would I?"

"Because I was on the clock and instead of helping you downstairs I was making out with a stranger?"

"It's about time," Gael snorted. "You're always sad that people don't accept you, but you're the one who closes yourself off first, Shade. Who cares that you kissed a virtual stranger? It's not like you were in the right state of mind to help us search through crowds anyway."

"Because I'm a broken Chitta."

"Stop it," for the first time there was a thread of anger in his tone. "I hate when you do that. Hate on yourself for no reason."

"I have a reason," he replied, waving toward the conference room. "Dario—"

"Cares about the case, yes," he stopped him. "But he's also worried for *you*. He doesn't think you're incompetent."

"Sure about that?"

Gael sighed and appeared as though he was gearing up to explain something simple to a child. "They had nothing before we got here. Now they have a solid lead and a clear suspect. They have a possible lead into how said suspect has been selecting his victims, and—"

"A lack of a clear motive," Shade began ticking off fingers, "let the suspect get away because I entered Repletion, no ideas on how to locate—"

"Your new boy toy," Gael said. "Stick by him and if Maxen shows, you'll be there to make up for letting him get away that first time, even though, and I'm serious, that wasn't your fault."

"If I'd been anyone else," Shade stated, "I wouldn't have lost my mind the second I entered that exhibit." He thought back to Apollo's words. "If I stopped using blockers on my off hours—"

"You'd have gone insane years ago," Gael sounded like he truly believed that. "Everyone needs a break from the voices in their head, S. You deserve that, same as anybody else. You were dealt a shit hand, okay? But you've done everything in your power to make your life your own. You've accomplished things Chitta who don't have the same skill level as you couldn't dream of. That means something. You mean something."

"Exactly what I've been trying to tell him, Inspector," Apollo's voice shocked them both, and they were startled. The door to the conference room was cracked open, but he was less than ten feet away, having managed to quietly sneak up on them.

"You didn't feel him?" Gael mumbled under his breath, accusatory, before smiling at the reporter. "Got impatient waiting?"

"I've been called into work," he said. "You aren't the only ones who need photos from me." He glanced over at Shade. "Are you coming, Detective? Or has your partner been unable to convince you I'm worth the extra care and attention?"

"I never thought you weren't," Shade assured him, realizing too late that it sounded an awful lot like an excuse.

"So, you're coming then?"

"He is." Gael pushed him in Apollo's direction. "I'll stay here and go over the evidence with Dario, put a list together of all the potential people we need to contact. Don't worry about a thing. We've got this."

Without giving him a chance to respond to that, the Inspector turned toward Apollo, giving him an apologetic look. "Please forgive any self-deprecating things he may or may not say while with you. He can be annoying like that."

"Hey!" Shade glowered. It probably did get annoying though, to constantly listen to him bitch and moan when the truth was, Gael wasn't entirely wrong. Shade iced people out on a personal level before they could get too close out of fear they wouldn't accept him.

All because he didn't accept himself.

What a mess.

"I'll help him see the light," Apollo winked at Gael, moving over to wrap long fingers around Shade's elbow, "you can count on that."

"Well," Gael clapped his hands, "all right then. Call if anything happens."

"I'm supposed to be the one saying that," Shade said.

But no one was listening. Gael had already turned back to the conference room and Apollo had begun to drag Shade down the opposite end of the hall.

Chapter 13:

He didn't need a mirror to know he was attractive as all hell, but Apollo took an extra minute to check himself in the one hanging over the sink anyway.

His dark hair was curled and damp from the shower he'd just taken, the white towel secured low on his hips to show off the lean length of his torso, and the way the hot water had given his skin a rosy tint. Corded muscle and a devilish gleam in his eyes reflected at him and he grinned, relishing in the anticipation.

It'd taken him a couple of days, but he'd finally convinced the detective to come up to his apartment. Up until now, Shadow had been stubbornly sleeping in his car parked in front of the building, a tiny act of defiance that shouldn't have bothered Apollo nearly as much as it had.

He'd been pissed though. Even knowing the only reason the detective had kept refusing was out of some misplaced sense of duty and fear that if they were alone, they'd end up in a similar situation to the one on the rooftop.

He wasn't wrong.

Apollo had been haunted by it ever since it'd happened. If he closed his eyes, he could almost picture the way Shadow had trembled against him, his shoulders quaking as he desperately fought against his own desires.

It'd been cute, but the appeal had lost its luster and both Apollo and his neglected dick were no longer amused by the other man's mulishness.

This was already a distraction, one he should be trying harder to untangle himself from, and yet…Unlike the detective, Apollo didn't fight against his own urges. Going to war with himself was a losing battle, one he'd long since realized wasn't worth the time or the energy. Still, this little obsession he'd developed was admittedly no longer little, and his plans for Shadow had practically consumed his every waking moment.

It was different.

Apollo wasn't used to wanting anything this badly, not even the hunt, and most days that was all he lived for. All that could get him out of bed in the morning amidst the otherwise dreary world. Everything and everyone was boring. Even things that had used to entice him, like the process of learning and picking apart another person's life. Trying to find exactly where things went wrong for them, exactly what made them snap.

He could pinpoint the exact events that led up to him turning out the way he had, and it was a sort of pastime of his to try and piece together what had caused that in others.

There wasn't always an obvious reason though, or even necessarily a reason at all. Some people were just evil from birth, and no amount of digging through their lives would be able to prove otherwise.

He wasn't sure if he fell under that category, because how could he be? For as long as he could remember he'd always been this. Always just been himself. But what was clear was, whether or not he'd been born with his devilish nature or if it'd been torn out of him, someone else was responsible.

His reflection peered back at him, expression suddenly dark, mouth pressed into a thin line as images of his sister flicked to the forefront of his mind against his will.

He'd taken care of that problem and he'd take care of this one.

Straightening, he finger-combed his hair one last time and then stepped out of the bathroom, a trail of steam following him into the living room where he'd left the detective earlier.

As per usual, the second he spotted Shadow an onslaught of emotion consumed him.

Arousal, excitement, anger, and this deep-rooted need all clawed at his chest, urging him to cross the room, take the detective by the back of the neck, and force him down onto the table so he could—

Shade glanced up, noticing him finally. "Hey. Sorry, I'll clear this away."

He was sitting in the center of Apollo's black leather couch, perched on the edge so he could glance between his multi-slate and the glass coffee table before him. The table, like most, doubled as a computer, and images and writing flickered over the surface.

Apollo caught a glimpse of broken limbs as Shade swiped his palm over the images, sending them into a digital folder in the corner of the glass. The pictures did nothing for him. Seeing the carnage never did. That wasn't what he was after. He forced his lips to lift in a partial smile, nonchalantly bringing the smaller towel he'd brought with him to the back of his head as he ruffled his hair.

"Don't worry about it. I'm not squeamish, and I promise not to look at classified information anyway." He'd already read through everything they had on the case. Getting close to Shade had been beneficial after all. It'd been almost too easy hacking into the man's multi-slate.

"I really shouldn't." Shade hesitated with his fingers hovering over the middle of the screen.

The most obvious observation Apollo had made about the detective was that he could easily be considered a workaholic. Not because he actually enjoyed his job—he didn't, really—but due to a lack of having any other interests.

Shade didn't do anything on his off time aside from going on long runs as far from civilization as he could manage and that was about it.

Where Apollo had learned to love and embrace being Chitta, Shade's overstimulated brain caused him to loathe what he was, unable to focus on much else other than feeling sorry for himself.

Typically, that would disgust Apollo, and yet, it'd had the opposite effect on him. He didn't want to punish Shadow for being weak and self-wallowing. He wanted to tempt him out of his shell and expose him to reality. The moment he'd heard Shade's parents had left him at an orphanage his fascination had exploded into a full-blown obsession.

They'd both been rejected by their families, the people who were meant to love them unconditionally, but Apollo had gone one way and Shade had gone the other. At first, he'd been curious about how different they'd turned out. Then the rooftop had happened, and he'd recognized the truth.

They weren't so different after all, it was just that the detective was afraid of his darkness. Afraid of what giving into it might make him.

For all his complaints over not being able to differentiate between his emotions and the people around him, Shade was very clearly terrified of his own feelings. Enough that he tried to pretend they didn't exist.

Was that due to his parent's rejection, or had something else caused it?

Apollo was going to find out. He was going to find out everything about Shadow Yor.

The best way to conquer something was to uncover them completely. Expose them to the things that made them uncomfortable. Shine a light on the skeletons in their closest and watch how they reacted when forced to confront them.

In the past when he'd targeted someone Apollo had played it smart, avoiding direct contact. There was nothing linking him to any of his victims, no trail for the police to even potentially stumble upon. He'd had to do everything from the sidelines, carefully weaving his web, luring his prey right where he wanted them before he could strike.

Things were different with Shadow. Not only did he not have to hide, but he also didn't want to. The distance between them was already too great, the thought of having to take a step back and avoid being in the same room with him?

Apollo's eye twitched in anger at just the idea, and he quickly covered it up by broadening his friendly smile.

He should have tossed the detective off the roof that day, but it was too late to turn back the clock and what was done was done. Apollo had given in to his base desires and now he had to pay the price. Or, really, Shadow did.

"The sooner you solve this the sooner you can stop following me around," Apollo teased, the smirk that twisted his lips when that had Shade dropping his gaze real.

Seduction was easy when you knew where to press and stroke.

"I didn't mean I don't like having you around," he corrected, making his tone come off somewhat apologetic even though he'd done it on purpose. "I'm sure you'd rather be doing other things though. Following me to and from work and sleeping in your car can't be fun."

"If it bothered me that much I would have taken Dario up on the offer to assign a protection detail," Shade told him softly.

Had the officer made that offer? It was a good thing Shadow hadn't taken it. Apollo wasn't sure what he'd have done if he had. To both him and Dario.

Apollo cocked his head, waiting for him to continue, but when it was clear he was done, he asked, "So then why do you seem so down all the time?"

He frowned. "Do I?"

"You're making a puppy dog face right now." He circled a finger at his own face and then went back to drying his hair, sure to stretch his arm out and flex at the same time.

Sure enough, Shade's gaze dropped to his chest, lingering there for a long moment until his pupils had dilated and his pink tongue popped out briefly to wet his lips.

"Maybe that was the wrong descriptor," Apollo pretended to reconsider, "not down, more like, distracted?"

"I'm working," Shade said.

"What about…?" He tapped his temple with the hand not holding the towel, muscles rippling from the motion.

Shadow's gaze lingered yet again.

Working. Apollo almost snorted.

"The migraines come and go," Shade told him, clearing his throat. He tore his gaze off Apollo's navel and met his eyes. "But I haven't had to worry about entering Repletion since I started following you around."

Apollo was the one doing the following here, but he kept that tidbit to himself. Something told him the detective wouldn't like hearing about how he'd been stalking him that entire week after their coupling on the rooftop.

"Even when you came with me to the office earlier?" Work had been bustling, with more people than he could count. He'd wondered about Shade the entire time, but the man had only openly winced a couple of times.

"Yeah," he let out a humorless chuckle, "who knows? Maybe I'm suddenly starting to fix myself."

"Anything happen to make you think that way?" Apollo grinned knowingly when a blush crept over Shade's cheeks. For a tough guy who acted cold around others, he was really just an easy target. There was next to no challenge in embarrassing him, no doubt a side effect of all that low self-esteem. "A break in the case, perhaps?"

They both knew he'd been referring to the roof, but Apollo gave him the out. Push and pull. That's how it was done. And he was a master at it.

"Unfortunately," Shade tapped one of the files on the table frustratingly, closing it, and dropped back against the couch, "no. We're still searching for Maxen but it's like the guy is a ghost. He doesn't have any known friends or family, and even though it's been running through facial recognition software since he escaped, there haven't been any hits."

And there wouldn't be. Apollo had taken care of that on his end. So long as Maxen continued to follow orders like the good waste of space that he was, he'd continue to do so.

Maxen was a tool every bit as much as Apollo's bone saw. The second a tool broke or stopped being of use, he tossed it and got a replacement.

"Afraid you'll be stuck with me for a while, Detective?" Apollo flung the smaller towel off to the side and it landed on the back of one of the dining room chairs.

The space itself was rather small, with the living room and the designated dining area bleeding into one. The kitchen was sectioned off by a half wall, with the entrance just off the single hallway that led to the bathroom and the bedroom. There weren't any other rooms.

Apollo kept his space neat and tidy, sports posters framed on the walls—even though he didn't give a single fuck about sports—and a couple of art pieces he'd been gifted from galleries over the years. Those he actually had a fondness for. Photography had been the best cover-up he could think of, which was why he'd gone into it, but he'd quickly realized there was something about artists he enjoyed being around.

They were raw and open. Different from most people on the planet in that sense.

Everyone was always trying to hide. From the world. From themselves.

Including the disheveled detective still seated before him.

And he wasn't just referring to the fact that, no, Shadow wasn't afraid he'd have to spend more time with Apollo, it was the opposite. He *wanted* to be in Apollo's company. It was clear as day even if he refused to say it.

Even if he refused to ask why nothing else had happened between them since that event on the roof.

The detective really was making this far too easy for him.

"You have a great place," Shade said then. "Do you rent or own it?"

"I own it," Apollo gave it a second and then added, "The building, I mean."

Shade blinked at him. "You what?"

"My parents left me their substantial wealth when they passed. Technically, I don't have to work. It just gives me something to do. What do you plan on doing once this is all settled?" he changed the subject for the millionth time, watching the confusion splay over Shade's face. "You seem like the planning sort. What's the plan? Keep climbing the ranks and then what?"

"Why are you asking?" Shade cocked his head.

"Just making conversation." He smiled and rested back against the edge of the TV stand pressed against the wall behind him. "Trying to get to know you better. Come on. I promise not to tell. What do you want?"

"What do I want?" He made a big show of thinking it over before stating in a mocking tone, "Domestic bliss?"

Interesting. Apollo hadn't been expecting that response. Another thing he'd learned about the detective, though. Everything about him seemed obvious, but then he'd throw out something like that and prove that looks could be deceiving.

Apollo needed to dig deeper.

"Take it from me, it's not all it's cracked up to be." His smile faltered and this time it wasn't on purpose. He inhaled slowly through his nose, trying to quell the sudden burst of anger that threatened to incinerate him from the inside out. He couldn't allow the detective to see, wasn't ready to show him that part of himself just yet.

Shade latched onto that reveal like a dog to a bone though. "Things weren't great in your family?"

"Before they died?" He snorted. "No."

He waited silently, obviously hoping that Apollo would open up on his own.

Damn it.

"My sister was abusive," Apollo said. "And when my parents found out they did nothing to stop it." When Shade's expression didn't change at all, curiosity got the best of him and he pressed his luck. "Want to hear the most twisted part? I was grateful to the fire that took them."

Shade continued to watch him, and in a rare occurrence, Apollo wasn't able to read what he was feeling. It was almost as though the other man had completely cut himself off.

"I bet you think I'm a monster now." Most people did when they heard him talk about his family, at least when he wasn't playing the part of mourning son and brother, a role that unfortunately was never-ending. Any time they were brought up he was forced to pretend to care about their loss instead of rejoicing like he truly wanted.

"Why would I think that?" Shade asked.

"I just told you I'm happy my family is dead."

"You also told me they hurt you," he pointed out, speaking as though it was the obvious answer to a simple problem. "It'd be weirder for you to feel bad for people who treated you poorly. I assume the abuse was more than your run-of-the-mill older sibling fuckery."

It wasn't a question, but Apollo found himself answering anyway.

"We were eight years apart and she was pissed when our parents told her she was no longer going to be an only child. She took that anger out on me. I've got burn marks on the bottoms of my feet from all times she and her friends put their cigarettes out on my skin. Once when I was four she locked me out of the house in a blizzard and I almost froze to death. Another time she shaved my head in my sleep the night before picture day at school. I was six that time."

As an adult who did horrendous things, Apollo could admit now that what she'd done was nothing in the grand scheme of things, that it could have been a lot worse if only she'd been creative enough. But that didn't change the fact that all of those events had culminated in causing something within him to fracture.

He *liked* who he was.

That didn't mean he had to be fond of how he'd gotten there.

It didn't mean he couldn't be glad that bitch and the assholes protecting her had burned alive.

"None of that sounds like domestic bliss," Shade said after a moment.

"Told you."

"No," he shook his head, "I mean you and I are both in the same predicament. We've never known the safety of a loving family. *That's* what I want."

He'd gotten from some of his eavesdroppings that Shadow had this deep-seated need to be wanted. It was a large part of what caused his low self-esteem issues. He thought he wasn't worthy of love and that no one would ever give it to him. That idea ate him up inside and caused those inner demons to turn on him.

"Our demons aren't meant to destroy us," Apollo found himself saying, voice dropping low and husky, losing the carefully crafted upbeat tone he was always so careful to keep. The only other time he'd slipped in the detective's presence had been up on that rooftop, and like then, the sound of it had Shade shivering. "You should focus on turning them outward instead of inward, that's what they're actually for. Own them instead of hiding from them. Trust me, Shadow, it'll be worth it when you do."

Shade shifted in his seat when Apollo straightened and started for him, but he didn't pull away, his head slowly lifting and tipping back as he got closer so that their eyes remained locked together.

"You want to be taken care of, baby," he drawled silkily, momentarily unleashing his true nature, allowing it to shine through so that the detective no doubt caught the glimmer of mischief and hint of excitement written across his face, "want to sit back and leave all the tedious stuff to someone else."

"I'm not a child," Shade stated, but his words lacked the bite he no doubt meant for them to have. His cheeks stained that deep pink shade all over again.

"I never implied you were. There's no shame in wanting someone to take the reins, Detective."

He winced and Apollo recognized his mistake too late.

Shade shot to his feet and rounded the table, stopping at the end so there was some distance between them.

Calling him detective reminded him of his reputation, which sent him scurrying back to that cookie-cutter image Shade obviously had of what a respectable person should and shouldn't be.

Noted.

"If you run like that," Apollo changed tactics, "how do you expect me to believe you when you claim you're not repulsed by my demons? You can't even stand your own."

"That's different." He didn't like the thought of hurting Apollo, running a hand through his hair in mild irritation. "We're not the same."

"Aren't we?"

"No. You're," Shade waved a hand at him, his shoulders noticeably curling in, "perfect. Everybody likes you."

"Nobody knows what I think about my family," he pointed out, only to have Shade shake his head.

"They wouldn't think less of you if they knew the whole story."

"Do you really believe that? You can't be that naïve, you're Chitta." He knew what people felt, deep in their blackened souls, same as Apollo.

"*I* don't think less of you," Shade insisted. "And I can't be the only one who'd say that."

"Maybe not," Apollo gave him that, "but you'd be the only one who meant it. If you do in fact mean it, that is."

"Of course I do." He seemed offended by the accusation. "I like you."

Apollo quirked a brow, surprised yet again. "Even though I'm not perfect?"

"You don't have to be," Shade said. "I want to get to know you too. That means being introduced to your demons, as you call them. Show me. I won't run away. Trust me, I've been a detective for a decade now. I've seen it all."

"Have you now?" For some reason, Apollo didn't like the idea of Shadow playing with other people's monsters. He wanted all of his focus, all of his attention. He didn't want to share anymore.

Not even with Maxen.

Definitely not with his overly clingy partner Gael.

That was…dangerous. For both him and his little Shadow.

Because at the end of the day, whether he believed what he was saying or not, Shade *would* try to run the second he discovered who Apollo really was. Just like Apollo's parents had. Just like his monstrous sister, the one who'd scarred his body and tarnished his soul, had when she'd looked him dead in the eye and labeled him a psycho with all the vitriol she could muster.

After that, he'd been tempted to burn her with sulfuric acid as poetic justice, but the fire had been the smarter way to rid himself of those particular nightmares. Every day since he'd been at peace with it too. He wouldn't have done it any differently if given the option.

His father had told him everything would be fine and that they understood. That they accepted him. Then he'd caught his parents discussing shipping him off planet to some medical ship for testing.

Him.

Not his sister who'd just that morning shoved him down the stairs hard enough he'd broken his wrist catching himself during the fall. They'd known too. His mom had watched the whole thing happen.

They'd sworn they accepted him as he was. That they still loved him. They'd lied.

Shade claimed he could accept him?

Heavens help him if he was lying too, because he might not yet be aware of it, but he wasn't up against your average run-of-the-mill demon.

Apollo was the Devil.

And the Devil took no prisoners.

Chapter 14:

"I finally got you to go on another run with me," Apollo teased a couple of days later as the two of them jogged a twisty and narrow path on the outskirts of the city. There was a dense forest off to their right, and a scene of the city streets to the left, so they weren't far from the rest of civilization.

Shade had been watching him for a while, bouncing back between the police station, his hotel room, and Apollo's work and apartment. During that time, over three dozen witnesses from the gallery event had been interviewed, but they still didn't have any leads.

This was one of Apollo's favorite places to run, but they'd been so busy trying to manage both of their schedules together, this was the first time they were getting a chance to get a workout in. Since Shade didn't have a problem waking up early, they'd stuck to the reporter's typical routine, and the sun was just now starting to peak from over the tops of the trees.

It'd been a little over a week now and so far there'd been no signs of Maxen. Dario and Shade had agreed to give it another three days or so before they were going to have to call this off. He'd put a protective detail on Apollo just in case, but since it didn't appear as though anything was going to happen, it didn't make sense for him to continue to follow him around.

A part of him was disappointed with the idea. He'd adjusted to seeing the reporter on the daily and enjoyed their time together. Things had flowed easily between them, the conversation light.

But there also hadn't been anything like what had happened on the roof either.

Apollo was always touching him, sure. A hand on his arm, his waist, or their knees pressed together beneath the table. But that was all. Just small brushes of his body here and there. He didn't even initiate another kiss. He seemed like he liked being in Shade's company, was friendly and open and constantly teasing him, however the lack of advances left Shade wondering if he was the only one who still felt the sexual tension. If maybe Apollo had realized they really weren't a good fit and had friend-zoned him without saying anything.

Maybe he just hoped that Shade would get the hint and that would be that.

It made him a little sad, which made him a lot annoyed. Because hadn't he been the one who wanted to pull away? Hadn't he been the one thinking about how he shouldn't get involved with the reporter because it would only complicate the other man's life?

Careful what you wish for.

"Hey," Apollo bumped into him, grinning when that caught Shade's attention, "where'd you go?"

"What?"

"You spaced out."

"Sorry." Forcing himself to concentrate, Shade scanned their surroundings. They'd moved further down the path which had led them deeper into the wooded area, and now the buildings seemed much further away.

"Relax, Detective," Apollo said, "nothing's going to happen."

"No one thinks they're about to get murdered before it's too late and they find themselves dead," Shade told him, internally ignoring the fact that he'd only just been thinking about how Apollo had been safe thus far.

He chuckled. "I don't know. Some people see it coming, I'm sure. But you and I will be fine. I run this path all the time and nothing has happened yet."

"Famous last words." Shade had realized during their time together that Apollo was rather fearless. He didn't appear to be the least bit concerned that there may be a known serial killer targeting him. In fact, every now and again, Shade swore there was even a slight glimmer of excitement in the other man's ocean-blue eyes.

Whenever he tried to look more closely the gleam was always gone, as if he'd imagined it.

"So," Apollo changed the subject, not even slightly out of breath talking as they jogged, "I've been thinking about your problem."

"My problem?" Shade frowned at him.

"Yeah," he tapped his forehead, "this one. I think I have a few ideas on how to help you. Interested?"

"I might be, if I knew what you were talking about." As it were, Shade was completely in the dark.

"Your inability to block," Apollo explained. "That's a pretty common mental tool Chitta use. We all do it with ease. But according to you, you can only dim the emotions you feel, and from the sounds of it, you're a lot more powerful than typical Chitta. Take now, for instance. We're the only ones here for miles. Feel anything?"

"Of course I do—" Shade stumbled, the rest of that sentence getting caught in his throat. He came to a complete stop, eyes searching through the trees.

"Detective?" Apollo slowed and came over to him, brow furrowed.

"Someone's here," he said, still looking for any signs they weren't alone.

"I don't see anyone." Apollo followed suit, turning slowly so he could check all sides.

They couldn't see them, but Shade could feel them. Whoever it was, they were upset, a mixture of nerves and anxiety. And a dash of anticipation.

"Can you tell how close they are?" Apollo asked.

"No." He absorbed emotion like a sponge, so instead of the steady stream most Chitta felt that could help them determine how near or far away the person feeling was, Shade only had the emotions to go off of and nothing else. Nothing useful. "They could be over thirty feet away or three."

"We can count out three," Apollo reminded. "If they were that close we'd see them."

"What's your range?" Shade couldn't believe he'd never asked that before, but when they spoke of their abilities, the conversation was typically on Shade.

"I don't have any, remember?" Apollo replied. "I have to make eye contact."

"Oh, that's right."

"Careful, Detective," he smirked, "your envy is showing."

He rolled his eyes but retreated in the direction they'd come. "We should go back."

"No way." Apollo shook his head stubbornly. "I'm not letting some random person scare me off."

"What if it's Maxen?" It could be. The emotions would be fitting given the situation.

"What if it isn't?" Apollo started walking backward, heading down the path as originally planned, grinning when Shade glared.

"Stop," Shade said, "we need to go back."

He clicked his tongue and shook his head. "You're not the only one who doesn't like taking orders, Detective. Although, something important I should note you'll need to keep in mind for future reference," Apollo stopped a few feet away, expression morphing into one of intensity, "I enjoy giving them. And I expect them to be followed."

Shade paused. Why was that hot?

What was wrong with him—

Movement just over the reporter's shoulder cut off any response Shade may have had to that. A shadowy figure was standing tucked between two large soot-colored tree trunks. He was wearing a baseball cap, and the second he realized that Shade had taken notice, he bolted.

"Shit!" Shade took off after him without thinking, sliding to a stop just as he was about to leave the path and enter the forest. "Go back to the car!" he called to Apollo before giving chase again.

Though the man he ran after was a decent distance away, Shade could make out the familiar stature of Maxen. The movement also matched what he recalled from that time in the gallery. He hoped there were no early morning yoga groups or anything like that out here that Maxen was planning to lead him to. Only because a bunch of scared and scrambling people would make it a lot harder for him to make an arrest. There was no fear of him entering Repletion now, not that Maxen could know that.

They didn't come across anyone though as they raced through the trees. Shade batted branches out of the way haphazardly, struggling to keep the fleeing man in his line of sight at all times. If he lost him now, he'd really feel like a failure. Letting the suspect escape not once, but twice? That would look so bad in his report, and no doubt the I.P.F would call him on it.

Shade's thighs began to burn, and at some point he slipped on some debris and twisted his ankle slightly. The pain was minimal, definitely manageable, and he ignored it as he pushed himself further.

Seeing that he wasn't going to catch him any time soon, Shade clicked a button on the side of his multi-slate that would automatically send his exact location to Gael, alerting his partner that something was up. As soon as he'd done that, he popped the earpiece attachment out and pressed it into his left ear, calling for good measure.

"Got it," Gael's harried voice boomed into his ear first, the sound of pounding footsteps coming through even as Shade continued to slap his way through the brush. "ETA twenty minutes!"

Shade let out a low growl and ended the call, not wanting the distraction of his partner in his ear when he needed to be concentrating on the figure sprinting ahead of him. It was a good thing too because one second they were surrounded by thick forest and the next he found himself bursting out onto a road, the change in terrain almost causing him to trip.

A wide tunnel was to the left, the windy road traveling straight through it. The sun was high in the sky now, but within the tunnel darkness still crept at the sides. He could see straight through and twisted on his heels as he pulled out his blaster when his eyes landed on Maxen.

The man wasn't even trying to hide. He was standing in the center of the tunnel facing away from Shade, his head tipped down slightly. From the rise and fall of his shoulders, it was clear he was out of breath from the chase.

"Put your hands in the air and turn around," Shade ordered as he slowly eased his way beneath the lip of the tunnel, keeping his weapon trained ahead. If he had to, he'd shoot the guy in the leg. They still had too many unanswered questions for a kill shot so he'd have to be satisfied with crippling him instead. "Do it, now!"

Maxen remained where he was.

Shade continued his careful approach. His handcuffs were at his left hip, beneath the hem of his sports shirt. He needed to subdue Maxen before Gael and the others arrived so they could take him in. And this time, he'd be riding in the back with him. No way in hell was he giving him the chance to hurt anyone else.

Thinking about Axel who was still in the hospital had a burst of anger blooming in his chest and his hand tightened on the blaster gun. On second thought, maybe a shot to the back of his skull wouldn't be—

Someone stumbled down the incline leading into the forest and entered the tunnel at Shade's back, loudly.

He spun, weapon still lifted, cursing when his eyes landed on Apollo.

The reporter must have followed him.

"What the hell—" he began, already in the process of turning back toward, Maxen, but was swiftly cut off by Apollo's warning.

"Look out!" He pointed over his shoulder, but Shade already knew it was too late.

Maxen dove at him, taking him down in one solid move that had Shade's head whacking against the cold concrete road. Stars exploded behind his eyes and the blaster skittered across the way, out of reach. He didn't have time to worry about that, though, not with the heavy guy on top of him, currently struggling to keep Shade pinned.

Knuckles dug into the side of his jaw as Maxen landed a punch, and while it hurt, it only served to piss Shade off more than he already was.

He fought back, slamming both palms against the side of the other man's head, right against his ears. When that had Maxen rearing back in pain, he shifted his hips enough to get out from under him, delivering a punch of his own.

Maxen's chin hit the ground, drops of blood left there when his head rebounded from the force.

Shade undid the cuffs, quickly leaping over to shove a knee against his lower back. He almost had him but the other guy was fast, rolling with enough strength to dislodge him. They both got to their feet, Maxen going on the offensive.

Waves of giddy pride swarmed off of the other guy, seeping into Shade's bloodstream. It confused him, made him wonder why the hell that was what he was feeling, but it wasn't distracting. One other set of emotions was nothing when he had to deal with dozens all at once on the daily.

"What are you so excited about?" he found himself asking as he evaded a swing of the man's arm. Somewhere down the line, Maxen had clearly done some boxing. His stance and attacks were very in line with that style of fighting, but he wasn't necessarily good at it.

Shade caught his arm on another swing, using his momentum against him to pull him in and knee him in the stomach. He shoved him back after, watching him crumple to the ground and popped open the cuffs.

As soon as he saw them, Maxen's eyes widened and he turned his head, catching sight of Apollo who was still standing on the outskirts of the tunnel. He sprung up and ran for him, causing Shade to swear again and rush to stop him.

Grabbing onto the back of his shirt, Shade yanked Maxen back, putting himself between him and the reporter. In the process, Maxen knocked the cuffs out of his hands, and they went flying. He managed to land another punch, this time to Shade's solar plexus, and then whacked him across the other jaw.

The hit was hard, dazing Shade long enough for the other man to get the upper hand. He was slammed to the wall of the tunnel, and then both of Maxen's hands were around his throat, squeezing like he was trying to pop Shade's head clean off his body.

He tried everything he could think of to dislodge Maxen's hold but nothing worked, and the lack of air started getting to him rather quickly. Black dots winked in and out of his vision, and he dug his nails into the other man's wrists, drawing blood.

Maxen hissed from the pain but didn't loosen. No matter where Shade hit him, a knee to the side, a stomp to his toes, he didn't let go, almost as if his own life was on the line and if he stopped now he'd die.

Realizing that he wasn't going to be able to break free, Shade shifted his gaze over to Apollo, planning on silently ordering the reporter to make a run for it while he had the chance.

But as soon as he did, Shade felt himself go cold.

A normal person would have either frozen in fear, run for their own life, or tried to help—either on their own or by calling the police. There'd been a few odd comments here or there, but for the most part, if asked, Shade would have said Apollo was as normal as they came. He worked a steady job, was well-liked by the entire community, was charming, rich...

The look on his face now was anything but normal, however.

Apollo's eyes were locked onto the hands squeezing Shade's throat, riveted. There was a sparkle in them that Shade had never seen on anyone but criminals before, the type that liked inflicting pain on others and watching them squirm and cry out. His lips, the same ones that had been on Shade's only a week ago, were curved up at the corners in an almost gleeful partial smirk that had Shade's instincts recoiling.

And when those eyes slowly traveled up to meet his? If Shade hadn't already been gasping for air, he would have certainly done so then.

There was a cold calculation written on Apollo's face, a twisted satisfaction that Shade didn't immediately understand.

"That's enough," Apollo's voice was steady, strong, and commanding. His gaze never wavered from Shade's but it was obvious he wasn't speaking to him.

The hands around his neck loosened slightly, but not enough for Shade to get a proper breath in. Honestly, it was a small miracle he hadn't already passed out.

"I said," Apollo repeated, a thread of darkness ringing that even Shade felt a spike of fear at it, "*enough.*"

"I can do it," Maxen told him a bit frantically. "Kill him now, and then he won't be a bother anymore—"

Shade's eyes fluttered, and as he struggled to remain conscious he missed whatever else the guy choking him was saying. It was important too, everything about this exchange was telling, and he needed to keep it together long enough to note it all, but…

His fingers, the ones that had so desperately dug into Maxen's wrists, lost their grip and dropped to his sides.

Then suddenly he was falling as Maxen was ripped away from him, too far gone to do anything to brace against the drop. He fell onto his side, left shoulder taking most of the impact so that he winced and moaned, but the sound was cracked and weak, his throat burning. He'd landed with his back to the wall, and couldn't get his body to move. As he came in and out of it, he struggled to process what he was seeing.

Apollo was beating Maxen. At first, it didn't even appear as though the other guy was going to fight back, he must have started though because Shade blinked—most likely passed out for a moment—and came to in time to see Maxen finally swing.

With an easy grace Apollo sidestepped, catching his upper arm and twisting hard enough there was a cracking sound loud enough even Shade heard it past the ringing in his ears.

Maxen screamed, cradling his injured arm and tried to stumble backward. He was speaking again, but the words were jumbled and sounded like they came from a million miles away.

Shade was going to pass out, but for real this time, he could feel it. He was going to pass out and most likely wouldn't wake up because he was alone in a secluded area with a serial killer and—

Apollo grabbed Maxen by the scruff of his shirt and hauled him forward. Something shiny flickered, silver catching the light to wink at Shade a split second before whatever it was vanished into Maxen's front.

A knife, Shade realized with a start.

Apollo had just stabbed Maxen with a knife.

Where the hell had he even gotten a weapon from?

Maxen dropped to his knees, Apollo staring down at him coldly.

He yanked the blade free and twisted it, eyeing the blood, ignoring the sobs Maxen was making as he settled a hand on his shoulder. He patted him but said nothing, and then he drove the knife in again.

Maxen's screams rang in Shade's ears as his eyes closed.

When he managed to peel them open again he caught sight of Apollo's running sneakers approaching. There was a splatter of blood on the right one, staining the white.

He had just enough time to think about how he was about to die before all the strength left him and the darkness took control.

Shade had wanted to get close to someone.

Careful what you wish for.

Chapter 15:

The detective was lighter than he looked.

Apollo had expected him to be heavy, what with all the corded muscle he kept hidden beneath his clothing. The sportswear he was in at the moment did a worse job of that in some areas, clinging more tightly to the curve of Shade's ass and the breadth of his shoulders, but the tank top didn't do his abs any justice, didn't cling to the dips and divots of his six-pack or his pecs the way Apollo would have liked.

Oh well. He'd rid the man of the pesky clothing soon enough anyway.

He hadn't gotten the chance to see him during their encounter on the roof, had only gotten a look at Shade's ass and the small of his back. The dimples just above those hefty globes…He almost groaned out loud thinking about it, barely containing his excitement as arousal, thick and heady, swept through him.

He hadn't seen it on the roof, but he'd caught glimpses of it behind frosted glass, had watched as Shade washed in the shower at his hotel, completely oblivious to the fact he wasn't alone.

They were going to have to work on that. With the constant stream of never-ending emotions Shade felt from everyone else around him, Apollo had already decided he was going to fix that problem. Not for Shade's sake, but for his own.

He didn't like the idea of not having Shade's full, undivided attention. Sharing? Wasn't in his vocabulary.

Apollo carried Shade through the woods, traveling on a path he knew by heart. He'd mapped it out earlier, walking it over and over again this past month to ensure he got it right when the time came. He hadn't wanted to allow for any errors.

The unconscious detective was tossed over his left shoulder, one leg at Apollo's front. He'd taken his arm and draped it over his other shoulder, and had his hand wrapped beneath Shade's knee so he could hold onto his wrist and a leg in a solid grip as he trekked through the wilderness, moving them further and further away from the city.

He'd seen Shade call for backup during the chase, hadn't been pleased about it, but had anticipated it already. He did things by the book, his little Shadow, and calling his partner was rule number one.

Apollo made it to the unregistered hovercar he'd parked there last week and yanked the door to the passenger side open, carefully depositing Shade into it. He buckled him in and paused, unable to help himself from staring.

Shade's features were relaxed despite the violent way he'd been knocked out. Bruises were already forming around his long neck, purple and blue blotches in the shape of Maxen's fingers.

Another man's fingers.

Apollo squeezed the top of the door hard enough the metal protested. To calm himself, he reached out and brushed a strand of Shade's mahogany brown hair off his forehead. The color was rich and pleasing, and in direct sunlight, like it was right now, the reddish undertone practically glistened.

In all his life, Apollo had never seen anyone so beautiful. He'd noticed it the very second Shade had stepped from the taxi that had driven him to the crime scene, the camera in his hands all but forgotten as he'd watched the tall man make his way to the building.

He'd been enraptured, unable to look away, taking in every movement, every reaction Shade had to the scene Apollo had left there only hours before. He'd even found himself wishing he'd taken more time with this one, done it up nice and pretty for the detective. Sort of a welcome to the neighborhood gift as a prequel to the much bigger present Apollo had in mind.

His obsessive personality was no great shock, Apollo was nothing if not self-aware, but he'd never found it aimed at an individual before, at least not one he intended to keep for long periods. He liked invading the minds of his victims, liked to claw his way in deep and hook into them before the final blow. Liked to force them to acknowledge their deepest, darkest truths.

But from that very first glance, he'd known things with Shade were going to be different. He'd taken it slow, watching from afar, keeping his distance that first day even as he followed him back to the station, and then his hotel. Things had escalated rather quickly from there, however.

He'd gone from wanting to make sure the I.P.F weren't on the right path to wanting to get rid of Shadow for being such a distraction.

Even that hadn't kept.

Apollo no longer cared about the progress of the case, and he didn't intend to kill the detective.

He was going to make the other man purr for him.

They were running out of time. As soon as Gael and the other officers arrived, they'd come searching. It wouldn't take them long to find the tunnel and Maxen's dead body in it.

Apollo scowled, frustrated at how poorly this had gone down all thanks to that idiot. He slammed the door and rounded the car, slipping into the driver's side and leaning over to snap the handcuffs he'd snatched from the ground around both of Shade's wrists. Once he was attached to the door and Apollo knew there was nothing to worry about even if he woke during the drive, he started the vehicle.

There were no roads or paths this deep into the forest, so he had to pay attention to where he maneuvered, doing a couple of long loops to throw the police off his trail and buy some more time once they found the tire tracks. After he was satisfied, he finally went in the direction that would lead him to an off-road, one that connected to several busier ones leading in and out of the city.

They'd never be able to find him. His windows were tinted and his car was a basic model, one owned by half the middle-class population of Uk. As a backup, he'd change the color as soon as he got them to their destination.

A full two weeks sooner than planned.

"Damn that fucking moron." If Maxen wasn't already dead, Apollo would kill him. Again.

Things weren't ready yet, the plan to kidnap the detective having only breathed to life after their time on the roof. Apollo had assumed he'd fuck the man to get him out of his system and then end things. He'd been prepared to shove him from the rooftop afterward—that had been the whole reason he'd brought him all the way up there in the first place.

In the state Shade had been in, no one would question it when Apollo told them he'd stumbled too close to the edge and had toppled off before he could stop him. Gael might have, he mussed, but he was confident enough in his acting abilities he was sure he could convince the Inspector to believe him after one or two conversations.

Apollo hadn't liked how all-consuming Shade was. Hadn't liked that he could barely think without thoughts of the other man plaguing him. Distractions were a risk, and the best thing to do about risks was to get rid of them.

But he hadn't been able to. Instead of killing him, he'd fucked Shade to completion. At least he'd had the foresight to keep the man's back turned toward him so that the detective couldn't see his face and catch on that he wasn't the average guy he was parading around as. And he definitely would have too, because that familiar darkness Apollo carried with him had sprung its demonic head and roared in pleasure the second Shade had come undone in his hold.

That darkness, which usually urged Apollo to kill and maim, had whispered other things into his ears. Still horrible things, of course, but the urges were different, nothing like what they were when he typically chose a victim.

Instead of pinning the detective down and slicing him open, he wanted to tie him up in his bedroom and keep him there. Wanted to have him in any way and every way he could imagine. He was a devil, but he'd never been the type who got off sexually when he tortured someone. It wasn't about that for him. It was about forcing his victims to be what they truly were.

Monsters, just like him.

But with Shadow…He didn't like thinking about how much the detective despised himself and his true nature. He should be embracing who was, not hiding from it, cowering under the mask of an I.P.F agent. There was no hypocrisy in his hatred either, Apollo wore his mask to keep himself safe, whereas Shade was slowly killing himself with his.

Suffocating himself.

Although, he admittedly looked rather dashing when his face was turning that off shade of purple and his eyes widened like glassy marbles.

He wondered what Shade might look like choking on his cock.

Apollo had realized at a very young age there was something wrong with him. His parents had realized too, after they'd come home to find the family pet deconstructed and arranged on the dinner table. He hadn't killed it—weirdly, he'd always had an affinity for animals. One of his victims had even become a target due to animal cruelty. The creature had been sick for a while and they'd been told it didn't have much longer to live. Apollo had been the only one home at the time when it'd taken its final, rattling breath.

After that...

He'd been trying to figure out how all of the pieces fit, had excitedly turned to his father to show how far he'd gotten. It'd been the horror coming off of the man in droves that had given him pause. He'd felt his disgust and his fear, potent and rich. Like warmed melted chocolate.

And he'd wanted to dip his fingers in it and lick it off.

Still, he hadn't been interested in the fear or the disgust. Outside observers hadn't meant very much to him at all. But the way his father had shivered when confronted with the truth of what his son was had never left Apollo's mind. Especially since he'd never given that reaction to Apollo's sister, not even when he witnessed her abusing his son firsthand.

No, he'd turned the other cheek and pretended not to see or hear.

He'd stupidly believed that meant he could be as true to his own nature as he wanted, that no matter what he did his parents would stand by him. He'd smartly kept that darkness on a tight leash outside of the home, of course, but in front of those who'd birthed and raised him and claimed to love him unconditionally, he'd decided to be his true self in the same way his sister was allowed to be.

His parents had been liars. They could blind themselves where his sister was concerned, but when it came to him, he was the demonic spawn they'd never wanted.

A bad taste entered his mouth and he clenched his fingers tight around the steering wheel as he brought them off the crowded road they'd been on the past ten minutes and onto a more secluded one.

Shade would have been no different. He stared at him with attraction in his eyes, but the moment he'd noticed Apollo standing here watching him getting choked by Maxen there'd been horror. Maybe that idiot fuck had done him a favor after all. If they'd kept up the rouse as long as Apollo had initially planned, he would have had Shade eating out of the palm of his hand by the time he tricked him into coming here with him. He would have had him willingly walking into the snare and springing the trap before even realizing there was one.

Apollo had thought that's what he'd wanted. That seeing the comprehension sweep over Shade's face, watching as that attraction turned into abhorrence, would finally trigger his inner darkness and set things right again.

Because surely seeing that, witnessing Shade turn on him after declarations of adoration and caring would have reminded Apollo of his parents. Would have infuriated him to the point he'd do what he'd meant to do that night on the roof.

Alas, those plans had gone to shit now. They hadn't spent nearly enough time together for a strong connection even closely similar to love to have formed for the detective.

Which meant Apollo was either stuck with this distracting and risky obsession, or he moved on to Plan B.

Since he was more important than anyone, including the unconscious man at his side—no matter how delectable he'd tasted—Plan B it was.

He was going to fulfill all of his dark desires. He'd have Shadow on his knees begging for him, begging to be hurt and loved and cared for and destroyed. He was going to twist the detective so tightly around his fingers, thoughts of anyone else wouldn't so much as enter Shadow's mind.

Apollo was going to become his everything.

He'd fix Shadow Yor, take him apart, figure out how the pieces went back together properly, and make him whole again.

And then he'd slice that beautiful neck and watch as the life drained from those pretty hazel-colored eyes and get back to his regularly scheduled program.

* * *

The warehouse was Apollo's sanctuary, where he could shuck the guise of being normal and just be himself unencumbered. He didn't perform all of his kills here, because doing so in the exact same spot over a dozen times was a recipe for disaster and just asking to get caught, but many of his recent victims had found themselves here.

The surrounding land was all privately owned under a dummy name that had no connection to him, and the area he'd selected was deep enough in the forest and far enough from the city that there was little to no fear of wandering hikers or campers accidentally stumbling on him either. Even with that, he'd put a lot of time and money into setting up an Invisi-Dome, an invisible force field that encased the entire two-story wooden monstrosity. It acted as a soundproof barrier as well as camouflage. At the touch of a button, it reflected the nearby trees making the warehouse disappear entirely.

Apollo turned that dome off as he drove up to it, parking the hovercar beneath a large oak tree where he typically left it. The detective was still unconscious in the seat next to him, which was for the best really. Made his job easier, in any case.

He rounded the vehicle and pulled Shade out, lifting him over his shoulders the same way he had before. There was no front door to the warehouse, just a giant square opening large enough to fit a two-wheeler through. While it could get rather chilly up here some nights, he had enough space heaters to keep himself comfortable.

His victims got to freeze. He liked the sound their teeth made when they chattered and how complacent they got. Half the time he didn't even need to resort to actual violence. One night half frozen and they'd give up their own mothers for a scrap of cloth.

Pathetic.

Shade had mentioned he hated the cold. At the time, Apollo had feared he'd given himself away with his reaction. He'd been far too excited by the thought of all the ways he could use that information against the detective. All the things he could do to him to get him to scream and eventually purr.

Because he'd been rather fond of those sounds Shade had made when Apollo's fingers had been stretching his hole. And the more frantic moans when he'd driven his cock deep and fucked him hard against the wall…He'd dreamed of those sounds, fantasized about them as he'd stroked himself in the shower, imaging Shade bent over for him, his round little ass up the air, begging to be stuffed.

With a curse he shook his head, glaring down at his dick straining in his pants. Now wasn't the time, there was too much to do and all of it needed to be done before the detective woke.

Inside was huge, with most of the space left empty. A couple of used mattresses had been dragged to the far corners and left there, forgotten, but the entire right side was set up and waiting. He'd begun putting this space together as soon as he'd realized this was where things were heading between the two of them.

The second he'd snuck into Shade's hotel room and caught the guy in the shower his mind had been made.

He was going to take him and break him and make him his. But it wasn't all selfish. He'd be sure to fix him in the process.

Shade was damaged. Apollo had hacked into the I.P.F Percy Branch main database to read his file, which was sealed to the public and anyone not a Class 9 or higher. It didn't hold as much information as he would have liked, but there'd been confirmation about his parents having abandoned him as a kid. Confirmation that he'd joined the Academy at the impressive age of sixteen and had risen to the top of the class within a couple of weeks.

He'd graduated within three years and would have been head of the class except he'd opted out of giving a public speech, no doubt to avoid having to stand up on a stage and look out at everyone. Gael had been his partner since the beginning, and the two of them were considered one of the Percy Branch's top teams.

On paper, his stats made him sound like the golden child.

Notes from his teachers and superior officers painted a different picture.

Shade was unfriendly. Cut off. Too much of a loner. He snapped at other students who got too close.

Argued against authority. The list went on and on. The teenage and young adult Shadow Yor had been filled with anger and bitterness and he hadn't yet learned to hide those things from the world.

But, despite those negative feelings, he'd solved every assignment handed to him with flying colors. Reports about him as an adult were sparkling, his professionalism praised by other officers on other planets, and even a couple of reports directly from Royals or Imperials, all stated he was intelligent and quick to solve their problems. Friendly and attentive had even been words thrown in there.

If he put his mind to something, his little Shadow seemed to be capable of anything, even getting people to forget that he was a Chitta and how uncomfortable having someone like that around made them.

When it came to convincing other people he was worth it, he could, but when he didn't seem capable of making himself believe that same nation.

Shadow didn't think he was good enough for anyone to want.

Apollo was going to prove differently.

He brought Shade over to the clean mattress he'd purchased specifically for him, set on the floor against a wooden panel he'd bolted to the wall. The wood was sanded and smoothed, ensuring it wouldn't rub uncomfortable against the detective's skin if he leaned against it. The others who'd been brought here hadn't gotten the same treatment by far.

The mattress was wrapped in a waterproof encasement because things were most definitely going to get dirty and he didn't feel like wasting time doing major cleanups. There were no blankets, sheets, or pillows, just the mattress on the floor and nothing else within a ten-foot radius.

Apollo eased Shade down onto the center, pulling him back until his shoulders rested against the paneled wall. Then he lifted one arm above his head and secured his wrist in one of the metal cuffs before following the motion with the other.

When he stepped back and stood to eye his handy work, he hummed in approval. He'd been a bit worried he'd gotten the height of it wrong, but nope. Where he'd placed the cuffs, they kept Shade's wrists only an inch higher than his head at either side. There was one thing about the picture that wasn't sitting right with him however…

Turning toward the long workbench table he had set twenty feet away from the area he'd designated as Shade's Space—he snorted just thinking about it—he grabbed up a pair of scissors and returned.

Cutting through the middle of Shade's navy sports tank top was easy, the material sheering away like butter. The tattoo on his right side coming into view.

The ink stretched across his ribs, a solid black rose, stem and all. The top of the bloom rested just beneath the side of his pec, the stem curving inward slightly and about five inches long. Three thorns and a single leaf were also included, colored in as well.

Apollo wondered if there was a personal meaning behind it or if Shade had simply wanted to test out his pain tolerance. If he'd been trying to get off on it, he must have been disappointed by the end of the session.

He balled the scraps of Shade's shirt and set them to the side before resting his gaze on the space between Shade's thighs. It'd been damn near torture keeping his hands to himself this past week, but he'd had to set the right tone, lure Shade into a sense of safety.

Or, at least, that'd been his intention before Maxen had fucked it up.

Angry all over again at the reminder, Apollo yanked Shade's shorts off of him roughly, the movement causing the detective to let out a small sound that had him stilling. He stared at his face, waiting to see if he was rousing, but after a minute where nothing happened, exhaled and lifted off the mattress.

He carried the clothing over to the side of his workbench and tossed them straight into the trash, dropping down into the swivel chair he had. He angled it so that he could rest his feet up on the bottom rung of the table, and tilted his head in Shade's direction, almost as if drawn to him.

A satisfied sigh passed his lips. The picture was perfect now, enough to have his hands itching to grab the camera that was set at the corner of the table. But he refrained. He hadn't made it this far by leaving traces of physical evidence that could be linked back to Reporter Apollo.

Snapping himself out of it, he got back to his feet. There was still so much to do before Shade woke. Things needed to be ready for when he did. Perfect.

Maxen may have put a wrench in Plan A, but there was always Plan B, and now that it'd come to it, Apollo was already starting to feel that familiar itch starting up just beneath his skin.

Who knew. Maybe he'd be thanking Maxen by nightfall after all.

Chapter 16:

Shade came to slowly, as if from a long-lasting deep sleep. Blinking, he groaned and shifted, wincing at the sharp bursts of pain at his shoulders. All that did was make him aware of his split bottom lip, a gift from Maxen, along with the bruise he could literally feel forming on his right side.

The light was brighter than expected, a golden hue that cast down upon him from somewhere extremely high up. He tipped his head back and stared at it, waiting for the light fixture to come into focus. A line of floating bulbs had been programmed to hover a good twenty feet in the air, bathing the section of space he was in so he could make out every detail.

Which, admittedly, he sort of wished wasn't the case.

Shade went cold the second he dropped his chin and realized where he was. The space was massive, darkness creeping in the far corners so that he couldn't make out how far it was until the room came to an end. The area he was placed in had been sectioned off with a long workbench that had a single chair set in front of it.

The workbench had an assortment of items carefully spaced out across the surface, but he couldn't get a good view of any of them and couldn't identify anything. To the left of the bench, turned so that together they created an L shape, was a desk made out of the same dark wood. A holo-screen computer monitor was on, the rectangular screen projected up over the center. Security feeds showed pictures of what Shade assumed were angles outside the building.

Tall rafters above and the concrete floor below. Tan wood walls, except for the piece directly behind him that seemed to be a new fixture made of golden wood instead. He could just barely make out the bottom of a staircase over at the far right of the wide open space of the first level, so there were at least two stories to the building.

Warehouse maybe?

A breeze blew in through the opening to his left, cold skating across his bare skin causing him to shiver.

And realize he'd been stripped down to nothing but his dark gray boxer briefs.

Shade swore and pulled at his wrists, cursing again when it hit him he was also bound to the wall. He turned and glared at the thick metal encasing him, tugging more furiously to see if there was any give at all.

There wasn't.

"Awake already, Detective?" that honey-toned voice, the same one that had been haunting Shade's dreams for weeks—in a *good* way—came from somewhere off to the left. A second later, Apollo stepped from the darkness holding a silver can. He popped the tab and took a deep swallow, eyes on Shade the entire time.

"You're working with Maxen." Shade remembered what had happened at the tunnel, even though he was fighting against it if only so he wouldn't feel so foolish. But no matter how his brain tried to spin it, the truth was clear.

He'd been played.

And he'd enjoyed every second of it. Like an idiot.

Apollo's expression darkened as he approached. "Don't insult me. That complete and total waste of blood and bone couldn't even pick his nose successfully, let alone another person's mind."

Shade frowned. All of the victims had been tortured and then killed, but they were only able to find out about the physical injuries. Was he admitting that other things had been done to them before their deaths?

"I can see the gears cranking around in there," Apollo circled a finger at the side of his head and then crouched down across from him. "Should I help you out?"

Shade knew without even trying his leg wouldn't reach if he tried to kick him, so he refrained, conserving his energy for the right moment. "By all means," he ground out. "Start with these damn cuffs." He jerked at them, but aside from a slight rattling sound, nothing came of it.

Apollo clicked his tongue and shook his head as if chiding a small child. "I like you right where you are, Detective. Autonomy can be earned, of course, but we're getting ahead of ourselves. We were discussing what took place in the tunnel."

"I thought Maxen was after you," Shade accused, "but that was a lie, wasn't it? You were never in any danger."

"No," he confirmed shamelessly, twirling the contents of the can absently as he rested his wrist on his knee. "Even if I had been his target, Maxen is no match for me. Neither are you, Shadow Yor."

"You played me." He hated saying it out loud, but it needed to be said, a burst of indignation blooming in his chest.

"Don't feel so bad," Apollo stood. "I played *with* you. It's not the same, and you didn't stand a chance. There's no reason to beat yourself up about it. I'll do enough of that for you in the days to come, so you may as well get over that petty self-contempt issue you've been hauling around with you. If you need someone to aim all that hate toward, I'm more than happy to fill the role for you, baby."

"Don't call me that." Shade clenched his fists tightly until his knuckles threatened to pop.

"You're wondering how much of it was a lie," Apollo guessed, casting his gaze down his body. The lust that sparked in his eyes had Shade stilling like a deer caught in headlights. "Not all of it."

"The roof?" He couldn't stand that he was asking, but he had to know. Was that why nothing else had happened since? Even when he'd been sleeping on Apollo's couch?

Those first couple of nights he'd foolishly hoped the reporter would sneak into the living room once the lights were off and climb on top of him. When it hadn't happened, he'd almost given in and snuck into the man's room to do it instead.

He'd held himself back.

Like always.

Despite what Apollo might think, Shade wasn't exactly a fan of the way he treated himself either. If it were that easy, to shut off all the self-loathing comments and feelings, he would have done so ages ago.

Apollo met his gaze once more. "I took you up there to kill you."

Shade sucked in a breath, hating the disappointment that hit him before anything else, but he wasn't finished.

"Clearly the plan changed." He took another sip from the can.

"Why?"

"Truthfully?" Apollo smiled, but it wasn't anything like the smiles he'd given before—the ones Shade was now realizing had been faked. It was dark and a little twisted, the promise of something wicked behind it. He'd seen it once when Apollo had been talking about his family. "It appears that I'm a little bit obsessed with you, Detective."

He was so fucked up because those words actually had a rush of relief coursing through him. Relief. Here he was, chained to a damn wall with a criminal before him, and he was *relieved*? Because at least that meant he'd really been wanted. Even if it'd been brief and by a monster. Which it was becoming clear was what Apollo was. He'd had them all fooled, every single one of them.

But he'd had Shade dreaming about being spanked and—

What the actual fuck was wrong with him?

"And if I tell you I hate your guts and want to stab you in the eye?" Shade goaded, only to grimace when Apollo's reaction was to laugh.

He bit his bottom lip, working it between his teeth as if taking a moment to calm himself down before finally replying in a smoky voice, "Gods, that's so hot, baby. Say something else."

Shade made a face. "You're sick."

"I'm a serial killer," he stated plainly. "Takes a certain kind of someone to enjoy doing the things I do to people. You've seen my work. You should understand that better than anyone."

His stomach turned and for a second he was actually afraid he was going to throw up. "It was you? All of it?"

He'd gathered that Maxen hadn't been a threat to Apollo, sure, but a part of him had been in denial about the other possible implications there. Things would be so much easier if Maxen was still the guy he'd been after.

He *had* seen Apollo's work. Some of the bodies had burn marks, others were slashed up close to being unrecognizable. One had every single bone in his body smashed so the crime scene photos of him were just a pile of—He gagged, only just managing to keep it down.

Apollo closed his eyes and let out a soft sound that came really close to satisfaction. "I could do without the disgust from you," he said, "but the fear…Keep that coming. I like it."

"I don't want to do anything you like," Shade snapped.

"That's too bad," slowly, he rose to his feet, "From here on out, I'm the master of your fate. Keeping me satiated is in your best interests. However," he took a single step onto the mattress, the material dipping beneath his weight, "in the spirit of staying truthful, I hope you fight, tooth and nail. I hope you try to dig those claws of yours into me, Shadow mine, if only so that making you purr will be all that more gratifying. Keep me interested and we could do this for a while. Don't and…Well. It's obvious what will happen to you, isn't it?"

Yeah. He'd kill him. Or he'd do worse and then he'd kill him. Either way, the outcome wouldn't be good.

He was ashamed to admit that he'd been so focused on the man's words Shade hadn't even considered trying to kick him now that he was in range. By the time the thought came to him it was too late, and Apollo was settling down over him, straddling his thighs.

"It's coffee," he said as he brought the edge of the can up to Shade's lips. "You hadn't had anything when we went for our run and that was hours ago. Your body needs it."

"Why?" Shade stubbornly asked, refusing to sip even with the metal pressed against his bottom lip. "To deal with whatever you have planned?"

Apollo tilted his head, expression settling into an unreadable mask.

Only, Shade got the impression it wasn't a mask at all but that he was seeing the real man for the first time.

"You really shouldn't push me," Apollo told him, "I'll like it too much."

Before Shade could say anything else, Apollo's hand shot out, wrapping around his throat. With his thumb, he forced his chin up and squeezed until Shade gasped. Without skipping a beat he poured half the contents of the can into his mouth, holding his head in that position as he gargled and choked on it until most of the liquid had made its way down.

The second he was freed, Shade coughed, loud hacking sounds that brought tears to the corner of his eyes. There was no doubt some coffee was swirling around in his lungs now. He glared angrily up at the other man.

"Don't cry yet, baby," Apollo cajoled. "We haven't even started. Besides," he shook the now empty can, "I made sure to buy the kind you like. Not too bitter," a wolfish grin morphed his features, "not too sweet. Tell me, Detective, is that your preference for all things, or just your coffee?"

"Get fucked, asshole!"

Apollo snorted and leaned in slightly as if to divulge some big secret. "Oh no, that's going to be you. You liked it, on the roof. Remember those sounds you made? I wonder if anyone ever noticed your come on the wall later. Do you think someone went up there and saw it? Do you think someone knows what a dirty little—"

"Stop." Shade's tone lacked all bite, but surprisingly, Apollo instantly shut his mouth.

"Sorry about that," he said a moment later, and it made Shade sick to his stomach at how sincere he sounded. "I forgot."

He tried to resist asking but the urge was too great and he ended up blurting, "Forgot what?"

"About your low self-esteem and how that translates," he lifted a hand and ran his fingers through Shade's hair almost tenderly, "I don't have a preference myself, so we'll avoid the degradation kink and focus on praise, sound good?"

"No," Shade said. "None of this sounds good. I don't want to be here, and I don't want to be anywhere near you."

"That would probably hold more weight if I wasn't aware of how much you hate yourself," Apollo drawled. "Am I supposed to be insulted that a man who can't stand being in his own company claims not to want to be around me either? Unlike some people, I know my own worth. It'll take more than that to hurt me, baby, but by all means, keep trying."

"I'm not your fucking baby."

"Keep saying that word too." Apollo licked his lips. "It turns me on."

Shade head-butted him. The impact had him hissing in pain right alongside Apollo, but it was worth it.

At least, he thought it was at first. Until the spots stopped swimming in his vision and he was able to get a good look at the man still straddling him.

He'd gotten him good, tearing a bit of skin over his right eyebrow so that a single drop of blood now rolled down between his eye and the bridge of his nose. Holding Shade's gaze trapped with his own, Apollo stuck out his tongue and caught the drop, sweeping it into his mouth. "That's one, Detective."

"You befriended me to eavesdrop on the case." It felt like he was being hit by too much all at once. Nothing that he'd believed to be true actually was and, the worst part?

He was more disappointed that Apollo had used him than he was by the fact he was a serial killer.

What the hell did that say about Shade? He caught criminals for a living and yet when face to face with one like this, all his mind could think about was how low he felt knowing none of that attraction was real.

Apollo had never actually liked him.

Of course not.

"Enough of that," Apollo snapped then, jerking Shade out of his spiraling thoughts.

The pathetic, needy ones that he was ashamed of.

"You being the one assigned to my case has nothing to do with why I want you," he continued. "Even if you'd been on planet for some other reason, the moment I saw you it would have been game over. We would have ended up right here, just like this."

Apollo eased off of him and left the mattress, heading straight for the workbench. The sound of metal and moving objects as he picked up and discarded a couple of items had fear racking up within Shade.

He swallowed the sudden lump forming in his throat and concluded that he regretted the head butt, if only because he'd been hasty. If he was going to fight back it should be in a situation where he knew it would cause actual damage, right?

That thought seemed to flee his mind as if it'd never been the second Apollo turned, a pair of pruning shears in his left hand. He turned it this way and that, as if inspecting the blades before nodding to himself.

"Hud Flore bawled his eyes out when I used this on him," Apollo said breezily, as if he were talking about that one time he'd tried baking a cake on his own. "I hadn't secured him down properly and he ended up squirming too much and making a mess of things. In the end, I had to cut the whole hand off just so no one would have to see my shoddy work."

Shade's eyes widened and his stomach plummeted. He'd seen the crime scene photos, of course, which Apollo well knew. Hud was victim number six—as far as they were aware—and had been found missing his right hand.

And his nose.

"Want to know what he did to deserve it, Detective?" Apollo slowly dropped down onto the end of the mattress again and crawled his way over, resting on Shade's knees.

He'd gone still as a statue, unable to move as he watched the sharp blade of the shears being lowered to his thigh.

"Officer Dario is a decent person, tries his best with every case that's handed to him, but he can only do so much. Secrets, real secrets, tend to be buried deep. You've got to get your hands dirty if you want to dig them out." Apollo slipped the bottom end of the shears beneath the hem of Shade's boxer briefs on the left. "Can't be afraid of the grime." Snip. "Or the blood." Snip.

Slowly, he worked his way up, cutting through the thin material one inch at a time as if he were trying to make a straight line and couldn't go off course even a bit.

Shade heard the snipping sound like gunshots ringing in his ears, his pulse spiking with every glide of the cold steel against his thigh.

"Monsters know how to hide in plain sight," Apollo continued, though Shade was only partially listening. "How to pretend. Hud Flore was a first-class nightmare. I'd have you ask his daughter, but she's dead."

That'd been in Hud's file. His daughter, age eighteen, had died in a hovercar accident only a month before his body had been discovered in a ravine next to a popular grocery store. It hadn't been looked into when she'd crashed because they'd assumed there were no connections. Driving accidents sadly happened all the time. The information packet left with Hud's body had proven it was no accident.

The waistband took a little more effort and Apollo reached up with his free hand and grabbed onto it, pulling it away from Shade's body so he could work the blade through. The material came apart with a snap, half of the fabric falling to the side of his leg, the other half settling over his middle, just barely covering his junk.

Without skipping a beat, Apollo moved on to repeat the process on the other side.

"Shouldn't you be questioning me, Detective?" he asked. "You're usually better at your job than this. I'm giving you answers. You should be paying attention. Unless there's something else that's more important?"

Shade clenched his teeth, a prickle of that anger from earlier worming its way through the panic that had been consuming him. While it was tempting not to play directly into his hands, Apollo had a point.

Since they were here and the asshole was talking, he couldn't miss the opportunity to find out more, if only for the victims' sake.

"How did you know he'd killed her?" he said, voice sounding far away to his ears even after the little pep talk he'd given himself.

"It wasn't all that hard, actually," Apollo divulged. "If the coroner had only paid a little bit more attention to the injuries, she would have easily picked up on the truth. That girl was covered in bruises from past beatings, some of them weeks old and already turning a golden green."

"Hud beat her?" All accounts from family and friends stated he was the best dad there was, doting and always bragging about her accomplishments to anyone who would listen.

"Surprised?"

Shade wanted to say no to be difficult, but... "No."

"Because you're a Chitta," Apollo said. "And as such, you've seen people's true emotions, the dark and dirty things they feel that they try to bury under false smiles and fake tears."

"You saw Hud Glitch," he surmised.

"At the grocery store. Saw her Glitch too. She was terrified of the man. Of her own father."

"Why do you care?"

"You mean because I'm a serial killer? I shouldn't have emotions because of what I do?" He cut through the other side of the waistband then and leaned back, eyes drawn to the apex of Shade's thighs where the tiniest bit of material still kept him from view. "I have emotions, just not many, and not in the same sense that you and everyone else do. And why did I care? I didn't. Not then. Not now."

"Then why—"

"Because I like to see how long it'll take to break someone, to make them tell the truth." Apollo remained fixated on that spot as he spoke, as if unaware of the way Shade was now staring at him and holding his breath. "I like to expose them for who and what they truly are and watch as they come apart when they're faced with reality and there's nowhere left for them to hide. Remember how I took you on the roof?"

The sudden change of topic threw Shade for a second, and he could almost feel the proverbial gears in his brain skipping and faltering.

"You moaned so prettily when I rubbed at your insides with my fingers," Apollo rested a palm over Shade's right knee and slowly eased his way up his thigh, "With my cock. Remember how it felt? The stretch and the burn and how good it was once you accepted me into your body."

"Stop." Shade's breath caught as the tips of Apollo's fingers finally made it to the top of his thigh and then brushed beneath the scrap of cloth, just barely grazing his balls. He didn't want to react, but his hips jerked at the light contact, completely out of his control.

Because he did remember, damn it, even as he tried desperately to block those images out. How could he, when he'd been replaying that scene over and over again on repeat for the past couple of weeks? It'd been like his own private porn clip when he'd been alone in the shower, stroking himself to completion while imaging Apollo behind him.

Apollo lifted the scrap of cloth away and Shade squeezed his eyes shut.

He needed to concentrate on the other part of this conversation. The one about severed hands and snipped fingers and dead bodies. His stomach flipped a little, but it was nowhere near the reaction he'd originally had when thinking about those crime scene photos. Bile rose up the back of his throat and he focused on that, on the disgusting taste and the way it burned unpleasantly and—

Shade gasped as he was grabbed roughly by the neck and pinned to the wall. At the same moment, Apollo brought the closed shears to his dick, slipping the cold blades beneath his shaft and resting it there. Fingers tightened around his throat, cutting off his air supply and he struggled for a second before the press of those shears had him stilling like a caught rabbit in a bear trap.

"We're at one, remember, baby?" Apollo asked low and sultry, tipping the blade so the narrow part of it stroked lightly against the underside of Shade's cock as he dragged it down. "You made me bleed, it's only fair I return the favor, don't you agree?"

He shook his head without thinking, though he only barely managed the motion with Apollo's fingers still keeping him in place.

"No?" Apollo lifted a taunting brow. "Think long and hard about how you want to answer. Anything you say can and will be used against you later." He smirked at his own stupid joke. "I'll ask again, just this once, you don't think it's fair I return blood for blood?"

Shade almost whimpered when he felt the shears stop at the head of his cock and press against his slit. They were closed and the only threat at the moment was the fact they were cold, and yet he felt like his heart was about to explode out of his chest. He shook his head a second time, the fear of what Apollo might do next getting the best of him.

After having seen those photos he'd been an idiot not to be afraid. Those images were permanently seared into his brain.

Surprisingly, however, that seemed to be the answer Apollo was hoping for, his grin widening as he pulled the shears away and tossed them down onto the mattress, close enough he could easily reach for them if needed, but at least no longer touching Shade.

"That's all right," he said smoothly, "I don't like playing fair, remember?" He shifted closer, dropping his knees at either side of Shade's hips. "You'll pay me back a different way then. One minute."

Shade frowned and Apollo clucked his tongue.

"Did you lose count already? You were at one, so I'll make it a solid minute. You last that long," he leaned in and ghosted his lips over Shade's, just enough for the sensation to be there and gone, "and I'll reward you. Don't," he tipped his head to the side, "and it's back to the shears after all. Got it?"

No, no he really didn't. This was all insane. Super insane. Not to mention happening all too fast. This morning Shade had still been stupidly in the crush stage of things and now he was chained to a wall being threatened with gardening tools by the guy he'd thought was a sweet and friendly boy-next-door type.

How had he missed all the signs? There'd been signs, right? Surely there'd been signs. The first guy he shows an interest in forever and of course it had to be a psychopath. He was a moron. A complete and total—

"Hey," Apollo narrowed his eyes, "enough of that. Want someone to hate, baby? Here. Hate me."

That was all the warning he gave before his fingers tightened, tighter than they had before, constricting airflow, pressing against the old bruises that were already there from Maxen. As if aware of that fact, he shifted ever so slightly, almost like he was appalled by the idea of copying Maxen and wanted to make fresh marks of his own instead.

Shade mindlessly struggled against his bonds, the metal digging into his flesh, completely unnoticed. His eyes bulged and tears dripped from the corners of his eyes.

The entire time, Apollo watched him as if enraptured, a bliss-filled sigh passing his parted lips. "That's the look. I've been jerking off all month to this picture right here. Almost there. A full minute, remember? If you pass out…"

It was a miracle Shade could even recall the shears less than a foot away with the way his lungs felt like they were on fire. He was starting to feel lightheaded, his vision winking in and out.

"Eyes on me, Detective," Apollo ordered. "I like the way you look when you're gasping for air. I've liked it since the first time I saw it. You're so sexy. So raw. So real."

What the actual fuck was he going on about?

He chuckled. "There you go, get angry. Are you mad that you're neck looks like it was made to have my hand around it? Mad that this is the only time you let your guard down and force yourself to show exactly what you're truly feeling? Or," he leaned in and brought his mouth up to the curve of his ear, "are you mad because I put my fingers here instead of inside that tight hole of yours?"

Just as Shade was sure he was about to pass out, Apollo loosened his hold. He didn't let go, kept his palm there, lightly against his throat as Shade gasped and sputtered.

"Good job, Detective." Apollo turned his wrist and stroked the side of Shade's jaw almost reverently. "Good job."

It hurt breathing and it hurt not breathing. His throat felt raw and his neck was pulsing, aftershocks of pain quaking through him as his lungs rattled in his chest. There was something else though, something lower, a sensation his frazzled mind couldn't compute for a solid ten seconds before it crashed into him like a tidal wave and he inhaled sharply in absolute horror.

At some point, Apollo had dropped his free hand between Shade's legs and begun to stroke him.

It took all his strength to force himself to look down and see the horrendous truth for himself.

He'd just been choked to the point of nearly losing consciousness by a proclaimed serial killer who'd threatened to snip off his dick with garden shears less than five minutes ago.

And yet, Shade was hard.

Chapter 17:

"Why are you doing this?" Shade tried to keep the pathetic and cliché comments to a minimum, but now that he was getting a boner five seconds after almost being murdered, he opted to put pride aside for a second.

He was used to being betrayed by his own body. His head was always achy even when he needed to concentrate, and his empathic abilities never dimmed when he wanted them to. His whole life he'd been a slave to being Chitta, but those were mental chains.

This was different. His dick had never done something like this before and he hated it. Maybe even more than his messed up powers because at least those he could hide from the rest of the world. There was no hiding his erection, especially not from Apollo.

"If it's because I saw what you did to Maxen, just kill me already." Death would be better. Although, even as he said it, Shade recalled the way Apollo had tortured his other victims before delivering the killing blow. He almost shuddered, catching himself at the last second.

But Apollo was Chitta too, and unlike Shade, he could read him.

"Are you forgetting the part about how I saved you from him first? I'm not going to kill you anytime soon so relax, Detective," Apollo said in a tone that really didn't help ease any of the fear collecting in his gut. "You did such a good job not passing out on me, don't you want the reward I promised?"

"No." He shook his head vehemently. "No I don't want anything from you except for you to let me go."

Apollo tsked. "Don't be boring. You're better than that."

"I'm not," he disagreed. "So answer the question. Why are you doing this? Do you do this with all of your victims, huh? Is this some sick game you like playing before you start chopping body parts off?" His eyes dipped back to the shears, another wave of fear trickling in.

"I'm not cutting anything off," Apollo said, and he sounded annoyed for the first time since the start of this. He rested his hands on Shade's thighs, stroking those long digits up and down, eyes locked on his bobbing cock.

Despite the fear, Shade was still hard as rock, and he bit the inside of his cheek when precome dribbled out of his slit and rolled down his shaft.

"I knew you were beautiful," Apollo told him, entranced as he reached out and dragged his pointer finger through the wet line, collecting it on his finger, "but I wasn't able to get a good look before."

On the rooftop, Shade had been facing the other direction.

"You don't actually hate yourself you know," he said, "You just hate your circumstances."

"I don't recall ever telling you I did." Shade didn't want to go there right now, not when he was already feeling like a complete fool for his body's reaction. It was because he'd already experienced it though, knew exactly what Apollo touching him felt like, and after years of there being nothing but him and his own fist…His dick must be momentarily broken, that was all. "You're right about the circumstances bit though. Get away from me."

"Why?" He tapped his crown teasingly, causing Shade to hiss. "Embarrassed that all I had to do was stroke you a few times to get you hard for me? This is nothing, baby. In due time, I'll have it so your dick is rising and ready at the sound of my footsteps approaching. I won't even have to touch you to get you to weep for me just," he rolled the pad of his thumb across the silky head, "like this."

Shade tried to close his legs and turn his body away protectively, but Apollo was having none of that.

He had his hands under his thighs and Shade's body bent in half in a heartbeat, pinning his knees practically to his chest. Since he was flexible the position didn't hurt, but it was humiliating, exposing his lower region to Apollo in its entirety. His struggles increased as he cursed, trying to kick out at him yet failing to dislodge himself from that vice-like grip.

Apollo lowered himself down and the first flick of his warm, wet tongue at Shade's entrance had the detective stilling instantly.

"Wait," he breathed out, words unsteady, "don't."

Apollo didn't listen, spreading him wider as he began to lap at him, lightly at first, just enough that he could feel him there before finally spearing past that tight ring of muscle. His tongue wiggled its way inside, curling upwards as he buried his face against him, nose making contact with the underside of Shade's balls.

He twitched at the intrusion, tears stinging at the corners of his eyes that he refused to shed. Shade dug his nails into his palms, hard enough he felt them leaving indents, and tried to focus on the sting there instead of the way pleasure was coiling tighter and tighter with every invasive stroke of the other man's tongue. Only, that added bit of pain seemed to make it worse, the intensity only rising.

No one had ever done this to him before. It felt dirty. Wrong. On the surface, he understood there was nothing shameful in the act itself, of course, but that was when there were two consenting partners and they'd both agreed this was something they were interested in. Shade wasn't getting a say here and—

"Nothing to be ashamed of," Apollo pulled back enough to say, groaning a second later when Shade felt his hole twitch at the sudden absence of attention.

He closed his eyes, cheeks heating at the knowledge that the other guy had noticed.

"Fuck off, you psycho!" Shade jerked in his hold, attempting to free himself all over again, stopping only when Apollo loomed up over him and he caught sight of the look in his eyes.

"What did you just call me, Detective?" Apollo's eyes were so dark they may as well be black, his lips twisted in an almost snarl. "Say it again."

Ten years doing this job and Shade had never known fear like this. He'd been in scuffles with criminals he'd been sent after before, been in sticky situations with them where things had gotten dicey and he'd had the fleeting thought that this could be it. Death wasn't something he was afraid of. He didn't *want* to die, but he'd always been able to acknowledge that was a distinct possibility in his line of work, and that when the end came, it may not be swift or painless.

This was different. The look on Apollo's face wasn't promising death, it promised regret. Suffering. Humiliation.

Shade bristled at that last one. The asshole knew exactly where to get him because he'd been feeling around his emotions all those times they'd been together. He'd been stupid and had assumed that because he couldn't read the other man, Apollo couldn't either, but he'd been wrong. Still, even after he'd discovered as much, he hadn't pulled away.

He hadn't wanted to be a hypocrite, saddened by all the times other people had distanced themselves from him simply because of what he was. So he'd pushed the discomfort down, and, honestly, a twisted part of him may have even been a bit curious. Curious to know what Apollo felt from him.

Shade wasn't curious anymore. Now he was scared and more than a little pissed off, at Apollo sure, but also at himself because as a detective of his rank he should have seen this coming and gotten the hell out of dodge long before they were ever able to end up here.

And, as per usual when he entered that state of mind, his temper got the best of him.

He looked Apollo dead in the eye and said in the stoniest tone he could muster given the fact his ass was still being held in the air and he was staring through his spread thighs, "You're a psycho. What you did to all of those people is sick. You're psychotic and you need help—"

Shade yelped when Apollo slammed a hand on the wall just above his head. He'd thought it was a warning, but less than a second later there was a soft beep, and with a frown, he glanced up to see a hidden control panel set in the wood blink a small orange light. There was a clicking sound as if something within the wall was giving way, and in the next instant, Apollo had grabbed onto his ankles and tugged him down the mattress.

He let out a cry of alarm thinking his wrists would protest but they didn't. Chains attached to the cuffs extended from the wall, pulling tight only once Apollo stopped yanking on him.

Apollo flipped him onto his stomach, causing his arms to cross in their bindings, and shoved Shade's head down onto the mattress with a hand on the back of his neck.

When his thighs were forced apart, Shade sucked in a breath and tried to crawl away, but Apollo held him firmly, his strength easily greater than Shade's. Considering he was still suffering from being knocked unconscious, and choked out twice, that wasn't too surprising. Not to mention the only thing he'd had to eat or drink that day had been the half a can of coffee he'd been forced to swallow.

Horrified, a pang of hopelessness hit him as it dawned on him there was no way he was strong enough to get away from this, that he was completely at Apollo's mercy.

"Wait," he scrambled to come up with anything to say, words catching in his throat when he felt something thick and hot press against his entrance. It was much larger than a tongue. "Wait."

"Wait for what?" Apollo practically snarled next to his ear, settling his entire form over Shade's back. He used a hand to lift Shade's hips off the mattress half an inch and reached beneath him to grab onto his dick. "You're still hard for me. You want this."

"No." Shade shook his head and tugged on the chains, still trying to get away. "No, I don't. I don't want any of this. I don't want you."

"Sure about that?" He gave him one solid pump of his fist and then brought his hand around, presenting his fingers in front of Shade's face. "Look at that. You're dripping for me, baby. Leaking all over the mattress."

"I am telling you," Shade gave it one last attempt, speaking clearly and steadily, "I don't want this."

Apollo hummed noncommittally. "You and I both know how easy it is to lie with words. I've long since stopped trusting them."

"I'm telling you no!"

"And I'm telling you," he growled against his ear, "I don't care what that pretty little mouth of yours says. I'm taking my cues from your body, Shadow mine. I'm taking my cues," he let go of Shade's dick and wrapped an around his shoulder, poking hard at the spot on his chest where his heart was located, "from right here."

It didn't take a genius to figure out he meant Shade's feelings. Which was ridiculous, because the only emotion he was feeling right this second was hatred.

"You're delusional! You—"

Apollo shoved his head back down to the mattress, cutting him off, and rested his forearm over the back of his neck. "I'll do most of the talking. I let you the first time because I needed you distracted so you wouldn't notice me slipping. But now that the cat's out of the bag, all you have to do," he pressed his lips to Shade's cheek and grinned down at him darkly, "is purr for me, baby."

Then he gave one hard thrust, forcing his cock deep into Shade's protesting body, stretching his hole without warning or the proper preparation needed to ensure it'd be a smooth glide in.

Shade screamed, the chains rattling as he grabbed onto them, desperate to get a hold of anything. But he couldn't pull himself out from beneath Apollo's heavy form, couldn't stop him from dragging his cock out of his depths slowly enough to ensure Shade felt every painful inch of him. Couldn't stop him from snapping his hips forward and doing it all over again.

The searing pain was like nothing he'd ever felt before, his mind blanking for a solid thirty seconds, tears streaming freely down his face completely unnoticed by him.

Apollo grunted over Shade as he continued to spear through him with his thick, curved cock.

The sound of their bodies coming together was sharp, mixed with the creaking of the plastic covering over the mattress, and filled Shade's ears as he gasped. On the rooftop it'd been uncomfortable, but Apollo had taken the time to open him up and the pain had been minimal at best.

He was doing this on purpose, showing Shade he could hurt him just as easily as he could make him feel good. Teaching him he didn't care which way it went, whether Shade got pain or pleasure out of it, so long as Apollo got what he wanted.

It was sick, but a tiny part of Shade perked to attention at that.

He chased sickos down on the daily, and yet here he was getting turned on by the fact a serial killer wanted him?

And he was too. At some point, the pain started to fade as his body adjusted, discomfort morphing into something else.

On the next forward thrust, Shade moaned, his hips tipping upward on their own as if to silently beg for more. He pushed back when Apollo retreated, chasing after that too-full feeling that only a moment before had made him feel like he was about die.

Apollo chuckled and eased up on his grip so that Shade wasn't being pressed so restrictively into the mattress. Then, without breaking stride, he leaned forward and planted another soft kiss on the rise of his cheekbone, clearly pleased.

"There you go, baby," Apollo's voice was husky, his breaths coming in sharp pangs as he rolled his hips, switching to sharp jerky motions that kept him buried deep and never fully pulling out. "Purr for me, just like that. You like it when it hurts."

Shade went still as if doused by a bucket of ice-cold water. Comprehension over what he'd been doing hit him and even though the pleasure was still building and intense, he locked his limbs in place and bit into his bottom lip hard enough to draw blood. Anything was better than giving Apollo the reaction he wanted.

Hell, the taste of his blood was better than giving the other man anything he wanted at all.

"Don't be stubborn," Apollo said, and when that did nothing to persuade Shade, he nipped at his cheek, right over the spot he'd kissed tenderly only a moment prior. "You're going to want to start moving again," he stated, low and threatening, "or I'm going to make you regret it later."

Shadow turned his head just enough to catch Apollo's gaze. "I regret it now."

Apollo pulled out and flipped him around onto his back, lining his cock back up with his hole before he could so much as blink. He drove back into him, making sure to bump against that spot inside that set fireworks off in Shade's body.

Shade bit into his lip even harder to keep from letting out the moans that threatened to crawl up his throat. Defiantly, he kept his eyes locked on Apollo's, giving him nothing, not even a repeat of his earlier resistance.

Sure, there were a lot of negatives that came with being an overly powerful Chitta. The inescapable feelings of self-hatred for not being strong enough to turn it off, the self-suspicion that came from never really knowing how far was too far and when his body would just give in and he'd enter Repletion.

But there were good benefits too. Positives that came from having to learn at a young age how to handle all the mean gossip and the whispered words from other students as he'd passed in the halls. Like being able to shut everything out, at least for a moment.

He focused on the dark shade of Apollo's eyes, the way his pupils were blown so big it was impossible to tell where they ended and his irises began. Concentrated on the anger building in their depths, instead of on the hand currently stroking his dick in rapid succession to the cock gliding in and out of him.

When he came, his body jerked, but he never tore his gaze away from Apollo's. His lips parted and he cried out, but even that came off detached sounding.

It didn't go unnoticed.

Apollo thrust into him a few more times before finding his own release, emptying into him, stuffing himself as deeply inside of Shade as he could get and staying there as they both rode out the electric aftershocks of their orgasms.

This time when Shade passed out he was grateful for the reprieve, and he didn't even need the help of a hand around his neck.

Chapter 18:

He woke in the same position he'd been in the first time, only now the pain wasn't just from his fight with Maxen. Shade winced and shifted, trying to find a more comfortable seated position and failing. His rattling the chains at either side of his head was what most likely gave him away, and Apollo swiveled around in the single chair across the mattress to face him.

"Morning, sunshine." He snorted at his own stupid joke and corrected, "My bad. Shadow. Morning, Shadow. How are you feeling?"

"Like I was raped," he ground out, forcing down the feeling of dread acknowledging that caused him. It wasn't nearly as hard as he'd imagined though. In fact, any indignation he felt was aimed directly at the man across from him. It was a struggle to maintain eye contact, but he made himself do it.

Apollo gave him a once-over. "It shouldn't be too bad. I took care of you after you passed out. The cream should have healed most of the tears."

"The tears—" He stopped himself and glared. "Asshole."

"Yeah," Apollo nodded. "That's where the tears were."

"I can't believe you're making jokes at a time like this."

He quirked a brow. "Are you serious, Detective? Out of this whole scenario, that's the part that's unbelievable to you? Not my seducing you and luring you into my clutches? The fact that I have a sense of humor is what does it? And you said I was the psychotic one."

Shade paused, waiting to see if he was about to snap at the use of that word. Yesterday it seemed to have acted as a trigger for Apollo, but it didn't appear to have the same effect when the man said it himself. Still, he wasn't about to drop his guard.

"What?" Apollo asked, and when Shade didn't immediately reply, added, "It looked like you wanted to ask me something just now. Go ahead."

"You were triggered..." Even though the other man was right and there wasn't actually any real pain, Shade remembered the pain of being forced to take it last night and shifted uncomfortably. "Is that what happened with your other victims? They said the wrong thing to you and—"

"No one has gotten close enough to the real me to even consider calling me names like that," Apollo cut him off. "There's only ever been you," his gaze hardened, "and my family."

"Your sister?" That made the most sense when he considered it. "She called you that, didn't she? Even though she was already—"

"Already what, Detective?" it was impossible to miss the warning in his tone.

Shade swallowed down the doubt and continued anyway. "She was horrible to you. Hurt you. Is that why you turn on other people?"

"I don't turn on them," Apollo rolled his eyes, "I just don't like them pretending that they're better than me or any of the others around them. Do you? When you catch a criminal and he pleads not guilty despite all of the evidence you've collected against him, can you say you're all right with that?"

Shade pretended to think it over but... "Honestly? I don't really care."

The grin he got for that answer had him shuddering and feeling like he'd walked into another trap.

"I did it, you know," Apollo said then. "The fire? I set it before I left for the library. Rigged it so it wouldn't get bad enough to be noticed until it was too late. The night before, my sister had pushed me down the stairs in front of my mother and I'd ended up in the ER. Know who was blamed?"

"Not her."

"Nope. She was the angel and I was the devil son, no matter how much damage she caused me, mentally, physically, it didn't matter. She was perfect in their eyes."

"I know what it's like to think you're not good enough," Shade replied before he could help it, only to have Apollo snort at him.

"I'm more than good enough," he stated. "It's not my fault my family couldn't accept me, it was theirs. And in the end, they paid the price for it. How about now, Detective?"

Shade frowned, silently asking what he meant.

"I just told you I murdered my family in cold blood but that it wasn't technically my fault because they drove me to it. Do you still stand by what you said before? Do you not care?"

"I think it's horrible that you killed them," Shade confessed. "But I also think it's horrible that they let your sister get away with torturing you for years just because they couldn't accept she needed help. Were they going to get you help?"

Apollo stood abruptly.

"You said they knew who you really are," Shade reminded. "Were they trying to send you somewhere against your will? Did you find out about it that same night your sister shoved you?"

"You're very perceptive, Detective," he drawled mockingly. "Too bad you weren't this observant when I was hunting you, you might have known better than to allow me to get close enough to learn what you feel like on the inside."

"You're doing it again," Shade pointed out. "Hurting me because of the pain caused by then."

"Great," he growled, "and now you want to play shrink on top of it all? Should we bring up your damaged parts while we're at it?" When Shade closed his mouth, Apollo hummed. "Yeah, that's what I thought."

Shade felt like he had a better understanding of why Apollo killed at least. There was something inside of him that demanded to be seen, and torturing his victims until they were forced to acknowledge that not only were they monsters, but so was he, gave him an adrenaline rush.

It was also why he'd targeted people who hurt other people. In a way, was he punishing his family all over again?

He wished he'd been lying just to get on his good side, but Shade meant it when he'd said he didn't feel a thing for Apollo's family. Had they gotten what they deserved? He didn't know, he only had Apollo's account of events to go off of. But if two grown adults had stood by while their eldest child broke the bones and burned the flesh of their youngest?

Yeah, Shade wasn't exactly in the mood to weep for such people.

Did that make him a monster too?

"Do you need to use the bathroom?" Apollo asked suddenly, and it was with great displeasure that Shade realized he did. "There's an Elec-Field placed around the entire perimeter of this building. If you try to make a run for it, it'll activate the cuff around your wrist and you will be electrocuted. Understand?"

Problems with his dead family or not, what he was doing to Shade was messed up.

"I'm going to arrest you and throw you in the smallest cell Pollux has, and if it isn't small enough, I'll file to have you shipped elsewhere where there is one." Shade tensed as Apollo approached, though he didn't bother trying to attack the other man when he activated the hidden control pad on the wall again.

The cuffs around Shade's wrists separated from the wall and his arms dropped to his sides. For a second, another wave of fear rippled through him when he found they were numb and he could barely feel them.

Apollo knelt at his side and started massaging his right arm. Carefully, he moved from his wrist all the way up to his shoulder before working his way back down again.

"What the hell are you doing?" Shade asked incredulously.

"You were stuck in the same position for too long," Apollo explained, as if that was the part that Shade didn't understand. "As soon as the blood flow is back you'll be fine, then I'll take you to the bathroom. It's about time for your shower anyway." He switched to his left arm.

At Shade's frown, he motioned with his chin over to the desk. There was a small clock next to the projected security feed that he was almost positive hadn't been there last night. According to the neon blue numbers it was nearing eight o'clock in the morning, typically the time when he'd shower before heading to the station.

Shade ran on a pretty set schedule, since he and Gael tended to stay up late working on cases, he slept in until about seven-fifty and then got up and had a quick shower before the two of them left for work together. He only showered during other times of the day when his migraines got worse and he needed fast relief.

But he hadn't stuck with that routine when he'd been staying at Apollo's, not wanting to intrude on the reporter's schedule.

"How do you know that?"

"Come on," Apollo helped him onto his feet, keeping him steady with a hand around his waist. When Shade struggled to move away, he clicked his tongue. "Stop it, the bathroom is all the way over there," he motioned to the far right corner, "and you'll never make it on your own. So unless you want me to stand back and watch you attempt to crawl—" he stopped himself, an idea formulating in his head. "Actually. I could just bring over a bucket. That would save me a lot of—"

"Let's go," Shade grumbled. He wasn't about to take a dump in a bucket out in the open. There had to be lines somewhere, even when it came to kidnappers who also happened to dismember people sometimes.

…Right?

"Why are you doing this?" He'd never gotten an answer and he still wanted one.

Daylight spilled through the opening to the warehouse, casting the whole place in a warm light. Now he could make out details he hadn't been able to in the dark, like the rest of the staircase set into the far wall, and the single door set in the corner beneath it. That's where they were heading.

All of the windows had been boarded up, with only slight cracks here and there which allowed the sun to filter in. None of them were large enough for anyone on the outside to peer through and get a good look at anything, which was probably why Apollo had left them as is. The smooth cement floor was surprisingly clean, no matter how far into the warehouse they went, and the reporter—no, the psycho—caught him noticing.

"Vacuum robot," Apollo explained. "Works wonders."

"Neat freak," Shade mumbled to himself, and when that earned him a questioning look, exhaled and said, "It was one of the possible character traits given to the killer's profile before we suspected Maxen. The drop sites were always so clean, and even though the bodies were all mutilated differently, even those came back free of anything that could be used as evidence to help us locate or identify the murderer."

"I like things to be in order," Apollo shrugged and then opened the door by placing his palm against the scan pad next to it. "It'll only open for me."

"Figured that out already," Shade drawled, mostly just to be difficult. He sure as shit wasn't going to make this easy for him, no matter how terrified he was deep down or how likely it seemed like he was nearing the same type of fate as all those other victims.

As just another gruesome photo on a crime board for others to poke and ponder over.

He was scowling when the door slid open and Apollo walked them in.

"You don't like it?" Apollo sounded legitimately curious, enough to snap Shade out of his dark thoughts.

He glanced around, surprised to find the bathroom had been decked out in all of the latest appliances and tech. It was also huge, with a glass shower stall with two stone benches set in one corner, and a bathtub large enough to fit five grown men in the other. On the opposite wall were the toilet and the sink, and then another door with a window in it.

"Sauna," Apollo said.

Shade hummed in understanding. "Taking bodies apart must be laboring work."

"Got to have some way of relieving all the aches and pains," Apollo agreed, not the least bit nonplused by the obvious jab. "Would you like to use that instead?" He glanced down and behind Shade, clearly staring at his ass. "The cream really should have worked…"

"Cut it out." Shade shoved him away, only realizing as soon as he had that he was wearing a pair of gym shorts and not naked. How the hell had he gone all this time without even noticing that he was in clothing?

"I'll take that as a no then." Apollo shut the door and then walked over to the shower stall, stepping inside to work the nozzles until the square showerhead came to life. The spray came down like sheets of rain, and he tested it with his palm before exiting and motioning Shade to get in.

He stared at him a moment and then shook his head. "I'm not showering with you in the room."

"Then you're not showering at all," Apollo stated.

"Fine," he retreated a step toward the exit, "then I won't—"

Apollo moved too quickly for him to react, grabbing onto his wrist and hauling him into the stall fast enough to give him whiplash. He yanked the shorts down Shade's legs and tossed them carelessly back out into the bathroom, then pushed him directly under the spray, laughing when Shade immediately started sputtering.

"Shampoo," he pointed to the small alcove cut into the sandstone wall. "Now. Do it properly, Shadow."

He was about to snap at him not to call him that, but then the name brands of the products caught his attention. Shade reached for one and picked it up, frowning at the blue and green bottle. "This is the kind that I use."

Apollo remained silent, which only made Shade more nervous because the man was incredibly fond of the sound of his own voice and seemed to never miss an opportunity to hear it.

Shade moved to the shower stall door, shoving Apollo's arm out of the way when he went to stop him and poked his head out. His gaze went straight to the sink where a rack was set beneath a long mirror with two toothbrushes.

"That's my toothbrush." The one he'd suspected Gael of dropping and tossing. "Did you go through my trash?"

Apollo made a face like *he* was the crazy one here and pulled him back in and under the spray. "Of course not, that's disgusting. Why would I let you put something that filthy in your mouth? Do you know how many germs can accumulate in a single garbage can?"

"Then where did you get it?" He was afraid he already knew, but Shade wanted to hear it. Needed to for the reality of his situation, even after the brutal events of last night, to fully sink in.

"I got it from your hotel room," Apollo said, "obviously."

"You stole it, you mean."

"Sure, if you want to get technical."

Shade glanced back over at the shampoo and conditioner matching set.

"I bought those," Apollo answered before he could ask. "You didn't bring enough with you for it to go unnoticed if I'd taken some. The razor though, that's yours."

He stared at the black razor hanging on the side of the cubby.

"If you even think about trying to use that against me," Apollo warned, "I'll make last night seem like it was our honeymoon."

"Last night was a nightmare." Shade blinked past the water smattering into his eyes and rubbed at his face. "*This* is a nightmare. And to think, I was *worried* about *you*." He laughed but the sound lacked any humor. "I thought you were the target of a serial killer but instead—"

"You aren't my target, Detective," Apollo stated, waiting until Shade had gathered the energy to look him in the eye. "Those things you saw done to those other people, I would never do anything like that to you. You're different."

"Forgive me if I don't believe you."

"You will. You just need time, that's all. It'd be weirder if you didn't."

"Did you do this to them too?" He picked up the shampoo bottle again. "Stock this place with all their favorite products? Fuck them even when they said no?"

Apollo scrunched his nose in distaste. "I wouldn't have stuck my dick in any of them if they'd offered to pay me twelve billion coin."

Shade had seen before and after photos. It was sick of him to even think it, but he'd seen what those people had looked like, how gorgeous some of them had been.

"I'm telling the truth," Apollo said, clearly knowing where his thoughts were going. "I got off on seeing what they were like on the inside, sure, but it wasn't sexual in nature."

Shade's brow furrowed and Apollo sighed in exasperation.

"I told you," he repeated, "you're different."

"Different how?"

"I stalked you. I hunted them. There's a difference."

"Is there?" Shade wasn't convinced. It sounded like the same thing to him.

"And if there isn't?" Apollo tipped his chin and took him in, his suspicion apparent. "You've been pretty calm since you woke up. Why? Do you think someone's coming for you?"

Of course he thought that. Gael would never abandon him. But Shade wasn't going to bother responding to a dumb question like that, so he set to washing up instead, figuring since he was already wet and there he might as well.

"I felt that," Apollo accused. "That wave of confidence that came off you just now."

"How much of me can you feel?" Shade wondered, pretending like it wasn't that big of a deal and he was only mildly interested in knowing. Hoping that he couldn't tell he was faking it and pick up on the brimming anticipation lying just beneath the surface of the stony mask he wore as he worked shampoo into his hair.

"After we've made eye contact I can look away and still feel you. But, it comes and goes," he surprised him by admitting. "Sometimes I can feel you strongly, other times it's weak, like you're incredibly far away…" His gaze hardened. "Last night, what you did. It won't happen again."

"I don't know what you're talking about," Shade stated calmly, shifting that new info around in his mind. If Apollo could only read him some of the time, he needed to figure out what controlled that and how he could put a stop to it or use it to his advantage.

"I'm not asking you," Apollo told him darkly, "I'm telling you."

"And I'm telling you, I don't know what you mean. Last night…I blocked a lot of it out." He was lying. He could remember everything right down to the smallest of details, like the musky, amber and moss smell of Apollo's sweat and the slick sound of his balls slapping against his ass with every forward stroke.

He washed the shampoo out and then hesitated to reach for the conditioner, noticing the cuts on his wrists from the cuffs weren't there when they should be. He pushed the gold metal away as much as he could, but there wasn't even a slight bruising.

"You moaned in your sleep when I stuck my fingers in you to deposit the sun cream," Apollo said moving a step closer. "And you sighed when I applied it to the bruises on your wrists, and your ribs, and your neck." He stopped in front of him and lifted his hand, hovering just over Shade's throat as if he was tempted to grab on and remake those very marks. Instead, he dropped his hand without making any sort of contact at all, his expression serious and intense. "You're the first person I didn't want to leave physically broken. The first person I've ever wanted to take care of.

"Why am I doing this?" Apollo said. "What makes you different?" He tapped his heart "This. This foreign feeling I've never felt before. That's what drove me to follow you to your hotel the day you arrived on planet, and what had me befriending you. What made me change my plans and fuck you on the roof instead of throw you over it like I should have."

Shade knew he was staring at him like he'd grown a third head, but he couldn't help it. "You aren't trying to say it was love at first sight or some other such bullshit, right?"

Apollo snorted. "Love? I'm not even convinced love is a real thing and I'm a Chitta. No. it's not love. If that's something you've dreamed about in that pretty head of yours, set it aside right now. I don't do romance, Detective."

"Oh no," he drawled sarcastically, not even sure why he was doing it, "how ever will I cope?"

"Preferably? With my cock up your ass."

The conditioner bottle Shade had been reaching for toppled off the shelf when that blunt comment caught him off guard, and he watched as it rolled over to Apollo, stopping once it hit his foot.

Slowly, Apollo bent and picked it up, the playfulness draining away as fast as the water currently swirling at Shade's feet. He was calculating by the time he straightened, his shoulders set in a determined and confident way that Shade didn't need empathic abilities to decipher. When he took a step forward, Shade withdrew without thinking.

The corner of Apollo's mouth tipped up, but it wasn't sweet or because he truly found Shade's instinctual urge to put distance between them funny. "Obsession," he announced, and his voice seemed to crack against the stone walls ominously. "I'm infatuated by you. Have been from the start. The moment you stepped out of that taxi your fate was already sealed, Detective."

Shade stumbled another step, not even ashamed by that fact when Apollo moved closer. His back hit the wall, the razor off to the side of his head, just within his peripheral vision.

But he didn't reach for it. Maybe he should have. Maybe he should have tried his luck and tested his skills against Apollo despite the earlier threat but…He couldn't get his arm to move, too entranced by the possessive gleam in Apollo's dark blue eyes. It was almost as if he was hypnotized. He couldn't look away.

"I've decided," Apollo announced and stopped in front of him, his body under the shower spray, his clothes drenched through within seconds, not that he seemed to notice.

"That you're going to kill me?" Shade asked.

"Kill you?" He shook his head and lifted his arm, the one not holding the bottle of conditioner, slipping his fingers through Shade's wet hair. "I want your life, but not like that. I'm not going to kill you. I'm going to ruin you, Detective. Totally. Completely."

"Those mean the same thing." Shade internally screamed to shut up, but he'd never been very good at listening to himself.

Apollo grinned and brought his face closer. "Entirely."

"Now you're just being annoying."

"Is that all you have to say?" Apollo trailed his fingers down the curve of Shade's jaw down to his chin, gripping him tight between two fingers and forcing him to tip his head back against the wall. The move brought his mouth up, closer to his, and his breath ghosted against his lips. "So set on hiding behind your bravado. But that's okay. I'll strip you of that too. I'll pick you apart and leave you bare until all you have left is me to keep you warm. Until you can't recall which pieces were yours initially and which ones I sewed into your psyche. I'm going to leave traces of me everywhere, baby. You wanted to be wanted?" He brushed his mouth feather-light against his. "Careful what you wish for."

Shade was so stunned, he took the conditioner when it was offered silently and watched as Apollo turned on his heels and exited the shower stall, clicking the glass door shut behind him.

Chapter 19:

"There's something wrong with you," Shade asked from his spot on the mattress, "isn't there?"

He'd been watching the other man closely all day, taking stock of his movements and the expressions that came and went from his face.

All three of them.

"There's nothing wrong with me," Apollo disagreed. He was sitting in front of the desk, typing something out in front of the monitor. He'd been there for a while, working silently, either unaware of Shade's gaze on him or uncaring. "I'm perfect."

Shade almost brought up that whole modesty thing again but kept himself from doing so at the last second. A line needed to be drawn, a definitive one that could help separate the man he knew now from the one he'd foolishly believed Apollo to be. Everything that had taken place between them before the tunnel needed to be categorized in a different mental folder.

Because Shade's slipup last night couldn't happen again. He couldn't allow himself to get lustful for his kidnapper and potential future murderer just because they'd had one amazing sex encounter on a rooftop. He wasn't that pathetic.

He couldn't afford to be.

"Since you aren't a fan of the P word, should I switch it to Sociopath?" They meant the same thing, but Shade wanted to see how the other man would react. He needed to gain a better understanding of Apollo's ticks if he was going to make it out of this alive.

Apollo's fingers paused over the holographic keyboard, hovering there for a split second before he started typing again. The look on his face never altered. "You said you were ostracized as a kid. Is that what made you the way you are? Why you get embarrassed so easily and why you think so low of yourself?"

"I held out for an impressively long time," Shade found himself replying, folding his leg so he could rest his arm on his upturned knee. "No matter how much the kids at school picked on me, or the whispers my relatives would throw my way when we were at family events, I believed my mother when she told me it was their problem and not mine. When she said they were jealous of what I was and wished they had a superpower just like me."

That caught his attention, and Apollo turned his head and quirked a brow.

Shade chuckled and rested his head back against the wall, staring sightlessly up at the rafters. "That's what she called it. My superpower. For a kid that made it sound exciting."

"You felt special," Apollo said.

"Yeah."

"You want to feel special again."

Shade glanced over at him, mocking smile never leaving his lips. "Guess I've always been gullible, huh?"

It sucked that Apollo had so easily picked up on that, on the fact that Shade had spent his life chasing after that same elated rush he'd gotten whenever his mom had patted his head and told him he was remarkable. The contented feeling he'd gotten at the implication he was perfect just the way he was.

"Don't be so hard on yourself, Detective. I've been doing this all my life. Fooling people is in my blood. You didn't stand a chance. Especially when that superpower of yours doesn't work on me."

He scowled and returned his sight to the rafters. "It's a curse," he corrected. "It's always been a curse. I realized that the day that same woman who always told me not to listen to the accusations dropped me off at an orphanage and never looked back. She couldn't handle what I was. So she got rid of me. I was a burden." He picked at a loose string on the crimson-colored gym shorts he'd been given after his shower. "I'm always a burden."

The murky late afternoon light painted the trees outside in golds and oranges, and when the wind blew particularly strong, the leaves chimed. Even though he hadn't been given any other clothes but the shorts, Shade was comfortable where he sat, unaffected by the mid-autumn weather.

"Gael wouldn't agree with that," Apollo's honey-toned voice cut through the silence then. He was watching him, leaning on the edge of the desk. He'd swiveled in his chair so that he was facing him, dressed in long black pants and a tight deep purple t-shirt that did nothing to hide how fit he was.

Shade hated the appreciation that swept through him, but the man was gorgeous, plain and simple. His shoulders were broad, his torso long, and his legs—

They'd been talking about Gael. *He'd* been trying to get answers. Damn it.

What the actual fuck was wrong with him?

He conjured images of the crime scenes, stomach turning—the way it should be—at the awful recollections. The man before him had done atrocious things. That's what Shade needed to focus on. Not what happened between them on the rooftop.

Hell, even last night, he'd taken him by force. That wasn't the type of person who deserved to be swooned over. Doing so wasn't normal, and there was already enough that set Shade apart from the rest of society. He didn't need to add anything else to the list.

"Gael and I make a good team," Shade admitted, smiling fondly at the mention of his partner.

"You think he's coming for you," Apollo picked up.

"He's more family to me than my parents ever were." From the very first moment they'd met, Gael had treated him the same as he had every other cadet in the Academy. It hadn't mattered to him that Shade could read his emotions against his will. "You want to know what he said when he found out I couldn't turn it off like every other Chitta? 'That must be really hard for you'."

It'd been the first time someone had thought of his feelings first. And he'd meant it. Gael had looked him straight in the eye, had said the first thing that'd come to mind, and it'd been the truth.

"I'm going to need you to wipe that lovesick look off your face, Detective," Apollo warned, and any of the casualness that had been in his tone only a moment prior was gone. His gaze had darkened as well, hands now fisted, like it wasn't just an idle threat but he was legitimately struggling to contain his temper.

"Gael is like my brother," Shade said, real fear for his friend urging him to set the record straight.

"He isn't coming."

Shade's spine straightened and he forgot all about placating him. "He would never abandon me. The fact that I've gone missing—"

"That's the thing, Shadow mine," Apollo leaned forward, propping his arms on his thighs, "if you'd gone missing, I might be a little bit concerned. Keywords there being a little bit. As it is, your *brother* thinks you've taken me into hiding after witnessing someone murder Maxen. You didn't get a good look at the perp, and because of that, you don't think it's safe for me to stay out in the open."

That…Was believable. Shit.

"I sent the message directly from your multi-slate, which only you have access to. Both it and your N.I.M. are tucked away safe and sound in a Faraday 2.3, so there's no chance of anyone tracing us. It wouldn't be the first time you've gone off the grid with no notice."

"How do you know that?"

"I read your files."

"You hacked into my files?" He could do that? Shade wasn't just dealing with a serial killer, was he? It would have been simple enough for him to use Shade's multi-slate with him literally right there, even if he'd been unconscious, but his files were kept behind state-of-the-art firewalls.

Sometimes when on a case Shade had to think quickly and didn't have the time to consult things with Gael. He'd taken potential witnesses and victims into hiding before. Had even slipped away himself a time or two to follow a lead that having two people around would have made complicated to achieve.

But because it'd happened so frequently, they had a process. He always checked in within a certain number of days, so the second he failed to do so—

"Before you start patting yourself on the back," Apollo drawled, "I know all about your schedule. You won't miss a check-in, Detective, and your partner won't be coming to find you."

Shade glared, feeling exposed and somehow even more played than he had before. "He'll figure it out eventually. You can't keep me here forever."

"You better pray he doesn't," he rose from the chair slowly, "It would be unfortunate if I had to slit his throat in front of you."

The handcuffs had been locked back into place against the wall, but Apollo had left him a little slack, a good three feet of golden chain connecting the cuffs to it.

At the threat, Shade leaped to his feet, only managing to make it to the center of the mattress before they prevented him from going any further.

"Does that upset you?" He advanced a solid step, ignoring when Shade pulled at the chains angrily. "If just picturing it affects you this much, imagine what it would be like actually having to witness it."

"You're insane!"

"That's why you should put those hopes of rescue aside," Apollo continued. "If anyone comes for you, if anyone gets close, I'll kill them. If that's not something you want, I suggest aiming that desperation you're feeling elsewhere." He'd made it to the mattress now and took a step onto it, clearly unconcerned with what Shade might do.

Shade was shoved back so quickly he almost fell over, slamming into the wall. He inhaled sharply when Apollo followed, sealing his entire form against his, so that their chests and thighs were pressed together.

"Try being desperate for me instead, Detective," Apollo suggested, lifting his arms to block Shade's view so that he was only able to look forward, directly at him.

When Shade moved to head-butt him a second time, Apollo's finger's latched onto his hair and yanked him back with enough force to cause stars to burst behind his eyes at the sharp pain.

He'd definitely torn strands out of his scalp.

"If you hurt Gael—"

"I won't stop there," Apollo cut him off. "I'll cut his throat so deep it'll be a miracle if his head stays attached to the rest of him. You know I'm not lying."

"All you've ever done is lie to me," Shade pointed out.

He believed him though. Something about the particular fury in his eyes and the way his fingers still curled in his hair domineeringly told him how serious this conversation was. If Gael ever did stumble on this place and Apollo was around…

"He's the only friend I have," he hated the slight quiver in his voice, but he wouldn't put his pride before Gael's life. Some things were more important than how other people viewed him.

It might have been his imagination, but it seemed like Apollo softened some, the tension in his face easing, his shoulders relaxing.

"Do you want to keep him, baby?" Apollo shifted over him, the mattress creaking beneath his feet. He was still pressed against him, but something about the touch changed, the air crackling with a different sort of tension.

"Why do you do that?" Shade searched his eyes, unable to look anywhere else with him standing so close. "You keep asking me questions as if it's going to make a difference what I say."

"Of course it'll make a difference," he corrected. "I want to get to know you better. How can I do that if I don't get you to engage in conversation?"

"And if I say something you don't like?"

"Then you get punished." Apollo shrugged like it was a no-brainer. "Try saying something I like instead. See what happens."

"You don't want to get to know me," Shade said tersely. "You want me to play the part of someone I'm not to indulge whatever this is."

"This?"

"This," he tapped his foot against the mattress and then moved his head as much as he could to indicate the room, "You. Whatever it is you're trying to accomplish here."

"I already explained, but clearly you weren't listening. Pay attention, Shadow. You're here because I want you to be. I took you because I wanted you, and I'm going to keep you for that exact same reason. You're going to be exactly who you are because that's the person who caught my attention in the first place. If there are bad habits we need to straighten out, we'll do that, no problem. It might even be fun. But you aren't going to stand here and lie to me to appease or humor me. I get you're used to being in charge, but let's set that record straight here and now."

Apollo lifted his other hand and rested it around Shade's throat, smirking when that had him wincing even without him needing to squeeze. "I'm in command here, baby. From this moment on, I'm your everything. I'm your damn sun and you're my little Shadow. Your whole world revolves around me, and in return, I'll keep you warm and comfortable and safe."

Shade must have hit his head on the wall a bit too hard just now, because he snorted derisively before he could think better of it. Both he and Apollo went stiff at the same time, though for different reasons.

"Something funny, baby?"

"Walk me through it," Shade said, trying, and mostly succeeding, to steady his voice as he did. "How's this going to work? What do you want from me, really? Why go through all of this trouble? This is different from your usual M.O., it's got to be." He indicated the computer. "You're a photographer. There's only so much work you can do from here before you run out of material and your shithead boss gets suspicious. Don't forget, you can be fired. Me? I'm an I.P.F agent, Apollo. Eventually, when I don't show up, the agency will send people for me. Highly trained people who won't easily walk into a trap."

"You're highly trained," he pointed out, "and I caught you just fine."

He glowered. "I was tricked. You going to befriend each and every agent they send to this planet and then do the same to them?"

"Nope," he popped the p and shook his head. "Don't want anyone else the way I want you. I never have. Pretty sure that's also something I told you. Since it still doesn't seem to be sticking, let me try again, using words you'll understand."

Apollo wrapped his hand more thoroughly around Shade's throat, his thumb and pointer resting just beneath the end of his bottom jaw. "You've become the obsession of a psychopath. Honestly, I'm a bit surprised this is the first time in your career it's happened, what with all the unmentionables you've met working cases over the past five years. But it's happened now and if you think there's a chance you'll ever be able to escape you're dreaming. I don't catch and release."

"You kill." The crime scene images came back again, only this time he wished they hadn't. His stomach flipped.

"Maybe I'll dispose of you eventually," Apollo hummed, "but eventually is not today. Today, we're coming to an understanding, you and I. Laying the groundwork for our future together."

"As your plaything?" Shade swallowed and felt his palm flush against his throat with the movement. "Pass."

"You don't get to reject me. You don't get any say at all."

"You can't keep me here like I'm some sort of thing." Shade insisted. "Even if you've stocked up and covered your tracks, we'll run out of food and supplies eventually. When that happens, what then? You sneak back into the city and hope no one notices? Not to mention the fact you'll go even more insane with it being just the two of us here."

"I don't care about anyone else," Apollo disagreed. "Before you, I preferred my own company. As for the rest, we'll deal with it as it comes. I make no promises about how long this will go on. I don't know the answer, Shadow. Believe me, I wish I did because then I'd know how long I have to deal with these foreign emotions I'm feeling toward you."

"Emotions?" He grunted. "They can't be positive ones. You don't do things like this to people you like. Kidnapping, rape, murder—"

"If you're trying to make me see the error of my ways, you're wasting your energy. I don't experience things like remorse or empathy. I've read the definitions in books, sure, I get the gist of it. But I don't feel it."

That caught Shade's attention. An empath who didn't feel empathy? "What about when other people do? Don't you read it and feel it off of them?"

"I don't feel anything off of other people," Apollo confessed. "I know what they're feeling, but I don't feel it myself. When you're scared, like you are right now, there's an almost bitter taste on my tongue, like overly ripe cherries." He smiled. "I like the flavor."

"You…taste emotions?" Shade had never heard of a Chitta's abilities developing like that before. But then, there weren't any others like him written in the medical textbooks on their kind either. They were both anomalies.

He refused to allow that to change his perception of the other man.

Refused.

"And people's overall energy. Know what you taste like, baby?" A pleasure-filled rumble made its way up Apollo's throat. "Chocolate. Chocolate all the time. Up until now, only one other person ever tasted like that. My father."

"I already know about your daddy issues, but honestly? Yikes."

"What? Don't like thinking that you remind me of my dad? Don't worry, you don't. It's similar but nowhere near the same. Your base note is unsweetened, but it changes with your mood and feelings. Chocolate-covered cherries when you're afraid, milk chocolate when you're happy, dark chocolate when you're mad, salted chocolate-covered caramel when you're in the throes of pleasure—"

"I get it." He was suddenly extremely uncomfortable, though he couldn't quite put his finger on why. It wasn't like this was any weirder than anything else he'd been told thus far, and yet, his insides felt like they were being scratched at.

And the worst part was, he couldn't tell if it was in an altogether bad way or not.

Damn his younger self for developing the need for attention.

"One more," Apollo said. "Do you know what you taste like when you look at me? That hasn't changed, Detective, not once, not even when you saw me gut that idiot Maxen, or when you woke up last night and realized you were chained and in my clutches. Chocolate-covered strawberries. A little bit sweet, a little bit bitter. A lot unsure, even from the start. From the moment you ran into me in the hallway, that's what you gave off when our eyes met. You liked what you saw."

"I didn't know you were a serial killer then," he reminded, but it was useless and they both knew it.

Apollo chuckled a bit cruelly, clearly not even willing to allow him to entertain the idea. "What about ten minutes ago, when you were eye-fucking me? All I was doing was sitting and you certainly knew all about my proclivities then. You even said it yourself. Psychopath."

Psychopaths displayed abnormal or violent behavior in social settings. They lacked the ability to distinguish between right and wrong, and typically acted on their impulses. If that truly was what Apollo was, and not just something Shade had been using to try and insult him, then nothing Shade said could convince him this was unethical. It wouldn't matter how many times the word no shot out of his mouth, Apollo would take and continue to do whatever the hell he wanted with little to no regard for Shade's personal wants or emotions.

"Chocolate-covered pickles," Apollo stated. "That's typically the taste of apprehension, pickles. Sweet and sour and pungent. What's wrong, baby? It finally hit you you've become the property of an actual psycho? Were you just throwing that word around before to be cute? It didn't work. It just pissed me off."

Shade's eyes widened slightly when the hand around his neck tightened. It wasn't enough, but the reminder of the threat he posed was visceral.

Apollo mimicked the people around him, figured out exactly what type of personality to present to the world to hide his true nature. Even if someone eventually became skeptical about Shade's absence, there was little to no chance they'd ever even consider Apollo a culprit.

When Shade had even shown a hint of suspicion toward him, Axel had immediately jumped to Apollo's defense. And Dario, a man with over thirty years on the force under his belt, smiled and called Apollo *kid*.

A Chitta who was unable to feel the full range of human emotion.

A Chitta who harbored one of the darkest, most twisted secrets Shade had ever heard of.

A Chitta who was a psychopath.

Just one of those things sounded impossible to Shade's ears, let alone all of them.

"Who *are* you?" he asked, but he was almost certain he didn't actually want the answer.

Sure enough, when Apollo's lips stretched into that now familiar wicked grin, Shade shivered.

"I'm the Sun or I'm the Devil, really depends on the way you look at it. As the sun, I'll burn away all that misplaced self-loathing you've got. I'll keep away all those unwanted foreign emotions so there's just you left swimming in that sexy mind of yours. I'll melt through your stubbornness and help you see that you're perfect just the way you were made. I'll keep you wrapped up in my warmth until eventually you'll be begging me not to exit your orbit. All you have to do is accept me, baby. Just give in to your fate."

He should stop this here, remain silent and refuse to give into this conversation or the morbid curiosity filling his mind with all sorts of things better left unknown.

He should stop.

But Shade was never good at keeping his mouth shut.

"And if I refuse?" He'd always been more of a night guy anyway. Less people out and about then.

Apollo tightened his grip on his throat, this time with enough pressure to leave him gasping, and leaned in to press that sinful mouth of his delicately against the curve of Shade's ear.

"Then I'll be the Devil," he whispered harshly, "and this will be your own personal hell."

Chapter 20:

Rain pattered against the roof, the single front light hanging over the entrance illuminating drops as they pitter-pattered down. A muddy puddle was already beginning to form just outside, and though rain was his favorite type of weather, Apollo scowled thinking about tracking any of that in with him when he left.

He'd already made a trip around the perimeter just to double-check that all his security measures were in place. Admittedly, Shade's confidence in Gael's abilities irked him, even knowing the best Inspector wouldn't be able to find them all the way out here.

His gaze shifted over to the detective, trailing down from his head to the curve of his plump ass.

Shade had fallen asleep less than an hour ago, curled up and facing the wall away from him. He'd been silent all through dinner—even though Apollo had gone upstairs and made him a burger and fries, his favorite—but he'd eaten at least. There'd been a chance he'd refuse and try starving himself, and while Apollo wasn't above force-feeding him like he'd done with the coffee the other night, he'd prefer not to have to.

The detective was a conundrum, even more so now that he had him where he wanted him. He'd thought things would become clearer once he got Shade here, but in a turn of events, the opposite had happened.

It was…interesting. Exciting.

It made him want to cut the other man open and crawl inside of him. He wanted to see and touch and feel everything. Wanted to pick him apart and figure him out like a pure white thousand-piece jigsaw puzzle.

And then he wanted to take that finished puzzle and paint over it in blood.

Obsession had been accurate. Even when he'd been walking around outside, gone for less than ten minutes total, there'd been this urgency clawing at him, screaming that he had to get back to Shade as quickly as possible and see for himself with his own two eyes the man was still there.

As if there was even a remote chance he'd managed to slip through his cuffs and escape.

As if there wasn't a security camera aimed directly at the mattress that Apollo could access from his multi-slate at any given moment.

Shade wanted to know what he was thinking, what he was doing, but the truth was, Apollo was operating on pure instinct.

He'd wanted Shadow Yor. So he'd taken him. And with the way things were going, he'd be keeping him. At least until that gripping sensation in his chest went away and he lost interest, but there was no telling when that would happen.

And if it didn't? If he never grew tired of the other man…Well. He'd worry about that if and when it happened.

Apollo was sitting in his chair by the workbench again. He'd been trying to get some work done while Shade was asleep, but the sounds of the other man's gentle breathing had distracted him and now that he was looking, he couldn't tear his gaze away.

It was tempting to wake him with his cock, teach his little Shadow not to turn his back on him, ever, but he refrained. Even a devil like him knew how to practice restraint when it was called for, and despite everything he'd said to Shade earlier, he *did* want to be wanted back. Not just because it would make things easier, but because a part of him he hadn't known existed demanded it. Craved it.

He was going to do everything in his power to ensure Shade fell totally and completely under his thrall, make it so the detective went crazy over him the same way he was crazy.

Shade had been mortified last night when he'd realized what Apollo was about to do. Usually, fear was something Apollo got off on, but he'd been angry about the accusation in Shade's tone, reminded of the way his dad had looked at him and called him a monster. The time his sister had told the whole school he was a psycho.

He *was*, but that was beside the point.

He'd only meant to give oral, reward him for how pretty he'd looked with his cheeks turning bright red and his eyes widening like saucers. The way his pulse pumped pleasantly against Apollo's palm as he'd squeezed…The plan had been to make Shade feel good after making him feel so bad.

But it seemed like Shade's real ability was being able to get Apollo to toss his plans out the window.

He didn't feel guilty about forcing him, didn't feel bad about the painful cries Shade had made or the tears that had flowed down his face.

What he hadn't liked, however, was the moment when Shade realized he was no longer being forced and he went still as a dead fish. Apollo had been doing all the work anyway, but the contrast to how it'd felt on the rooftop to how it'd felt when Shade had refused to participate beneath him…

The metal coffee can in his left hand crunched as he squeezed it. Another first, getting angry over sex.

Up until now, sex was something Apollo did to pass the time. If someone approached him and he was bored enough, he'd go home with them, then be gone by morning. No exchanging of numbers, no flirty texts or goodbye notes. Just one and done. Forgotten by breakfast.

He didn't have any problems getting it up, had experienced lust before, of course. When he'd been a horny teen, he'd jerked off just as much as the next hormone-overloaded kid. But he'd never been desperate for it. Had never woken in the middle of the night, hard, hot, and aching, humping his pillow like some virgin.

The very first night after seeing Shade at the crime scene, that's exactly what had happened to him. Apollo had come to and discovered he'd rolled onto his front and positioned his pillow between his legs. He'd opened his eyes, hips still pumping, his headboard slapping against the wall loudly, and had growled at the ridiculousness of it all.

Best orgasm of his life though, at least, up until that time on the roof.

Last night had left him wanting, and he wasn't a fan of wanting. If there was something that caught his fancy, he made it his, always had. Always would.

It was time Shadow Yor learned that lesson as well.

* * *

The storm had increased by morning, loud booms of thunder echoing throughout the warehouse. It was either the noise that finally pulled Shade out of sleep, or it was the chill bite to the air.

Even from where he stood over by the desk, Apollo could see the way it nipped at Shade's bare skin, goosebumps rising on his flesh.

He was hardly ever jealous, but the emotion ripped through him now. He wanted to be the one biting him, not the damn air. Stomping over to the workbench, he lifted his multi-slate from where he'd left it and clicked the button that would activate the force field at the entrance. It was invisible but glowed a soft blue for a split second to show it'd turned on.

The sound of the wind sweeping through the trees dimmed, and the breeze was cut off. They could still hear the storm, but it wasn't nearly as loud. Apollo hadn't been after silencing it anyway, just getting rid of the cold that was causing the detective to start to shiver.

It was fine though. Apollo planned on heating him up soon enough.

He'd brought out the heavy dining table and set it up on the other end of the workbench, so together with the desk it created a U shape instead of the L shape it'd originally been. At first, he'd thought about placing it elsewhere, but Shade wasn't ready to be let off his leash just yet, couldn't be trusted to behave without the chains secured around his wrists, even with what Apollo had in mind.

So he'd been forced to compromise, moving it within the bubble of space that he'd measured the chains to reach when he allowed it. Right now, he'd left Shade with five feet so he could sleep more comfortably, which meant as he sat up, there was plenty of room for him to stretch his arms and legs before shifting around to face outward.

The second he spotted Apollo standing there watching, he stiffened.

"Still haven't gotten used to not being able to read me?" Apollo asked, already knowing that was the case. Shade had spent his entire life hyperaware of every living creature within a fifty-foot radius. Of course he still forgot that Apollo was an exception to that.

Shade didn't reply, merely sat there on the edge of the bed and stared back.

Apollo nodded toward the table he'd just finished setting up. "I made breakfast."

He'd gone all out too, filling the table—big enough to fit a body on— entirely with dishes both traditional to Pollux and ones he'd looked up from Drax, where he knew Shade was originally from.

"You left when you were sixteen," he mused, taking in some of the dishes, even knowing from where he sat, the other man probably couldn't get a good look, "but that's old enough to remember what your favorite food was. I hope I got it, but if not there's always tomorrow."

Shade still didn't grace him with a comment, but that was okay. Apollo knew it took him a while to snap out of it when he woke up in the morning. He wouldn't even talk with Gael first thing, needing a hot shower and a cup of coffee to start his day off before it was safe trying to start up a conversation.

Apollo was blowing right through that routine on purpose. They needed to start building their own routines, needed to begin the process of getting his little Shadow to not only accept his new life, but to crave the attention Apollo gave him.

It shouldn't be too hard since Shade was already so starved for affection, a byproduct of the shit hand the universe had dealt him.

There was already a space for him inside the detective, but he couldn't just barge in, no, he'd run the risk of being shoved right back out of he did that. He needed to move slowly, give and take. He wasn't into catch and release, but he rather liked the idea of giving

Shade a little slack before reeling him in. How had the other man put it? Playing?

Apollo couldn't wait for the real games to begin.

He tapped another button on his multi-slate, this one controlling the locking mechanism in the wall panel behind Shade. The clicks of the chains unraveling finally caught Shade's attention enough to get a reaction.

The detective rose to his feet and frowned, tugging at his right wrist as if to test it. Chain spilled from the wall, a good couple of feet clanking to the mattress.

Gold. Apollo had gone with that color on purpose. Had pictured what Shade might look like bound by golden chains specifically, all that shiny metal matching the hue of his sun-kissed skin.

He hadn't been disappointed.

Suddenly he was starving, but not for breakfast. He needed to speed this up so he could get to the good stuff.

"Come here," he ordered, keeping his voice light so as not to scare the other man away. He liked the way Shade shivered when he was frightened and unsure of what Apollo planned to do next, but now wasn't the time for that. The goal at the moment was to coax him into a sense of security.

Still, Shade hesitated.

"It's just breakfast, Detective," he smiled, keeping the expression easy. "You've got to eat."

His eyes narrowed. "Don't do that."

Inwardly he swore, outwardly he kept up the relaxed disposition. "Whatever do you mean, Shadow mine?"

"There," he pointed at him, "that. That nickname gives it away. You're not nearly as clever as you think you are now that you've exposed yourself. I learn quickly."

Apollo was counting on it. "Are you saying you'd rather starve yourself?"

He'd eaten last night, but if he chose to be stubborn today, it'd throw a serious wrench in Apollo's plans and he would not be pleased.

Fortunately for him, Shade blew out a breath and ran a hand through his hair haphazardly before stepping off the mattress and making his way over to the table. He was cautious about it, but he came.

What a good little shadow.

Apollo had brought a wooden chair over as well and set it on the opposite side of the table, width-wise. He planned on using his, so he rolled it over, putting himself within the U shape and Shade just outside of it. His chains wouldn't reach much further than that anyway, but it kept him away from the desk where his computer was still setup.

Even if he managed to get his hands on it, Shade wouldn't be able to use it to call for help since it was bio-locked, but there were still a lot of things Apollo didn't know about him. Too many things for him to take unnecessary chances.

It took more than just average intelligence and good aim to reach the level in the I.P.F. that Shade had. He was a clever one, even if he spent most of his time trapped by his own mind, slave to the constant migraines.

Apollo would cure him of that though. All in due time.

Shade stared at the spread on the table, lips pursed, as if he was considering whether or not it was safe to eat. His gaze lingered a little longer on one particular dish, one of the ones Apollo had looked up from Drax, but that tight expression never wavered.

"It's not poisoned," he said dropping down into his chair first, hoping it would help hurry the other man along.

Sure enough, Shade lowered into the opposite seat, his back straight and his shoulders spread like he was taking photos for a book on perfect posture. Just, without a shirt.

Actually…

Apollo allowed his hungry gaze to drift down the hollow of his throat and chest, stopping only once Shade's torso disappeared beneath the table. He scowled at himself, and made a mental note to get one in glass next time before Shade spoke again, cutting through his thoughts.

"Could be drugged," he mused, though he didn't actually sound all that upset by the notion. He lifted his fork and then noticed the plastic knife Apollo had made a point of setting out for him. His brow dipped in annoyance when he saw that Apollo had a real one next to his plate.

"What?" He picked the knife up and set the sharp tip of the blade onto the wooden surface, spinning it idly. "Think I'd trust you with a weapon? I'm not a moron, Detective. I'm also not going to waste my energy drugging you. What'd be the point? Anything I want you to give, you're going to give me. Drugs won't be necessary."

"Like hell," Shade sneered, because as Apollo was coming to pick up on, the poor guy just couldn't help himself.

Shade cared an awful lot about sticking up for himself. It was almost as if his mindset was still stuck in the past, when he'd been a kid being picked on at school. If someone said something to him he didn't like, he snapped back. Didn't matter who it was.

Like that time at the station when Dario had invited Apollo without letting Shade know. He'd been frustrated because the older guy had ruined his plans to ice Apollo out, and he hadn't held any of that frustration back, he'd merely morphed it and made it sound like something understandable.

His reaction was legitimate when it was a superior scolding an officer for possibly risking classified materials.

It wasn't though if it was simply a man mad that the lover he'd been trying to ghost had been invited over despite his best efforts to avoid him.

Dario had been none the wiser and had felt bad about going behind Shade's back. He'd felt grateful toward the other man for allowing him to remain on the case, since typically I.P.F agents appeared and took over. Because of that, he'd been disheartened for causing Shade trouble.

Shade had to have felt all of that too though. Probably more strongly than Apollo had.

The detective liked to pretend he wasn't as big of a manipulator as Apollo was, but that was a lie. Every time he winced due to a migraine but smiled at his partner like everything was fine, he was lying. When he'd finally texted Apollo back a few days after ignoring his messages and claimed he'd been too caught up in the case?

Liar liar.

Apollo lifted his fork and speared one of the tiny round sausages that Shade had seemed to be interested in earlier, holding it up for him.

Rolling his eyes, Shade refused the offering, stabbing one himself. He put it in his mouth and chewed furiously, no doubt picturing it as one of Apollo's eyeballs instead.

Chuckling, Apollo ate the sausage himself and repeated the process with another dish. Same thing happened. Shade refused to be handfed, but he'd immediately get some of it himself. Which meant he was eating.

Exactly like Apollo wanted.

If the detective noticed what was happening—and he was too smart not to have picked up on it—he pretended not to, keeping his eyes cast down and his mouth constantly chewing one thing or another. He sipped at the coffee Apollo had poured earlier and set out for him, cream and three sugars, but didn't say anything about how it was made just right.

That was fine too. Apollo hadn't done it for verbal praise. He'd done it to make a point.

He knew Shade's likes and dislikes. He'd paid attention. Who else in Shade's life could claim that?

"Stop staring," Shade mumbled around a mouthful.

"Not my fault you look so delectable, Detective. I could just eat you up." He grunted when that had the other man tensing. "Not literally. Even I have my limits. Cannibalism isn't one of my kinks, thankfully for the both of us."

"Fine with slicing and dicing but draw the line at actually doing a taste test?" Shade asked. As soon as he had he scrunched his nose, clearly seeing how messed up that statement had been even though he'd been the one to say it. "I must be losing my mind."

"A bit early," Apollo said. "It's only day three."

Shade's hand tightened on the fork, and he paused for a moment before forcing himself to keep eating.

To keep up appearances, more like.

Truthfully, he was freaked out. Even though he'd slept like a log last night, he was mentally exhausted and confused. He was wary of Apollo and his intentions, but too stubborn to use that sexy voice of his and ask about it, so instead, he was going to sit there and stew and work himself into a tizzy, all while presenting the perfect picture of "I don't give a fuck, do your worst, it's just another day ending in Y" he could.

Shade may be able to see through Apollo's fake nice act now, but Apollo had seen through his masks first. There was no hiding from him, and shortly, he'd teach the man as much.

"Forgive me for finding the company of a psychopathic serial killer unpleasant." Shade drained the rest of his coffee in one go, setting the mug down with a sharp clatter.

"Is that what it is? Unpleasant?" Apollo shook his head. "Every time I touch you, you go still like a caught bunny, but we both know it's only partially due to fear. You like a little pain, like not knowing what's coming."

"You're delusional."

Apollo simply lifted a brow and waited.

"Fine," Shade acknowledged, and it was obvious by the way he was shaking slightly that it took a lot of willpower for him to admit it out loud, "I do, but the keyword there is *little*. What you did the other day? That shit *hurt*."

Apollo had momentarily lost his cool, but did he regret it? Hell. No. He'd do it again if the mood called for it, anything to force his Shadow into place. Besides, he'd brought the other man here to test his limits, to figure out how far he could push him and how much pain he actually liked.

Shade had cried and begged for him to stop at first, true. But that'd lasted less than a minute because Apollo had opted to take it easy on him after all and had started rubbing his cock. The combined stimulation of pain and pleasure had quickly had Shade changing his tune.

Right up until he'd realized what he was doing and that stubbornness had set in.

Apollo had hated it and had sworn to himself from here on out, he was going to have the other man sobbing for him, either in agony or rapture. It was up to Shade and his actions to decide, but either way, Apollo wasn't going to allow him to close up on him like that again ever.

"That was a punishment," he shrugged. "And you enjoyed it."

"I did not! I didn't enjoy any of that."

"Downplaying now? Your defense mechanisms are a bit predictable."

"That's rich coming from you," Shade said cryptically. He set his fork aside and leaned back in his chair, muscles flexing as he moved.

It took all of Apollo's willpower to keep his gaze from wandering and remained locked on Shade's face.

"Day three," Shade spoke as though playing with the words, testing them out on his tongue. "Know what that means, Psycho?"

He was doing it on purpose, but even knowing that couldn't stop Apollo from flinching. His hands tightened around the fork and knife. Typically, it wouldn't bother him that much, but something about the way Shade said it in particular reminded Apollo of his sister when she had sneered the word at him.

"It means I already had a chance to read the room. How did you put it the other night before you almost killed me?" Shade tilted his head as if contemplating the answer. "Ah, right. Reward." He tapped the table. "Here's the good. Which means there's a bad around the corner, just waiting for me to drop my guard. Not." Tap. "Going." Tap. "To." Tap. "Happen."

Yes, his little Shadow was definitely smart. Too smart for his own good.

Since he'd had both lunch and dinner on the mattress last night, he'd easily figured out Apollo must have a motive for hauling out a table and setting it up all pretty and proper. That's why he'd been suspicious of the dishes, not because he'd believed Apollo would drug him.

He'd been the one fishing, and Apollo had been so wrapped up in the anticipation of what was to come, he hadn't noticed.

Hubris. Even he suffered from it a time or two.

Instead of getting mad about that, however, all it did was stroke his ego and make him want to rise to the challenge.

Shade wanted to call him out and speed things along?

All right. He'd oblige.

Slowly, Apollo set his cutlery down and stood, staring at Shade until he saw the telltale signs that he was cracking under pressure. The moment he saw that self-doubt sweep through Shade's gaze, he struck.

Wordlessly, Apollo swept all of the dishes onto the floor.

Chapter 21:

Shade sprung back from the table as food and platters went flying. When he looked at Apollo like he'd grown a second head, Apollo almost laughed.

"I like it when you're scared, baby," he taunted, watching as Shade tried to move around the table, only for the chains to pull taught and stop him. That's why Apollo had sat him where he had. The only way for Shade to go was closer to the other end, where he'd be there waiting for him. "I was going to give it another few minutes. You're the one who pushed for this."

"Hold on." He held up a hand as if that would stave Apollo off, but all it did was draw attention to the shiny golden cuff secured around his wrist, and the long length of his well-defined arm.

"You work out a lot?" Apollo asked, easing around the table like he had all the time in the world, grinning when he saw Shade's breathing increase in tempo. "You've got an amazing body."

Shade opened his mouth to reply—no doubt with something else quick-witted—but whatever it'd been died in his throat when he saw Apollo take up the knife he'd discarded and drag the tip against the wood over to him.

Apollo kept it there, carving into the surface of the table as he gradually made his way to the end of the table and then turned so they were finally on the same side.

The detective tugged at the chains, eyes stuck on the weapon.

"Keep your guard up," Apollo said darkly. "I'll shatter through that pesky resistance of yours the same way I'll be breaking through everything else. What do you say? Want to start finding out where your limit is? Where that line starts to veer from pleasurable pain to just plain suffering?"

The chains were hovering in the air at his waist level and Shade hadn't seemed to notice the danger in that. Before he could, Apollo caught them up, twisting them around his hand and giving one strong tug that had Shade falling toward him.

He twisted them in a flourish, so the chains were now at both of their fronts, and then bent Shade over the table. Glancing down quickly, he grinned, pleased that he'd gotten the measurements right. The table was just high enough that Shade's ass was put at the same level as Apollo's cock.

At the sight, he swelled instantly, the teeth of the metal zipper biting uncomfortably against the root of his dick. In preparation for this, he'd forgone underwear, and knowing he'd never provided any to the detective, and all that stood between him and sliding in home was two pieces of fabric…He growled, the sound guttural, feral.

It had something going off in Shade, maybe instincts, and suddenly his struggling increased. He bucked against Apollo, trying to peel himself off of the table, slapping blindly back in an attempt to dislodge his arm from where he had it pressed against his shoulder blades.

Apollo shifted to use his hand to keep him pinned instead, slamming him down by the neck as he kicked out at Shade's heels, forcing his thighs to part.

Shade hissed and cursed at him, trying his best to get free despite the impossibility of his situation. At least he was moving though, participating.

"Keep fighting, baby," he twisted the knife in his hand so the sharp part was against his wrist and he could safely pull Shade's pants off, the shorts dropping to the ground with ease, "That's what I want."

He danced his knuckles over the curve of his left ass cheek, letting out a low whistle. Hand slipping lower when Shade bucked again, his fingers grazing the other man's balls.

"You're a fucking monster!" Shade snarled, glaring back over his shoulders, only just able to catch sight of him, no doubt.

Apollo brought his thumb to his mouth and swirled his tongue around it, getting it nice and wet. He'd considered making the detective do it, but something told him he'd try to bite it off, no matter what kind of threats Apollo made first. Better to get the lesson started and learned, then later he could test that limit.

Breaking someone physically was the easy part.

Breaking someone mentally? Now, that required finesse. Though, since his victims were always dead by the time the cops found them, there was no way for any of them to have clued the police in on that part of Apollo's process.

How long would it take Shade to realize what was going on, he wondered. He'd already picked up on it a little, had been able to see the trap that breakfast had been for what it truly was despite all of Apollo's best efforts.

Thinking about the detective's mind had him just as hard as the view of his body bent for him did, and he groaned when he pressed his thumb against Shade's hole, forcing his way in, instantly engulfed by silky heat.

Shade swore and floundered, trying to move away, digging his hips into the edge of the table in an attempt to escape as Apollo watched, riveted, as his thumb disappeared into his body.

"Look at you eating me up like a good little Shadow. You're so pretty. Your ass is so perfect, like it was made for me. Say you were made for me, baby."

"Go fuck yourself," he growled, but his hole fluttered around Apollo's finger at the praise.

"Now why would I do a stupid thing like that when I have you here practically begging for it?"

"You're delusional. I don't want you! Let me go!"

He pumped a few times before pulling out, and set a hand on Shade's lower back, just above his crease. He forced him flush against the table so his ass lifted a little more into the air, allowing him to catch sight of the impressive organ swinging between Shade's legs.

"Want a recap on why I don't trust anything you say, Detective?" Apollo licked his lips, loudly to be sure the other guy heard. "A few choice words and a thumb was all it took to get you dripping for me."

Shade's dick was caught between his body and the table, hanging low. As if summoned by those words, a pearly drop of precome slipped free from his slit and plopped to the cement floor between his feet.

He coated his fingers in Shade's juices, his own cock twitching in his pants when the contact had Shade sucking in a sharp breath. He gave him light touches only, barely rolling his fingers around the flushed crown, until he'd collected enough to be satisfied. Then he stuffed all three fingers into Shade's entrance, splaying them and curling them up to find that spot that'd have the other guy mewling for him like a kitten.

Sliding them out, he returned two, opting to go a bit easier on him. He set a steady pace, taking his time to stretch him nice and good, wanting for him to be open for him this time so things could go according to plan.

Apollo was the one who was left a hot needy mess though, moaning whenever he pulled his fingers out and Shade's body struggled to suck him back in, like it didn't want to let him go either. The squelching of his juices mixed with the rain, and though it was softer than that day on the roof with the storm ragging around them, he was reminded of it all the same.

Reminded of that feeling of complete and total bliss. The very same one he was chasing right now.

He didn't feel very much very often, but that didn't usually bother him. Emotions only seemed to get in the way, and he'd personally witnessed how they turned people into idiots and fools. Everyone always tried so damn hard to present their best selves to the world, not for the same reason Apollo did, not because it was fun or necessary for their continued survival—he might not feel empathy, but he understood if he was caught he'd be given the death sentence without fail. No, regular people did it because they were too afraid to be honest with themselves. Too scared of their true natures and how the rest of society would react if they ever found out about it.

Shade was no different. Shade hid behind his tough exterior and flippant words. But really, he was a little bit twisted on the inside, same as Apollo. He liked being pinned down and roughly taken, because it meant he didn't have to get stuck in his own head. Didn't have to overthink and over plot how he needed to be and whether or not it'd be safe for him or if Repletion might be an issue.

He'd never have to worry about Repletion again with Apollo.

"There you go, baby," he removed his hand and reached for his pants, slipping the button free and practically tearing the zipper down so that his cock sprung out, angry and red. The vein at the bottom looked like it was about to burst, and though he'd teased Shade about it earlier, he was the one who had a massive wet spot staining his jeans now. "Just like that. You don't have to worry about anyone else. Just you. Focus on how you feel."

It was the wrong thing to say.

Shade tensed up beneath him, going still in a repeat of what he'd done the other night.

But Apollo was prepared for it this time.

He lined up his cock and drove into him, gritting his teeth against the tight clenching of Shade's inner walls. The hot heat and the way he was compressed from all sides almost undid him, but he forced himself to remain focused, seating himself fully before moving the hand he'd been using to hold Shade in place.

Proof that the detective was doing this whole dead fish routine on purpose came when he didn't bother trying to get away even once Apollo's hand was off the back of his neck.

"I'm not fucking a damn pillow here," he stated, snapping his hips to make a point.

Shade clenched his jaw bad gave no other reaction.

"Oh, baby," his voice dropped into a husky drawl, "I was hoping you were going to play it like this. You really never disappoint, do you?" He gave him a split second for that statement to set in, for the frown to begin to mar the detective's face before he acted.

Apollo pealed Shade's front off of the table, one hand going to his hip to keep him steady while his other wrapped around his left shoulder and flicked the blade. He pressed the sharp edge right up against Shade's throat, noting the exact moment he realized what was happening by the way his muscles squeezed around him and his spine stiffened.

Keeping his hand in place, Apollo thrust again, hard enough that Shade's body was forced forward, right up against the knife.

Shade's skin was nicked and he hissed, instinctually pulling back to avoid making the cut deeper.

Effectively causing him to chase Apollo's cock, forcing another inch back inside.

Before he could lock up again, Apollo repeated the motion, even harder this time so that his pelvic bone slapped against Shade's ass cheeks loudly.

The detective tried to hold on to his stubbornness, he really did, allowing the blade to slice through until rivulets of crimson rolled down, staining Apollo's fingers where it gripped the handle. He only lasted ten seconds before he was sucking in a sharp breath and retreating from the weapon and back onto Apollo's waiting cock.

"Keep bucking back just like that," Apollo crooned, moving the knife a quarter inch closer so as to deter Shade from trying to defy him a second time. "Remember the sounds you made on the rooftop? It felt good for both of us when you cried out. Why are you holding yourself back, Detective? Who are you trying to impress here?"

"Fuck," he slammed back onto Apollo to escape the knife, only this time he also shifted on his feet, finding a more comfortable stance, "you."

It didn't seem like he was aware he was doing it, so Apollo decided not to tell him, liking the way Shade had tilted his hips up ever so slightly, causing him to stroke in even deeper than before.

"I'm the only other person here," he reminded him. "It's just you and me. I already told you what I want. How you can make me happy. Wouldn't you rather be good for me? Be my perfect little Shadow? Who are you trying to impress?" he repeated.

Shade growled and fucked back onto him with more force, almost as if he were trying to punish Apollo instead of the other way around.

Had he noticed Apollo had stopped thrusting? Shade was doing all the work now, which, admittedly was a bit hypocritical since Apollo had started this due to his anger over the other man's refusal to participate, but curiosity was getting the best of him. He wanted to see how far Shade would go on his own.

"Myself," Shade answered, and he sounded pissed. "I'm trying to impress myself."

He was pissed, when Apollo opened up his ability and did a quick read of him he could taste it. But he was also turned on like crazy, maybe even more than he had been on the rooftop and that—

Apollo *really* liked that.

"Why so judgmental?" He made a big show of sighing right against Shade's ear, just the way he seemed to like. "I've realized something, Detective. Well, actually, I've known it for a while now. I like watching you choke. Doesn't matter on what, and I'm looking forward to trying it with my fingers and my cock. Bet you'll be so pretty. Maybe I just have a thing for your neck in general." He brought the blade a little closer again.

They were both practically standing now, Shade's hands just barely still flat against the surface of the table, at either side of his hips. He was only partially bent, the nearness of the knife preventing him from leaning too far forward. As a result, their thrusts had turned shallow, Apollo's cock never fully leaving him, his head constantly beating against his prostate.

"Will you purr for me?" Apollo asked. "That's what I want. I want to hear you, baby, and if you're not going to give it to me...Should I slice your throat open instead? Watch you choke on your own blood?"

Shade's breath hitched.

"Oh, but then playtime would be over too quickly, don't you agree? And there are so many things I want to try with you still." He rolled his hips, ignoring the way his balls tightened, and focused on the short exhales Shade was giving instead. "Purr, baby," he urged, a bit more desperately this time. "Do it quick before I change my mind and see what you look like bathed in crimson after all."

Shade must have misunderstood his desperation as meaning he was being serious with his threat and losing control over his killer nature—he wasn't and he hadn't been, but whatever the detective needed to believe to get the job done, he supposed.

"Get rid of the knife," Shade said, speaking for the first time without any anger in his tone. "And I'll do it."

Apollo hesitated, though he knew he had him. He just didn't want Shade to know that he knew. "If you're lying to me…"

Shade shook his head, rubbing that already cut spot on the blade and grunted. "I'm not." He swallowed and then seemed to struggle to admit, "I'm close."

That was all he needed to hear since Apollo was at risk of blowing his load any second now. He tossed the blade across the room, uncaring of where it landed in that moment of desperation and shoved Shade back down to the table.

Shade didn't protest this time, didn't need to be held by the neck and forced. Instead, he reached out and gripped the opposite edge, holding on for dear life as Apollo was able to pull all the way out to the tip again and slam home.

He fucked into him brutally, the table legs scrapping against the floor as it was propelled by his momentum. It probably looked ridiculous, but Apollo didn't care. With every plunge of his cock, Shade pushed back to meet him.

And he was purring.

Well, he was moaning wantonly, but same thing. Shade had rested his cheek against the wood and closed his eyes, his lips parted as the sounds slipped freely from him.

Neither of them had been lying about how close they were.

With one final shove Apollo buried himself as deep as he could and exploded, his cock emptying itself as pangs of pleasure jolted through him. Beneath him, he felt Shade reach his own peak.

The detective cried, jerking around Apollo's burning cock as he emptied onto the floor, come splattering into a puddle.

Apollo didn't even care that he was going to be the one to have to clean it up. Maybe he wouldn't. Maybe he'd leave it there as physical evidence of what transpired here. Something he could point to whenever his little Shadow got snippy with him and tried to pull that dead fish act again.

Even the thought of him not having learned his lesson sparked a rage in his chest and Apollo dropped his body over top of his, not carrying when Shade sucked in a breath, probably getting crushed beneath his weight.

Instead of relieving the pressure, Apollo captured his mouth, driving his tongue inside in a mirror of the rough fucking they'd just finished. He bit and nibbled at Shade's bottom lip, at one point hard enough to draw blood, swallowing that and the other man's sharp cry. He needed Shade to know who he belonged to, needed to quell this particular act of rebellion while the iron was hot so they could move on to another lesson.

He kissed Shade like breakfast had never happened and he'd been starving himself for months. Kissed him long enough that one second he'd been spent and the next he was getting hard all over again, lengthening still inside of Shade's tight hole.

Shade whimpered and that was all Apollo needed to hear to get him to start thrusting, short but deep movements all he could manage without breaking the kiss, which he so wasn't about to do.

It wasn't until they were both grunting and twitching through another orgasm that Apollo realized that all the while, Shade had been kissing him back.

Chapter 22:

Shade found himself back on the mattress later, the cuffs keeping him tight to the wall as Apollo kneeled next to him, seemingly hyper-focused on the task at hand.

Which was applying ointment to the thin cut on Shade's neck.

"Did I hurt you, baby?" Apollo asked when he caught him watching.

"Yeah. On purpose. If you didn't hold a knife to my neck in the first place," Shade found himself saying, "you wouldn't have to bother doing this."

"I don't have to do it now," Apollo paused and smiled at him, but then he went back to gently cleaning the wound with the wet cloth he'd brought over before reaching for the small tube of cream. "I want to take care of you. It's not a chore."

Shade eyed him for a moment before gathering enough courage to say, "You also want to hurt me."

That smile turned wolfish. "I do."

"Why?" He licked his dry lips. "Why do you want to hurt anyone?"

"Are you asking as the detective or as the guy I'm currently fucking?"

"Forget it." It was true Shade was scared. He was worried about how things might escalate and couldn't stop thinking about the possibility of becoming a carefully laid out body for his partner to find at a construction site or outside a grocery store.

"You aren't that scared," Apollo corrected him, as if he could read his thoughts though there was no chance of it. At Shade's frown, he shrugged. "You're afraid of course, it'd be idiotic for you not to be. This is scary. A man you were interested in turned out to be a psychopath and now you're chained in the middle of nowhere."

"I'm not seeing the part where I'm supposedly not that scared," he drawled. "There isn't a single part of this that's not 'that scary'."

"Sure there is." Apollo's fingers carefully spread the ointment over the cut and then moved to tend to the bruises around Shade's wrists from when he'd been struggling against them on the table. "How's your head, Detective?"

"My head?" Shade's brow furrowed even more.

"Any signs of entering Repletion?"

Oh. "I can't read you and you're the only one here for miles."

"Or," Apollo switched to the other wrist, and Shade let him, "the sex is helping you relieve all that pent-up anxiety. Wasn't that one of the suggestions your last psychiatrist made? Find something that'll help pull you out of your headspace? She was certain your heightened ability to read people and your body's inability to properly sort through those readings and keep you stabilized was because of some mental issue."

"I'm not a mental patient," Shade snapped.

"Don't put words in my mouth," he said. "You're the only one here who thinks little of yourself. We've all got baggage from our past that we need to sort through eventually so we can move on with our lives. That's nothing to be ashamed of, and it's not all that special."

Shade stiffened.

"That's not what I meant." Apollo clucked his tongue. "You're a lot of work, you know that? I'm not saying you're not special, Detective. I'm saying you're not abnormal. There are cases of other Chitta experiencing the same thing you are right now, typically after a traumatic event. It's like a version of PTSD."

The rest of what he'd said before finally hit Shade and he snatched his hand away, ignoring the way Apollo sighed at him, as if he were a child fighting against taking his medicine or some such nonsense.

"You hacked into my medical files too?" Just how far was this guy going to go? "They're private."

"Nothing about you is private from me," Apollo corrected. "I want to know everything there is to know about you, and I'm going to. You can take that as a promise or a threat, it doesn't matter to me one way or the other."

"Why? Because you want to hurt me?"

Apollo sat down and tossed the tube of ointment to the other side of the mattress before crossing his legs. He rested his arms on his knees and motioned with his fingers. "All right. Ask me."

"I just did."

"No, ask me using specifics. I'll answer anything you want to know."

Shade tilted his head, suspicious.

"It's only fair," Apollo said.

"You very clearly told me you don't like being fair," Shade reminded him, but he wasn't about to waste this chance, so quickly added, "Why do you want to hurt people? Why do you want to hurt me?"

"I like it?" He shrugged and thought it over some more. "It's like there's this itch I can't scratch when I see people sometimes. It doesn't happen with most people, mind you. It's not like I want to go around seeing inside of everyone and their grandmother. Just the ones who hide things from the world. When they glitch and I can see their true faces? That's when my interest is piqued. I have to know what they look like when the mask is ripped off their face."

"So," Shade tried to follow, "you torture them until they show it?"

"I do research first," he admitted, though he was talking as if they were discussing how he spent his holidays and not how he selected and kidnapped his victims. "A lot of it can be found online. People post all kinds of things on social media. And what I can't find there, I find the old-fashioned way. Follow them around a bit to be sure I'm not wrong about them."

So Shade had been right about Imagine.

"Wrong that they're bad people?"

"Wrong that they're interesting people," Apollo corrected. "But if you feel better thinking about it that other way, by all means."

"Why?"

"Because I want you to like me, Detective."

"You failed then."

Apollo grinned at him. "Not yet. I'm still worming my way into you. Give it time."

"Confident."

"Always."

"Because you've done this with others?"

Apollo's flirty expression dropped and he scowled. "Never. I've never wanted to do this with anyone else before. I've never had the urge to tie someone up to keep them. It's always been about bringing them here and taking them apart. Once I've done that and I've seen all there is to see, I put them back together as best I can and then I discard them."

"You also expose all the horrible things they've done."

"I'm not a vigilante," Apollo said.

"I've realized." Shade had. In the beginning, he'd thought maybe that was what the killer was, sure. Even after meeting Maxen for the first time, there'd still been a chance. But the second he'd woken up here the truth of the situation had been impossible to miss. "It provides you cover. People are less likely to pressure the police into finding the culprit when they know he's only killing scumbags."

"Rapists and murderers rarely get any sympathy from the public," Apollo agreed, ignoring the pointed look Shade tossed his way then. "I fought against these urges for a long time for that very reason. I didn't want to be this way, Detective, I just am. Not being able to empathize with my victims makes it a hell of a lot easier. I don't care that I hurt people, and it's not the pain itself that I get off on. It's the look in their eyes when they realize that all the hiding in the world isn't going to save them from what's to come. From being exposed. You get that look sometimes."

Shade's heart skipped a beat, but not in a good way.

"Relax," Apollo said. "It doesn't spark the same reaction in me that the others did. I want to get inside of you, yes, but I don't want to slash you open and blindly feel around to do it. I want you to unfurl for me."

"No."

He leaned back on his palms. "You'll do it for me eventually."

"I won't."

"You'll enjoy it every bit as much as I will," he stated, then with a knowing look that Shade couldn't place, repeated, "How's your head, Detective?"

"The only way you're preventing me from entering Repletion is by keeping me here against my will away from society," he told him. "If that's your grand scheme, to hide me away forever, that isn't going to work. If that isn't it, and you're seriously trying to convince me you have a magic, healing dick or some such bullshit, you really are a psycho."

"Being a psychopath doesn't mean I'm dumb or delusional," Apollo retorted. "There are plenty of people like me who function just fine in the universe. That's not the part of me that makes me like killing, it's just the part that makes it so I don't feel useless guilt after the fact when I'm left standing over a mutilated corpse dripping in their gore."

Shade rolled his eyes.

"Interesting that that's your reaction," Apollo pointed out.

"I've seen a lot worst on the job before." Not entirely true, but not a complete lie either. "People can be terrible to each other. That's nothing new."

"You mean I haven't single-handedly obliterated your belief in humanity?"

"Sarcasm, really?"

"Why? Because we're talking about me being a serial killer and you dealing with horrible things like that all the time? You said you took this job because you had to. Still think that?"

"Are you asking if I like what I do?" Shade wanted to lie and say he did but the other guy would see right through him, so why bother. "Not really. I like being able to work with Gael and I like the praise I receive after each case that I solve, but that's about it."

"Still thinking you're going to solve mine, is that it, Detective? Trying to be subtle about it?" Apollo leaned back in, propping his elbow up on his thigh. "Want to know why that's not going to happen?"

"You plan on keeping me here forever?"

"I plan on keeping you with me forever," he nodded, "but the location doesn't matter. That's not what I was going to say."

"I don't want to hear what you were going to say." Shade was certain he didn't. That glimmer of mischief had reentered Apollo's eyes and he got a bad feeling in his gut telling him not to listen to whatever he was about to tell him.

"The tattoo didn't do it for you for a reason," he motioned to the ink trailing down Shade's right side. "That's why you only have one, isn't it? You went there hoping the pain would ease something inside of you that's been coiled for a while now, but it didn't, and you left dismayed and never tried again."

"How could you possibly know that?" That certainly hadn't been in any digital files Apollo could have hacked into. He hadn't even been able to tell Gael, too embarrassed to go into the details, especially when it'd been over and he hadn't felt anything from the experience except for burning, unpleasant, pain.

"Any old pain won't cut it," Apollo ignored him and continued. "There's a method to everything, even madness—again, not that I think you're crazy, you aren't. There's nothing wrong with liking it, Shadow."

"I don't." If he had, the tattoo would have done the trick.

"It's okay if you're not ready to accept it, but, baby? The reason you're not going to toss me in a prison cell like you threatened before is simple." He shot forward, forcing Shade to gasp and press back against the wall. Apollo slapped a hand next to his head, hard, his knees planting onto the mattress between Shade's now-opened thighs. The fingers of his free hand reached out, tweaking Shade's nipple, lightly at first, before pinching hard enough to have him cry out.

Apollo continued to twist and pull, smoothing his thumb over the sting now and again before starting the process up from the start. He shifted forward, knee bumping against the spot between Shade's legs, and started to rotate in slow circles, applying the barest amount of friction to his dick.

Shade tried to resist the pull of desire, he did, but before long the burning sensation at his chest wasn't enough to block out the friction against him down there, and he felt himself swell and push against the stretchy material of his shorts.

"I'm the only one who knows exactly how to touch you right," Apollo said.

It took Shade way longer than it should have for him to connect that sentence with the ones the man had been speaking before he'd put his hands on him, but once he had, he only had a second to feel irritation before Apollo was tugging him free from the confines of his pants and dropping his mouth down on him.

He swore, back bowing when Apollo swirled his tongue around Shade's flushed crown, and for the rest of the evening, everything else completely vanished from his mind.

Chapter 23:

There really was a method to any kind of madness, even the one sparking between Apollo and Shade.

Apollo had fought against it at first, despite all of his comments about owning his nature. He hadn't liked the way wanting the detective had made him feel, distracted and desperate and on edge. He'd gotten his system down pat, hunting a carefully executed art form he'd perfected over the years, and the thought of all that hard work going down the drain all because he lusted after Shadow…

He'd been angry about it for a while, but that anger had long since dwindled. Giving into his desires made everything easier, and this situation was no different.

A few days after he'd admitted to Shadow that he'd stolen his medical files, Apollo watched the security footage of the other man from the bathroom. He'd gone in alone and turned the shower on, but he'd been finished for a while now and was merely stalling.

Shade was getting more and more squeamish with every passing second. His gaze kept flickering from the workbench and the table where the computer was kept to the bathroom door. He even tested his chains a time or two, as if they'd somehow loosened and he could get free.

Apollo watched as he sat on the edge of the bathtub, staring down at the small screen of his multi-slate, anticipation bubbling up in his gut.

There were two things he was waiting to see, and so far Shade had shown him one of them already.

He didn't feel bad that he was manipulating Shade, but he did want to test out how well that manipulation was taking. He'd put a lot of work and energy into this whole thing, into getting Shadow here under his control, and since he'd already come to terms with the fact that he fully intended to keep him, his plan had to work.

Shadow had wanted him prior to discovering who he really was. He'd wanted the friendly, charismatic Apollo who everyone else liked having around, sure, but he'd also liked the Apollo who pinned him to the wall and bit at his throat and took him unapologetically.

The more Shade's mouth said no, the more his body screamed yes, and Apollo took pleasure from that fact.

Was it wrong? Fucked up? Forced?

Sure.

If he was a better person he would care. But he wasn't and he didn't. What he cared about was making Shadow Yor his, and to do that, he needed to drill into the stubborn detective's head that he wanted this every bit as much as Apollo did.

Because that was the truth.

Apollo could taste it in the air, knew what Shadow was feeling even if he was in denial. The more he took care of the detective, the deeper those feelings seeped into him.

Which was also why he'd put them on a schedule. He wasn't sure if Shadow had noticed it yet—he probably hadn't, since he was too busy fighting against himself and his inner demons—but Apollo was making good on his promise to acclimate the man to him.

Every other day he touched Shade, he licked him and kissed him and got him off on his fingers, his tongue, and his cock. He made him come more times than either of them could count, until Shad had turned pliant in his arms with tear tracks staining those rosy cheeks.

Apollo would always leave behind marks, even if he fucked him slow and steady, sure to deliver the right amount of pain to have Shade purring and arching in his hold, completely lost to arousal. It was the best way to quiet those damn voices in the detective's head, and also the best way for Apollo to slowly turn into an addiction for him.

There was a reason people loved sex so much. It was every bit as psychological as it was physical, and Apollo was sure to touch on all of those hidden places inside Shadow that had been neglected over his lifetime.

He bit and spanked and choked him. Fucked him hard enough to make him scream, sometimes even beg for him to stop. But he always made sure Shadow came, and afterward, Apollo took great pleasure in taking care of him.

Aftercare was something he hadn't been aware he'd be interested in himself, but there was something special about pulling Shade in close and whispering comforting words into his ear, feeling his racking sobs as he buried his face against the curve of Apollo's neck—a move which had started as hiding but had quickly morphed into something else.

Now, when they were done, Shade came to him without prompting, seeking out comfort and connection.

And Apollo was always there to give it to him. To brush his hair off his damp forehead and clean up the mess from both of their releases. He applied ointment to any of the bruises he'd left behind, brought Shade snacks and water.

For all his arguing in the beginning, less than two weeks later and Apollo had already made serious progress.

On the days when he didn't fuck him, Apollo still stuck close by, answering more of Shade's questions, most of them about the case. The detective was still determined to uncover everything he could about the victims, which meant he still intended to arrest Apollo the first chance he got.

Apollo would just have to make sure that chance never came.

Still, there'd been no need to force-feed him like he'd had to that first night with the coffee. No struggles when he unchained him from the wall and led the detective to and from the bathroom.

Shade had asked once what was kept upstairs, but when Apollo had shrugged and said "nothing much" he'd let it go. If he was still interested, he didn't say.

At night, when Apollo snuggled in close at Shade's back, holding him hostage against himself, there were still often snarled words and empty threats, but with each passing day, those threats lost more and more bite. Maybe the detective didn't notice, but Apollo did.

The change in Shadow could easily be explained. It was Apollo's doing, after all. He was forcing this, tricking him into a sense of ease and comfort. Logically, Shadow must know that this was messed up and he was a captive, but illogically…His body would have stopped caring.

Case in point, the fact that his dick twitched to life in his pants whenever Apollo approached. The longer he went without touching the detective, the needier he became, and that meant he became meaner as well.

It'd sort of become a tell, the moment Shadow started cursing him openly and calling him a psycho, that was Apollo's cue to hold him down and fuck him.

His little Shadow liked being shown who was boss, it was actually comforting for him, even if he'd never admit it. In a universe where no one had ever shown even the slightest bit of interest in him, knowing there was someone who wanted him bad enough to *take* him got Shadow off like nothing else.

He thought he was doing a good job of hiding it.

He was wrong.

Apollo had pegged that about him before they'd even come to the warehouse though. Shade had never stood a chance.

It was Apollo's change that was unexpected.

Not only did he enjoy those softer moments between them when he was cleaning the detective up and cuddling after, but everything else as well. That obsessive yearning didn't dim the longer they were together, there was no calming of the storm as he'd anticipated. He wasn't growing bored or losing interest, if anything the exact opposite.

Apollo wanted more. He could take and take and take from Shadow and he was starting to think it would never be enough.

And in the same way Shadow's ability was finally stabilizing, that devil inside of Apollo seemed to be as well.

He hadn't lost his edge, still liked choking the detective and watching his eyes bulge, but he could satisfy that darker part of himself simply by bending Shadow over his knee. The sound of his palm whacking against his skin, the way the detective jolted, and the delicious red handprints left behind…all of that soothed that wickedness within him, satiating it.

Apollo had no interest in hurting anyone else, in making them show their true selves to the world. Every day he woke up, excited to make Shadow show him, and that was enough.

So they settled into a routine, both of them secretly dealing with their own inner demons, Apollo more welcoming to his than Shade was to his own. He picked himself apart in those hours where he pretended to work and Shade was left alone on the mattress with only old paper books to keep him distracted—Apollo had given them to him so he'd stop complaining of the boredom, go figure. Every other day, he'd fuck his little Shadow, and on the days that he didn't, he'd catch the other man getting hard and trying to hide it, clearly annoyed at the both of them.

It couldn't last forever, of course, eventually, they'd need to leave this place and find another or risk eventual exposure, but Apollo wasn't too worried about that yet. Besides, if he had to drug Shadow, knock him out and carry him out to the hovercar to move them, he would.

And if a small part of him shook its head at that idea, sulking a bit, well screw that part. They were too deep in this and Apollo wasn't going to risk letting Shadow out of his clutches.

The detective was his, and he wasn't too afraid to acknowledge that maybe a sick part of himself was also becoming the detective's as well.

Apollo gave it another ten minutes until he could see Shade visibly getting concerned, gaze no longer touching the bathroom door but lingering on it now.

From this distance Apollo couldn't taste his emotions, was going purely off of sight, so he stood and made his way to the exit. He'd gotten what he'd needed anyway. Proof that Shadow was still intent on escaping.

And that he was developing an attachment to his captor.

* * *

"What are you doing?" Shade asked, glanced up from the book he'd been reading from, and gave him a suspicious look.

It was one of the days that Apollo wouldn't be fucking him, however, so ignoring the way the detective's gaze dropped pointedly down to the hard-on pressing against Apollo's jeans, he replied, "I'm going over how much remote work I have left."

Shadow set the book aside, calculation entering his eyes. It was too obvious that he was choosing his next words carefully.

There was still much progress to be made between the two of them. He got off on Apollo's viciousness in the bedroom, but he still very clearly didn't trust him.

"Meaning you'll have to return to the office soon or risk getting fired," he finally said.

"Don't get any misplaced hopes," Apollo drawled.

"If you show up, I have to as well," Shade pointed out, ignoring the warning. "Or are you trying to think up a way to explain your being there without me?"

"I'm not going to kill you." He knew that's where this was headed and hated how that caused a pang in his chest. He didn't like thinking about the detective worrying over whether or not he was going to become the next victim in the news.

"Why not?" Shadow asked.

"Because you're mine." Slowly, he stood from his chair and stretched his arms over his head. "And I don't break my own things."

"Just other people."

"When are you going to stop pretending that bothers you?"

"When it actually stops bothering me," Shade countered. "So never."

"Do you think about the people from your past cases?" Apollo asked.

"No," he admitted.

"Never?"

Shade glared, figuring out where he was going with this. "It's not because I don't care, it's because I have too much going on to think about every single person I've ever come into contact with. Speaking of, did you have something to do with what happened to Axel?"

Apollo was surprised it'd taken him this long to ask. "I was with you, remember?"

"Sure, but Maxen was your guy—"

"You're my guy," he corrected. "The only one."

He watched as Shade swallowed, his throat working, and considered breaking his own rule and fucking him after all.

"How did you and Maxen meet?" Shade said, clearly struggling against the attraction he was feeling as well. He shifted on the mattress, crossing his legs as if he could hide the growing bulge from Apollo's notice. "Did you see him and—"

"The only interest I've ever had in him is how I can use him," he stated dryly. "Stop, Shadow. You're the only one for me. The only one there ever was."

"Want me to swoon?" Shade grunted. "Feel all tingly inside because you're making it sound like I'm special and you waited for me?"

"You are special," he insisted, "but no, I didn't wait for you. I didn't want this any more than you did."

"So put an end to it."

"And damage us both?" He clicked his tongue. "I don't think so. The trauma you suffered being abandoned once was enough, don't you agree?"

"The difference is I loved and trusted my parents," Shade told him. "I don't feel anything for you."

"Baby," Apollo sighed, "I can read you, remember?"

Shade pursed his lips, switching the topic back over, obviously too much of a coward to continue on that particular path. "Does Maxen like seeing inside of people too?"

"In a way," he nodded, "but we're not the same. Sometimes he helps me if I call, but that's the extent of our relationship. I asked him to come to the press conference and told him how to react to get your attention. Then I ordered him to make a run for it."

"Leading me straight to you."

"Exactly." Apollo glanced pointedly at Shade's side. "Why a rose?"

"Axel really liked you, you know."

He rolled his eyes. "I had nothing to do with that."

"If Maxen was brought back to the station, he could have turned on you."

"He wouldn't have."

"How can you be so sure?"

"Because he idolized me," he said with a shrug. "And while he enjoys seeing the blood and the guts, he's too squeamish to do any of the hard work himself. He would have kept his mouth shut and trusted that I'd figure out how to get him out of there."

"There was no way—"

"Did you forget the part about how I have lots of money?" Apollo was loaded. "There isn't anything in this entire universe that can't be bought."

"I can't be," Shade stated stubbornly.

"Not with money," he agreed, "no. To fully answer your question so we can drop it, did I care when I heard Axel was in the hospital? No. But did I orchestrate how he got there? No. I wasn't paying attention to the case or the best ways to avoid getting caught, Shadow, I was paying attention to you. You know that's the truth because if it wasn't, I—"

"Would have tossed me off the rooftop like originally planned," Shade waved him off grumpily, but it was clear by the way his shoulders slumped slightly that he finally believed him, "yeah, yeah. I got it."

"Look at me," he demanded, wanting to know if that reaction was due to relief or a lack of fight, pleased to find it was the first when Shadow dutifully lifted that hazel gaze.

He was glaring, but he'd followed the command so...Apollo would let it slide.

"Now," he leaned back against the edge of the desk and crossed his arms, "tell me about the tattoo."

Shade immediately dropped his eyes, picking at the threads of his purple shorts.

"Tell me."

"Or what?" Shade snapped.

Apollo grinned and shook his head. "Don't think you're going to get me to touch you, Shadow mine. It's not going to happen. In fact, if you keep refusing to be honest with me, I might just make you sit there with that," he motioned to Shade's erection, "all day tomorrow as well."

It was obvious by the look he sent him he didn't think Apollo would be able to contain himself that long, and Apollo laughed.

"I didn't say I'd abstain," he clarified. "I'll just keep you chained right where you are and work myself into orgasm just out of reach. You can watch me rub my cock and squirm over your neglected one. How does that sound?"

For someone like Shade, it would sound awful. He got off on being touched. It made him feel wanted. Skin-to-skin contact, of any kind, even if it hurt, was Shade's particular love language. Denying him that was worse than any other threat Apollo could've made, especially now that Shade was so used to coming on the regular.

Before this, he hadn't been very sexually active. Now that his body had a taste of what it was like...

"Black roses symbolize major change and new beginnings," Shade bit out, pissed off about being backed into yet another corner.

Apollo felt his lips stretch into a knowing smirk. That's why he'd been too embarrassed to tell him right away. "Aren't we the perfect pair, Shadow mine?"

"No," he said. "We aren't."

He tsked. "Our tattoos may be different, but they mean relatively the same thing. What was it you asked me? Why not a phoenix? So, why not?"

"They can also stand for life after death," Shade replied, "and I don't want life after, when it's too late. I want life now."

"I'll give it to you, baby," Apollo found himself saying, the urge to make promises so fierce within him he couldn't stop the words from flowing. "We're almost there. Just a little bit longer and you'll be willing to accept everything from me and yourself. Then I'll give you the life you've always dreamed of."

"What? Pretending not to care when you sneak off to kill someone?" Shade asked.

"I won't." He was just as shocked to realize that he meant it as Shade was to hear it. But it was true. "You're all I need."

There was just one more job to complete, more like a chore now than anything, and then Apollo was willing to step away from the hunt if it meant he'd get Shadow's approval. If it meant he could coax the other man to willingly run away with him.

"You're all I need," he repeated, holding Shade's gaze hostage as he added, "and I'm all you need too."

Chapter 24:

Someone was yelling. Shade furrowed his brow in his sleep and tilted his head toward the noise. No, his mind corrected, not yelling. Crying. It sounded like they were hurt.

He blinked, needing a moment to adjust to the harsh light of day before the sounds caught his attention and helped drag him the rest of the way out of his sleepy daze. He rolled up and winced when the bruises on his hips from the edge of the table yesterday where Apollo had fucked him after dinner smarted. But he didn't have long to think about his own discomfort.

The sobbing, because that's what it was now, heavy, full-on sobs, was coming from the computer screen on the desk. It'd been turned to fully face him so he could see everything taking place there.

For a moment he was trapped, unable to look away from the horrific scene playing out before him. Then there was a loud bang and the sobbing came to an abrupt halt and before he knew what was happening, Shade was hunched over on the floor emptying the contents of his stomach.

"I'd tease you for being a detective who can't handle a little gore," Apollo's warm voice cut through the pounding in his ears, "but that one was admittedly a lot, even for me."

Shade whipped his head in the direction of the voice, accusatory glare already prepared.

Apollo was leaning up against the table, arms and ankles crossed. The pose was casual, but there was tension in his broad shoulders and at his firm mouth that gave him away. When he glanced over at the screen, he scowled and lifted the multi-slate set on the chair behind him to shut the video off.

"Why the hell would you show me that?" Shade demanded, still feeling a bit sick.

"Because you would never have believed me if I hadn't made you see it for yourself."

"Believed what?"

"That that," he pointed to the screen, "is the type of vile garbage you're trying to get justice for, Detective. Him, and all the others like him deserve everything they have coming to them and more."

Shade rested back on his heels, stunned into momentary silence.

"If you tell me you're actually an avenging angel, or a vigilante, or that you're doing this for the betterment of Polluxians all across the planet, I will throw up again." Speaking of, Shade gaged at his vomit and tossed the blanket Apollo had given him last night over top of it.

He was wearing a shirt too. He wasn't exactly sure why, but something told him they were meant to act as rewards for "good behavior", aka, for fucking him back.

Shame threatened to rise but he shoved it down, focusing on the taste of bile on his tongue and the horrible video he'd just watched.

Apollo looked at the blanket and sighed in obvious disapproval. "Don't worry, I'll get you a new one."

"That's the least you could do after springing something this messed up on me." He pointed over his shoulder at the screen, not even wanting to face it even though it was off now.

"You seem all right."

"I threw up!"

"From the shock, not from the actual sight of it."

"That's…" Shade didn't like what that said about him *if* it were true. So far, he wasn't a fan of anything that had happened to him since waking up in this place.

As if to protest, memories of the sex they'd been having played through his mind, and he couldn't deny that he'd enjoyed it. That the orgasms had been amazing but the after, when Apollo held him close and acted like he cared, brought him dangerously close to that blissful state of being he'd been chasing ever since he'd been abandoned.

Because Apollo had a knack for making him feel cherished and wanted even as he was abusing his poor as and tightening the chains. With each passing day, Shade felt more and more comfortable with the idea of this being his future and he couldn't allow that to happen.

He *couldn't* want it.

He couldn't be sexually attracted to the type of man who'd wake him with a video of a guy smashing someone's skull to bits *while they'd still been alive.*

"You see monsters all the time, Detective," Apollo said, pushing off the table to wander over toward the workbench. As he rounded the dining table, his fingers trailed across the knife marks he'd left on the wood almost fondly, though it didn't appear as though he noticed what he was doing. "So do I. We just…handle them differently."

"You can't just go around killing people," Shade stated, "no matter what they've done."

"No?"

"No." Shade got it—he fucking hated that he did, but there it was. He understood what Apollo meant by seeing monsters too. He didn't mean in the literal sense, with his regular eyes or through footage like the video he'd just played. He meant through the empathic ability they both shared.

Shade had seen monstrous true faces with the Glitch, some of them aimed at animals, others at children. It made him sick to the stomach each and every time, but in most cases, there was nothing he could do unless an actual crime was committed. He'd learned that lesson the hard way, when he'd broken a kid's nose in high school for having twisted feelings about a girl who wasn't interested in him.

The principal had pointed out that feelings didn't equate to actual thoughts or legitimate action, that even though Shade was certain he'd been considering raping the poor girl, he hadn't, and therefore Shade was the one in the wrong.

The thing he'd always hated the most about becoming a detective was that he still had to wait on the sidelines for something bad to happen before he could do anything about it. Preventative measures? What a joke. Reports came in all the time about stalking incidents and domestic violence. The first were typically told to wait it out and ignore it, the latter weren't taken serious unless there were physical marks, and even then, they had to be serious and backed by a medical professional.

Henry Ight, one of Apollo's victims, had been beating a colleague, and Shade hated that just as much as the next person in his positon would. But even *if* that was the reason Apollo had targeted him, and it was a big if, that still didn't make what he'd done to the man *right*.

On the other hand...No one had known what Henry was doing. Even when they'd investigated after his body had been found, the police hadn't uncovered anything suspicious. He'd been that good at covering his tracks. At hiding the demon lurking within...If Apollo hadn't taken action, would it have been Suli's body they'd discovered murdered outside that grocery store instead?

"How do you even know what people are feeling if you can't feel it yourself?" he asked, trying to cover up the way his own feelings were twisting into confusing knots. "You had to have identified the smells somehow."

"I can see it through the Glitch," Apollo said. "It was easy enough to match up the similar scents that way.

And it's not that I can't feel anything at all. I do have feelings, Detective. I feel happiness, excitement, boredom—"

"Jealousy, arrogance, anger—"

"Lust." Apollo crossed his arms and gave Shade a pointed stare.

Recognizing it now, Shade scrambled to keep the conversation going. It'd already been a couple of weeks and what Shade needed was to try and find a way out, which he couldn't do with the other man's dick constantly inside of him. Something he sort of got the impression Apollo was doing on purpose. He wanted Shade distracted, wanted him to spend all of his waking hours wondering when or if he was going to have sex with him again so that he wasn't thinking about escape or how to do it.

"So you just," Shade shrugged, "what? See a weird Glitch and go that's the one? That's the next person I'm going to brutally murder? People do shitty things all the time. How do you choose? And where do you even find them? Henry Ight didn't have a criminal record. There was nothing to link him to the things he'd done until—"

"His victim came forward?" Apollo quirked a brow and waited for Shade to read between the lines.

"You want me to believe she did that because of you?" He snorted.

"No," he corrected, "she did it because of you. Because I needed to get close to you and a break in the case was a good way to do it."

"And all of these people really leave no clues behind beforehand? There was no other option but to kill them yourself?" Shade pointed to the computer screen. "That can't be true. There's no way that many people were able to keep their shit hidden that well."

"You don't actually believe that, Shadow," he stated dryly. "You can't possibly."

"Why not?"

"Because you're no fool. You're Chitta. You've seen how easily people hide in plain sight. Hell," he held out his arms, "look at me."

"You're a rare breed," Shade said, but…Apollo was right about that too, damn it. Half the cases he was put on were about horrible people whose neighbors told the media they would have never guessed.

Apollo didn't report these people, not because they most likely wouldn't be convicted, or out of some twisted sense of justice. No, he didn't call them in because he wanted to punish them his own way, wanted to use them to satisfy his own needs. If they were all monsters, he was the devil who lorded over them, and a part of him had to get off knowing that as well.

But there was a softness to him too, a side that he didn't let out too often. A side he only showed to Shade…

Self-hatred pricked at him, but the worse part was how brief it actually was. The problem with knowing you were being conditioned was it didn't help. It made him feel worse about himself, sure, but that was the extent of it. It couldn't stop his brain from conforming, couldn't stop his body from adjusting to Apollo's ministrations.

Shade was being conditioned to accept things about himself he'd rather pretend didn't exist, and to accept his new circumstances and eventually welcome them.

He didn't want to, but...His body ached those days he went without Apollo's touch, and not simply because he went to bed hard. When Apollo took care of him afterward, when he stroked those fingers down Shade's spine and whispered how good he'd been for him and how pleased that'd made him...Shade felt safe.

Safe. In the arms of a serial murderer.

"Gonna puke again, baby?" Apollo thankfully cut through his thoughts, pulling him out of his spiral.

"Walk me through it again." Shade really, really didn't want him to, but even chained and defiled like he was, it was impossible to shake free from the mindset of a detective.

"The urges have always been there," Apollo surprised him by complying, answering lightly. "Ever since I was young, I've always been interested in taking things apart, seeing all the pieces laid out before me, and trying to put it all back together again. Everything is just a puzzle, Detective, even people, you just have to know where to find all the parts and figure out how they all fit together. Then anything you don't like you can simply," he made a pinching motion with two of his fingers, "pluck out."

He may actually be about to throw up again, yes.

"This has never been about justice for me," Apollo said. "Not once. I like knowing I'm taking out trash, that I'm not lowering myself to their standards by picking on the weak and the innocent, but that doesn't mean I wouldn't do it if it came to that. If someone pissed me off or said the wrong thing and I snapped. We aren't the same, Detective. Not in that regard, anyway."

"I'm not in it for the justice either." Shade had no clue why he'd just admitted that, but since he had and there was no turning back, he dropped his gaze and forced out. "I only took this job because my options were limited. Join the Academy or try to make it on the streets. The first seemed the easier of the two."

He was no saint. Did he like being thanked at the end of a case? Did he like knowing he'd saved someone and they could go on with their lives because of his help? Sure. It was nice. But it didn't set his heart on fire or urge him to keep crawling out of bed in the morning. Shade was a detective because he'd been trained to be one and he was good at, great at it, really. It put food on the table and provided him with a place to stay. On Percy, the man-made planet where most of the agents of the I.P.F in this galaxy lived, people in his neighborhood knew him.

No one batted an eye when he walked into the grocery store, or shied away from him when they both went to test to see if the fruit was ripe. Because they were all used to living amongst a Chitta. It didn't mean they were friends, people were friendly toward him, but it rarely ever escalated into friendship, however it was comfortable. If Shade didn't have that, if he had to live somewhere surrounded by strangers who always either frowned because he was wincing or whispering behind his back, trigging his PTSD and his paranoia...None of that sounded appealing.

"If that's what you've thought of me all this time," he chuckled humorlessly, "sorry to disappoint, but that's not who I am. I don't get off knowing other people are suffering, but I don't lose sleep over it either."

Shade's entire life, he'd had enough of his own problems to keep him awake without needing to tack on anyone else's.

Apollo was quiet for a long moment, and the tension seemed to soar to new heights, making it hard for Shade to breath. But then his voice cut through the silence, drawing Shade in like a moth to the flame, even as he recognized the danger for what it was.

"You're perfect, Detective. Don't fret. I wouldn't ask for you to be any other way. There's nothing wrong with you, nothing wrong with being an empath who doesn't put empathy as their topmost concern. Look at all the people out there who do worse than that? You could never disappoint me for being who you are."

Shade bristled even as warmth settled in his chest and seemed to wash outward, throughout his entire body. "I know what you're doing."

Apollo was stroking that part of Shade that craved love and affection. Acceptance. He was telling him all of the things he'd longed to hear from someone, anyone, ever since he'd been a kid abandoned on the side of the road outside of the orphanage. Sometimes Gael told him he'd done a good job. His captain back on Percy said the same when he solved a case. But they were empty words, fleeting.

Shade worked his ass off time and time again just so he could hear that one phrase at the end of it all. That one phrase that came and went, uttered only half seriously before he was tossed another case and his accomplishment over the one he'd just solved was wiped away and he was forced to start fresh. Always a clean slate. Always a slate he tried to get the word "good" stamped across.

He'd accumulated enough of them that he'd earned his neighbors and coworkers acting like it didn't bother them that he could read their emotions. The privilege of simply walking down the street and not having others recoil? He'd earned that.

He'd had to.

Yet here was Apollo, giving it away like it was free, like it was a no brainer that he accept Shade for who he was, and even commend him for it. And someone help him, Shade knew that's what he was doing. Knew he was being manipulated and strung along and pulled like saltwater taffy but...

That warmth in his chest continued to spread, a pleasant glow that settled inside of him like a live thing. A thing that soothed his inner child and seemed to say, "Look how much he cares? Look how much he accepts you? Look how well you are loved?"

Which was laughable, because Apollo didn't love him. That's not what this was. Great fucks did not a soulmate make.

"I know you do," Apollo said, "I want you to know."

"Why?" Shade shouldn't have asked. He wasn't going to like the answer, he could already tell.

"Because I'm twisted, Detective. I intend to own you, body, mind, and soul. I'm well on the way to the first and the second. The third is a little harder to achieve but I'll get there, I promise you, I will. And when I do, when I have you lapping at the palm of my hand, attached to my heels like my true little shadow, it'll be all the sweeter knowing you knew what I was doing the whole time and yet it happened anyway."

"No," Shade's voice shook, words coming out breathy and even he couldn't tell if it was from fear or…something else. Something he still didn't want to admit even in his own headspace. "No, it won't."

"What do you think is going to happen then, Detective?" Apollo cocked his head, eyes narrowing slightly. "You think you'll figure out a way to save yourself?" He clucked his tongue. "The only way to salvation is through me. Shadows can't survive in the darkness, baby. You've tried your best. You've been trying. You know better than most that shadows are nothing in the pitch black. But in the light, they come alive."

Apollo held his gaze, steady, almost hypnotically as he took a single step closer to where Shade still sat, frozen on the mattress on the floor. "Come alive for me, Shadow. I'll be your light. You just need to focus on being *mine*. That's all. Just be you and be mine. My pretty little—"

A thud almost directly above them abruptly cut him off, and Apollo paused, eyes closing momentarily as he inhaled as if seeking patience.

Shade was busy staring up at the ceiling, frowning. "What the hell was that?"

He did not have a good feeling about this, and any of the warmth or anticipation that had been building in his body prior vanished in a puff of smoke as tendrils of apprehension took their place.

Which of course Apollo noticed. Man probably fucking tasted it even.

"That," he pinched the bridge of his nose, "was Gunther Hynth."

Shade stared. "Who?"

"The man from the video," Apollo motioned to the computer as Shade literally recoiled.

"He's here?!" He glared up at the ceiling. "What the fuck?! For how long?!"

"Almost a month," Apollo said nonchalantly.

"…I've been here for less than three weeks."

"Don't be jealous," Apollo told him, purposefully misunderstanding. "He was here before you because I didn't intend for you arrive so soon. Maxen really messed with a lot of things. I should have done worse than simply stabbing him in the stomach, but I was on a time crunch, since you'd already called the Inspector and he was on the way."

"You're telling me," Shade just wanted to be sure he was hearing this right, "there's been a man held captive upstairs this entire time?"

"Always quick on the uptake, baby. I love that about you."

"Shut up."

"The way you fight me at every little turn like that…" Apollo snorted and grinned. "Nope, actually. I like that a lot too."

Another bang, louder than before, cut the conversation short, this time for real.

"Wait here," Apollo ordered, as if Shade actually had a say in whether or not he followed through. "I've got to deal with our friend for a bit. He's been patiently staying nice and quiet, which means there has to be a reason he's risking making a racket now. Want to make a bet of it? I'm guessing he's simply lost patience. People are like that. Can't stand having to wait, even with their life is on the line. You?"

Shade scowled. "I'm not making a bet out of someone's misery."

"Even after seeing that video?" Apollo clucked his tongue. "That's okay. We'll find a game you like later."

"Pass."

"What did I tell you before, Shadow mine?" He smirked at him. "You don't get to pass. I won't be long." He started heading for the stairs and then seemed to think of something, turning slightly to gaze at Shade cryptically over his shoulder. "Behave, Detective. You wouldn't like it if I decided to choose a game I want instead."

Shade didn't bother with a response, simply kept the glower in place, aimed at Apollo's back even once the other man had turned again. He didn't allow his shoulders to droop until he'd disappeared completely up the steps. Not that being alone with his thoughts was much better than being forced into the company of a self-proclaimed psychopath.

He'd taken this case because no one else had wanted it, the same way he'd taken all the other cases no one had shown an interest in. So why had this one gone so wrong?

What had Shade gotten himself into? And more importantly, how? There was no right answer though; it didn't take a genius to see that his was a matter of wrong place at the wrong time. He'd done nothing to attract the interest of a murderer initially. That day at the crime scene? He'd gone about his business as per usual. Had done his job and nothing more.

Apollo had seen him and wanted him and that was all there was to it. Shade hadn't needed to *do* anything.

In a way, that made it so much worse, because there wasn't even a way for Shade to blame himself. Nothing he could put his finger on and be like "oh yes, remember not to do that next time". Not that he thought there was a chance he'd attract another psychopath in his lifetime, but still.

He couldn't be held accountable for his actions initially either. Apollo had been pleasant and attractive and warm. He'd come with glowing recommendations from Avery and Dario who'd both clearly thought highly of him. Avery had even kicked things off by trying to set them up as running partners. Of course Shade had fallen for him and wanted to get to know him better.

Of course he'd been open to more that day on the rooftop, when he'd been messed up from Repletion and vulnerable. When Apollo had touched him so lightly, tenderly, and spoken to him in hushed tones. No one had ever treated Shade like he was important or delicate. Like he was lovable.

Like he was worth running into a crowded room and making a public fool of themselves for.

But that day, Apollo had come to his rescue like some cliché knight in shining armor and Shade had eaten that shit up out of the palm of his hand. And then, to make matters worse, to ensure Shade thought about him even once the day had ended and they'd parted ways, Apollo had slept with him. With that one act alone, he'd successfully crawled underneath Shade's skin and burrowed deep.

Shade had given into the fear after that, had shied away thinking he didn't deserve a perfect person like Apollo—laughable now when he thought back on it—but the damage had already been done. All it'd taken was for the other man to show up at the station under the guise of having been called there by Dario and Shade had been right back where he'd wanted him.

He'd been kidnapped, raped, and threatened, but their sexual encounters always ended the exact same way, the same way it had that day on the roof.

With Shade screaming out Apollo's name, letting go, and giving into the pleasure. Sick as it may be. Twisted as that made him. No matter how much he struggled against the other man's hold, no matter how much he fought against himself, the end result was him turning into a puddle of needy mush beneath Apollo's ministrations.

Letting go wasn't something he was used to. That rush of adrenaline that came without the emotions of other people clouding his judgment or clogging his mind. When he was with Apollo, there was only him in his head, only his voice and the voice of his captor. There was only this and the moment and them—

Shade needed to get the fuck out of here.

This line of thinking was dangerous, telling. Had he always secretly been this weak? This pliable? Had the potential to roll over and become someone's bitch always been in him, or was that something Apollo was etching into his soul bit by bit?

Hadn't he threatened to do just that? He'd said he was going to take Shade apart and piece him back together again in his preferred image. Was that was this was? Had it already taken affect? It must have, since thinking back on the violence of their first time here, when Apollo had pinned him down and forced himself inside despite his protests…

Shade's dick twitched in his shorts.

Conclusion? There was something seriously wrong with him, and whether it was something now being unlocked by this situation, something that had simply been lying dormant within him all along, or a byproduct of Apollo's influence, Shade couldn't stick around and wait to find out. He needed to escape, now, before it was too late.

Before even playing grotesque movies in the morning wasn't enough to scare him away.

He'd never been privy to violence, was better known for being cold and unmovable, scaring people with a look rather than his fists. He could fight, of course, had been trained by the best at the Academy and come away with top marks, but he wasn't the most skilled in that department, and since his cases came in a range of flavors and didn't always involve beefed up fighters, that had never really been an issue in the past.

But just because he wasn't overly interested in it didn't mean violence bothered him. It was more…indifference. He'd kept that tidbit to himself over the years for fear what others might think of him, yet it was the truth. The reason most crime scenes didn't get to him was because he could easily remove himself from what he saw. When one had the ability to home in on another's emotion, it was pretty easy to get lost in their head.

Shade made his attention to each crime clinical, forming a wall between him and whatever horror he was dealing with. He had to in order to make it through the day. In order to maintain that sense of indifference.

Only, now, there was on one here for him to lock onto. No one here other than him and Apollo and that guy trapped upstairs he'd somehow been unable to pick up on all this time. The question of how was something he'd have to figure out later, when he was free and no longer at risk of completely and totally falling apart the exact way Apollo wanted him to.

And if that man had been here the whole time, that meant he'd been just a floor away when Apollo had spread Shade's thighs and forced him to—

He needed out.

Right now.

Chapter 25:

Shade worked quickly, unsure when Apollo might return. He kept one ear peeled toward the stairs as he searched for literally anything he could use. He'd done this before, of course, but everything that could even possibly double as a weapon or a means of escape was always kept just out of reach, almost as if Apollo was taunting him.

He most likely was, the bastard.

It was by pure happenstance that Shade opted to check beneath the mattress, simply because there was nowhere else for him to look. He hadn't actually thought it would lead to anything, so when he caught sight of something silver in the far corner, tucked beneath, he paused. With a frown, he dropped down and lifted the mattress out of the way, sucking a breath when his eyes landed on the dinner knife Apollo had used on him weeks ago.

He'd tossed it once Shade had given in and must have forgotten all about it after the fact. Shade certainly had. How it'd ended up here was beyond him, but it made sense that neither of them had noticed it before since it wasn't like they slept on the corners, and the most movement the mattress had gotten up until this point was when it slid an inch or two on the cement ground when Apollo—

Shade swore, not wanting to go there. If he started thinking about how good the other man could make him feel, that trickle of doubt he'd been pretending didn't exist would rear its ugly head. Now wasn't the time for second guessing.

He pulled the thin knife from where it'd lodged itself and held it up, checking the blade. Should he stash it and try to find the opportunity to use it against Apollo?

That wouldn't work. Apollo was quick on his feet, and what's more, he had the advantage of being able to read Shade. All hiding it would do was piss the other guy off and get him tossed over another table. Or worse.

Shade's gaze wandered over to the wall where his chains were set, an idea formulating when he recalled the control panel hidden there. Sending a glance over toward the stairs, he rushed to it, searching in the wood for any small crease that would indicate where the panel was. It took more time than he would have liked, but he found it eventually, digging the pointed tip of the knife into it to wiggle it free.

The face of the panel popped up, and he eased it clean off so he could get to the controls beneath. He might not win any martial arts awards, but tech? Tech he could do. Years and years as a child with no real friends had made him turn to other things for amusement, and computers had been one of them.

He had the system cracked and the chains clicking softly as they unlatched from his wrists in less time than it'd taken to find the damn panel location.

Shade spun on his heels and stepped off the mattress, pausing for a moment to listen. There weren't any sounds coming from the top floor, so there was no way of telling what may or may not be happening or whether or not Apollo was on his way back.

Deciding he couldn't wait any longer, he set his attention on the computer, cursing low when he clicked it on only to find the device had a bio-lock. He wouldn't be able to bypass that in the short amount of time he had before Apollo returned and caught him, which meant finding another way.

It was probably for the best that he couldn't call for help anyway, considering the threats Apollo had made toward Gael. Threats Shade one hundred percent believed he would follow through on if given the chance.

Shade might not be privy to violence, but Apollo clearly got off on it. That much was obvious in how hard he got whenever Shade struggled or uttered the word "no". His end goal might be to break him, but he was enjoying the process of getting there far too much.

He'd seen Apollo use his multi-slate to access everything, but of course that hadn't been left lying around when he'd gone upstairs. But those devices connected to other things, meaning the system that controlled the Elec-Field had to be around here somewhere. If he tried to bombard his way through that type of force field, he'd not only end up electrocuted and tossed on his ass, but there'd also be a sound loud enough to have Apollo come running.

Sure enough, the controls were separate from the main computer, set to the side of the workbench. With a single click of a button, Shade felt the first taste of freedom settle on his tongue.

Closer, but he wasn't there yet.

Still gripping the knife, he made his way slowly over to the large entrance, cautiously waving his hand beneath the lip of the opening just in case. When no sparks flew and he remained standing, he let out the breath he'd been holding and sent one last glance over his shoulders. The moment he saw Apollo still hadn't shown up, he bolted.

Shade had no clue where this forest was even located on a map, how near to or far from the main city he was, but none of that mattered. His bare feet sliced open on twigs and rocks as he pushed himself into a mad run, his brain barely processing the pain as fear and adrenaline pumped through his veins rapidly.

He had no idea where he was going and there was no path for him to follow. He turned every now and again, careful not to accidentally loop his way back around, and ran until his lungs felt like they'd been filled with fire and his thighs burned.

Low hanging branches slapped at his face and he slashed them away with his hands and the knife he still held, only partially aware that his legs and arms were covered in scrapes. He should probably be stealthier, move less frantically so there wasn't any sort of path behind him, but that franticness spurred him on like prey running for their life from a predator, and logic wasn't enough to burst through that bubble that had formed around his mind.

For a while, he was so gone to it he thought the humming sound he heard was simply his heart pounding in his ears. The very second he realized it wasn't, that it hit him it was coming from somewhere else, he slid to stop.

He couldn't tell where it was coming from, either behind him or off to the sides. Spinning in a circle he tried to locate it but to no avail. Was it coming from the warehouse or was there someone else out here? Someone who could maybe help him? He didn't feel anyone, but then again, he hadn't felt Gunther Hynth either…

There was no way. Apollo wouldn't be that stupid. He brought his victims out here to torture and murder them, after all. He wouldn't risk setting up shop if there were neighbors. Which meant it had to be the warehouse…

Had Shade sprung an alarm?

He cursed, taking off once more, intent on putting as much distance between himself, that sound, and the warehouse, as he could. The only slight comfort was in knowing that he'd gotten a serious head start.

Time lost all meaning as he practically flew through the forest, so there was no telling how much of it had passed when he finally made out the telltale signs of hovercar engines up ahead. A relieved sound left his lips and he forced himself to keep going, climbing a small incline, eyes locked on the trees at the top.

He'd flag a car down and then ask them to take him straight to the station. He couldn't afford to stick around and put whoever it was at risk of Apollo's wrath, so he'd just have to take the chance that in the time between his leaving and bringing reinforcements back with him that the other man would flee.

He stubbornly disregarded the small voice inside of him that whispered it didn't want Apollo to get caught anyway. They'd toss him in a cell for life or worse, kill him for his crimes and—

No. He couldn't care. He had to stop.

The sounds of a somewhat busy street grew louder and just as he was about to reach the top something large and dark appeared out of the corner of his eye.

It darted forward, slamming into Shade before he could even get a cry of alarm out, taking them both back down the incline at a roll. He landed on his back with a hard thud, the figure recovering his baring faster than he, hands and legs already resituating over him in an attempt to dominate and pin him in place.

Shade saw red, instincts taking control as he fought tooth and nail. He punched and clawed, even bit with his mouth at an arm that got too close to his head. The screams that came out of him were guttural and desperate and filled with enough terror he may have been embarrassed about it if not for the fact he was too far gone, drowning in sensation.

Fear…and something else.

Something a lot like excitement.

No.

Apollo didn't go easy on him, fighting back with just as much ferocity, growling and hissing above him like an actual beast. The look in his eyes certainly mirrored one, the wild fury there turning them a dark, never ending black that threatened to swallow Shade whole. He wasn't gentle as he planted a knee onto Shade's stomach.

Shade saw stars, but he returned the blow with one of his own, using his fist instead of his hand. He connected with Apollo's jaw but all that ended up doing was pissing the other guy off even more.

He roared and dropped down, teeth latching onto the spot between Shade's neck and his left shoulder. Then he bit him.

Not a hot, sexy bite either, but full on, teeth tearing through skin, jaws latching on like he was a piece of meat, bit him.

Shade screamed, the pain sharp, and battered his hands against Apollo's chest, his back, his arms. No matter where he hit him, however, the other guy didn't budge, didn't flinch.

He simply dug that knee in even harder and clenched around the mouthful of flesh he had until blood was practically spurting into his mouth.

Recalling the knife he'd been holding, Shade's hand blindly searched the ground, praying that it'd fallen close by when he'd been knocked over. The second his fingertips touched the cold handle of the blade he almost cried out, lifting it and twisting to slam the knife into Apollo's side.

Apollo saw it coming though, even with his face buried against Shade, he somehow knew, twisting at the last second so the weapon ended up slashing over his hip instead of imbedding into him like Shade had intended.

They both froze at the exact same time.

Shade didn't need to be an empath to know he'd made a mistake. The man above him coiled, his face contorting into a sheer mask of rage and all of Shade's senses seemed to narrow in on him, so that everything else bled into the background and it was just the two of them, alone, with no hope in sight.

He'd never been the type to bow out of a fight, even if the odds didn't appear to be in his favor. That was something he couldn't afford, since he'd needed to maintain his image so badly to keep the people around him from whispering like those kids had back at school. Before now, he would have snorted in someone's face if they'd told him that was even something he was capable of doing.

But Shade's hand unfurled from around the handle as if possessed, the weapon plopping to the bed of leaves they were currently wrestling on top of. He was shaking, he realized, sweat from the run causing the debris to stick uncomfortably all over his skin, his breathing coming in short, shallow gulps as if he were afraid to make too much noise and set the man on top of him off.

No, not man. Devil.

One currently covered in blood.

It was impossible to miss now that he'd noticed, the red streaks up and down Apollo's arms and smeared across his left cheek still wet and glistening in the beams of sunlight trickling through the canopy about them. The tear in his shirt from where Shade had cut him with the knife was damp as well, but it was clear this was the only spot on him where the crimson painted over his skin was his own blood.

It'd been so quiet upstairs when Shade had been planning his escape…What the hell had Apollo done to that man to get that much blood on him and have there be no sounds?

He actually opened his mouth to utter an apology as a wave of fear rolled over him, but his stubbornness set in just then, apparently finding that bit going too far and he snapped his jaw shut before a single word could make its way out.

As if drawn by the sound, Apollo's head tilted, his dark gaze lifting from the discarded knife and finally settling back on Shade's panicked one. For a single moment, tension hovered in the air between them, as if the world had come to a complete standstill. Then a sort of frenzy entered Apollo's eyes and Shade knew the exact second he was about to snap.

Not that it did him any good.

He cried out and tried to kick as the other man tore the shorts clean off of him with ease. He flung them over his shoulder and they vanished in some bushes, leaving Shade naked from the waist down. With no effort at all, he was flipped onto his stomach.

"Stop!" He shoved back at Apollo as his legs were forcefully pulled apart, his ass tilting up into the air, exposing him. A cool breeze blew by and against his heated flesh it was like a gust of icy wind that had him shivering.

Or, maybe, that's not why at all.

The air licking against his skin and the familiar position had his dick swelling despite his minds protests. Within seconds his body was ready, his balls hanging tight and his ass tipping as if in silent welcome.

He trembled, dreading what was about to happen even as he screwed his eyes shut and inhaled deeply in a poor attempt to prepare himself.

The hit was harder than that day on the rooftop, as if Apollo had been testing the waters then, holding back to get an idea of whether or not Shade might be into it. And Shade, naïve as he had been, hadn't realized the danger and had, for the first time, given into those urges within him and into the sensation.

Shade tried to crawl away, the slaps against his ass increasing in severity, enough that he felt the welts already beginning to form. He held out for as long as he could, but a sob ripped from his lips and once it had, there was no stopping the rush of emotion that sprung from him like a waterfall.

Apollo dragged him back into positon each time he attempted to wiggle away, grip on his hip tight enough to bruise all on its own. "Stay still," he growled when he'd finally gotten tired of dealing with Shade's struggles, "or I'll go and find a branch to use instead of my hand."

He sucked in a breath but, his body followed the order even before his brain had fully registered the full threat.

Forcing his knees further apart in the dirt, Apollo picked up where he'd left off, firm hand coming down with a sharp crack, jostling Shade with each impact. It wasn't until the last couple that he started to ease up a bit, at such a slow rate that it went unnoticed at first until he'd shoved Shade flat onto the ground, and his spanks had turned into gentle touches against his abused flesh.

Apollo smoothed over the damage, the contact still painful after that kind of mistreatment but a lot better than the strikes had been. He cooed to Shade, voice close to his ear as he made soft shushing noises, as if to comfort him.

The tingling in his ass started to change, altering to a low burning fire that seemed to grow with every careful massage of those skilled fingers, until Shade was close to humping the dirt beneath him just for some type of relief.

As soon as that happened, Apollo cut the comforting tactic. It was like ripping off a bandage, the flip so shocking it momentarily had Shade disoriented. One minute the man's warmth was on top of him, his attention gentle, and the next he was gone and there was nothing for a moment except cold air against Shade's flushed skin.

It didn't last long.

The zip of a fly cut through the forest like a gun shot and then Apollo's thick crown was there at Shade's entrance, shoving itself in deep and raw before Shade could even process the new danger.

Not only was the stretch enough to make him feel like he was being torn apart, but the added agony when Apollo's hips pressed against the battered flesh of his ass had his mind fracturing. Black spots burst behind Shade's eyes as his spine bowed, a silent scream parting his lips as tears welled in his eyes and spilled before he could even think to hold them in. The pain was worse than that first time and it felt like he was being shredded from the inside out as that thick cock fucked in deep and hard.

"Please," someone was begging, and he was pretty sure it was him, "stop. Please."

When he forced himself to blink through the tears and look over at Apollo, he whimpered, noting the complete lack of care or empathy written across his face. Shade clawed at the ground and tried to push him out but nothing worked, the other man merely flipped him over. He speared into his hole again before he could get used to being empty, and flattened over him, nearly bending him in half as he pinned him to the forest floor.

"It's too much!" Shade hit at his shoulder, the pain starting to make him feel nauseous.

Apollo pulled something from his back pocket then and slipped his cock almost all the way out. The sound of squirting fluid came next, and Shade realized he was emptying a bottle of lube on the two of them.

"No." He tried yet again to move away, but one glare from Apollo had him stilling instantly.

The second he tossed the now empty bottle over his shoulder, Apollo thrust back in, pounding with the same level of ferocity as before.

Shade hated himself more then than he ever had because the emotion that sprung up inside of him as soon as he adjusted to that large cock with the help of the lube wasn't disgust or anger.

It was relief.

He was relieved that Apollo had taken pity on him in the end and given him lube.

As if that was some great, romantic thing.

As if it was kind.

"You shouldn't have done that," Apollo growled over him, and Shade's attention snapped to his face.

No, no he shouldn't have. Shade had been foolish, thinking he could get away.

"I'm going to make it so you're afraid just thinking about trying to leave me," Apollo threatened, and it was possessive and abusive, the type of thing someone in a domestic violence case Shade might be called to would say.

So why the hell did his heart leap and his muscles clench in anticipation?

Once he'd applied the lube, Apollo didn't last long at all, maybe a couple of minutes at most. But it felt like an eternity before he yanked himself out and rose up over Shade. He stroked himself with his palm, quick jerky motions, aiming for Shade's brutalized hole, and unloaded with a guttural groan that Shade felt all the way to his core being.

Shots of come hit him in the ass, splattering on his raw flesh, stinging against the welts, and against the underside of his balls. He wasn't released, however, and before relief that it was over could sink in, he felt one of Apollo's hands against his skin, collecting globs of the stuff.

He shoved three coated fingers deep into Shade, rubbing against his battered insides, jackhammering in and out of him.

The duress Shade felt the second his cries of agony switched gears on him, seemingly out of nowhere, was like being hit by a tsunami. He started mumbling the word no to himself over and over again, shaking his head back and forth, uncaring about the tiny twigs poking into his scalp and at his ears. But just as it'd been impossible to physically fight off Apollo, it was just as futile to fight against himself.

His dick twitched, flushed a deep red, and precome dripped from the tip like a leaky faucet.

As soon as he was at full mast, Apollo pulled his fingers free, settling a hand at each of Shade's knees to keep him spread wide so he could stare down at him.

Shade covered his face with an arm, sniffling and biting down on the inside of his cheek in an attempt to get a hold of himself. He'd just been fucked, at first without lube, and was no doubt bleeding and torn, yet he was still getting off?

And it wasn't just because of the physical stuff either, like the way Apollo was prodding purposefully against his prostate. It was the mental aspect of it all that was really what was helping to push him over the edge of sanity. It was thinking about how he'd tried to escape and how Apollo had come for him with such intensity that the other guy appeared completely out of his mind.

…No one had ever wanted Shade enough to completely lose their minds over him. To pin him down and take him even as he screamed and fought back.

This wasn't healthy. It wasn't normal. He'd heard of consensual non consent before, knew it was a thing some people were into, but that's not what this was. No part of Shade had started this off consenting. This was a straight up crime, yet even if his brain acknowledged that, the rest of him didn't seem to get the memo.

It didn't care how he'd gotten here, only that he had. His entire being narrowed down to the seesawing of sensations he was being forced to feel and nothing else.

Peeking over his arm, he locked eyes with Apollo who was watching him, his breaths harried, his body tense as if ready to pounce all over again. There was a frenzied edge to the set of his jaw and the wildness in his gaze.

Shade had done that. Shade had made him this crazy and out of control. It was fucked up as all hell but he—

"Something enjoyable about this, Detective?" Apollo sounded like the Devil himself when he spoke. "I felt that burst of pride you just had. This was meant to be a punishment, a warning. I see you didn't get the memo."

"No." Shade tried to scramble back, flailing his legs. He managed to get one of them free and rammed his heel against Apollo's face, twisting and clawing at through the dirt and the leaves until he could make it onto his feet. He'd only managed three steps before he was shoved hard against a nearby tree, the rough bark skimming the sensitive flesh of his thighs and his dick uncomfortably.

Then Apollo's cock was back at his entrance, thrusting inside at the same time that he wrapped those long fingers around Shade's neck and squeezed. He rutted into him violently, blocking off all air flow as he choked him simultaneously with his hand at his throat and his cock in his ass.

Shade felt like he was about to pass out from the lack of oxygen, but his dick didn't care about that either, and every time it rubbed against tree bark the friction had his balls tightening. He even liked that it stung a bit.

He was going to die. Apollo was well and truly going to kill him this time and he was going to both die here and come at the same time. Even through the terror and the pain he could feel himself slinking closer to the edge, any second now and he'd—

Apollo released him as quickly as he'd taken hold, giving Shade a heartbeat to suck in a breath and cough before he grabbed a fistful of the shirt he was still wearing and dragged him back to the ground.

Too stunned to fight, Shade found himself resituated on his side with Apollo sealed at his back, his cheek cradled by the other man's firm arm. His right leg was lifted and then that heavy cock was spearing into him from behind all over again. Pumps deep and measured.

Apollo wrapped the arm beneath his head around his front, his other hand keeping his leg high in the air, manipulating Shade's body like it was nothing.

There was no pain at his entrance now, though that might be more because of how aroused Shade was. The slaps against his marked ass cheeks stung but in a way that only served to spur the heat inside him further. His dick bounced with every thrust, slapping against his stomach, the brief contact not nearly enough to give him what he wanted. He thought again about how wrong this was, how sick in the head he must be to enjoy being abused this way.

But the harder Apollo pummeled him with his cock, the higher that elation inside seemed to grow, inflating like a balloon until it was stretched so thin it was at risk of bursting.

Before it could, Apollo dropped his leg and wrapped his ring finger and thumb tightly around the base of Shade's dick, compressing and cutting off blood flow. He pulled his cock free and stilled with just his head left poking at Shade's hole.

A whiny sound worked its way up Shade's throat and he actually tried to push back, to get that cock to return where he wanted it, but Apollo shifted easily and tightened the arm he had around his front.

"I figured out why I like choking you so much, baby," Apollo whispered against his ear, that delicious honey tone back as if the devil he'd been only a few minutes ago had been a figment of Shade's imagination. He slipped his cockhead back into Shade but stopped there. "It's not about that at all. It's this." His tongue darted out and lapped at Shade's wet cheek. "It's these fucking almost tears. Something about you struggling to hold them back is so damn sexy. I want to bend you over my knee and beat you for trying to get away. Break your legs so you can't ever do it again. But because of this," he licked him again, "because of these," and let out a groan, "I want you bawling for a different reason."

He fed him another inch of himself. "Say you're sorry, baby."

"I'm sorry," Shade's voice came out a mess, ending with a sob. He pinched his eyes shut and tried to block it all out, but the feelings were too strong.

And all his.

Every last one of them.

The fear, the anticipation, the desire…All of those emotions pinging inside of him, rushing through his bloodstream, they all belonged to him.

When was the last time he'd felt anything real?

"Again," Apollo demanded, gliding in another inch.

The stretch and burn had Shade moaning, but it wasn't enough. "I'm sorry."

"Are you sorry only because you've figured out I'm not going to let you come," he jeered, following it up pulling back out to his crown.

Shade shook his head and reached blindly, hand clutching at the dirt as he struggled to keep himself together. "I'm sorry," he swore, unable to ignore the desperation in his tone, the reediness in his voice, "please."

What was happening to him?

Why was he spending so much energy on caring?

What he should be doing is focusing. Focusing on the way his dick was throbbing, still trapped between Apollo's clenched fingers, and the ache it was causing. The discomfort. Focus on the frustration building within him and the anguish.

Who gave a shit what was normal when *he* was the one going through all of this? Every emotion that flickered through him, even the bad ones, seemed to flip switches inside that he hadn't known were there, let alone off. Here he was, half naked in the middle of a forest covered in blood and come and dirt, coming alive like a damn Christmas tree in December.

And Shade no longer cared. All he could think about was how he wanted more.

"You tried to escape," Apollo reminded, and Shade vehemently denied it even though it was ridiculous for him to even bother.

"No," he shook his head, "no."

"What was the plan, Detective? Run back to your partner and pretend this never happened? And when this greedy little hole of yours acted up, what then? Were you going to find a random stranger on the street and beg them like you're begging me now?"

"No." He reached down and pressed on the hand Apollo had on his dick but he didn't loosen his hold even a little. "It hurts."

It might even hurt more than when he'd been fucked up the ass with no preparation, because that had come with one solid sensation, pain, but this...the absolute turmoil Shade currently felt was several times worse because of how complex it was. He wasn't used to these emotions, wasn't used to being forced to feel things at full blast and his mind was struggling to sort through all of the sensations even as his body zeroed in on one thing and one thing only.

He needed to come.

Shade latched onto that thought like a kitten to milk. If he could achieve an orgasm then all of these feelings would go away and he could think clearly again. He could breathe again.

"You're shaking," Apollo rested his chin on Shade's shoulder and blew air against the curve of his neck. "And you're covered in sweat. Imagine if someone else saw you like this, unraveling, this pretty cock of yours weeping for attention. That's what it comes down to, doesn't it, baby? You crave attention."

Shade didn't deny it. It was no great secret at this point.

"Were you going to bend over for the first guy who gave you a little lip service and beg him to stuff you full of his cock, rough, the way you like? Give your body to someone who isn't me?" Apollo's voice was slowly taking on that edge again, the scary one from before. The one that threatened pain over pleasure instead of the satisfying mix Shade had just come to the acceptance he appreciated.

"It's never been like this with anyone else," Shade said, struggling to come up with the right thing to say to pull Apollo from that darker place.

Apollo growled and hauled Shade back against him, his cock slamming all the way in so that Shade's mouth popped open. "And it never will be." He lowered his mouth to his ear again. "But telling me what you think I want to hear isn't going to be enough to save you now."

He rolled them again, forcing Shade onto his stomach, and kept his vice-like grip around the base of his cock even as he started thrusting. Apollo rolled his hips and used Shade's body to stroke himself, keeping his pumps shallow enough to avoid that spot inside of Shade that would have him singing.

Instead, he sobbed and begged beneath the other man in a mirror of how he had earlier, only with one major difference.

He wasn't pleading to be released, he was pleading to be taken.

His prostate was neglected, his cock so painful and angry now that it felt like he'd either explode or it would fall off altogether. When he tried to hump back, he found his face crushed into the dirt, Apollo's fingers tangling in his hair.

Apollo came shortly after, pulling out and repeating what he'd done before as well, denying Shade even the pleasant warm feeling of being filled with his come. Like he'd thought there was a slight chance it would have been enough to have Shade coming even with his dick being choked the way it was.

Maybe it would have been.

Shade had never been able to orgasm without stimulation to his cock before, but he hadn't thought he'd experience arousal being taken like an animal in the dirt either so…

Apollo pulled him up, sitting him back on his heels with his back to his front, and kissed the curve of his jaw lightly once, before nipping him with his teeth hard enough for it to smart.

Jerking in his hold, Shade moved his head away and reached down towards his dick with one of his hands.

"Do it," the Devil said, back full force, the rumble in his chest vibrating through their shirts and skittering up Shade's spine, "and I'll drag you kicking and screaming to the warehouse, slash open Gunther's bloated stomach, and fuck you in his entrails. He'll be awake for the start of it before dying, which means there will be an audience. Someone else will know how secretly depraved you are, Detective Yor."

Shade gulped. He'd never called him that before. It felt…wrong, almost like a threat in and of its own which made no sense since it was only his name. But he felt it. He felt the peril in the air and the rigid, corded muscular body at his back.

"He'll see it in your eyes too," Apollo continued, "I'll make sure of it. I'll make sure the very last thing Gunther sees is the humiliation on your face. We both know that's what you'll feel. Not disgust, not pity for his end or his suffering last breaths. What you'll feel is shame that someone else got to see your perversion."

"Please," Shade's throat had gone so dry it hurt to speak, "please."

"Please what, Detective?" He squeezed his dick smirking against the curve of his ear when he received a strangled cry in return. "Please don't kill that man? Please don't fuck you in his blood? Please don't embarrass you?" His grip loosened ever so slightly. "Or—"

"Please let me come!"

It was the right answer, and with a dark chuckle, Apollo finally obliged. He worked him in quick movements, his hand easily gliding up and down Shade's stiff length thanks to all the precome that had run rivulets down the root of his dick.

It didn't take long at all, a couple flicks of his thumb against his slit and a few good pumps and Shade was toppling, the orgasm crashing into him, ripping him away from reality as he came, and came, and came. And all the while, Apollo continued to stroke him, ringing out every last drop.

Chapter 26:

Shade had passed out. It was beginning to become a habit.

For once though, the usual guilt and embarrassment didn't drown him. Streaks of sunlight blinded him when he managed to peel his eyes open sometime later. Wincing, he buried his face against the warm curve of Apollo's throat, snuggling in closer, too blissed out to sum up the proper energy needed to feel ashamed at doing that either.

It wasn't really his fault. Apollo just smelled so damn good, like moss and salt. Shade felt like he could inhale that scent forever and never get enough of it. But it wasn't just the smell. Even though they were close in height, the other man carried him like he weighed nothing, easily stepping over rocks and fallen tree branches as he presumably made his way back to the warehouse.

For a fleeting second, the thought that maybe Shade should try to run again, now when Apollo's guard was down, entered his mind, but he dashed it before it could fully form. His ass was sore and he was covered in bruises from the tumble and fighting. He was in no shape to try any of that again and…

He hated to admit it, so swore he'd only do it in his innermost thoughts, but…He couldn't really recall at the moment why it'd seemed so important for him to get away in the first place. He was sure he'd had reasons other than duty and honor and blah, blah, blah, but whatever those reasons had been, they'd seemed to have discharged from his mind the same way his come had finally shot from his dick.

But that realization had something ugly finally unfurling its tendrils inside of him just as they made it back to the warehouse.

Apollo set him down, keeping an arm around his waist to hold him steady as he activated the Elec-Shield, sealing them both inside. Then he turned to stare at Shade, inspecting him, no doubt reading the subtle change that had started to take root.

Had he realized it before Shade had, even? It was possible.

"You want to run, baby?"

Shade shook his head curtly, but that only had the other man's eyes narrowing.

"You want to run," he corrected. "I can taste it on you."

"I don't." He did. But not in the sense he figured Apollo meant. He might be able to read Shade's emotions, but he couldn't read his mind, which meant the most he could do was piece those feelings to an action that made sense in his head, not Shade's.

Shade didn't want to run from Apollo—not so soon after being taught what would happen to him if he failed and was caught. He wanted to run from himself.

Because the ick was starting to funnel its way through the hazy, bliss-filled headspace he'd been lost in only a moment ago, and it was telling him he was a disgusting piece of garbage. That he was weak, a freak, a monster. Just like everyone had always told him.

What kind of normal person would snuggle against their captor? Their invader?

Good Light. What kind of person could look at the man who had done those brutal things to him and call him an *invader* in his head instead of what he really was?

Shade hadn't wanted it.

Until he did.

But he hadn't at first, and that's what counted, right?

...Right?

Apollo opened his mouth slightly and inhaled. "Think you still can, baby?"

Shade frowned, not following at first, too caught up in the self-loathing taking shape. What would Gael say if he found out? What if Gael burst through the door right now and saw and somehow *knew* what had happened here?

What if he knew that a part of Shade liked it?

"Run," Apollo shook him slightly, snapping him out of it before shoving him away.

Shade stumbled and hit the cement floor, wincing as pain zapped up his hip upon impact. It had the desired effect, however, and when he got back on his feet and retreated, self-preservation snuffed out all the woe-is-me talk in his mind. He didn't have time for it, not when he was potentially going to have to fight for his life again.

"Your punishment's not over," Apollo said. "I warned you if you didn't behave that we'd be playing a game I like instead. Run. If you manage to get away, you win."

Shade glanced pointedly over Apollo's shoulder at the only exit, which was currently blocked not only by his tall form but also by an electric force field.

Apollo shrugged, seemingly saying without words, "tough".

"There's nowhere for me to go," Shade stated bitterly, backing up another step when Apollo took one forward.

"There never was," he informed him. "I was going to have you the second I set my sights on you. Same way I'm going to have you now."

He held up his hands as if that would make a difference. "You just got off twice in the woods."

Apollo tilted his head, thinking. "Is that the game you want to play? Should we count how many times I can blow my load in that tight, little ass of you—"

Shade twisted on his heels and ran, racing across the warehouse, bare feet slapping against the stone floor. He slid to a stop at the stairwell, already starting up it before he recalled the threat Apollo had made back in the forest. If his punishment wasn't over, did that mean he'd make good on *that* threat if given the chance?

Not wanting to risk it, he dove to the side, just avoiding Apollo's hand as it reached for him. He hit the ground on his knees, teeth clenching against the sharp pain, but forced himself back into motion. His eyes searched wildly for any kind of out. He couldn't keep this going, as exhausted and spent as he was. If it came down to a race against stamina, Apollo would win by a landslide and he knew it.

The bathroom door caught his attention and he swerved, veering toward it. If he could get inside and slam it shut behind him, he might stand a chance.

Running this time was different than back in the forest. Then, he hadn't been aware he was being chased, hunted. He'd thought he'd put a good amount of distance between himself and his captor and been more concerned about the burning in his lungs. But now…

He could feel the sharp outtakes of breath fanning against his nape whenever Apollo got too close and almost caught him, hear the beats of his shoes eating up the space between them. A thrill shot through him, the excitement palpable.

In his haste, he'd completely forgotten the door was locked, but it was too late for him to try something else. When he slammed his palm against the control panel and the door opened for him anyway, he let out a surprised sound, slipping into the room.

But before he could shut it, Apollo was there, slamming a palm against the frame, forcing Shade to stumble back as he invaded his space, filling the doorway.

Shade tried to run to the side toward the sauna, yelping when a hand wrapped around his arm and tugged him back. He fought, swinging a fist, but that was caught too and the next thing he knew he was being shoved into the shower stall, the door shut and locked behind him with Apollo on the other side.

Panting, he stood there, watching with suspicion as Apollo went over to the bathtub and pressed some of the controls.

Water started pouring from the faucet, filling the tub as he stepped back and tugged his t-shirt over his head, dropping it to the tiled floor. He turned back to face Shade, an enigmatic expression set in place as he deftly undid the snap at his pants and stripped those off as well. He kicked out of them and then, standing in all his naked glory, tipped his head as if silently daring Shade to drink him in.

Stubbornly, his eyes met the challenge, sweeping over the bridge of his nose, across the broad stretch of his shoulders and his long, defined torso. They caught at the dark trail of hairs leading straight down from his navel, all the way to his proud cock which was already erect again, ready for him.

Shade swallowed, the sound audible past the ringing in his ears, unable to look away even when Apollo started moving toward the shower stall. He only snapped himself out of it once the man was a few feet away, quickly retreating to the far corner, as if that would somehow save him from whatever the other man planned.

Instead of getting annoyed that he was still resisting, however, Apollo smirked, coming after him and hauling Shade back out as easily as he'd shoved him into the stall to begin with. He tore Shade's shirt over his head, the only piece of clothing he'd been in since losing his pants to that bush in the forest, and then dragged him over to the tub.

The water had automatically shut itself off as soon as it was full, steam wafting off the surface. There was a hint of rose coming off of it, a pleasant smell, nothing altogether nefarious looking about the situation at all, and yet...

Shade continued to struggle. Not because he thought Apollo planned on drowning him or anything.

He struggled because he *wanted to*. Because something inside of him raged that he had to for this, whatever this was, to be all it could be.

"Are you resisting me," Apollo asked, looping an arm around his waist and lifting him over the lip of the tub, stepping in immediately afterward, "or are you resisting yourself?"

"Shut up!" He didn't want to hear that, didn't want to go back to that place. This was better. It was better when he had something to focus on.

"Let it in, Detective," he coaxed, pulling Shade down so that water splashed up around them and they were both submerged to their mid-chests. "You don't have to be afraid to feel." His hand wrapped around his front, found his dick and gave it a single pump.

Shade was hard for him almost instantly. He thought back to the forest and made a sound of protest. Edging and orgasm denial weren't things he was a fan of and he really didn't want a repeat.

As soon as they'd entered, the water had taken on a twinge of pink, and seeing that he'd noticed, Apollo bit at his shoulder, gave his dick another pump, and said nonchalantly, "It's the blood."

A second ago, Shade had been thinking it was pretty.

Pretty.

Apollo was covered in Gunther's blood—and a bit of his own, thanks to Shade, and a bit of Shade's, thanks to him—and now it was mixing with the water, and they were bathing in it.

And Shade had thought it was pretty.

He tried to stand, wanting out, but was wrested back, skilled fingers finding the beaded bud of one of his nipples and tweaking it to distract him.

It worked.

He cried out, leaning back into Apollo as one of his thumbs traced the vein on the underside of Shade's dick and the other swirled around his nipple. Just as he was starting to get into it however, those hands stopped. Tears sprung to his eyes, a mixture of anger and bitterness and that desperation again, as he was bent over the edge of the tub.

Apollo mounted him, his cock prodding at his hole before it found his entrance and pushed inside, slow and steady. He pressed a kiss to Shade's shoulder as he leisurely seated himself all the way, as if he had all the time in the world and there was no hurry.

When Shade made another sound of protest, Apollo snorted at him and ran the bridge of his nose against the curve of his jaw.

"Who was it saying we got off in the woods already so should be satisfied?" he teased, and Shade bristled under him. "Stop running, Detective. You want me. You want me to do bad things to you and you want to both hate them and love those things at the same time. There's no shame in that."

"Shut up." Tears spilled and he felt them roll down his cheek. He hung his head, hands tightening on the edge of the tub for purchase as Apollo rolled his hips, bumping against his insides, the crown of his cock tapping against his prostate. Before he could even think about what he was doing, he rocked back and widened his thighs around Apollo's hips so he could get him to go deeper.

He froze.

"Don't even think about it," Apollo growled, the hint of the devil scratching the surface.

When he thrust forward again, Shade dutifully pushed back.

They both moaned.

The fit was so tight, Shade's body clinging to Apollo's, the heat building in his lower region like this was normal. Like they were regular lovers having playful afternoon bath-time sex.

But they weren't, and they'd never be, and why the hell wasn't Shade more bothered by that fact?

Apollo growled behind him, no doubt tasting his feelings again, and then picked up the tempo, slapping against his ass bruisingly. "You want this."

Shade shook his head. It was one thing to let the thought plague himself, but to say it out loud…to give it purchase and make it real…He was a monstrous freak.

"You want this," Apollo insisted, fingers digging into his sides. "You want me."

"I didn't," he snapped, the words ending on a cry as Apollo fucked him with more vigor.

"I wasn't using past tense," Apollo told him, "You want this. Tell me."

"No."

Apollo peeled him off the edge by his throat, one hand remaining there while the other dropped to his dick, fingers taking position locked around the base of his cock in a mirror of earlier.

Shade sucked in a breath, eyes wide and tried to turn to peer at him over his shoulder, tried to silently plead with him.

Apollo merely thrust up into him.

How had he gone from being an eighth class, respected detective to *this*? This mewling mess of a person practically drooling for a murderer's cock? And now, on top of that, the murderer wanted him to admit it? Verbally?

Shade pressed his lips into a thin line, blinking through the onslaught of tears that poured out of him.

"I won't have you running again, Shadow mine," Apollo said. "If I'd lost you…" a breath stuttered out of him. "Do you think it's easy for me? I'm not used to these emotions either. I'm not used to feeling desperate. Before you, the only thing I even came close to being obsessed with was the urge to see inside people. But I don't just want in you, baby, I want to own you. I want you wrapped around my finger, purring my name even in your sleep. I'm a devil with a weakness now, don't you see how complicated that is? You aren't the only one here having an identity crisis."

It wasn't the same. It couldn't be.

"You think because you're a good person it's different?" Apollo asked. "Bullshit. Everyone is a monster behind a mask. None of us are different. We're all hiding behind brightly colored masks, praying the world never glimpses our true face. Praying if they do, that at least the people around us won't turn their backs. Normal? Good? These are just social constructs. Who gets to decide what's right and wrong? Who gets to tell you that you're gross for wanting to be owned?"

"I don't." He maybe sort of did though... There was something about the idea that someone could want him so much, that Apollo could want him so much, that he'd even want to have all of him. To take all of him.

Keep all of him.

Damn his fucking abandonment issues turning him into this freak.

And damn Apollo for forcing him to face it.

He'd been fine before they'd met. Unhappy, unfeeling more than half the time, but *fine.* He'd had Gael's friendship and coworkers who maintained eye contact and respect. Sure, he wanted what others had sometimes. Wanted a lover who looked at him and only him. Wanted to feel wanted. And if he sometimes broke down when he was alone? Sometimes had nightmares about being that kid, left at the doorstep of a strange place while his mom drove away without even looking back once…So what? Everyone had baggage. Nobody was perfect.

But where his parents had driven away from him, had run from him, Apollo had done the opposite. Shade had tried to leave, but he'd come after him. Had held him tight. His mom had always lied, telling him what she thought he wanted to hear. Placating him when in reality she'd considered him a burden.

Apollo didn't lie, at least not about this. Proof of that was in the way he'd punished him in the forest, the way he'd unleashed his true feelings and turned all that anger and fear on Shade without hesitation…

Anger that he'd run.

Fear that he'd almost lost him.

Fuck, it was so wrong. So wrong to find comfort in that when logically Shade knew this was all kinds of messed up and yet…

"You're perfect," Apollo told him.

A moan slipped past Shade's lips.

"Accepting you have a painful past doesn't make you weak," he continued. "Just like acknowledging you like to be forced to take my cock doesn't make you a monster."

"You kill people," Shade reminded, but he didn't know which of them the reminder was for anymore.

"Would you like me to stop?"

He frowned. "Don't make promises you can't keep."

"Would you like to come?" Apollo still had that grip on Shade's dick, preventing him from doing so, and that coupled with the negative internal monologue and the ping-ponging conversation Shade's head was spinning.

On top of that, he was still crying. Practically sobbing now, from both the lack of release and the hot glide of that steel-like cock penetrating him.

"You're confusing me," he admitted, and they both knew he wasn't referring to the switching topics.

"I was honest from the start," Apollo said.

That's true. He'd said he was going to take Shade apart and put him back together again.

"I just hate myself more now than I did before." The words left him on a sob. But there was no one else to share that with, and Shade didn't think he could take being haunted by that fact on his own much longer.

Before, he'd hated how he couldn't control his abilities. How he made everyone in the room uncomfortable because of them.

He'd hated how even when that wasn't the case, like with Axel and Dario, who'd been nothing but sincere and kind to him since his arrival on planet, a part of him rejected that notion anyway.

He'd been confident as a detective and nothing else, and he didn't even like being one. He hated constantly traveling and meeting new people and listening to their problems when he couldn't even solve his own damn issues.

But at least before all of this he'd been able to lie to himself about that last part. Had been able to pretend since he'd been so out of touch with his own emotions, either too busy drowning in the people around him or numbing it all with blockers. Apollo had stripped him of those security blankets and forced him to confront his own demons and frankly…

He was already exhausted by it all.

He was tired of fighting a losing battle. It was becoming clear in the end the only one who would wind up suffering was himself, and if that was the case, then who cared what other people thought of him? Who cared if he was right or normal or average or any other bullshit word.

Why couldn't he just be himself?

The universe wouldn't come to a screeching halt if he was, right?

"I want to come."

Maybe it was a reward for being honest, or maybe Apollo simply liked the sound of Shade's sobs, either way, in the next moment he took pity on him. Shade recognized that's what it was the same way he recognized the bath water had started to cool.

"Look what you do to me, baby," he crooned, and even knowing it was an attempt to placate him, to ease him back into a sense of comfort, Shade found himself slipping into that honey tone anyway. "See what you turn me into?" He released his dick, hand roaming up the center of Shade's chest instead as he fucked into him leisurely. "See how badly I want you?"

"I know what you're doing," Shade said—ever the broken record, he realized—hissing and dropping his head back against Apollo's shoulder when the other man's hand returned to his dick and started rubbing him in time with his thrusts.

Apollo knew saying those words would stroke at something different, something even deeper inside of Shade. Something otherwise untouchable.

He wanted him.

He was wanted.

"I'm all you'll ever need," Apollo promised, his breathing labored as he approached climax, hand jerking at Shade faster so that he would get there as well, "You can fight me all you need to. But you are going to be mine, fully and forever. I am going to have all of you, and you're going to give me it."

"This is insane." Shade reached back and grabbed Apollo's hair, but not to push him away. He clung to him instead, riding him as he felt that familiar tightening creep up.

"Let's be insane together then. You can be right or you can be happy. You've tried the first, is that really the life you want? Is that really what you're struggling so hard to go back to? Anyone who looks at you and doesn't see how fucking gorgeous you are is the crazy one."

Shade grunted.

"If I can't convince you you're not a monster, baby, that's okay. You can be a monster." Apollo latched onto the side of his neck and sucked, sending electrical tingles sparking throughout Shade's entire body. Then he brought his mouth to his ear and growled, "The Devil always embraces the wicked."

Shade had thought the orgasm in the forest had been intense.

He'd been mistaken.

He screamed so loudly it'd be a miracle if Gunther Hynth—that filthy disgusting kid killer—didn't hear.

And afterward, when his vision was blurry and he felt like he was untethered and floating, Apollo turned him around and cradled him against his chest, holding Shade close and whispering comforting words about how perfect he was while he sobbed.

He wasn't even sure why he was crying, whether it was because he was horrified and trapped, because of the abuse he'd just endured, or for another reason.

One that seemed entirely more terrifying than any of the others.

One he wasn't quite sure he was ready yet to face.

One he knew he was going to have to.

Chapter 27:

"Shh," Apollo cooed, planting a soft kiss to the shell of Shade's right ear as his fingers slowly prodded his entrance. They were gentle, easing in and sweeping over his walls, trying to avoid causing as much discomfort as possible. "I'm just putting in ointment, baby, don't fret. We're done for the day."

"Hurts." Shade buried his face against his arm, trying to hide the way he winced at every press of those careful fingers. They'd moved to the shower and were draped over one of the long stone benches, Apollo between him and the wall.

They were lying on their sides with the other man spooning his back, a tube of sun cream in one hand, the other methodically working the ointment over Shade's cuts and bruises. Time had started to bleed together and Shade had no clue how long they'd been in there, just that the steam from the shower spray, which only barely hit them from where they were lying, had filled the closed stall, wrapping him in a satisfying warmth.

"I got angry," Apollo told him, voice low and soothing. "You do that to me."

"So it's my fault." Shade kept his eyes closed, shifting when those fingers pushed in a little deeper. His dick twitched, and he bit his lower lip, still hiding his face from the man at his back.

"Do you want me to tell you it isn't?" Apollo asked.

"It's manipulative of you to blame me for your actions," he pointed out, but he didn't sound accusatory or even remotely upset. The comfortable surroundings and the soothing feeling of the ointment settling into his skin lulled him into a sense of calm despite everything he'd just experienced.

"I'm not a good person, Shadow. The sooner you come to terms with that, the better it'll be for the both of us."

"How do you figure?"

Apollo slipped his fingers free and then reached out to rinse them under the shower spray, unsettling Shade enough that he was forced to lift his head and steady himself or risk slipping off the bench. Ignoring the slightly frustrated glare sent his way, Apollo scooped up more cream from the tube and began to smooth it over the cuts on Shade's arms from running through the forest.

"You'll stop feeling so guilty and I'll stop having to feel you feeling so guilty," he explained.

"So it's for you then." Shade lowered his head back down, only for Apollo to resituate so that his cheek ended up pillowed against his arm instead. He didn't argue over it, eyes slipping shut again. It stung in some areas more than others, his ass one of them, and even though Apollo was being as gentle as possible, there were still moments Shade flinched.

Tears pricked the corners of his eyes, but he wasn't even sure if it was due to the pain or just a matter of being overall overwhelmed.

"Not completely," Apollo corrected. He kept speaking in hushed tones, fingers dancing down to Shade's leg, over more scrapes. They slid forward, close to the apex of his thighs but if he noticed how Shade had started to grow semi-hard, he didn't point it out. "Believe it or not, I don't like seeing you distressed, baby."

"I don't," he grit his teeth as the cream was worked into a bruise over his right knee, "believe you."

"Even though I'm taking such good care of you now?"

"You're only doing it so you can break me again later." Shade hadn't even been aware of that thought in his head, but the second the words were out he realized that's exactly what this was.

To his credit, Apollo didn't deny it either. He merely hummed lightly and planted a feather light kiss to Shade's shoulder. "That's true. In part. I'll have you falling to pieces in my arms again in no time, because I like that, a lot. And then I'll comfort you again," another kiss, this time a little closer to his neck, "help seal those pieces back together. We can do it as many times as you need. For the rest of our lives if you'd like."

"You said you'd kill me eventually," he reminded, and Apollo stilled around him for a brief second before picking up his ministrations as if the pause had never happened. Shade let it stretch on until the silence became too much and threatened to burst the sedated bubble that had formed around him. "Why aren't you saying anything?"

"Because I'm trying to keep you at ease," he admitted, "and I'm not sure responding will be conducive to that goal."

Shade licked his suddenly dry lips. "Tell me. I'm not stupid. This was my only chance to escape and I failed."

"Are you telling me you're prepared to die here, Shadow?"

He nodded his head, refusing to appear weak despite the fact he was currently pudding in the other guys hands anyway.

As if to further prove that, Apollo danced those fingers up the inside of Shade's thigh, causing Shade to arch back into him.

"You aren't going to die," he said then, firmly, as if there was no question about whether or not that was the truth.

Shade's heart skipped a beat and before the self-hatred for that response could kick in, he forced the conversation to continue. "What?"

"I'm going to keep you," Apollo told him. "Forever. For always. My perfect little Shadow," his hand slipped around to trace the definition of Shade's stomach, "how could I not? You were made for me, and I was made for you. Don't," he shushed him when he went to argue. "I won't make you say it right now, I know you're not ready. That's okay, baby. We can keep going on just like this for the time being. You can keep pretending you don't like the pain."

Shade shook his head but words stuck in his throat.

"Do you know why some people are drawn to it?" Apollo asked softly. "To pain?"

"I don't like being hurt," Shade denied, voice shaky and weak.

"No," Apollo surprised him by agreeing, "it's not the pain on its own that attracts you. You need a bit more to reach that sweet spot, that altered state of consciousness where your worries don't seem so heavy and it's easier for you to toss them away. Pain helps reduce blood flow to a certain part of the brain, the dorsolateral prefrontal cortex. Do you know what that is?"

"It helps control a lot of functions," Shade said stubbornly.

"It's partly responsible for helping to distinguish self from other." Apollo flattened his palm against the center of his chest and snuggled in deeper at his back, smiling against the curve of Shade's neck when he didn't bother attempting to pull away.

Admittedly, Shade was too curious to hear where he was going with this, too content and comfortable where he was, his muscles loosened from the steam and the sun cream.

"I'm no doctor, but I'm guessing this altered state of consciousness cuts off part of the connection you have to your abilities, severing you from the rest of the world without that nasty numbing side effect that you get from blockers."

He pursed his lips. "What makes you think that?"

"Gunther," Apollo started rolling the pad of his thumb lightly over the rosy bud of one of Shade's nipples when he tensed at the name, having him back to being pliant in a matter of heartbeats. "He was up there the entire time, just above you. The ceiling is high, yes, but with your range you should have still been able to pick up on his emotions here and there."

"But I didn't."

"Nope."

"You sound rather pleased with yourself."

"I'd suspected pain might be the way to go, but hadn't been certain. Though I suppose until it's tested further, it's still just a theory and nothing concrete."

"I don't like pain," Shade repeated. "What you did to me that first night," he shuddered, "and what you just did in the forest—"

"Claiming you?"

"We both know what that really was."

"Brutal?" Apollo turned and inhaled deeply against the side of Shade's neck. "Devilish?"

"I didn't like it."

He paused. "Are you sure?"

"Yes. It hurt."

"What about after?" Apollo persisted. "When I had you purring for me like a cat in heat?"

Shade felt his cheeks flush.

"Hey," he cupped his chin and tipped his head back so their eyes could meet, "none of that. There's no reason for you to feel embarrassed. It's just me here, baby, just us." His fingers brushed aside a lone, angry tear as it spilled free. "If it makes you feel any better, it's not just the pain. You need more than that. And you're not into it if it hurts too much; it's not like I'll ever take things so far as to lop off a body part or actually slice you open."

A whimper slipped past his lips before he could help it—because it reminded him who he was currently cuddled against and what that person was capable of—but Apollo pressed a finger to his mouth.

"Don't be scared, baby," he settled his forehead against his and breathed him in a second time, as if Shade was some drug he couldn't get enough of. "I'll hurt you, but I'll never *hurt* you."

"How can you possibly expect me to believe you?"

"Because that's not what you need," he insisted. "That's not what you like. It's not just the pain. It's what comes with it. You need a constant stream of both pain and pleasure. You need to feel wanted, but not just. It needs to feel desperate."

Shade felt himself go still, eyes widening as he searched Apollo's face as he spoke. The truth he'd thought he'd been keeping so close, so safe and hidden, sounded like no big deal coming from Apollo now. Like they were discussing his favorite foods and not his twisted sexual desires.

"I want you, baby," his hand slid across his jaw line until his fingers reached his hair and he cupped the back of his head, cradling him closer, "*desperately*. I want you so bad, all it'd taken was one look to know I had to make you mine. To know I had to claw my way inside of you until there's no chance of anyone ever untangling us from one another. Until escape won't even be a fleeting thought in that pretty head of yours."

Shade wouldn't have been able to break eye contact if his life depended on it. Maybe it did.

"I want your love—no, I need it. Crave it even. And you're going to give it to me. You're going to give me everything, return every frenzied touch and ache and kiss. Every feeling. Every want. I'm going to have you mad for me. Going to make it so that it's just you and me in here," he tapped at Shade's temple and then lowered his palm to the spot on his chest where his heart was located, "and here. I'm going to consume you, baby, and do you want to know the best part?"

A shaky breath came out of him but he was too hypnotized by that speech to fight against the mixture of guilt and curiosity within himself. He shook his head slowly.

Apollo grinned at him, expression coming alight with so much emotion, beautiful in its wickedness. "The best part," he lowered those warm lips to Shade's, the kiss brief and teasing, "is that you're going to beg me to do it. You're going to yearn for me to devour all of you, and I'm going to oblige. Know why, baby?"

Shade should put an end to this. He should be mortified, or frightened, or want to fight back.

He should feel anything really, other than what he actually felt.

Captivated.

"Because deep down you know I'm the best choice you could ever possibly make. I'm everything you've ever wanted, Shadow. I'm the only one who soothes the storm in your brain, can make you feel bad," he nipped at his lower lip, "in the exact way you like. So bad that it's good. I'm the only thing standing between your dull and unsatisfying life and the freedom you've always desired. I'm your ticket to a world free of Repletion and having to drop your gaze in front of strangers. With me at your side, you'll always hold your head high and proud. With me at your side, you'll want for nothing."

"You kill people." Right. How had he forgotten that, even for a second?

"You aren't the only one whose inner demons are soothed by our bond. I get off on bringing you to that state of bliss, hurting you and soothing the sting. Watching you struggle to hold back those tears." Apollo closed his eyes and breathed in, letting out a low groan after that sent shivers skating down Shade's spine. "I haven't felt the need to pick anyone else apart since that day I first watched you from afar. You want me to stop hunting?"

Shade allowed the other man to resituate them, laying him flat on the bench so that he could lift himself over him, settling his body atop of his, careful not to crush him beneath his weight.

Apollo brought his arms to either side of Shade's head and then kissed him again, coaxingly, with a little more heat and suggestion in it than the other couple of times. "Stay with me."

Stay with him so he wouldn't feel the need to kill, he meant.

"You're trying to blackmail me."

"I'm trying to call on that pesky empathy you've been saddled with," Apollo corrected, that grin returning full force. He didn't feel bad about it, wasn't bothering to hide it from him. "Use it to my advantage. But I'm only planting the seed," he kissed him again, "for now."

Shade felt the hard length of the other man bump against his abdomen, the responding heat sweeping through him like a wildfire. "You said we were done for the day."

"I'll get off like this," Apollo promised, rolling his hips so that his cock rubbed against Shade's stomach.

As if they had a mind of their own, Shade's hands lifted, settling themselves on Apollo's hips. He shouldn't be doing this. Shouldn't even remotely want to, and yet… "Those thoughts are starting to creep back in."

"Which ones, baby?" Apollo stroked his damp hair off his forehead, continuing with his leisurely movements against him, as if he really would be content with finding his release that way.

But he knew, it was clear as day in the way his gaze sharpened, those blue irises darkening and turning to tiny deep oceans, sucking Shade in, promising protection from the chaos of his own mind.

"The ones that say I'm a monster for listening to this." Shade dug his fingers into Apollo's hips. "The ones that say I'm grotesque."

"Don't listen to them," he said.

He inhaled, giving himself the chance to turn back before he did something those voices really wouldn't like. Before he did something he was positive he'd regret later, when the bliss he was currently feeling was over and he was returned to the cruel reality of the world.

He didn't take it.

"Help me," Shade whispered. "Make it so I can't."

"You sure, Detective?" Apollo waited, coiled and still, the anticipation written all over his gorgeous face.

The face of the Devil.

The face Shade saw in both fantasies and his nightmares.

A devil always welcomed a demon, wasn't that right? Which meant he wouldn't judge Shade for caving, just this once.

"Yeah," he said, "I'm sure."

Apollo lifted one of his legs and lined his cock up with Shade's hole faster than he could blink. Then he grinned and stared down at him with more longing and possessiveness than Shade thought possible for a single being to ever feel.

With a solid thrust he impaled him, stroking deep and hard. He set a quick rhythm, as if too lost in a frenzy to bother with slow or steady, his movements almost sloppy, though he was sure to bump against Shade's prostate with every pound in and out.

"You know what you've just done, baby?" he leaned in and growled, the satisfaction making his voice sound more like a deep purr than anything.

The orgasm snuck up on Shade, tossing him over the edge so fast there wasn't a chance of him holding back the scream as he came apart beneath the other man. As he rode the waves of pleasure, the intensity of it making him almost delirious, Apollo's words buried themselves deep within his soul.

"You're mine now," Apollo rumbled. "All mine. Forever."

Chapter 28:

His life as the reporter had helped him a lot, and not just in covering up his true nature. The fact that he'd been well liked, trusted, and respected was what had initially drawn Shade to him like a moth to a flame. Now that he knew him better, Apollo easily saw that it was because he'd had everything his little Shadow had always secretly longed for.

People liked Apollo, sang his praises, wanted to be around him. Axel had seen the two of them standing together once and immediately tried to set them up. That was the reason Shade had tuned his instincts out every time Apollo had said or done something that could have been seen as suspicious. Shade was already the type of person who didn't trust himself.

That had worked to Apollo's advantage in the beginning, but now he needed a way to break through that stubborn self-loathing. He needed the other man to be open to his own wants and needs without second guessing whether they were real or valid. It was the only way he was going to be able to keep him, at least, the only way he could keep him and keep him whole.

He wasn't sure when he'd realized that he didn't want a broken Shadow, no matter how fun picking him apart and sorting through the pieces might be. Wasn't sure when he'd switched gears, when he'd stopped trying to break Shade and instead begun to put him back together.

It'd only been a month, and suddenly it was as if the detective had become his whole world. He thought of him when he was asleep and when he was awake, and ever since Shade's attempt to escape, that urge to always keep him in his sights had intensified.

Before, he'd slept on the chair at the workbench those days he didn't fuck him, but he stopped doing that, hating even that brief amount of space between them. There'd been the chance, and still was the chance, that Shade would attempt to strangle him in his sleep with the gold chains, but it was a risk Apollo was willing to take.

He didn't have a death wish by any means, but when he wrapped himself around Shade and clutched him close enough he could feel the pounding of the other man's heart through his chest? It was worth it.

Besides, there'd been a change in Shade ever since that day. He still cursed at him and acted like he didn't like being touched—at first—but he turned to mush in Apollo's hands faster than before, with fewer struggles. The fighting didn't stop, neither of them wanted it to completely, but it was clearly becoming a game to the detective as much as it was one for Apollo. They were starting to sync up and get on the same page.

Shade still wasn't ready to come to terms with himself or his wants, but they were making faster progress than Apollo had even suspected they would. He was easily able to keep the damn Inspector off their backs by sneaking out while the detective was sleeping and send off the needed message so Gael would know he was safe and not come running, so that was covered as well.

Everything was working out the way he'd hoped, with only one caveat, the same one Apollo had become aware of before.

Shade wasn't the only one who kept changing.

Sometimes, when Shade cried out and it was obvious it wasn't an entirely good cry, Apollo instinctually reacted. It'd started with that time in the forest, when he'd been so lost to the furious haze clouding his mind he hadn't even realized he was fucking Shade without prepping him until it was too late and he was already balls deep. Even then, when it had registered, the sight of the other man's blood coating his cock had been enough to have him almost coming right then and there.

But then Shade had made a sound, one of pure agony, and he'd begged in a shaky voice so different from the one he usually had, and something in Apollo had broken apart. He'd almost felt it snapping inside of him.

He'd pulled the lube from his pocket and, not wanting to risk seriously injuring Shade any more than he already had, he'd emptied the entire bottle on his aching cock. Three weeks ago, he would have relished in the other man's weeping. If anything, it would have spurred him on to inflict even more pain, just to see how quickly he could make him come undone.

The idea of Shade suffering now, however, made Apollo's hands tighten into fists.

Next to him, Shade shifted in his sleep and mumbled something under his breath. A second later, his brow furrowed.

Was he having a bad dream?

Was it about him?

Apollo didn't like that. He'd won Shade over as the friendly neighborhood reporter, so he'd always known there was a strong chance the detective would recoil the second he was made aware that was all an act. Hell, that's exactly what he'd expected. What he'd wanted. It hadn't bothered him before.

It did now.

Shade couldn't leave him no matter what he thought of him as a person—Apollo wouldn't allow it, period—but it would be ideal if he stopped wanting to. He'd meant what he'd said the other day. He wanted the man to be just as lost in him as he was for Shade.

He needed it.

This was an altogether new emotion and Apollo still wasn't sure whether or not he liked it, not that it mattered either. He wasn't the type to fight against his instincts. If he wanted something he'd have it, and what he wanted right now was more than simply Shade's submission like he'd first believed. He wanted his adoration.

The two of them were on the mattress again, Shade stretched out and asleep with Apollo sitting back against the wall. He'd been going over some notes on his multi-slate for work, sorting through the photos he had left that he could get away with submitting. Shade was right though. They'd been here a while and he was running out of material. In his defense, he hadn't anticipated it lasting longer than this.

While it was true he hadn't wanted to take the detective apart the same why he had his other victims, he'd assumed once he'd gotten the man here, that would change and those usual proclivities would sink into his brain. Was it risky, kidnapping and murdering an I.P.F agent? Yes. But Apollo hadn't been able to resist.

Now…He needed to figure out a way to get them both through this before people came looking. Preferably a way off planet. They'd need to leave, start somewhere fresh.

Rebirth. The corner of his mouth tipped up at the corny thought and he inadvertently reached out and ran the pads of his fingers over Shade's rose tattoo.

Would Shade fight him on it?

The detective was still a conundrum. Apollo could read his emotions fairly well, but sometimes he got the reasoning behind them all wrong, which was something he wasn't willing to admit out loud. Earlier, in the bathroom, when Shade had finally given in, there'd been a rush of relief coming off of him, the taste rich and dark and decadent.

But what was that relief actually for?

Would Shade still leave him the first chance he got?

Could Apollo even blame him if he did?

Damn it. This wasn't how it was supposed to be. These emotions weren't ones Apollo was familiar with and he found he didn't like them. It wasn't empathy, per se, he knew he wasn't capable of that, and it wasn't exactly guilt but…It was something close enough to it that he felt apologetic toward the detective.

Not for everything he'd done, but for the struggle it'd forced the other man to endure. Apollo was used to accepting his true nature and embracing himself, but Shade wasn't.

Apollo had put him through that with no real long term plan, and that was the part that bugged him now. He hadn't thought that far ahead because he'd been arrogant and certain that this obsession would run its course as soon as he fed the demon within him. He'd been wrong, and now they were both going to pay the price if they were discovered by the police.

He swore under his breath and stood, pausing when one of Shade's hands snaked out and latched lightly around his ankle. Apollo peered down at him, watching as the detective mumbled something else in his sleep.

Shade's lips were pursed and whatever dream he was in, it didn't look like it'd gotten any better in the past few minutes.

Apollo lowered to the mattress and eased the other man onto his back. Carefully, he lifted one of his eyelids so he could make eye contact quickly. The taste of chocolate and tart citrus exploded on his tongue and he dropped his hand.

Distress.

He didn't like it, didn't like Shade feeling that even if it was in a dream. Gently, he removed their clothing, wanting to feel him skin to skin, and settled his body over the detective's. When his fingers trailed up the other man's inner thigh, Shade's brow twitched.

Not good enough.

Apollo watched closely as his fingers sought out Shade's entrance, slowly easing his way inside that velvet heat. The grip was tight despite their earlier activities and he almost groaned as those inner walls clutched at his digit. He played with him a bit, coaxing him out of whatever dream he'd been having, only adding another finger the moment that frown started to smooth away.

Shade made a sound of protest when Apollo pulled his hand away, but he didn't leave him wanting for long.

He took a moment to apply more lube from the bottle they'd left on the floor by the mattress earlier, and then lifted Shade's left leg up. His cock sought out his hole and he glided in, relishing the clenching grip as Shade's body sucked him in.

"What are you doing?" Shade's voice was tired, and a bit scratchy from all the screaming he'd done earlier. The frown returned, but it was different this time, more curious than upset, and when he blinked up at Apollo and wrapped his arms around his neck it wasn't to struggle or push him away.

"What does it look like? I fuck you every day, Shadow. Today is no exception. Got to get you nice and used to my cock. Nice and dependent, so you crave it and can't go more than twenty-four hours without me filling you with my come," despite the words he said, his voice came out in a murmur, and he brushed his lips over Shade's face between sentences, just a brief press here and there.

"You fuck me every other day," Shade corrected. "Don't think I didn't notice."

"Did you?" He hadn't been sure.

"This is new though." The question was there even though he didn't openly ask it. Instead, he shifted on the mattress, angling his hips up to meet Apollo's leisurely strokes.

"Bad new?" Apollo wondered if he needed to apply some pain, if maybe this approach was too tame for his little Shadow. Was he not enjoying it? "Do you always need it rough?"

"If you'd asked me that before I would have said yes."

"You wouldn't have said anything at all," he corrected. The detective had been too ashamed. It was a wonder he was saying any of this now.

"True." Shade grinned at him and then sucked in a sharp breath when Apollo's cock rubbed against his just right. His fingernails curved at the back of Apollo's neck, but he didn't dig them in. "Plain sex was boring before."

"But it's not now?" He rolled his hips. "This isn't?"

Shade shook his head, the dark tendrils of his hair against the white of the mattress and his blown pupils making Apollo pick up the pace a little, rocking into him harder.

The detective was perceptive. Of course he'd picked up on the fact they only did this every other day. He no doubt understood Apollo's motives behind it as well, though he'd never brought it up. He was bringing this up though. He wanted to know why the pattern had changed, why Apollo was touching him tenderly.

"Quit stalling," Shade told him. "Tell me why you're doing this."

He didn't want to, but while he was many things, hypocrite wasn't one of them. So he rested his arms at the side of Shade's head, brushed the pad of his thumb beneath his eye before saying, "You were having a nightmare. Do you remember?"

"Apparently I have them frequently," Shade said, and at his questioning look explained, "Gael has mentioned it."

Apollo pulled all the way out to the tip and rammed himself back inside, hard enough to send Shade's body sliding up the mattress.

He gasped, hands dropping to Apollo's side for better purchase.

"Gael—"

"Stop talking," Apollo ordered darkly. He'd started this to help Shade out but possessiveness blinded him now as he pictured the damn Inspector close enough to *his* Shadow, on multiple occasions, to recognize he had nightmares recurrently. "You aren't allowed to think of anyone else when I'm balls deep inside of you. You don't get to do that when the only thing, the only person, I ever have on my mind anymore is you."

"Thought you were trying to comfort me here?" Shade teased, and it was clear that's what he was doing, since he never dropped his hold, even when the tempo of Apollo's thrusts increased enough to have the mattress shaking beneath them. Before he could get a reply, he tossed his head back, exposing the long length of his throat, and moaned.

The sound was loud enough it seemed to echo around them, spurring Apollo on. His mouth latched onto his neck, sucking and biting. He swirled his tongue over every nip, soothing the sting, before repeating the gesture. He'd wanted this to be soft, but apparently neither of them was very good at that sort of sex.

They also weren't going to last much longer.

Apollo felt his balls tighten and reached down to work Shade's length with quick pumps of his fist, needing to get him off first.

The second the detective cried out and Apollo felt his thick ropes of come splatter against his lower abdomen he toppled over the edge himself.

The orgasm had him bucking wildly, as if he was trying to burrow into Shade's body, he emptied himself deep, panting against the curve of Shade's neck as the spasms zipped through him like electricity.

For a moment there was nothing but a heated white blanket surrounding him. Just that and the inferno of the man beneath him. Then he felt a hand at the back of his head and he froze, yanked from that euphoric state.

Was Shade…petting him?

Nimble fingers threaded through the inky hair at the base of his skull, then traveled up to delve through more of it. Shade made a satisfied humming sound, the type of sound that made its way all the way down to Apollo's toes.

When he risked pulling away enough to glance down at him, it was to find Shade's eyes closed, a dreamy, content expression on his face.

Sensing he was being watched, Shade cracked his eyes open, staring back at him from beneath hooded lashes. "Next time you want to wake me from a bad dream, you can try something other than your cock to do it."

Apollo tensed, but before he could say anything, Shade laughed.

It was a real laugh too. Open and rich, like wind chimes on a warm, breezy mid-summer afternoon.

As soon as it ended, Apollo wanted to hear it again.

"I'm not saying I didn't enjoy it," Shade told him, seemingly completely unaware of the awe Apollo was now feeling, "I'm merely pointing out that sometimes fucking isn't going to be possible and there are other, more subtle ways to make a person feel better when they're down than just sticking it in them."

"Such as?" Apollo asked, part of him wondering if this was really even happening. The last time they'd had an easy, normal conversation like this where he hadn't needed to pull proverbial teeth from the detective's mouth first had been before he'd kidnapped him.

But the man underneath him now, the one still absently playing with his hair, who'd let his eyes drift shut once more, letting his guard down around Apollo completely, this was the man he'd encountered that day in the bar. Later during their first run. He was that guy, and yet so much more.

Compliant and relaxed.

Apollo wanted to capture this moment in a jar and preserve it. He wanted to keep this forever, for always, wanted—

"You're doing it again," Shade's words had him snapping back to attention. The detective was looking at him. "I'm right here," he said once their eyes met, "I'm already in chains," he rattled his wrist, sending the gold links clinking as if to prove it, "and you've got me pretty pinned at the moment." He jutted his chin out to indicate their positions. "I'm not going anywhere. Breathe."

He inhaled as though he hadn't taken a breath in a million years, only then realizing that he must have stopped at some point. He frowned.

"You do that sometimes," Shade explained to him, "it's been less often as of late, but it still happens once in a while."

"Do what?"

"Get that scary look in your eyes, like you want to skin me alive and wear as a suit or something equally gruesome."

"I would never do that," Apollo reassured him. "I would never hurt you like that."

"Yeah," he smoothed his fingers through his hair one final time and then dropped his arm to his side, "I know."

"Do you?"

"I was dreaming of the day my parents left me," he said suddenly. "The nightmare you woke me from? It was that. It usually is. My dad pulls the hovercar up to the orphanage, he doesn't look at me, doesn't say a word as I step out with my mom. She takes me by the shoulders and she makes me meet her gaze, but it's different, I can't only feel it with my abilities, but I can see it clear as day. She feels guilty, sad, disappointed, but more than that? She feels relieved. Relieved to be rid of me. Her monstrous child. I was the only Chitta in the family."

"There's nothing monstrous about being a Chitta," Apollo told him. It wasn't the Chitta part of him that made him enjoy killing people any more than it was the Chitta part that made Shade hate himself. "Your mom was the one in the wrong, Shadow. Not you. It was never really about you. *Her* demons convinced her to be a shitty parent and abandon you, not yours."

Shade was silent for a long while before he exhaled and draped an arm over his face, hiding himself. "There's definitely something wrong with me, because I actually believe you."

"So?"

"You're a serial killer? Of course you don't think there's anything wrong with me. The things you've done are way worse than anything I have."

Apollo may have been offended, but when he pulled Shade's arm away so he could read the other man, there was nothing but the taste of smooth milk chocolate on his tongue.

"You aren't upset," he pointed out. "Are you accepting it finally?"

"What?" He quirked a brow. "That just because I like a mix of pain with my pleasure doesn't mean I deserved to be rejected by society? Or—"

"You like the pain and the pleasure that *I* give you," Apollo stated, holding his breath all over again as he waited for a response.

"This is conditioning," Shade told him. "I know that. I've known it from the start. Logically, I can still see all the reasons this is fucked up and I should push you away. But just because I knew it doesn't mean I could fight against it. Just because there's no way for this to actually work doesn't mean I don't want to give in and see how long we can make it. I already tried running."

Apollo growled before he could help it.

"Don't worry. I learned my lesson."

"And what lesson is that?" he asked.

"My demons can follow me wherever I go," Shade said, "at least with you, they're contained. When I'm with you, I don't have to hate myself. I can pretend to hate you instead."

The keyword there was pretend, but Apollo wasn't going to make a big deal of it, not willing to risk pushing him too far when this was the first time he was actually coming to terms with everything.

"Bring me a coffee," Shade brought them back around to their earlier topic without skipping a beat. "If you want me to feel better, bring me a coffee."

Apollo glanced at the darkness just outside the warehouse. "It's three in the morning. I wasn't going to wake you up and shove a cup of caffeine into your hands."

"Next time, do."

"Getting kind of bossy, Shadow mine."

"You don't get to pick and choose," he said. "You either take me as I am, or we go back to me fighting you every step of the way. I'm not a slave, Apollo, not even yours, and I refuse to be one."

"No," he grinned, "you're my captive. My conquest. My—"

"Those mean the same thing."

Apollo laughed.

Chapter 29:

The top level was an open floorplan just like the lower one, and just like down there, Apollo had sectioned a corner off.

Only, here it was done with plastic sheets on the ground. Two even hung from the ceiling, creating flimsy walls at either side of the station he'd created. The plastic billowed at their approach, catching the attention of the man currently seated in the very center of the large tarp on the ground.

Shade could feel him.

It was murky, like standing on the edge of a cliff and peering down into the waves crashing against the rocky shore, but it was there. The sensation was…not entirely unpleasant, despite the types of emotions coming off the other guy.

The one currently tied to a chair across the room with thick ropes that bit into his tender and raw flesh. The man was twice the size of Shade, with a balding head and a round nose set over thick lips. He couldn't tell his eye color, since both of his eyes were practically swollen shut, but aside from the damage to his face there didn't appear to be any other obvious injuries.

Gunther Hynth was a bank teller at Central Ux North, one of the largest banks in the city. He was forty-seven, a widower with no children, and didn't have a criminal record.

But according to Apollo, he was also a pedophile who made his own home movies. One of which being what he'd shown Shade that day over a week ago.

Where he'd watched a small form being brutally butchered for fun before the final killing blow had been delivered. Even thinking about it had Shade's stomach churning. Knowing there were people like that out there, hiding in the dark, completely under the police and the I.P.F's radar made him livid.

He'd been trying to avoid this, but ever since he'd found out Gunther was up here, he'd known he would eventually have to confront it. As a detective, duty told him to untie the man and demand Apollo call for an ambulance. But as a person…

Gunther didn't deserve help.

"Did you only punch him?" he found himself asking, tipping his head toward Apollo who was standing just slightly behind him.

There was a workbench off to the right, set between them and Gunther. An array of tools was laid out carefully across the surface, sorted by size over type. Shade scanned them, noting a few corkscrews and more than one blade before returning his attention straight ahead.

They were only a ten or fifteen feet away from the man in question, the tarp taped down to the cement floor beneath the metal chair he'd been placed on mostly clean aside from a few dirty boot prints and a couple dried puddles of blood. It certainly didn't look like any of the crime scenes Shade would expect from the same serial murderer who'd killed those other people in the photos he had.

"Why do you sound disappointed by that, Detective?" Apollo drawled.

That caught Gunther's attention and he perked up some. "Hello?"

Apollo clicked his tongue. "Don't speak to him. You don't have the right."

"Please, help me!" Gunther tugged on his bindings, no doubt digging the rough ropes deeper into the ruined skin at his wrists and ankles, though Shade couldn't see with his arms behind him. He wasn't wearing any shoes and his toenails could use a clipping. The dress pants were wrinkled and smelled, and his dress shirt was stained in a mixture of grime and blood. "Detective?! Please, he's crazy! He's going to kill me!"

"Like you killed that boy?" Shade asked, and even he didn't recognize the almost deadpan tone of his voice. He tried to summon up some kind of pity for the tied man, but... there was nothing. "How old was he anyway? I couldn't tell from the video."

Gunther's bottom lip trembled and he deflated in his chair. Clearly he knew exactly what video Shade was referring to.

"How you feeling?" Apollo leaned in closer and asked against the curve of Shade's ear, not in a sexual way, but a comforting one.

It felt like he was there for him, that if anything went wrong, Shade could count on him to get him out of there before Repletion could set in. He waited for the usual fight to hit him, for his gut reaction to urge him to pull away, but it didn't. He didn't move in closer to him or anything like that, but he didn't move away either.

Something had broken in Shade that day in the forest. He'd been thrown to the ground and brutally fucked like an animal, the pain had been searing and excruciating…and marvelous. He'd shattered and come apart around Apollo, and afterward he'd literally felt the pieces coming back together.

The ones he hadn't wanted to keep? He'd left them in the debris. And any lingering ones that had clung to his skin? Apollo had washed those away in the tub.

The other night, when he'd been woken by Apollo's caresses and his cock, Shade had kept the best part of his dream to himself.

He'd seen his parents abandoning him like he'd said—it was a dream he had frequently. Except with one major difference. How it had ended. Shade been screaming after his parents retreating car, begging them to come back. In reality, that's when someone from the orphanage had heard and come out to retrieve him, but in the dream…A hand had settled on his shoulder, and he'd turned expecting to see the pitying look of Jo Lorn, the kind woman who'd taken him in, but instead it'd been Apollo standing there.

The instant relief he'd felt at seeing him, at knowing he wasn't alone anymore, had forced Shade to acknowledge another truth he hadn't been willing to accept up until that point.

He was falling for Apollo, not lightly or gently, but the way someone tripped and stumbled down a flight of stairs. It was painful and a struggle and more than once on the way down he prayed for it to finally end, but the landing was there. He'd reach it eventually. And when he did...

Another hard truth? Shade was a detective who should feel bad for this guy, no matter what atrocity he'd committed. He wasn't the judge, jury, and executioner. His job was simply to solve cases and make arrests.

But he'd seen that video, and it'd stuck with him in the days since.

When Apollo had wordlessly led him up here, Shade had known the reason without having to ask. He could have said no, could have tried to resist, but he'd been curious as well.

His abilities hadn't picked up on Gunther from the bottom level. Would they fair better face to face?

"I can read him," he said, opening those floodgates within himself a little more. The other man's emotions came in stronger, but nothing Shade couldn't handle. There wasn't even a slight aching at his temples. There was just the terror from Gunther and the interest from Shade, and the two were very easy to distinguish between. "He's going to piss himself."

Apollo snorted. "You can't possible know—" He stopped, eyes going wide when Gunther whimpered and a second later his trousers started to get wet. "I stand corrected. How did you know?"

"His fear is rising," he glanced at him, "can't you tell?"

"Not with his eyes like that." Apollo waved a hand in front of his own face and grimaced.

That was right.

"So you don't know what I'm feeling right now either." Since Shade was facing away. Sometimes Apollo could still sense him for a bit after they'd made eye contact, the connection strong enough between them to linger, but he could never figure out how long that timeframe lasted.

Apollo stilled behind him. "Do you?"

Shade took a second to double-check, just in case, but it wasn't necessary.

"Yes." The layers used to describe how a Chitta's abilities worked were clear within him now, and…. "It's familiar. How simple this is? I'm pretty sure I've felt it before."

"This was how you used to be, before your parents."

"And the trauma of it all, yeah." That answered that question. He hadn't always been overly stimulated after all. The psychiatrists had been right about him needing to make a breakthrough mentally. "If you make a comment about your magic dick, I'll find those sheers."

Gunther made another scared whimpering sound.

"Oh no," Apollo said, "Am I starting to rub off on you, Detective?"

"I still know what you're doing." He was calling him by his title on purpose, trying to see if he'd react to it the way he used to.

Being a detective was all he'd had going for him in the past, the only thing he had to help keep the monsters from fully consuming him. He'd gotten praise for a job well done, attention for being of such a high rank, and that mixture of respect had helped to quiet the self-doubt in his mind, at least on and off.

"This doesn't prove I'm fixed," he stated. "Just because I can properly read one person now doesn't mean I can handle a crowd. I could go back out there and instantly be bombarded and right back at square one."

"Only," Apollo wrapped a possessive arm around his waist and pulled him against his side, "you wouldn't be going out there alone. You'd have me. And if anything did go wrong, I would get you out of there."

Shade's heart kicked up a notch but he tried not to get his hopes up. "Does that mean you're going to let me out?"

Apollo was silent for a moment before he planted a chaste kiss on the rise of his cheek and said, "One step at a time, Shadow mine."

He was afraid Shade was going to make another run for it. He didn't need to be able to read the other man to figure that out. Apollo didn't want to lose him, didn't want to have to chase after him and drag him back kicking and screaming.

Shade wasn't the only one who'd been altered during their time together.

Interesting.

"What are you going to do?" He jutted his chin out toward Gunther.

"I've never kept anyone this long," Apollo admitted. "I sort of got distracted and forgot all about him, to be honest." He rested his chin on Shade's shoulder a second time. "What would you like me to do with him?"

"You can't let him go." He'd been around too long, knew too much. Even if he hadn't gotten Shade's name, he'd clearly seen Apollo's face. If they freed him, he could go straight to the police and give a description and—

With a start, he realized where his thoughts had been leading. Sure, Shade had never been the caring sort, the one who was in this for justice or in the name of doing the right thing. He felt bad when he saw someone wronged or hurt, found it absolutely disgusting what Gunther had done to that kid in the video, but that had never been the sort of thing that'd kept him up at night.

No, that had been the pain from his ability and the voices in his head that told him no one liked him and he was a freak. The second a case was closed, that was it for him. He rarely if ever thought of it again.

"I don't think you're rubbing off on me," he mused, tone flat, "I think this is who I've always been."

His abilities had made him unstable, confused. But without all of that hanging over his head, he was able to really feel his own emotions without anything else getting in the way. And what he felt toward Gunther wasn't anything close to what someone in his position should be feeling.

Not only did he not give a shit about the man's pain, he actually felt like, maybe he deserved it.

"That video was one of the worst things I've ever seen in my entire life," Shade said, this time loud enough to be sure the man tied to the chair could hear. "People like that shouldn't be allowed to roam the streets with the rest of society."

People like that were the true monsters, not Shade.

"You—" Gunther stuttered over his words, a flare of anger seeping through the fear. "You're just as bad as I am! You're a freak!"

Apollo growled and made to storm over, but Shade caught him around the arm and stopped him with a shake of his head.

"It didn't bother me," he told him, surprised to find that was the truth. Before, any negative comment toward him would have sent him spiraling, but now the accusation rolled off his shoulders as if it were nothing. Why shouldn't it? "Why should I care what the likes of him thinks of me?" He tugged on Apollo until the other man turned back to meet his gaze once more. "What do you think of me?"

"You're perfect, baby." Apollo gave his back to Gunther, cupping Shade's face and resting his forehead on his. "There's nothing wrong with you."

"Bullshit!" Gunther yelled. "Help! Someone help me!"

"He must think there are other people here," Shade guessed. "Since I came out of nowhere and all."

A snapping sound was all the warning they got before Gunther sprung out of the chair. His ankles were still tied together, but he'd somehow managed to break through the rope around his wrists. He must have been working on doing so for a while.

Gunther practically tossed his body at the workbench, blindly grabbing for anything before he found the rounded handle of a screwdriver. With a snarl he flung himself at them, his head tipped back so he could see through the small swollen slit of his left eye.

It all happened so quickly, Apollo barely had the chance to turn, let alone understand the danger for what it was.

Shade saw though, saw the pointed end of the screwdriver arch toward Apollo's neck, and more than that, he felt.

The rage and terror coming off of Gunther filled him to the brim, and before, that would have been enough to snuff his own emotions out, but not any longer. He could still feel himself there under the surface, so when a burst of fear shot through him he reacted.

He shoved Apollo out of the way, hard enough to send the other man sprawling onto the plastic sheet.

Shade didn't watch him fall, however, still acting on instinct as he grabbed onto Gunther's wrist. Using the man's own momentum, he shoved at his elbow, angling with his hold on his wrist.

The screwdriver ended up in Gunther's neck instead of Apollo's.

The man stumbled away, gasping, hitting the workbench with a thud as he yanked the screwdriver out.

Big mistake.

Blood burst from him like a sprinkler, spraying Shade in the face and all over the floor. Gunther's shirt was soaked through within seconds, and his mouth opened and closed like a fish gasping for air. All in all, it couldn't have lasted longer than a minute or two, but it felt like an hour had passed by the time Gunther's body dropped to the ground on his side and he ceased all movements.

Crimson pooled beneath him, flowing outward toward the edge of the tarp where Apollo still sat. Some of it even reached his foot, but he didn't seem to notice.

Apollo was staring up at Shade like he was seeing him for the first time and he was the most awe-inspiring thing he'd ever laid eyes on. His lips were slightly pursed, his chest rising and falling in a quick crescendo as if he was full of barely contained energy just waiting for the chance to explode out of him.

The darkness of his eyes mirrored back a stunned Shade.

He was covered in blood and…He gulped, head shifting slowly back toward the body on the ground.

It wasn't the first time he'd killed someone. His job was dangerous and sometimes he had to use lethal force. But all those other times had been different. This…He'd murdered this man for—

"You just killed someone for me," Apollo's honey-toned voice cut through Shade's thoughts like a razorblade, slashing through any of the resistance he'd been trying to build inside of himself.

It was one thing to admit that he enjoyed being manhandled by the other guy, it was another to discover his body's reaction when finding Apollo in danger.

Shade hadn't blinked an eyelash attacking Gunther. He'd seen Apollo in harm's way and his gut reaction had been to protect him. Defend him.

Slowly, Apollo rose to his feet, seemingly not even seeing when Shade shook his head and retreated a solid step. There was a haze over his eyes, a reverence there that was freaking Shade out a little.

Alarm bells screamed in his head, telling him to turn around and run, completely ignoring the fact that the last time he'd tried that, he'd ended up right where Apollo had wanted him anyway.

He backed away another step but didn't have a chance to decide what to do from there.

In less than a heartbeat, Shade found himself lying on the tarp, back pressed against the partial pool of blood, with Apollo hovering between his spread thighs. When he tried to lift himself into a sitting position, his palm slipped in the puddle and he fell back.

"Stop," the word came out breathy as he watched Apollo strip his t-shirt over his head, and Light help him, even with everything going on, the second his gaze snagged onto Apollo's cut body, his brain fritzed out for a second.

It was long enough for Apollo to unzip his pants and then yank Shade's shorts clean off. Grabbing a fistful of Shade's red shirt, he pulled him up so he was sitting after all, but only so he could remove that final article of clothing. Then he planted a palm around his throat and shoved him back down, rising over him with a wild glint in his eyes that instantly brought Shade back to that time in the forest.

"Wait!" He pressed against Apollo's chest, desperation growing. "Too much pain!"

Amazingly, Apollo froze above him, mind seeming to catch up to the moment, he stared down at Shade, taking in his panicked expression.

"I don't like it when it hurts too much," Shade managed to say, wondering if he was getting through to him or not.

Apollo sucked in a breath then, seemingly coming alive, and some of the intensity in his gaze softened. His hand found Shade's dick between them, and he twisted his fingers around his flushed cockhead before he dragged his palm down to the base and back up again. He worked him carefully, in easy gliding motions.

Shade grew hard, a moan slipping out as some of the tension in his shoulders eased. When he dropped his head back to the tarp, there was a squelching sound, but he couldn't even be bothered to care, not with Apollo's hand pumping him like that.

"You look like a damn wet dream, baby," Apollo growled. "The Devil's wet dream."

"Thought you were the Devil," Shade somehow managed to tease through the pleasure rising within him. In the back of his mind, a little voice was screaming that this was a different level of fucked up, but he wasn't really sure what that voice meant, and honestly? Who fucking cared? He especially didn't when Apollo released his dick, causing him to whine and gyrate beneath him in a plea.

Apollo had made him this way. Had made it so no matter what kind of sick and twisted bullshit was taking place around him, the second he touched Shade everything else faded into the background. It was all just white noise in the face of the Devil.

"My devil," he whispered, reaching for Apollo to drag him down to him. Their teeth clashed as he pried his mouth open with his tongue, stroking in deep, just the way he wanted Apollo to touch him. He rolled their tongues together and sucked on Apollo's bottom lip.

An explosion of sensation ricocheted through his being, the same as it always did when they kissed. Even that first time, Shade had felt it all the way to his core. It'd frightened him then, and it still did now, but there was something else lurking beneath the surface that he'd been viciously fighting against all this time.

Shade should care that this man manipulated him into wanting him with this sort of fervor.

But he didn't.

He should care that Apollo was a wanted criminal capable of horrible crimes.

But he didn't.

And if nothing else, he should, at the very least, care that he was about to be taken on the ground in a pool of blood.

But that didn't matter either. Not even when he thought about Gael and how disappointed he'd be if he ever found out.

Shade opened his legs wider, and took one of Apollo's hands, lifting it to rest lightly around his throat. Silently, he urged the other man on, his neglected dick already painting trails of precome across Apollo's lower abdomen.

Apollo's fingers found his hole and shoved in, stretching him and curling until he was a writhing mess beneath him. Then he replaced them with his stiff cock, thrusting inside brutally. He settled himself overtop Shade as he fucked him fast and hard, staking his claim on his body and mind.

As if there was even a slight chance that Shade could still pretend not to know exactly who he belonged to by this point.

Shade cried out and clawed at Apollo's back, only causing him to pound in harder. His head rolled to the side, and he caught sight of Gunther's body but Apollo quickly grasped his chin between two fingers and dragged his gaze back to him.

"Eyes on me, Detective." He grinned. "I get to see you painted in blood after all."

Suddenly, Apollo leaned back, switching their positions, pulling Shade on top so that he straddled him, his cock still buried deep inside his silky heat. "Ride me, baby," he ordered. "Show me who's my perfect little Shadow."

The blood had continued to pool around them and Apollo had rested back in some himself. Red coated his shoulders and the backs of his arm, a smear across his cheek when he rubbed at it with the back of his hand. Then he placed those hands on Shade's hips and dug into his flesh hard enough to leave bruises.

Shade started moving, his heavy dick bobbing between them as he rode Apollo at a frenzied pace that rivaled his earlier one. He chased after his release, gazing down into those ocean eyes, lost to their pull as he felt himself swell and threaten to burst.

He clenched around Apollo's cock as he came, spurting come across the other man's chest, fascinated by how he looked splattered in the stuff. A thrill shot its way down Shade's spine, a possessiveness he hadn't been aware he was capable of coiling in him so that when he slammed his palm to the ground at the side of Apollo's head, he almost didn't realize what he was even doing.

"You can't do this with anyone else," he stated.

Apollo's eyes gleamed. "You're the first person I've killed with, baby."

"And you're the first person I've killed for," he snapped. Before that fact could catch hold and drag him into the darkness of his mind, he pushed on. "You got what you wanted. Everything you did worked. Are you happy now?"

"Almost." One of Apollo's hands left Shade's side, gripping the back of his nape to force him down over him. He captured his mouth in another savage kiss that had Shade's mind reeling and his dick springing instantly back to life between them.

Apollo took hold of it and stroked him as he continued to thrust up into Shade's ass, meeting him and grinding against him in a way that had both of them groaning.

Shade came again a second before he felt the warmth of Apollo's come bathing his insides. He spasmed, riding through the intense waves, and then practically went boneless over him, unable to lift even his head anymore as he settled it just beneath the curve of Apollo's jaw.

He was positive he'd be abhorred later when he was in his right headspace and thought about what they'd just done—what he'd just done—but for now, he'd rather just cling to the man beneath him and accept that, maybe, Apollo wasn't the only devil here after all.

Chapter 30:

"I'll be back as soon as I can," Apollo's warm voice drifted over to where Shade sat, leaning against the wall on the mattress.

The golden cuffs had been secured to the chains once more, keeping him locked in place, not that he noticed. He hardly noticed anything, too lost in his thoughts to bother. Shade didn't even know how long he'd been like that, but it must have been a while since Apollo was ready to leave.

There was a large black plastic suitcase being dragged behind him and Shade's eyes caught on it momentarily.

How many bones had Apollo needed to break to contort a guy the size of Gunther to fit in that?

Why was that his only question?

He searched within himself like he'd been doing since he'd stabbed the man in the neck, but...there was nothing when it came to Gunther. No remorse, no regret, no pity.

He couldn't even really say he was glad the man was dead, it was more just an...indifference.

Shade had done what he'd had to in order to protect Apollo.

Apollo, the man who'd lied to him, captured him, and manipulated him.

The man who, even now, was about to go dispose of a dead body as if he were going for a stroll in the park.

Apollo's eyebrow twitched, a show that he was irritated, and it was obvious by the hardening of his ocean eyes that it was toward Shade.

"If you crawl back into hiding," he warned, "I'll drag you out all over again."

"I'm not." Shade could tell he didn't believe him, but that was okay. He only partially believed himself. It wasn't like he wanted to go back to being that self-deprecating person, he didn't. Eventually, you could escape the torment from other people, but if the bullying came from within? You were trapped.

Shade didn't want to continue to trap himself. That didn't mean there weren't some serious things he needed to consider. Like where he went from here and what he wanted next.

"I murdered someone," he reminded. "I'm going to need a minute."

"For what?" Apollo asked. "Do you regret it, Detective? Regret saving me and ending that scum? Would you have preferred he take me out so the two of you could run off to your precious—"

"Enough." He closed his eyes and rested his head back against the wall, needing something solid to lean on.

Surprisingly, Apollo listened. Silence stretched between them, tense and uncomfortable.

It'd never been like that between them, even when he'd first arrived here and discovered the other man's betrayal. The air around them had always seemed electrically charged, pushing down on Shade from all sides so that the only thing he could focus on was Apollo and the things he elicited within him.

"I'll be back," Apollo finally broke the tension, all of the accusations that'd been in his tone only a second ago leeched out now. "When I am, we'll talk."

It wasn't a question, but Shade gave a curt nod of his head anyway. He listened to the sound of retreating footsteps and the rolling of plastic wheels as the other man left, not opening his eyes until the engine of a hovercar signaled he was well and truly gone.

This was the first time he was being left completely alone in the building, and he waited to see if that urge from before hit him, the one that had screamed at him to run.

It didn't.

Shade sighed and stretched out his legs, feet dangling off the side of the mattress. The black shorts and tang top he was in were different from the ones he'd worn earlier. Those had been covered in blood by the time he and Apollo had finished with each other. They'd most likely been destroyed along with the rest of the evidence upstairs.

He'd gone quiet as soon as that second orgasm had hit him, a mixture of shock and revulsion overwhelming him to the point he'd gagged and thrown up.

Right next to Gunther's lifeless body.

Apollo had no doubt cleaned that up as well. His vomit.

After he'd puked, Apollo had smoothed the sticky tendrils of his hair off his face and led him wordlessly downstairs to the bathroom. He'd washed him in the shower, removing all traces of carnage from Shade's skin before bothering to work on cleaning himself. It'd been the same with getting dressed. He'd brought Shade a change of clothes and had helped him into them, naked and dripping the entire time.

Then he'd secured Shade to the chains and had disappeared on the top leave for...a while. Only returning with the suitcase. It'd been obvious what he'd done and where he was going.

Shade had murdered a man, had sex in his blood, and had sat back and watched as all of the evidence was destroyed. That wasn't just grounds for expulsion from the I.P.F., if it was discovered he'd be thrown in a dark prison cell to rot for twenty years minimum.

And the worst part? The part that had him throwing up all over the place?

He didn't care.

That revulsion he'd felt hadn't been because of what he'd done. It hadn't been about the fact he'd looked into Gunther's lifeless eyes while Apollo had been pounding into him, fucking him with a dead body less than five feet away while the man's still warm blood sloshed beneath them.

The fact that he didn't care was what repulsed him.

What kind of person did something like that and didn't feel disgusted? He'd killed Gunther, a child rapist, and murderer, to protect Apollo. Okay. Fair. But the second it'd become clear what Apollo intended to do afterward, Shade should have shoved him away. He should have protested. But what had he done?

He'd asked Apollo to prep him first.

He'd asked him to make it feel good.

Not, "hey, let's take this downstairs" or "no thanks, I just stabbed a man with a screwdriver, I'm not in the mood". Apollo had flipped him onto his back and despite everything, Shade had *wanted it*.

He ran a palm down his face and cursed. Apollo had warned him not to hide again. Shade didn't think he could even if he wanted to.

So, hard truth time.

Be it Stockholm Syndrome or grooming or whatever, the fact of the matter was Shade had feelings for Apollo. Was it all kinds of fucked up? Yes. But he had them and that was that. Pretending he didn't wouldn't solve anything. He'd spent his whole life pretending and look where that'd gotten him. Miserable and alone.

He should hate the other man for all of the things that he'd done, not just to him personally but to others, and yet…he couldn't. He didn't want to.

Apollo had forced him to confront his inner demons in a way no one else ever had before. He'd pushed him to the edge and then over it, and then he provided the lifeline Shade needed to save himself. It was calculated and manipulative, but that was only further proof that Shade wasn't normal, because thinking about that only made him like Apollo more.

No one had wanted him, not even his parents. No one had bothered getting to know him or taking from him without asking because they couldn't stand being apart. Apollo was a criminal and this thing between them was toxic and twisted, but damn if Shade's insides didn't ignite just thinking about his handsome face or the way he whispered to him in the dark.

Before today, there'd still been a sliver of a chance that Shade could wake up from this one day and realize he no longer wanted the nightmare. That he could wake up and see the devil for what he well and truly was, and this time, it would disgust him.

Now even that remote possibility was gone. Dead, just like Gunther.

And the best part?

Shade had been the one to kill it.

In that heartbeat of time, he'd had a choice to make, and he'd chosen.

He'd chosen Apollo and the dark promises he'd made. He'd chosen a lifetime on the run with a dangerous, wicked man who may or may not one day decide he no longer needed Shade around. Obsessions could end just like anything else, right? Yet even knowing that Shade had sided with him.

Shade had picked the devil.

He'd picked himself.

And that was the true crux of it all.

Shade didn't want to be normal. He wanted to be happy. Even if that happiness meant saying screw it to everyone else. Even if it meant turning his back on the things he'd foolishly believed mattered all this time. None of it did. None of it was real.

His life back on Percy? Those awards and accolades for a job well done? Shade had only ever been after acceptance and praise. He'd wanted the whispers people sent his way to at least be about how good he was at being a detective and not about him being a broken Chitta. Maybe he was still broken, and not being able to read Gunther all this time was a fluke, or maybe the onslaught of emotion Apollo had forced down his throat had actually worked and he'd stabilized in that department. No matter the outcome, it wouldn't make a difference now.

Shade didn't want to be a detective anymore. He didn't *need* to be one anymore.

He could just be himself—his twisted messed up self—and he was okay with that.

All this time he'd been so scared of rejection that it'd blinded him to the truth. He'd abandoned himself that same day his parents had. He'd turned his own back and he'd hated and loathed the person he was.

He didn't need anyone else to accept him.

He needed to accept himself.

Want himself.

Shade had fought for others, but he'd never fought for himself. In this context, perhaps starting to made him selfish, but he'd been waiting for that familiar guilt and self-loathing to seep inside of him and take over his mind for hours now and…nothing.

Apollo was right. They were going to have to talk, and then—

Movement on the ground just outside the warehouse entrance caught his attention, cutting his thoughts short. A N.I.M. ball rolled toward the opening, pausing just outside the doorway. A green light flickered out, keeping low at first before rising. The Elec-Shield crackled.

Slowly, Shade got to his feet. N.I.M.'s weren't available to the public yet, which meant—

The shield popped, sparks flying everywhere as the device hacked through it. The ball rolled forward, safely entering the warehouse, and not a moment later a familiar form was rushing around the side, gaze wildly searching and landing on Shade.

Gael.

Shade's enter body went still as he watched his friend run across the concrete toward him, at least a dozen other officers dressed in combat gear coming in after him. They fanned out, searching and calling out to each other.

"Are you all right?!" Gael grabbed Shade by the shoulders and pulled him from the wall, the chains clanking heavily. He glared at them and swore, lifting one of Shade's arms to check his wrists, seemingly confused when they weren't red or raw.

They wouldn't be, in part because he'd long since stopped fighting against his bindings, but also because Apollo was always sure to treat any minor injuries he may have gotten during one of their rough sex sessions. If anything, aside from the flush to his skin at being discovered here, like this, and a barely visible smattering of bruises around his throat, Shade looked physically unharmed.

He expected the embarrassment to hit him then—even though he was fully clothed he was still basically chained to a bed—and he'd always cared so much about what people thought of him, and here were a ton of people to see his current state.

But it never came.

What did he have to be embarrassed about?

"I'm fine," he said, surprised when he sounded calm and at ease.

Gael frowned at him. "Are you really? What happened to you? What did that bastard do? And where the hell is he?"

Shade opened his mouth to answer but closed it. How much did Gael know?

"How did you find me?" he asked.

"Maxen Schwan," Gael said.

"He survived?" Shit. Apollo must have been sloppy that day in the tunnel. Too desperate to get the two of them away before Gael arrived. He wouldn't have made such a monumental mistake otherwise.

"Yeah," he confirmed. "He was unconscious for a while, so we had to wait for him to wake up, but once he was the bastard wouldn't shut up. We know it was Apollo this whole time. Maxen said he was trying to warn you when Apollo stabbed him. Is that true?"

Shade snorted. "No. Maxen attacked me and Apollo is the one who stopped him before he could kill me."

Gael blinked at him. "Really?"

"Why would I lie?"

"But," he glanced around the warehouse, "he's the one who's been holding you here, right?"

He was considering whether or not he could get away with making up some story about the two of them being abducted together, but then Gael continued, blasting that idea right out of the water.

"We were able to find him heading this way in an unregistered hovercar, that's how we knew to search this area."

"Apollo isn't here right now," Shade said, seeing no other way around it. He glanced toward the exit and spotted a few police cruisers in sight. "How many officers did you bring with you?"

"Practically the entire force," Gael told him. "Hey," he called to one of the men standing by the workbench, investigating the items there, "figure out how to get these cuffs off."

"There's a panel," Shade pointed over his shoulder at the wall. "It's bio-secured. You can jimmy something sharp and pop it open though."

"Did you do that?"

"Once."

"He caught you?"

"Obviously."

The man by the workbench came over, unsheathing a short knife from his belt. He looked directly at Shade as he approached, a mixture of sympathy and relief that it wasn't him in this situation coming off of him.

Shade couldn't blame him for the latter. Most of the people in this room were feeling the same way. No one wanted to be kidnapped and held hostage.

"Drop your gaze," Gael snapped at the man when he noticed they were making eye contact. "Damn it, I briefed all of you beforehand!"

"It's okay," Shade reassured him.

"It isn't, you've got to be—"

"I'm fine," he repeated. He waited for understanding to hit Gael as the officer stepped between them and began working the hidden panel free with the tip of his blade.

Gael's brow furrowed. "Even with all of these people in here?"

Shade hadn't even sensed them coming, but he kept that part to himself. "Yeah."

He didn't appear to believe him, but after a closer inspection of Shade's face, seeing that he wasn't wincing or sweating or showing any other of his usual signs that he was overwhelmed, he had no other choice but to. "How?"

"We can talk about that later." The cuffs clicked and Shade was able to remove them. He sent a grateful smile toward the other officer and then dropped the cuffs so that they dangled from the wall. His gaze lingered on them for a moment longer than they should have, a swell of sadness engulfing him out of nowhere.

This, being rescued, wasn't what he wanted.

How ridiculous.

He sighed and turned back to his friend and partner. "Apollo isn't here," he told him a second time. "And he won't be returning."

Shade sincerely hoped that was the truth. If he was caught…He didn't even want to think about that.

"Let's get you out of here for now," Gael suggested, wrapping an arm around Shade's waist to help him off the mattress, as if he thought he'd be too malnourished or exhausted to walk on his own.

There was nothing wrong with Shade, but realizing that wasn't in his best interest, he didn't push the Inspector away. Instead, he made a big show of leaning on him for support as he was led out of the warehouse and carefully helped into the backseat of a cruiser.

But he couldn't stop himself from looking back at the massive wooden structure as he was driven away.

It was the place where the old version of him had died, and also where this new version, this *real* version, had finally been freed.

Chapter 31:

"It's like he never existed!" Dario slammed a fist down on the conference table, causing the content of the mugs set before all of them to slosh.

Shade watched as a drop of coffee dribbled down the side of his white mug. It was his first time back in this room since he was found last week, all the other meetings having been held in his hospital room where he'd been ordered to stay. They'd run all the tests they could think of on him, had even contacted a doctor who specialized in Draxen. When it'd become apparent that there was nothing physically wrong with him, they'd called in one of his old psychiatrists. He'd been forced to have a session with her over comms. They wouldn't have cleared him for active duty if he hadn't.

He couldn't afford not to be put back on the case, not with Apollo still missing.

For some reason, he hadn't returned to the warehouse. Shade hoped it was because he'd figured out the police were on to him, but there was a part of him that had started up with those voices again, the ones that whispered he wasn't worthy. They came alive at night, when it was just him alone with his thoughts in the dark.

They told him that Apollo had abandoned him. That it'd all been a game. That Apollo had played him the entire time.

It didn't help that those words straight from Apollo's mouth kept repeating in his head over and over again.

Keep me interested and we could do this for a while.

Was that it? Had Apollo lost interest? Was Shade no longer worth it now that he'd returned to being Detective Shadow Yor?

Apollo hadn't been lying about his wealth, that was for sure. That same day Shade had been rescued, his bank accounts had been emptied, the funds sent somewhere completely untraceable. It looked like they'd merely vanished, same as the man himself.

There'd been nothing in his apartment to hint at where he might have gone, and any personal computers he'd had there had been wiped by the time Gael had gotten to them after Maxen had woken and spilled what he knew. So there was no lead to go off of there either. What's more, any and all images that had been available of Apollo on the internet and his workplace's website had also been deleted.

It was making sending out a BOLO alert next to impossible since they had no photo of him now that could be used.

It was as Dario said, in the span of a couple of hours, it was like Apollo had never existed.

Had he started that process before he'd left to dispose of Gunther's body, or after?

Shade couldn't live like this, not again, with those damn hate-filled voices aimed his way. He needed to find

Apollo to get answers, to ask him point blank if what had happened between them was even remotely real. And he needed to do it before any of the others found him first. If they did, they'd arrest him and there'd be no way for Shade to help him from there.

He wanted to help him. There was no question about that. He was the detective assigned to Apollo's case and yet he fully intended to do everything in his power to ensure that Apollo was never caught. They couldn't have him.

He belonged to Shade.

"Are you sure you're all right to be here, Detective?" Dario must have noticed him spacing out.

Straightening in his seat, he forced himself to focus and offered a brief smile. "I'm fine."

"The doctors gave him the all clear this morning," Gael added for him.

"And…" Dario tapped the side of his head. "What about this?"

"They think I made a breakthrough while being kidnapped," Shade shrugged, "who would have thought."

"Guess something good came out of it, in any case." Axel had woken and been cleared the same day that Shade and Apollo had disappeared. The cast had come off his arm yesterday.

"You're really okay?" Dario had apparently worked closely with Gael in trying to locate Shade. The two of them had spent many sleepless nights combing over grainy security footage, digging into Apollo's past for any clues.

And while they'd been doing that, Shade had been sleeping with the enemy.

And liking it.

"I'll have to go back for more testing in a week or so," Shade said, "but as of now, it seems like I'm better."

"So," Axel rested his arms on the table, "you can only read me when you meet my gaze now?"

"I can still read you without needing to," he corrected. "For instance, I'm looking at you but Dario is feeling relieved."

"I'm happy that you don't have to worry about being in constant pain anymore," Dario told him.

When Shade turned to see for himself, there was no Glitch, proving that he was telling the truth. "You're a good man."

He didn't deserve Shade's deception. That wasn't enough to stop him, but he could acknowledge it at the very least.

"I can still read within a ten-foot radius, but nothing broader than that," Shade said.

"That's a lot shorter of a space than before." Axel hummed. "Does it suck not being able to do the same things you could before?"

"No. I'd rather be limited than have to worry about migraines or Repletion ever again."

His psychiatrist had concluded the shock of being tricked by someone he'd called a friend and then taken against his will was what had given him the breakthrough he'd been seeking all this time. Somehow, it'd jolted his system, almost as if resetting him, chipping away at the trauma he'd been carrying all this while.

He hadn't bothered to correct her and explain a lot of that had been thanks to Apollo actively trying. His methods had been devious and selfish, sure, but he'd gotten the job done. He'd said he was going to put Shade back together and look at him now.

All that effort couldn't have been done in vain. Sure, Apollo had told him not to bore him, but he'd also told him more recently that he intended to keep him forever.

Forever hadn't even started.

That asshole had better show up.

Shade had tried to be left alone a time or two over the past week, knowing there was no way for Apollo to appear if he was constantly surrounded by police and doctors. But even after he'd convinced Gael he'd be fine on his own at night, there'd been nothing since he'd still been at the hospital.

They weren't going back to the same hotel as before after this since Apollo knew about it, and there was no way for Shade to argue there without coming off suspicious so…He just had to keep searching on his own and hope Apollo would eventually come to him if he couldn't locate him first.

There was a good chance he'd already made a run for it though.

Shade didn't like to go there. Didn't like the way his chest ached whenever he did.

"What about Maxen?" He'd yet to meet with the guy himself and was hoping to avoid doing so. There wasn't really a need to, since the others had already squeezed as much information out of him as they were going to get, and since he'd rolled on Apollo already, there wasn't a great chance of him sharing anything else that could help Shade find him. Hell, Maxen hadn't even known about the warehouse. It was obvious he'd never been told anything useful.

"Right, we haven't given you the whole story yet." Dario got up from his seat and rounded the table, stopping at the small snack bar across the room to top his coffee off. Looked like they'd gotten used to being in here so long while Shade was away, they'd added it to save time. He held up the pot for them, silently asking if anyone else needed a refill, but they all declined. "According to him, he and Apollo met in college in one of his figure drawing classes. The two of them hit it off and kept in touch even after Maxen dropped out."

"He supposedly didn't know about the murders in the beginning," Axel picked up the story as Dario came back to the table. "Apollo would call him up every once in a while and ask for a small favor, nothing suspicious. By the time Maxen realized he was helping to cover Apollo's tracks he confronted him."

"And Apollo didn't kill him?" Shade quirked a brow. He'd seen the dynamics between the two in that tunnel. Maxen had looked at Apollo almost as if he were a god in his eyes.

Guess that had changed the moment his god had tried to kill him.

"Maxen didn't have any other friends," Gael said. "Apollo was nice to him and offered to include him in— and this is a direct quote—'the fun'."

Bile rose up the back of Shade's throat but he banked it down. That sounded too familiar for comfort. Apollo had said it wasn't something he usually did, that he didn't target people like Shade who hadn't committed any crimes. But what if...

"What kind of relationship did they have?" he forced himself to ask.

"From the sounds of things, Apollo only ever contacted him when he needed something," Dario said. "He was using him. Maxen was just too stupid to see that until there was a knife sticking out of his gut."

"Kind of hard to overlook evidence that solid," Axel remarked.

Maxen could have been lying about their relationship, the same way Shade had been lying all week. Their situations were similar. Neither of them had many friends and they'd both been lonely when Apollo had approached them...

No. No, he refused to believe that Apollo would do that to him. He might not have been able to read him, but Apollo had more than proved he cared in his actions...

Which could have also been a manipulation tactic. Fuck.

"Shade?" Gael leaned over and rested a hand on his arm. "You good?"

"Yeah." He inhaled and lifted his coffee cup. "Just need more caffeine after all. I'm still pretty beat."

"After everything you've been through that's to be expected." Dario continued to catch him up on things as Shade went to fill his still half-full mug. "Maxen confessed to making that painting, the one we found in his closet? The signature on it was his doing, but the actual one, the one found on all the bodies wasn't his."

"It's Apollo's," Shade said.

"Bingo."

"It's a butterfly." He wasn't sure when he'd figured that out, probably subconsciously over the weeks he'd been held captive. "He's got a butterfly tattoo on his wrist. There's a strong connection to both life and rebirth behind it. He's fond of them."

But was he fond of Shade still?

Pathetic. He chuckled at his own stupidity and slumped back into his swivel chair.

Everyone was giving him a funny look now.

Shade had reported that nothing all that interesting happened between him and Apollo during his time with him. Since there hadn't been many marks on his body to say otherwise, they'd had no other option but to take him at his word. Still, now and again he swore he felt suspicion from one or more of them. It was always gone faster than he could pinpoint who it came from, but it was there, constantly reminding him to be careful.

Apollo had done a good job cleaning up after Gunther, but since he hadn't anticipated Gael and the others arriving, he hadn't completely disposed of everything. A team was still trying to break into his computer, but they'd found a couple of drops of blood in the bathroom from when he and Shade had cleaned up. When asked about it, Shade claimed Gunther had already been there.

In the end, it worked in their favor since it'd given him a believable story about why Apollo had brought him there but hadn't tortured or killed him. He'd been working his way up to it, playing with Gunther first.

It bugged him having to lie to Gael, but the alternative was entrusting him with the truth, and if he agreed not to tell, then ultimately turning him into an accomplice.

Gael was different from Shade. It'd been his dream to attend the Academy and he came from a long line of I.P.F agents. His mother and father had been a team themselves before they'd gotten married and settled down. He'd always wanted this job and he loved having it.

But Shade didn't have to ask to know that he'd risk it all if it helped Shade out. Gael wasn't just his only friend, he was the best friend anyone could ask for. Shade had been the idiot for not noticing that sooner.

"He told me about its meaning," Shade made himself explain to the others, touching his right wrist, "when we met at the bar that day. I just didn't put two and two together."

"Right," Axel snapped his fingers, "I've seen it. It looks nothing like the signature on the bodies."

"That's because it's carved with a knife," Dario grunted. "Not as easy to move around. He simplified it. Doing so also helped to cover his tracks."

"How did Maxen know about it if he wasn't present for the kills though?" Shade asked. They'd kept that detail out of the news and as far as he knew, there hadn't been a leak.

"That's the interesting thing," he said, "turns out that's how Apollo used to sign all of his work at school. If we'd released the image to the public, someone may have recognized it from back then and given us a call."

"We couldn't have known that," Axel reassured him, patting his shoulder. "What I want to know is why he took that kind of risk. None of us would have ever suspected him, hell, we didn't even believe Maxen in the beginning."

"Took the guy proving it by telling us how he knew about the signature," Dario agreed. "We sent some people to the college to check."

"It's been years," Shade frowned, "they still had some?"

"One piece the school had purchased," he nodded. "It was hanging in the east wing of the political science building. Hundreds of students walk by it every day."

Apollo had marked the bodies knowing there was a very good chance he'd eventually be made. Why? Shade couldn't figure it out. He'd gone to great lengths to cover his tracks, even creating a false, nice guy persona to help him fool everyone around him.

That meant he had to have had an escape plan. He wasn't the type who'd take a risk, even for shits and giggles, without leaving himself some sort of out. Maybe draining the account and wiping his image from online servers on planet had been as easy for him as a touch of a button. If that were the case, he really could be halfway to another planet by now.

Had he left Shade behind?

His fists tightened over his thigh beneath the table. If that fucker thought for a second he could put Shade through all of this and then leave he had another thing coming. He'd hunt him across the damn galaxy if he had to.

"Shade?" Gael was giving him the look, this new one that he seemed to send Shade's way a lot since walking him out of that warehouse.

He'd spaced out again, hadn't he.

"We were holding off on releasing photos of Apollo to the press until we found you, but now that we know you're all right," Dario began, though the concern in his gaze mirrored Gael's, "we've had a sketch drawn up and are spreading that around, it's not exact of course but it's really close, and with facial recognition software constantly running, we'll catch him eventually."

Would they? They'd used all of those tactics with Maxen as well and he'd managed to evade them just fine. It didn't take a genius to know who he'd learned those skills from.

"We've got the tip line open and people working around the clock. We'll get him, Detective."

There was no way of knowing exactly what Dario believed happened to Shade in that warehouse, but it was obvious he knew Shade was keeping tightlipped about it. He was trying to be reassuring, was outraged on his behalf.

It made Shade question whether or not he'd been as alone and disliked as he'd thought all this time, or if that'd merely been his own twisted perception fooling him. Hadn't Gael tried to tell him that on more than one occasion? He hadn't been willing to listen then. Ironic that now that he was it was too late to make a difference, at least where this team was concerned.

Shade had already made up his mind not to stick around. As soon as he settled things with Apollo, he'd quit the I.P.F and leave. Where to, he wasn't sure, but he doubted he'd stay on Pollux, not when there'd be nothing keeping him here. This wasn't even his planet. He didn't really have a planet, since Draxen held more bad memories for him than good ones.

"How about we call it," Dario suggested, rising from his chair and making a big show of stretching. "There's nothing more we can do at the moment. Axel and I will go meet with the team combing through the CCTV footage."

"I'm going to meet with the officers sorting through the items found at the warehouse," Shade said, getting up as well. When Dario and Axel shared a look, he quirked a brow. "I'm still in charge of this investigation."

"Of course," Axel chuckled uncomfortably. "We're just concerned for you, that's all."

"If you need more time to recuperate—"

"I don't," Shade cut Dario off but forced a smile, "but thank you. I appreciate that you're worried about me, I do. I'm not going to be able to rest until I've found him though, so there's no point in my even trying."

"We'll get him." Axel held up a fist.

No, Shade would get him. They just needed to stay out of his way.

He smiled again and nodded his head in agreement before turning toward the door.

"I'll go with you," Gael offered, following after him.

They were halfway down the hall before the Inspector handed over a box. "Here. They never found yours so I picked up a new one."

There was a multi-slate inside, and he pulled it out and secured it to his wrist, turning the device on as they walked so he could start programming it.

"You'll have to hook it up to your drive back at the hotel to download all of your contacts," Gael said. "I wasn't able to do that."

Shade sent him a look and he snorted.

"Yeah, I tried. You've got all of that under lock and key though. I've always hated how good with tech you are. You could have had any position in the agency yet you went with detective. I'll never understand that. Waste of your talents."

"There are far more talented people out there," Shade drawled. A thought hit him and he paused just as they were about to turn down the hallway that would lead to the room where the items brought from the warehouse were being stored. The location itself had already been swept over and cleared before anything had been removed from it, and so far there was nothing that could even hint at where Apollo may be hiding.

There also hadn't been any evidence about what had taken place between the two of them, which Shade was grateful for. He may have gotten rid of most of those pesky dark thoughts, but that still didn't mean he wanted the entire Ux police force watching an impromptu sex tape of him getting railed by Apollo.

He'd panicked a bit when they were told they'd found security cameras, but no one had been able to hack into Apollo's laptop, so they hadn't been able to check any of the footage.

Shade needed to get to Apollo before they did that, which meant he didn't have any time to waste playing the role of dutiful detective, and Gael had just given him an idea.

"Actually, I'm going to head to the hotel now and get this situated first," he waved his wrist with the multi-slate on it, "and I'll meet with you after."

"Why don't I go with you?" Gael took a step toward him but Shade shook his head.

"You know how important solving this thing is to me," he told him. "I'd feel more comfortable knowing that one of us is overseeing the sorting. You never know what might turn up and be important, and if it's overlooked…"

"Good point." Still, he hesitated.

"What?" Shade finally pressed when it became clear he wasn't going to immediately speak.

"Are you really okay?" He held up a hand before Shade could reply. "Look, I know you're going to say you are, and I get that you probably just don't want to talk about it, but I'm here for you, you know that, right? For anything. I'll never judge you."

"Never say never."

"I'll *never* judge you," Gael insisted. "You're my best friend. I'll always have your back."

Shade felt the determination wafting off of Gael and knew it was the truth. "Thank you, that means a lot. And thank you for all this time. Always standing by me. I don't think I've ever properly told you how much that's meant to me."

"See this," Gael pointed at him, "is why I'm convinced something is wrong with you. You've been far too relaxed since you came back, even when you were at the hospital. And the hospital. The super crowded, always filled to the brim with people with heightened emotions, hospital…Those used to be your least favorite places on any planet. Yet you stayed in one without complaint for six whole days."

"I was fine," Shade said.

"I know that because I was paying attention. You were more than fine. You didn't have a single headache the entire time."

"The doctors already explained why that is. I'm better now, that's all. Isn't that a good thing?"

"Is it?" He held up his hands and retracted. "I mean, of course it is. I hated seeing you hurting. All I'm saying is, you've been different. The lack of pain is great, but the rest...Half the time you're spacing out and when you are paying attention it's almost like you're seeing right through us."

Shade cocked his head. "Are you trying to say you think I now lack emotion?"

Gael nibbled on his bottom lip. "Do you?"

"I can feel you right now," he reassured him. "And I can feel myself too. You're worried I'm going to be offended—I'm not, by the way—and I'm growing impatient because I really need to get this thing programmed so I can check in with headquarters."

"You can use mine."

"No, I want to call from my own device," he lied. Then he sighed, not liking having to keep things from the Inspector. "I am different, okay? And yes, stuff happened to me, stuff I don't want to talk about. Some of it was bad, and some of it..." He stopped himself from saying good outright, but it was implied. "I don't know. The point is, I've changed. I feel..."

"Tethered?" Gael supplied.

"Yeah—" He inhaled sharply.

Tethered.

Shit.

"What?" Gael reached for him. "What is it? A headache? Now?"

"No." He pulled away. He really was the best friend a person could ask for, not only had he given Shade one great idea, but two. "No, I just remembered something that's all. I've got to go. I'll be at the hotel and then I'll meet you back here, all right?"

"...Yeah, okay." Gael frowned. "I'll see you later."

"Later," Shade promised.

Only, if things went the way he hoped, that would be another lie.

Chapter 32:

"This is your Captain speaking, how may I be of service to you on this fine evening?" The teasing voice coming through the earbud made Shade roll his eyes, even though the speaker couldn't see his reaction. "Oh, actually, is it evening where you currently are, Yor?"

Only Fox ever called him by his last name, something Shade never bothered to correct since the two of them hardly knew one another, despite the overly friendly way he'd answered his comms a minute ago. Though, that's what Shade had been hoping for, that not only would his call be answered, but that the man on the other end of the line would remember him at all.

Shade had run into Fox Axford a little over three years ago on a job. The two of them were both detectives in charge of their own teams, and they'd followed leads for separate cases to the same planet just outside of their galaxy. Fox's galaxy, the Crystal Sea, neighbored theirs, and he'd popped in to keep up with his case without informing the higher-ups. In return for not reporting him, Fox had offered to owe him one.

At the time, Shade simply hadn't wanted to get involved, so he'd turned the other cheek and had made Gael do so as well, but now that offer might come in handy.

There were different Academies stationed throughout the universe, one for each galaxy, so of course the two of them had attended separate ones. They also lived on separate I.P.F stations for the same reason, but that didn't mean Shade hadn't learned a thing or two about the other detective.

Fox was supposedly an ace at computers, even better than Shade. Rumor even had it that he could hack into the highly protected Demeter Station, the information hub put together and protected by the International Conference. All data collected by every I.P.F branch in every active galaxy was stored there, this way even if the criminal came from another galaxy, they'd be able to ID them if they had history.

Since he'd entered their galaxy without clearance, Shade was praying that proved the rumors were true.

"Are you a captain now or still a detective?" Shade asked, checking for the millionth time out the window of the small hotel room he was in. He'd locked the door for added protection, not wanting to risk Gael showing up and overhearing this conversation.

When they'd met, Fox had shared that his true dream had always been to captain fighter ships, but due to familial pressure, he'd ended up with the I.P.F. instead.

"Nope," Fox stated brightly, "still a detective. Just making sure you didn't forget me, Yor. You never write, you never call...Way to leave your friends hanging."

That gave him pause. Were they friends? They'd spent a week tracking potential leads together one time but that was the extent of it. Though, he supposed since he was calling to ask for a massive favor...

"Sorry about that," he said, "you know how life is."

"Work, work, work," Fox grunted. "Gotta take some time to play. Trust me. Does wonders."

"Yeah," he cleared his throat, "maybe."

Fox was silent a brief second and then, "What are you calling for? Must be a big deal for you to take the time. Don't tell me you've gotten yourself into trouble?"

Shade crossed his arms and propped a hip against the wall, staring down at the parking lot. There weren't many people out despite it being mid-day. "And if I have?"

Fox mumbled something to someone he was with and there was some shuffling before he came back loud and clear through the line. "Okay, I'm secure. You?"

"Made sure of it before I called." He might not be as skilled as Fox, but Shade could work tech better than the average person. He'd blocked the call location so that even if he lost this device or someone got a hold of his logs, they wouldn't be able to tell he'd made this communication at all. "Ghost mode."

"Love ghost mode," Fox didn't sound concerned about what he might be asked to get into, instead he sounded a bit excited. "How can I help?"

"It's sort of a lot," he began tentatively.

"I never forget a favor," Fox said.

"There are favors and then there's my asking you to help me do something illegal."

He chuckled. "The more illegal the better. I've been complaining to Nova all day about how boring things have been lately. We talking risking our job illegal or—"

"More like life imprisonment." Nova was Fox's Inspector, and at the mention of her, Shade couldn't help but feel a little bad for dragging Fox into this. He'd gotten the distinct impression that she already spent most of her time cleaning up after her detective's messes.

"Really?" Fox let out a low whistle, but before Shade could get nervous he was going to decline he added, "If I'd known you were this fun, I would have contacted you myself a hell of a lot sooner. Something seems different about you, Yor."

"You can't possibly know that," Shade told him. "I've only said a handful of sentences since you picked up."

"It's the fact that I had the opportunity to pick up at all," he corrected. "You know doing something illegal could tarnish your sparkling record, right? No longer care so much about that? It was practically the only thing that mattered before. Solving your cases and getting that gold star pinned to your chest."

"We don't get gold stars," he drawled, even though he knew the other man was being a sarcastic ass on purpose.

"I got my point across."

"You did." Shade sighed. "Let's just say there's something more important to me now and leave it at that, cool?"

"Is it revenge?" Fox lowered his voice conspiratorially, and even though it was obvious he wasn't being serious about that either, Shade found himself replying anyway.

"Yeah."

The line went quiet again. "Damn. I'm liking this new you. We should get together sometime, cause a little trouble."

"After what I'm about to ask for," Shade said, "you'll agree we shouldn't see each other again for the foreseeable future."

"Ah, contacted me because we have no paper trail." No one knew they'd met except for their teammates because they'd agreed not to write it in either of their reports. That paired with the fact they were from different galaxies, it'd be next to impossible for anyone to link them together. "So, what's the favor?"

"Can you hack into Demeter Station?" He held his breath as he waited for the answer, a bit taken aback when Fox merely snorted.

"That? That's easy. And here I thought you were going to ask for something super dramatic."

"That part's coming," he promised.

"Do tell."

"I'd rather not say out loud." Shade had no reason to believe anyone was bugging the room, but with something like this, he'd feel more comfortable playing it safe.

"That's more like the old you," Fox laughed. "All right, send it through this same communication. All evidence will be wiped as soon as we're through with this talk."

"What if you can't do it?"

"You wound me, Yor. Of course I can do it."

"You don't even know what it is yet."

"And yet I am confident I can oblige."

Shade shook his head. "I forgot how cocky you are."

"Now that's just insulting. Do you want my help or not?"

"I'm sorry," he corrected, "I did not forget how cocky you are. I think about that fact every day."

"Better. There's even a hint of honesty in your tone. You really have changed."

Later, when this was all settled, Shade would take the time to mull over that more but for now, he needed to stay focused. Time was of the essence. For all he knew, Apollo had already fled the planet.

"Since I've been entertaining, mind if I tack on another ask?" Shade had planned to all along.

"Sure," he could practically visualize the blond detective shrugging as he said, "what's the difference between one or two broken laws between friends? Send me the details about that one the same way."

"I'll need a response on this part," Shade told him.

"Keep the line open then. Ten minutes."

"Seriously, your confidence is astounding." He lifted his multi-slate and began typing out instructions to

Fox, attaching it through the same line they were using for the call. "Done."

"Let me look over this and get back to you. Stay tuned."

"Will do."

Now all Shade had to worry about was whether or not he'd go insane from impatience.

* * *

Shade trudged through the dense forest on the opposite side of the city, following the tiny red dot glowing on his multi-slate over an image of a map. It'd brought him far from the location of the warehouse he'd been kept in before, and nowhere near anything that was related to Apollo, but he just had to trust the signal was accurate and hadn't been messed with.

There was always the chance it had been and this was a carefully laid out trap for if the police came sniffing. Not that the police had been any use where this was concerned.

The last thing Shade had asked Fox for was for him to see if he could hack into his N.I.M. and switch its locator device on. Since N.I.M.s were still so new and only used by the I.P.F, the police had no clue how to do any of that or what information they would need to even give it a try. Fox, being an agent himself, had easily been able to comply, sending over the tracking link to Shade before wiping their entire chat log. Before they'd hung up, he'd promised to have the other thing he'd asked for settled by end of day Shade's time.

That was fast approaching. Tipping his head back, he tried to spy the sky through the trees, but the canopy was so thick it was nearly impossible. Going off the clock on his multi-slate, however, he was looking at another two or three hours of daylight if he was lucky.

According to the little red dot, he was close, but there was no way of knowing if he'd actually find what he was looking for. At this rate, it was beginning to seem a lot more likely this was nothing more than a dump site Apollo had used to rid himself of Shade's stuff. Since they hadn't found his multi-slate or the N.I.M. at the warehouse, it was safe to assume Apollo either had it on his person when he'd gone to dump Gunther's body or he'd hidden it somewhere else.

Shade didn't think that last option made much sense, considering he'd kept up with his communications to Gael in order to trick the Inspector into believing Shade was all right—which Shade now knew Gael had played along with to prevent tipping Apollo off. Up until their last day together, Apollo had never left Shade alone in the building for longer than ten minutes, that he was aware of, which meant he had to have been keeping N.I.M. close.

Taking all of that into consideration, it was easy to hypothesize that Apollo had the N.I.M. on his person that day. The only real question was did he still?

When Shade was a few meters away from the dot, he unsheathed his blaster, popping off the safety as he slowed his steps. He moved more carefully over shrubs and around thick tree trunks, keeping his eyes and ears peeled for any sign he wasn't alone as he approached his destination.

Even though his ability had stabilized, it would be of no use here. Apollo couldn't be read, whether because of his psychopathy or for other reasons Shade hadn't figured out yet. Either way, it meant there was no way for Shade to sense whether or not the other guy was around beforehand. He had no other choice but to keep moving forward, whether this ended up being a trap or not.

Just as he was about to reach the spot where the dot was flickering, he shut his device off and took a deep breath. The trees were packed too closely together here, with their low-hanging branches shielding anything that may be on the other side from view. He'd come too far to turn back empty-handed due to a little unknown.

Pushing between two of the larger branches, he shifted his head to the side to avoid getting stabbed in the eye by the thick, waxy leaves. Some of them were nearly half his size, which was why it was so difficult to navigate through this place and why there weren't any manmade trails. There was nothing out here but unused acres of land.

Shade came out the other side, blaster lifted in front of him protectively, and stopped in his tracks.

There was a small wooden building a couple of dozen yards ahead of him, more a shack than anything else. No windows and a thatched roof. Also no door on the side he was standing. He listened for a moment until he heard sounds of movement within and then his heart picked up the pace and he found himself practically throwing caution to the wind as he made his way around until he found the entrance.

It was wide, with double doors left open at either side to allow a full view into the tiny space. There was a cot set in the far right corner and a desk in the opposite one, turned to block off the space in the other corner. There was a pile of blankets and some camping gear nearby, along with a computer—though Shade had no clue how he was getting electricity out in the middle of nowhere in an unmarked building. The N.I.M. and his multi-slate were set on top of a small end table, next to a hunting knife.

Shade was eyeing the items when the man standing in the center of it all turned and noticed him. They both froze.

Apollo glanced at the barrel of the blaster aimed his way and then cocked his head. He didn't look like a man on the run, his hair carefully combed and his gray t-shirt wrinkle-free, tucked into black jeans. His charcoal boots were caked in mud at the bottom at least, but that was the only thing about him out of place.

Shade was tempted to take a better look around and see if he could find a shower, that's how clean and put together he was, but he refrained, not willing to risk taking his gaze off the other man just yet.

"Detective," Apollo broke the silence first, tossing a quick look over Shade's shoulder.

"I came alone." And in secret, but he didn't need to add that part. Didn't need to make it known that he'd snuck around behind the rest of the team and Gael's back to come out here without them.

"I see." His expression remained enigmatic, his thoughts and emotions completely sealed off from Shade.

He never thought there'd come a time when he'd want his empathic power, but now was it and a part of him raged on the inside that it wouldn't work. "You said you were coming back."

"Sorry to disappoint," Apollo replied coolly. "Were you waiting for me with all of your friends, Detective?"

They were between a rock and a hard place, the both of them, neither sure who to trust or if trust was even a possibility. Shade was a detective and Apollo was the man who'd held him hostage. They were on opposite sides of the law and from the outside looking in, there was only one way for things to go from here.

"The ocean at my back, the devil at my front," Shade murmured to himself, shaking his head slightly when the corner of Apollo's mouth finally tipped down. He took a step forward, bringing him closer to the entrance, and by doing so caught sight of something strange sticking out from behind the desk.

A leg.

"Gunther?" he demanded, keeping his weapon steady.

Apollo didn't have to turn and look himself to know what he was referring to. "Afraid not."

Shade swore.

"If it helps, I didn't personally kill this one." Apollo shrugged when Shade didn't immediately praise him. "Although, I'm sort of wishing that I had. If it was going to be my last kill before you pull the trigger on me."

"You promised you wouldn't do that anymore," Shade reminded tersely.

"That's why I didn't," he said. "Really."

"So you just, what? Found a dead body on the side of the street and brought it home with you?"

Apollo clicked his tongue. "I wouldn't exactly call this home, more like a temporary arrangement while I got my ducks in order. The bodies came from the university—Med Ux U? They get deliveries for teaching purposes. The body was legally donated."

"But not legally stolen," Shade pointed out. "Can it be traced back to you?"

Another crack in that stony exterior, this time when his brow furrowed. "Why?"

"Just answer the question."

"I don't—"

Shade took another step, bringing the gun closer. "Answer. The. Question."

"When have I ever been sloppy, Detective?"

"With Maxen," he said. "You failed to kill him in the tunnel. That's how they knew to look for us."

Apollo's jaw twitched in irritation before he could contain himself. "That's how."

"Yeah. Good one."

"That almost sounds like you're annoyed with me."

"I'm furious," he corrected.

"I can see that." Apollo held his ground. "If shooting me will make you feel better, by all means. I won't fight you. Not you."

"Why not?"

"You know why."

"No," Shade practically growled, "I don't. *You said* you were coming back."

"I was," Apollo exhaled sharply. "I did. Only to find the place surrounded by the police. You were already long gone. I assume rescued by that partner of yours, the one you care so much about."

"His name is Gael."

"Forgive me for not giving a fuck."

"Do you?" Shade surprised them both by asking then. "Do you give a fuck?"

He wasn't talking about Gael and he saw the moment Apollo picked up on that fact, his blue eyes darkening as he pursed his lips.

"Don't play with me, Detective," he warned.

"Why?" Shade quirked a brow. "You seemed to enjoy it when the roles were reversed."

"Is that what this is?" He motioned with his chin to the blaster. "Is that why you came out here alone? Payback? You going to wrap those pretty hands of yours around my neck and squeeze the life out of me? Or are you planning on taking that hunting knife and—"

Shade ate up the short distance between them, pressing the barrel directly against Apollo's chest.

"Going to shoot me in the heart then?"

"Depends." Shade tilted his head, "Do you have a heart?"

"Want me to get a note from my doctor?"

"Think I'm going to let you talk to anyone else before this is settled?"

That caught Apollo's attention. "…That makes it sound like you don't plan on shooting me."

"Give me one good reason why I shouldn't." He applied more pressure to the gun, watching the other man wince as it dug into his skin. "One."

"The body behind me," Apollo began, only to have Shade snort derisively.

"That's not exactly a mark in your favor."

"It isn't the only body."

Shade's brow knitted.

"Does that matter?" Apollo licked his lips, a spark of hopefulness there and gone in a flash. "Does it make a difference?"

"I…" Shade shifted on his feet. "I don't know what you're trying to say."

"There are two bodies back there. One for me," he held his gaze, "and one for you. I paid someone to switch my DNA sample, someone who works for the Ux police."

"You what?"

"Dirty cops are everywhere." He shrugged. "Don't act surprised. There are dirty people in every profession. That's just how the universe works. And as you already know, I've got a lot of money. There are very few things I can't buy."

"Not me. You can't buy me." Déjà vu.

"I know that," Apollo agreed. "If there was a chance that I could have, do you think I would have gone through all the trouble of kidnapping you?"

Shade gave him a look.

"Fine," he admitted. "I probably would have. It was fun. Come on, I wasn't the only one enjoying myself. Don't deny it. You—"

"I wasn't going to," Shade cut him off.

This time it was Apollo's turn to frown. "What?"

"I enjoyed it." He lifted a single shoulder, careful to keep the blaster firmly in place. "Guess what? Ran a few tests while you were away. Gunther wasn't a fluke after all. Doctors think you miraculously fixed me."

"Please tell me you told them it was my magic dick."

"I told them you'd wiped away my trauma by giving me new trauma."

Apollo flinched but collected himself quickly. "So you are here to kill me."

"You said you were coming back? When?" Shade brought their conversation around.

"Tonight," he replied without skipping a beat. "You were only let out of the hospital yesterday and up until then, I couldn't get to you. There were cameras everywhere. I tried to sneak in and avoid them, but that partner of yours wasn't leaving anything to chance."

"What do you mean?" Shade asked.

"He never left the premises. Was always either in the waiting room right down the hall from your room or pacing in front of your door."

Shade hadn't known that.

"Did you think I'd forgotten about you?" Apollo stared at him as if trying to wiggle inside his mind to read his thoughts. "Did you start to feel relieved with every passing day thinking you were finally going to be rid of me? Sorry to burst your bubble, baby, but it's not that easy. I may have been forced to buy my time, but no matter what, I was coming for you—"

He acted without thinking. In a flash, Shade lowered the blaster and stepped forward, capturing the other man's mouth with his own. He moaned against the familiar feel of those warm lips the second the smell of brine and moss filled his nose.

Apollo hadn't forgotten or gotten over him and it hadn't all been deception.

Shade was wanted.

And he wanted back.

It took Apollo a little longer to process what was going on, but as soon as Shade's tongue darted out, trailing along the seam of his lips, he opened for him. His arms came up around his waist, tugging Shade hard against his front as their tongues fought for dominance.

That dull cloud that had seemingly been hovering over Shade's head all week long began to dissipate, a lightness filling him up in its stead. He felt…free. Full.

Like himself.

Was it crazy that it'd taken a psychopath like Apollo to snap him out of the fog he'd been living in? Yes. But it also made sense, at least to Shade. Whether it'd been by force or not, Apollo had helped him come to terms with his abandonment and rejection issues. For the first time in as long as he could remember, Shade didn't hate himself.

Ironic, that making out with a murderer was finally something that warranted hatred, and yet...He couldn't be bothered. Life was too short to waste energy worrying over what other people thought of him. It was too short for him to waste energy thinking about what he thought of himself.

Shade was done with all of that. From here on out, he was going to do what Chittas did best.

Feel.

He pulled away and waited for Apollo to open his eyes and meet his gaze. They were both partially out of breath, their cheeks stained pink with excitement, and maybe even a little awe. It was nice seeing that Shade wasn't alone in that.

That he wasn't the only one here who wanted or was wanted.

"You're the devil," he said, grabbing a fistful of Apollo's t-shirt when Apollo went to step away. "And this is my personal hell. So what do you say we get the fuck out of here?"

Apollo searched his expression as if waiting for the trap to be sprung. When Shade didn't offer up anything else, he asked, "Together?"

He gave a single nod. "Together."

The corner of his mouth started to tip up, but before a smile could fully form, something caught his attention over Shade's shoulder.

Chapter 33:

Shade was already turning to find out what it was when the harsh voice called out.

"Hands in the air!" Gael was standing just outside of the shack, his blaster aimed at Apollo's head. "Do it, now!"

Shit.

Apollo grabbed the hunting knife in a blur of motion, spinning Shade around so he was pressed back against his chest. He shoved the sharp edge beneath Shade's chin, right against his neck, and glared at Gael.

A flicker of fear raced through Shade before logic helped him bank it. Apollo had been telling the truth a minute ago. He wasn't going to hurt him.

Shade rested his hand on Apollo's wrist, the one holding the knife. "Put it down."

He held firm.

"Drop the weapon!" Gael yelled, and Shade sent him a withering glare that had him faltering.

"Apollo," Shade kept his tone even, "for once just listen to me. It's okay. Put it down."

There was another weighted moment of hesitation and then he shocked them all by actually doing it.

Admittedly, Shade hadn't been entirely sure he was going to.

As soon as the knife was no longer at his neck, Shade's arm shot up, his blaster now turned on a wide-eyed Gael. Regret and guilt swirled through him, but he refused to let them govern him.

"Shade…" A look of pure betrayal followed swiftly by a sharp sadness that punched Shade in the gut came off of Gael. "What are you doing? It's me."

"I know that," Shade told him, making sure to sound as apologetic as he felt. "You followed me."

Gael nodded.

"You shouldn't have."

"I was worried. You've been acting weird since you got back."

"Weird how?" Apollo's frown could be heard in his voice, but Shade didn't risk glancing at him over his shoulder.

Instead, he kept his body firmly between the two. His best friend and his devil.

"I can feel other people's emotions less strongly now," Shade filled him in. "I can also feel my own emotions."

"Are you sure about that?" Gael countered. "Because it hasn't seemed like it. You're always spacing out and losing focus. Your facial expression is always blank. He did something to you to make you this way." He held out his hand. "I'm trying to help you."

"You can't arrest him," Shade said.

"He's a serial murderer," he reminded. "He has to pay for his crimes."

"You're the one who said we should be thanking him for his work," Shade pointed out.

"You know I wasn't being serious. You can't just turn the other cheek here, Shade. I don't even understand why you would want to."

"He's mine." It was really simple. For the very first time in his life, he had something simple. Maybe not from the outside. He could see why it didn't seem that way to Gael, but for him...

"He's a killer."

"You're not hearing me," Shade reiterated. "He's mine."

"Shade—"

"You're the one who helped me come to that realization," he interrupted. "Back at the station earlier, remember?"

Gael was confused, but he tried to figure out what he meant and it was clear when he finally had, his mouth dropping open slightly in a gasp. His gaze flicked between the two of them as if seeing them both for the first time.

"What's going on?" Apollo leaned in closer and asked, his warm breath tickling across the back of Shade's neck.

"You're tethered," Gael blurted before Shade could even decide if he wanted to share now or not.

He was met with silence.

"You didn't feel any differently?" Shade sent the question over his shoulder, this time too afraid to turn and look for another reason. What if this was one-sided after all? Was that even possible? He wouldn't put it past himself to be the first, with how shitty his luck had always been. "When you and I were apart?"

Apollo thought it over. "I felt...restless. My abilities were heightened. I could read people further away than usual. I just thought it was in my head or something."

"The tether bond is formed between two Chitta who are unstable and in need of balance," Gael said, still shocked. "It's a natural occurrence that scientists are still trying to fully figure out. Since Shade's ability was so heightened and yours was low, you must have aligned without realizing it. That's why he's stabilized but is weakened on his own and you're—"

"Out of control?" Apollo finished for him. "I almost killed a lady who cut me off on my way to the hospital yesterday."

Which was out of character. He had a tight grip on himself, which was how he'd managed to sneak under the police's radar all these years. He would never do something as risky as attack some random person in broad daylight.

He placed a hand on Shade's shoulder and forced him to turn slightly, finally meeting his gaze. There was a flash of vulnerability in his blue eyes that had Shade's chest constricting. "You're saying we *can't* be apart?"

"We could be," he corrected. "People can untether if they spend enough time away from one another."

Apollo let out a low, threatening growl, and they both heard Gael raise his blaster again, though neither of them paid him any mind. "Try it, Shadow mine. Let's see how far you get."

"As eventful as that time in the forest was," Shade drawled, "I'm going to have to pass on a repeat."

He blinked at him.

"What? You didn't think everything I'd said up until Gael showed up had been a lie, did you?"

"I'm a serial killer," Apollo told him, repeating Gael's earlier words.

"We've agreed you're going to stop doing that, remember?"

"Shade," Gael called to him. "You can't be serious."

"I am." He turned back to his friend. "I'm sorry. I don't mean to disappoint you. But I hate my life. I want to start fresh."

"With a psychopath?"

"I promise I'll keep him from killing in the future."

"Shade."

"Let us go, Gael. Please."

"Or?"

"I don't know." He didn't want to hurt him. He couldn't. "I guess we'll be at a stalemate."

"Unless you get him to take me out," Gael jutted his chin over at Apollo.

"I wouldn't kill Shadow's only friend," Apollo stated. "You haven't done anything wrong, Inspector. I might kill people, but I have a specific preference I'm unwilling to deviate from."

"Tell that to the lady from yesterday."

"I can," he replied, "because she's still alive and kicking."

"I can think of someone else I'd love to be kicking right now," Gael muttered, but they heard him. With a curse, he dropped his weapon, and then stared at it and holstered it for good measure. "What's the plan?"

"You're going to let us go?" Shade hadn't seen that coming.

"I assume you have a plan? I'm not getting any more involved than I have to. You may hate your job, but I don't. I get you wanting to start a new life and since you're tethered to that," he waved at Apollo, "you feel like he's your ticket, but I'm not throwing myself in the mud along with you. Got it? And let's be clear, the fact that you've only ever gone after despicable monsters is the only reason I'm backing down and trusting my partner."

"He's my partner," Apollo corrected, then before anyone could say anything to that turned to Shade. "I haven't figured out how to get your DNA sample swapped. I was working on that problem when you arrived."

"I've got that covered already," Shade said.

"How?" Gael held up both hands as soon as the word had left his mouth. "Nope, nope, nope. Just kidding. Don't tell me. I don't want to know."

"There are two bodies in here," Shade said then, ignoring when Gael tensed at that bit of information. "Apollo didn't kill them. Anyway, we're going to light the shack on fire. Wait until it's almost entirely burned down before calling it in. You'll say you got worried and you trailed me, but by the time you got here, it was too late. You heard us screaming and recognized my voice. They won't be able to prove the remains don't belong to us."

At least, they wouldn't so long as Fox kept his word. It was too late to worry about that though.

"And what about you?" Gael asked.

"We'll escape while it burns. Should give us enough time to get away."

"I have new IDs." Apollo clicked at his multi-slate and then showed Shade the screen before tapping it against his. "I've sent you yours. I've also purchased tickets on the first spaceship off planet."

"As soon as we're marked as deceased, Apollo's sketch will be dropped from the wanted list," Shade told the both of them. "But we won't be able to leave before then."

"Tickets are scheduled for tomorrow morning."

"I can fast-track it," Gael jumped in. "Make sure it's taken down in time. Then the two of you go." He swallowed, clearly upset but trying to keep it together. "I can't believe we're doing this. I must be losing my damn mind. Are you sure this will work?"

"I have enough money in a safe account to take care of him for the rest of his life," Apollo promised Gael. "And our new identities are solid. As long as you can ensure we can make it off planet, we won't get caught. Ever."

"The second I hear about a killer with your M.O. out there, the deal is off," Gael said darkly, "and I come for you. Understood?"

Apollo clearly wanted to make a joke, but he kept the snide remark smartly to himself and only said, "Of course, Inspector."

Gael took a step to the side. "Go."

"Gael—"

"I can't. I can't pretend to understand what you see in this guy. I'm still torn over if I should try and stop you from leaving with him or not. But…If there's anyone in this universe who knows what you've been through, Shade, it's me. You've been different this past week, but it hasn't all been in bad ways. I don't want you going back to that, to the pain and the suffering from before. So, if staying with him is what will help keep you from that darkness, I don't need to understand everything. I just need to know that."

Shade had decided to run away with Apollo before he'd left the hotel earlier, and yet, now, standing across from his best friend, he couldn't seem to get his feet to move.

"I don't know what to say either." Gael gave him a forced smile. "Let's not worry about that right now. Once you're settled somewhere and you know that it's safe and secure, contact me then."

"I promise I won't do anything that'll risk your career." If Shade couldn't get a secure line, he wouldn't reach out, no matter how much he missed Gael.

"I know. I trust you."

"Even now?"

He nodded. "Yeah. Hell if I know why. But yeah, even now."

"We're all just a little insane it seems," Apollo cut in, earning glares from both of them.

"Go," Gael repeated. "I'll wait for a bit to give you some more time before I light this."

"There's a jug of gasoline in the corner by the door," Apollo informed him. "A blaster shot is hot enough to set it off."

Gael considered it. "If Shade came here to arrest you and the two of you were struggling, the gun could go off. You might not notice the flames right away if you were really fighting. But, how do explain how Shade found you."

"I tracked my N.I.M.," Shade answered, going over to Gael to show him the map on his multi-slate. "I've disabled all tracking functions. There's no way for anyone to find me using this, so they'll have to take your word for it."

"There's video footage of us talking at the station," Gael said. "I can say that's when you told me you might have a lead but you want to check it out yourself."

"I wasn't sure it was going to work and convinced you to stay back."

"But I followed anyway."

"Not entirely a lie." Shade clapped him on the shoulder, leaving his hand there a little longer than necessary. "I'm going to miss you."

"Stay in touch," Gael ordered. "I changed my mind. I don't care if it puts my career at risk. You're family. Stay in touch, Shade. Or the threat I gave your psychopath applies to you too."

"I got it." Shade smiled. "Thanks for being the only one keeping me going all this time."

"You don't give yourself enough credit." Gael mirrored his move and patted his arm, scowling when Apollo cleared his throat at the contact. He stepped in closer to Shade. "You're sure about this?"

"Yeah." He chuckled and pulled away. "I am."

Apollo must have grown tired of their display of affection, for he walked to them then and held out a hand to Shade. "Last chance, baby. It's two against one here, you can always change your mind and take me out."

"It is two against one," he agreed before he rested his palm against his, "but we're the two."

"Just go already," Gael mumbled heading into the shack to look for the gasoline. "You've got ten minutes to get as far as you can before I start it. Then I'll have to make the call within fifteen to avoid suspicion."

"Got it." Shade gave him one last long look. "I'm sorry."

Gael opened his mouth but then seemed to think better and closed it again. The last thing he did was wave them off.

Apollo tugged on Shade's hand lightly and then waited.

This was Shade's choice. To stay or to go. To be a detective or…was he a devil really? Maybe.

He turned away from the shack and began walking toward the trees, giving his back to his best friend and the life he'd always known.

They'd already made it out of the woods and were at a parking lot attached to a mall where Apollo had left an unregistered vehicle—not the one he'd used before—when Shade finally dared to glance back.

Smoke trails twisted above the canopy, coming from far away.

"Detective," Apollo called him softly, still holding his hand.

"He's dead," Shade said, meeting his dark blue gaze. "And so are you."

"Then let's rise from the ashes," he leaned forward and kissed the tip of his nose, "together."

"This is real, right?" He couldn't help himself from asking, needing that one final reassurance before he climbed into that hovercar.

"Who do you belong to, baby?"

"Myself. I belong to myself," Shade said without skipping a beat. But then he cupped Apollo's face and sealed his mouth over his. He poured all the desperation and the hunger he felt into it. By the time he pulled back, they were both panting. "But," he drawled, low and husky, "I'm not above making a deal with the devil."

Apollo's grin was bright and vicious. "Careful, Shadow mine, I can be obsessive."

"That's all right. As long as the only thing you're obsessed with from here on out," he brushed his lips against Apollo's in a fleeting kiss, "is me."

"And in return?"

"I'll let you keep me warm?" He'd meant it as a joke, but the glint in Apollo's eyes and the pleased sound that rumbled up his chest proved it'd been the right thing to say.

"Be yours," Apollo said, "but be mine also. My perfect little Shadow." His finger pulled at Shade's full bottom lip. "Deal?"

"You're the devil, and I'm the devil's shadow." Shade pretended to mull that over before he smirked. "Deal."

"I'm never letting you go," Apollo warned as Shade pulled away and headed to the passenger side of the car.

"Are you forgetting which one of us stalked the other today?" He popped open the door and slid into the leather seat, already buckled by the time Apollo followed after him.

He started up the hovercar and shook his head at Shade. "I was coming for you."

"Not fast enough."

"I was trying my best."

"I thought maybe you weren't going to," Shade said, that vulnerable truth slipping past his defenses before he could stop it.

"Hey," Apollo captured his chin and forced him to look at him, "I dumped the body and headed straight back for you, I swear. My feelings for you are real. I promised to take you apart, but I didn't realize until it was too late that you were doing the same to me. I can't live without you, Shadow., and not because we're tethered. Tell me I don't have to."

"You don't."

"You won't change your mind? The last time we saw each other…I lost control. It was…"

"A lot," he supplied for him.

"You didn't like it." Apollo went to pull away but Shade caught his wrist, keeping his fingers on his face.

"I didn't want to like it, but I did. Kind of like how I didn't want to like you, but I do."

"And you're all right with that?"

"I'm learning to accept myself and my desires," Shade explained. "It's my life. Who cares what anyone else thinks about it."

"Still, if you do change your mind—"

"I won't."

"—I'll chain you to the bed again," Apollo finished.

"I'm adding another stipulation to our deal," Shade decided.

"You can't."

"Are you sure?" He lifted a brow. "Don't you want to hear what it is first?"

The mischievous look on his face must have been enough to convince him because Apollo chuckled and then finally started driving out of the parking lot. "On second thought, I'm all ears, baby. Tell me what you want. I'll do anything for you."

As they made their way down the windy road, Shade glanced back into the rearview mirror, watching that spiral of smoke flicker up toward the darkening evening sky. He inhaled, letting the scent of the forest and the man at his side fill his lungs until a peaceful feeling he'd never experienced before rushed over him.

They weren't in the clear just yet, and wouldn't be until they were on that spaceship tomorrow, but for the first time in a long time, Shade *felt* free.

Realizing Apollo was still waiting for a response, he rolled his head on the headrest to look at him and grinned. "Anything?"

"Anything," he confirmed.

Shade laughed. "I'm going to hold you to that."

"Deal."

"Deal."

Epilogue:
One Year Later

"Hurry up and come to bed," Apollo's voice dipped low and suggestive as he sauntered up to Shade, stopping at his back.

"Almost done." Shade's fingers flew across the holographic keyboard, typing out the final details to Gael. "I've already sorted and attached all of the files so it's just a matter of filling him in and making sure I don't forget anything important."

"Too late," he drawled, leaning down to rest his chin on Shade's left shoulder.

He snorted. "I haven't forgotten you, I just need to finish this."

It was the third case they were sending Gael's way and in order to ensure there were no loose strings that could be traced back to them if anyone else got their hands on it, Shade had spent the past couple of hours sitting in front of the computer screen.

Instead of settling on a single planet, the two of them had purchased a ship—using Apollo's money, since all of Shade's had been frozen after he'd been declared dead—and had spent the past year traveling throughout the galaxy. They'd avoided any of the planets that surrounded Pollux to be safe, but their new identities had held up and no one ever questioned them when it came to showing their IDs.

They'd traveled to several planets and had yet to find one that felt like home. Neither of them minded too much, happy to seclude themselves on their ship in their room or a hotel. Right now it was docked at a shipping station, sort of like a campsite only for spaceships, and from the window of their bedroom where they were typically met with the dark star-studded universe, there was a sunset in the distance on Xian, their current location.

Xian was a beautiful planet with vast beaches and seaside casinos. The nightlife was every bit as lively as the daytime was, but the station they'd chosen overlooked the Celestial Sea, one of the planet's largest oceans. The water lapped gently at golden sandy beaches as the sky turned shades of pink and darkening blue.

Shade had worked all through the day it seemed. He grimaced at that realization. No wonder Apollo had grown impatient.

He really did have enough money to keep them both living more than comfortably without needing to work. But within a couple of months, the two of them had grown a bit restless, and to fill that void—Shade's from his detective days and Apollo's from...well—they'd taken to hunting the way Apollo had used to. With one major difference.

Instead of dealing with the criminals themselves, they collected the information, made it nice and tidy, and then sent it Gael's way through a secured transmission.

His best friend knew who it came from since the two of them had spoken more than a few times once the proverbial dust had settled, and he'd used those cases to climb the ranks.

Gael had switched jobs and become a detective, saying he could never fully trust anyone to take that role like he had Shade, and he'd been assigned a new Inspector soon after. From the sounds of it whenever one of them checked in with the other, he was doing well.

Shade was pleased to hear it. There'd been a lot of guilt and worry for his friend in the beginning, and knowing that Gael was happy and he hadn't inadvertently destroyed his best friend's life was a balm to his sorry self. Not that he would have changed anything about the last day they'd seen one another. He wouldn't.

Gael wasn't the only one content with the way his life had turned out.

Coming to terms with his trauma had cured Shade of being unable to stabilize, but being tethered to Apollo was what dialed his ability down to a manageable level. In return, being tethered to Shade helped boost Apollo's reading, so he could maintain the connection longer after looking into someone's eyes.

He'd stopped killing as promised, but he still got his kicks out of seeing the shocked expressions of the people they hunted down and exposed on the news after Gael arrested them. As an I.P.F agent, Gael was allowed to travel across the galaxy as well, meaning they could send information packets to him from anywhere and trust that he'd take care of it.

No sooner had Shade hit the send button than Apollo's hand was in his hair, forcing his head back with a tight grip.

He yelped, hissing at the lingering burn from having his hair pulled. Before he could say anything, Apollo dropped his mouth to his, sucking at his top lip and nipping when he didn't open for him fast enough.

Apollo dragged Shade out of the chair, ignoring when the plastic clattered to the carpeted ground. They both stumbled back, falling onto the bed in a tangle of limbs until he resituated them with him on top, pinning Shade into the mattress beneath him.

Their bed was twice the size of the plain mattress they'd used back at the warehouse over a year ago, and there were silky violet sheets and pillows, but one thing they'd opted to keep were the golden chains attached to the head of the bed.

Shade stretched his arms above his head, staring up at Apollo challengingly as he waited for him to take the hint.

With a chuckle, Apollo climbed up his body to reach for the handcuffs, securing them onto his wrists with a definitive clicking sound that had shivers of anticipation racing down Shade's spine.

"There you go, baby," Apollo said softly as he came back, stroking a finger over the curve of Shade's jaw. "Right where you belong."

Before Shade could reply, the computer dinged, and he lifted his head to peer at the screen only to have Apollo move into his line of sight.

"I don't think so, Shadow mine," he stated. "I only agree to this because it's fun for the both of us, but I refuse to allow Gael to get in the way of—"

Shade snorted, cutting him off. "Only you would consider hunting down monsters a fun pastime."

Apollo lifted a brow. "Is that so?"

Shade grinned. "What can I say? I guess I liked my old job more than I thought. Go figure." He got a kick out of putting bad guys in their place, only now it wasn't so he could get praise from others. In fact, no one could ever even know of his involvement since Shadow Yor was technically dead and needed to stay that way for both him and Apollo to be safe.

"Know what I like?" Apollo settled himself over Shade again, slipping one of his knees between his legs to slowly force them apart.

"Hurting me?" Shade pretended to guess. "Tying me up? Making me—" Another startled sound was ripped from his mouth when Apollo suddenly unhooked the cuffs and yanked him off the bed, hauling him over to the floor-to-ceiling window.

Apollo lifted him and wrapped Shade's legs around his hips, pressing into him so that Shade was pinned with his back against the glass and his front sealed to his. He kissed him, wildly at first, all teeth and tongue, before he brought their frenzied pace down a couple of notches.

"I like you," he said finally, pulling away enough to breathe the words out. "I like all of you. Everything about you. I like holding you like this and watching you work and the way you murmur my name in your sleep."

"I do not." Did he?

Apollo thrust his hips forward, rubbing the hard bulge in his pants against Shade's center, causing him to moan. "I like that sound you make and the way your eyes roll back whenever I take you rough and vicious, just the way you—"

"Just get to the part where you tell me you love me and then fuck me already," Shade interrupted, fingers already working on the buttons on Apollo's dress shirt, an annoyed growl climbing up his throat at how many there were. After the fourth one, he lost patience, tearing the material instead, causing buttons to go flying.

Apollo chuckled and lowered his arms to drop the shredded material before he tugged the t-shirt over Shade's head. By the time he'd finished with that, Shade already had his pants open, his hand dipping beneath the band of Apollo's underwear. He sucked in a sharp breath the second his fingers made contact and then leaned forward, pressing his forehead against Shade's.

"I love you," he whispered with a groan. "My perfect little Shadow. So forward and keen on getting what you want."

The word "now" went unspoken, but Shade knew what he meant. Ever since leaving the warehouse that day, Shade had come to an understanding with himself. He'd kept his word and hadn't gone into hiding again, and even though once in a while that familiar self-hatred reared its head, it was easy enough for him to tune it out now.

Shade wasn't afraid of who he was or the things he liked.

Or of the person he loved.

Apollo dropped his feet back to the ground only long enough to strip Shade's pants off, then he had him back up again, his thick cockhead lining up with Shade's entrance as he sucked at that spot at the side of Shade's neck hard enough to get him to bow off the window. They did this often enough now that the sting was minimal when he slid himself home.

Shade cried out and dug his fingers into Apollo's shoulders as Apollo fully seated himself inside and then sucked in a breath as the other man gave him a moment to adjust to his girth. When Apollo pinched his nipple he gasped, and that was all the encouragement Apollo needed to start flicking his hips.

They'd done this a thousand times, maybe even more, already and it never got old. Shade could spend the rest of his life just like this in fact, and the best part was, so could Apollo.

"Tell me you want me," he ordered, and Apollo sucked at his neck and chuckled against his skin.

"Of course I want you, Shadow mine," he drawled between pants, "Why else would I be fucking you like this?"

"Tell me—"

"I'm never going to stop wanting you," Apollo took over, not needing him to voice those old fears that sometimes crept up on him when he least expected them to. He was good at chasing them away whenever that happened, and this time was no exception. "You're going to be mine until we're both old and gray and then even after that. When we die, I'll find you in the next life. I'll hunt you down and make you mine all over again, baby. I'll never let you go. You'll always have me. You'll always be my perfect little Shadow."

"I love you," Shade said. It wasn't the first time they were exchanging those words, but every time still felt like a small miracle, a moment he had to hold on to in case it turned out to be a dream and he ended up returning to the nightmare that had been his life before.

But it never did, because it wasn't a dream and this was real.

He was wanted.

And he wanted.

Without shame or fear, because Apollo wouldn't abandon him, and he wouldn't ever abandon Apollo. They were monstrous in their own ways, but they were tethered by their hearts and their minds and their souls.

Together.

As the sun set at his back and the ocean waves broke against the shore, Shade embraced his devil and came apart in his arms.

Chani Lynn Feener

Between the Devil and the Sea

Chani Lynn Feener has wanted to be a writer since the age of ten during fifth grade story time. She majored in Creative Writing at Johnson State College in Vermont. To pay her bills, she has worked many odd jobs, including, but not limited to, telemarketing, order picking in a warehouse, and filling ink cartridges. When she isn't writing, she's binging TV shows, drawing, or frequenting zoos/aquariums. Chani is also the author of teen paranormal series, *The Underworld Saga*, originally written under the penname Tempest C. Avery. She currently resides in Connecticut, but lives on Goodreads.com.

Chani Lynn Feener can be found on Goodreads.com, as well as on Twitter and Instagram @TempestChani.

For more information on upcoming and past works, please visit her website: HOME | ChaniLynnFeener (wixsite.com).

Printed in Great Britain
by Amazon